I0586305

About the Author

Rachel Armstrong has always loved making up stories and has never wanted to be anything but an author. She writes contemporary romantic fiction ranging from rural to suspense. Rachel enjoys creating epic feel-good stories and has a weakness for an adventurous holiday escape. Helping her characters find their happily-ever-after is her life's joy.

Rachel lives in Townsville, Queensland, with her border collie, Jacob, where she helps people live their best lives as an exercise physiologist. In her spare time, she is either reading on her treadmill or plotting out her next novel while grooving at Zumba. Rachel's a keen traveller and has enjoyed many holidays exploring historic London, flying through the Grand Canyon, and hiking volcanos in Bali.

Rachel enjoys connecting with readers on social media and through her website.

www.rachelarmstrongauthor.com.au

RACHEL ARMSTRONG

Home
Among the
Palm Trees

Pink Paws
Publishing

First published 2022
ISBN 978-0-6453555-0-5

HOME AMONG THE PALM TREES
© 2022 by Rachel Armstrong

The reproduction or utilisation of this work in whole or in part in any form by any electronic, mechanical or other means, now known or hereafter invented, including xerography, photocopying and recording, or in any information storage or retrieval system, is forbidden without the permission of the publisher.

This book is sold to the condition that it shall not, by way of trade or otherwise, be leant, resold, hired out or otherwise circulated without the prior consent of the publisher in any form of binding or cover other than that in which it is published and without a similar condition including this condition being imposed on the subsequent purchaser.

All rights reserved including the right of reproduction in whole or in part in any form.

The characters in this book are a work of fiction and have no existence outside the imagination of the author and have no relation whatsoever to anyone bearing the same name or names. They are not even distantly inspired by any individual known or unknown to the author, and all incidents are pure invention.

Published by
Pink Paws Publishing
Rachel Armstrong
Townsville QLD 4810
Australia

A catalogue record for this book is available from the National Library of Australia
www.librariesaustralia.nla.gov.au

For Dillon

Dear Reader,

Welcome to Elizadale, North Queensland! I'm so glad you've decided to visit and I hope you enjoy your time here as much as I do. Ana and Liam have been with me for over a decade now, so I'm thrilled to finally be sharing their story.

Ana is a survivor who, despite removing herself from a difficult situation, continues to feel victimised. Fear leads her to flee interstate and start over. Thankfully, Liam is just the man to help her considering his protective instincts and his sixth sense to recognise a troubled soul. Violence is a serious issue in our world and something too many of us have been exposed to in some form. I can only hope I have handled Ana's situation with respect and done it justice.

But while this story developed around a dark theme, it has kept its original light-hearted essence about a woman's relationship with her beloved dog. I was born with a border collie big sister, Laura, so there was no other breed I'd have chosen to tell this story. Louis was inspired by my childhood border collie, Dillon. He was perfect in every way, obsessed with chasing balls, chewing sticks, and was far too intelligent. However, since he passed away, my baby boy, Jacob, has nosed his way into these pages with his cheekiness and fiery personality. It was within his herding instincts and obsessive barking that I found the inspiration to save this story.

I wish you happy reading, warm puppy cuddles, and yummy banana treats.

Rachel xoxo

Chapter One

Anastasia Hamilton stepped out of her car, opened the back door, and smiled at her border collie. 'We made it, Louis. We're safe.'

Louis looked at her with his big brown eyes, tilting his black-and-white head as Ana glanced down the main road of the small North Queensland town where she intended to make herself and Louis a temporary home. Heat radiated from the bitumen and up her legs, but after three days of constantly checking the rear vision mirror, her knuckles white on the wheel, Ana's pulse began to slow. She'd done it. She'd escaped Sydney and would find solitude in Elizadale.

Where, hopefully, he wouldn't find her.

Ana shook that thought away, unclipped Louis' harness, and led him across the road towards the historic Queenslander. *Riley House*, the wooden sign by the steps read. *Est. 1878. Elizadale Town Centre.*

Ana stepped beneath the shade of the wide verandah, wrapped Louis' lead around a pole and rubbed his head before going inside to collect the keys to her new home. It was as though the house had transported her back a century as the gleaming floorboards creaked beneath her feet. Her online research had told her it still belonged to the Riley family and that Ron Riley was Elizadale's representative with the Mareeba Shire Council. Ana smiled as she glanced around the ornate entryway. They sure took great pride in their heritage.

She approached the reception desk and greeted the lady behind the counter. 'Hi, I'm Ana Hamilton, the new schoolteacher. I'm here to see Deborah Maguire.'

'Of course.' The woman stood. 'Welcome. I'll take you through.'

Ana followed her down the panelled hall to the large meeting room where two women sat at an antique dining table. Charcoal drawings hung on the walls and windows overlooked lush green gardens. The receptionist introduced Ana and the older of the two women stood and extended her hand.

'Hello, I'm Deborah.' She smiled warmly. 'How was your trip?'

Deborah appeared to be in her mid-fifties and with greying blonde hair, she had the air and grace of a formidable school principal.

Ana smiled and shook her hand. 'Good, but long. You have a lovely town.'

'Thanks, I think so too. The school opens next week, so I'll get you to fill out paperwork then. Now, this is Meg.' She gestured towards the woman beside her, who was about Ana's age. 'Her family owns Jackson Villas, where you'll be staying. She's willing to take you there and show you around town, if you like?'

Meg flashed Ana a bright smile. 'It might look like there's not much to see, but every corner of this town has a story I could share with you. As long as you don't mind.'

'Not at all.'

Deborah placed her hand on Meg's shoulder and smiled fondly. 'Meg grew up here and is our grade two teacher, so unless you have questions, I'll leave you in her capable hands.'

Ana shook her head. 'Nope. No questions.'

'Lovely. Welcome aboard, Ana. Hopefully, you'll enjoy your time here and we might convince you to stay for another year.'

Ana smiled but was reluctant to make any promises. She'd signed a twelve-month contract with the school and that's as long as she'd risk staying when her future remained out of her control. She couldn't dare put down roots. It was best she kept moving.

But Ana didn't say that. 'You never know. So, Jackson Villas?'

'Yes!' Meg clapped her hands together, her blonde waves bouncing off her shoulders. 'Let's go. Thanks, Deb. We'll see you Monday!'

A spring filled Meg's step as Ana followed her out of Riley House. They returned to the verandah where Louis stood from a seated position and wagged his tail.

'Oh, hello! And who are you?' Meg grinned as she rubbed Louis' ears with enthusiasm. His eyes closed in pleasure, his tongue hanging out the side of his mouth. 'Aren't you beautiful? Yes, you are.'

Ana's heart swelled. Yeah, Meg seemed like someone she could get along with. 'This is Louis.'

'He's gorgeous.' Meg straightened as Ana untied his lead and they started towards the car. 'I have a Pomeranian who's my baby. Louis will love Elizadale.' Meg gasped and spun to face Ana. 'I should introduce you to Liam! He has a border collie too and runs the Dog Sports Association, which he'll surely pester you to join. Especially with this beautiful boy.'

Ana raised her eyebrows as she opened the bright yellow door to her Toyota Yaris and Louis jumped onto his seat. 'Are there many dogs here who train in sports?'

'There are now that Liam has the association going.' Meg rounded to the passenger side and slipped into the car with Ana. 'He does agility and obedience training. Turn right just here at the school.'

Ana followed Meg's directions, eyeing the school through the passenger window before turning. 'I guess I can walk to work.'

'Yeah, you can walk anywhere in Elizadale. It's only little and I could talk about my hometown all day. My great-great-great-great-great-grandfather—' Meg counted the 'greats' off on her fingers '—settled Elizadale in 1878, naming it for his wife Elizabeth. He thought it'd be a nice place to graze cattle, which most people did until some farms started to diversify. Tobacco was big once, but now we grow a variety of fresh fruits. Stuart Riley developed Elizadale and my family has been here ever since. Turn here, Ana.'

Ana turned into the driveway of a magnificent block of townhouses built of sand coloured brick. Meg directed her to the one on the far right, the unit built at a slightly different angle to the rest, and Ana parked in the open carport.

'Thank you, Meg. I should get Louis settled, but after that, could you show me where I could get some lunch? I'm starving.'

'Absolutely!' Meg brightened as they walked towards the unit, the keys jingling between her fingers as she searched for the one for the flyscreen door. 'We'll go to the Royal Hotel.

They have good meals. Although, come with me later and I'll introduce you to some people. My friends and I always get together on Monday afternoons.'

Nodding, Ana tried to force the knots in her belly away. It couldn't hurt to make friends, as it'd been a while since she'd had a social life. She might not plan to stay, but she didn't want to spend her year in the tropics alone either. 'All right. Sounds like fun.'

'Sorry.' Meg slipped another key into the deadlock. 'There are a few keys. I've suggested we get them all to match, but Mum hasn't got around to it.'

'It doesn't matter,' Ana said, knowing she'd only use one lock regardless while she was out since she liked the convenience of easy entry. But she was grateful for the deadlock as she'd certainly lock up tight while at home. Old habits die hard, she thought as she stepped inside.

The place was as cosy as described with white tiles spreading throughout the unit and a gleaming wooden staircase that led to the upper floor. Two red sofas occupied the living room and a round dining table sat by the spacious kitchen. Pulling the screen door closed behind herself and Meg, everything inside Ana softened.

The place was perfect. A haven. *Safe.*

'Look, Louis. Come outside.' She slid open the door to the patio overlooking the small yard. 'There's plenty of room to play.'

It wasn't true. Ana pressed her lips together, her heart sinking as Louis sniffed the buffalo grass. A large hibiscus shrub provided shade, but the yard was no bigger than a large living room. It certainly wasn't right for Louis. Ana hugged herself and watched his black-and-white coat blow in the warm breeze. She took a deep breath, then let it out slowly.

Everything would be okay. It had to be. She wouldn't survive if she contemplated the worst.

Meg joined her on the patio. 'There's a dog park on Station Drive where you can take Louis. Another insistence from Liam when he joined the town committee.'

Ana's shoulders relaxed. 'That sounds wonderful.'

'It is handy,' Meg agreed with a nod. 'Well, we turned the power on last night, so the fridge should be cold. The unit's been cleaned and if you have any problems, call the number on your lease. That'll put you through to my mum and she'll take care of anything you need.'

'Thanks, Meg.'

'No worries. You want to get that lunch?'

'Yep.' Ana wasn't sure if the pub would have a decent salad, but she needed food and company would help keep her mood bright. 'Just let me get Louis his water bowl and we'll get going.'

Once Louis was settled, Ana and Meg set off towards the pub. On foot. Ana frowned as she pulled her hat over her face. Was Meg crazy? It was the middle of summer! But Ana wouldn't complain about stretching her legs after spending three days sitting in the car.

'I'd ask Isabella to join us if she wasn't working,' Meg said, glancing across the wide driveway of Jackson Villas. 'She lives in unit one and is a close friend of mine. You'll meet her this afternoon. Her dad's also a teacher and her mum's the local doctor, so the Brennans are a big part of the community. Just remember this, Ana. Family dynamics rule this town.'

'Isn't that how small towns usually operate?'

'I suppose. You'll also find many Maguires around as they run the region's largest property, Shadow Creek.'

'Like Deborah?'

'Yep. Deborah's married to Cliff, one of the brothers who runs Shadow Creek. They grow bananas.'

Ana smiled. 'I love bananas. There were many banana trees as I drove in. They were beautiful.'

'You'd have driven in past Tropic Sun. Shadow Creek's bananas are north of town. Both are two of the biggest banana farms in the region and yeah, I think they're beautiful too. I hang out with the Maguires, so you'll meet them all eventually. Just beware of the Kelly family.'

'Why's that?' Ana asked as she spotted the wide verandah of the pub ahead. Her mouth watered at the impending taste of a cold drink.

'If you hang out with me, you'll be part of the Maguire clan and we're sworn enemies of the Kellys. But don't worry. Only the men get thrown out of the pub for fighting.'

Ana's breath caught as they slipped into the shade beneath the pub's verandah. Her pulse began to pound. Fighting? Really? She'd made a friend and found herself part of a social group within less than an hour of being in town, yet had also become enemies with people she didn't even know?

Her chest tightened. 'That's hardly reassuring.'

Again, Meg shrugged. 'Don't worry, it's not as bad as it sounds. Now, let's see what the lunch special is today.'

* * *

Ana sent her mum a text message to inform her she'd arrived safely, then started unpacking. Her heart ached as she lugged her suitcases upstairs. After tearful goodbyes with her family, Ana couldn't bear to hear her mum's gentle voice as she hung her clothes and aligned her shoes in the wardrobe. Thankfully, Nadia understood that as she replied with a lengthy message filled with reassurance, best wishes, and love. Ana smiled as she hung a lime green towel in the bathroom and texted back hugs and kisses. It'd been hard, but she'd made her decision to leave and would call her mum once she had settled in.

Unloading her crockery, Ana reminded herself to visit the shop to buy fresh produce. At least they shouldn't be in short supply in a town that thrived on fruit farming. But it was unlikely she'd get around to it today because she was meeting Meg at the pub again.

After spending two hours with her new colleague, Ana had identified Meg as the crowning jewel of Elizadale. She was Megan Riley, heiress of the Riley Empire that owned many businesses and rental properties in town. Added to that, her mother came from a large avocado farm, which could potentially be Meg's one day. Susan Riley operated the local homewares store and her father was Ron Riley, the unofficial town mayor and part-time solicitor. Her sister Christina lived an hour away in Atherton and had a young family. Meg was as local as they came, popular, and knew everyone.

Ana could do worse in a self-appointed best friend.

She leaned against the kitchen counter and glanced around, absorbing the comfort of her new home. It was perfect. Peaceful, private, and in a town where no one would think to look for her.

She clenched her hands tight and let out a deep breath. Even though she might feel safe, she couldn't afford to be complacent. She knew better than that.

Moving to the back door, she sat and called Louis over to play. He lay at her feet and pushed his tennis ball towards her, his dark eyes focused as he readied for his favourite game.

Smiling, Ana threw the ball and Louis took off after it to the small garden, retrieving and returning his prize proudly.

She played with him for a while and the game effectively improved her mood. When five o'clock drew near, she threw the ball one last time before scooping food into his dish, kissing his soft head, and stepping inside.

Since it couldn't hurt to put some effort into her appearance, she changed into a pair of denim shorts and threw on a pretty blue top. After pulling her long blonde hair into a ponytail, she slipped into her bejewelled sandals, locked up, and began walking to the Royal Hotel.

Despite everything she'd been through, a spring filled her step. Her heart lightened and freedom burst through her.

It was time to get her life back.

Chapter Two

The Royal Hotel, like any iconic Australian pub, was grand, old, and on the corner of the highway—locally known as Abbott Street—and Stuart Road. It was busier than it'd been at lunch as men who'd just knocked off work crowded around the bar and music played on the jukebox. Ana spotted Meg in the far booth with two other ladies.

'Ana!' Meg grinned and waved her over. 'Come. Sit. Meet.'

As Meg scooted over, Ana slid into the booth beside her.

'This is Isabella Brennan.' The young lady in the corner smiled shyly. With her platinum blonde hair and youthful face, Ana wouldn't put Isabella much older than twenty. 'And my lifelong bestie, Lucy Maguire.'

'Hey, it's nice to meet you.' Lucy smiled over her bottle of Great Northern beer. 'We heard that Meg's lured you into our group and showed you around town.'

'Yep. She took me for a tour down Riley Road.'

'That's pretty much where everything is,' Lucy said, brushing dark hair off her face. 'I hope you like Elizadale.'

'I like it so far.'

But that quickly became an understatement when a man

slid into the booth beside Lucy. Ana's breath caught. He was tall and not at all hard on the eyes, filling his T-shirt and jeans as though they'd been moulded for him. His sandy hair was an inch too long and he bore the gorgeous face of a country heartbreaker.

Ana's heart began to race. Crap.

'Afternoon, ladies. How're we doing?'

Meg grinned and clapped her hands together. 'Liam, you must meet Ana. She's our new teacher. Ana, this is Liam Maguire and, Liam, Ana has the most *beautiful* border collie.'

Ana swallowed as Liam's piercing blue eyes locked onto hers and his mouth curved slowly.

'Hey.' He extended his large hand and she took it shyly, a tingle of heat shooting up her arm. Double crap. 'Nice to meet you. I'm glad you have a perfect taste in dogs.'

Ana's shoulders softened. It was easy to win her over when Louis and dogs were the closest things to her heart, but this wasn't good. The last thing she needed was to be attracted to a man.

Somehow, she managed to find her voice. 'Nice to meet you too. Meg mentioned you have a border collie and do dog sports.'

Liam quirked his eyebrow. 'Well, Meg likes to gossip.'

'No, I don't.' Meg picked up her drink. 'I just told Ana about a few people in town.'

He smirked. 'Has she mentioned the love of her life yet?'

Ana glanced at Meg, who rolled her eyes. 'Liam, be nice and get us a round of drinks, will you?'

Laughing, Liam slid out of the booth and confirmed orders with the other ladies before turning to Ana. 'And what would you like?'

Ana wriggled in her seat and swallowed. God, what was

wrong with her? But she knew better than to insult him by insisting on paying her way. 'A Diet Coke, please.'

With a nod, Liam turned and strode towards the bar. Oh yeah, he was definitely hot. Wide shoulders, narrow hips, firm legs clad in snug jeans ...

Ana tore her gaze away and tuned into Lucy's story about a training session today with her mare Esme. She may not know the first thing about horses, but it was a far safer subject to contemplate than that of a man.

'Are you still going to breed her?' Meg asked.

'Maybe next year,' Lucy sighed, crossing her arms over the table. 'Not sure yet.'

Ana smiled at the thought of a baby horse as Liam placed three cans of Diet Coke on the table. 'Be back with the rest.'

She opened her can and when Liam returned, he slid into the booth beside her. Pouring the Coke over ice, she did her best to ignore the heat rushing over her skin.

'What's your dog's name?' Liam asked, taking a swig of his beer.

'Louis, named after the kings of France.' She forced herself to make eye contact. 'He's three now and such a good boy.'

'Steph's almost two. She's an extremely intelligent girl.'

Lucy blinked. 'Extremely intelligent? She's practically human! You go to Liam's house and it's Steph who answers the goddamn door. As in, she actually opens it.'

Ana's eyebrows shot up. 'Seriously?' She'd heard of dogs doing this kind of thing but had never known one.

Liam grinned. 'Come by and see for yourself. I'll admit, she's well trained. I made sure she was. And unlike this lot, she's a female who'll actually listen to me.'

Lucy smiled. 'We don't have time to listen to you, Liam.'

'She's a good girl though, and sometimes too smart for me.'

'All females are,' Meg said and Lucy laughed.

Liam ignored them. 'But you should bring Louis to agility training, Ana. He'll love it. It's on Sunday afternoons.'

Meg nudged Ana with her elbow. 'See? Told you he'd want you to join.'

'At least Louis may provide Steph with some decent competition since she seems to be the only dog who can actually *do* agility.'

'Have you seen how short Lola's legs are?'

Ana imagined a Pomeranian at agility and stifled a laugh.

'And Evie doesn't like to get her paws dirty,' Isabella said, defending her pup.

'Roger provides Steph with enough competition, thank you very much,' Lucy said. 'He'll totally kick your dog's prissy butt.'

Liam took a swig of his beer. 'Doubt it.'

Lucy narrowed her eyes at him, then glanced at Ana. 'Why can't big brothers just let their sisters win?'

'They should, hey?' Ana agreed, grinning as she turned her gaze back to Liam. 'But agility sure seems like fun. We only have a small yard, so Louis would enjoy learning something new.' Besides a few behavioural issues, Louis was a good boy and deserved to have an activity of his own. He'd always enjoyed learning basic commands and tricks, so he should love jumping hurdles. 'Does your association have many dogs?'

'Lots. It really took off because it's so much fun. The agile dogs are learning, such as Luce's German shepherd, but Meg's fluffball and Iz's cavalier have no talent.'

'Lola's trying, I'll have you know,' Meg said. 'But it is an enjoyable afternoon, Ana, so you should come.'

Ana relaxed into the booth and sipped her drink. Taking Louis to agility training wouldn't require any commitment to Elizadale, and after losing her social life, joining a community club may be just what she needed.

'We'll be there.'

* * *

Liam waved goodbye to the ladies as they left the pub. Daylight lingered, so he didn't mind letting them make the short walk home as he climbed into his old LandCruiser.

He gripped the wheel until his knuckles turned white. His heart pounded hard and low.

Damn, he was in trouble.

Glancing through the windscreen, he watched Ana as she walked with Meg and Isabella up Stuart Road and released a long breath. She sure was something. Ana had caught his eye the moment he'd stepped inside the pub, as a man would have to be dead six months to not notice a beautiful woman at his regular table. Her sparkling blue eyes, honey-blonde ponytail, and bright smile had brought him to a halt. Strange twisting sensations had taken over his body while talking to her, which had only tightened as they'd discussed their dogs.

Shoving the car into gear, Liam shook his head. *City girl*, he reminded himself. City girls never lasted in small towns. He knew that from experience and wouldn't make that mistake again.

But … would it be a mistake? Ana would be in town for twelve months. Other city folk had stayed, his mother a prime example. And he hadn't been able to take his eyes off Ana all afternoon.

Liam chucked a U-turn and pulled onto Abbott Street, heading for home on Station Drive where single-acre lots overlooked the eighteen-hole golf course. Even though Elizadale was small, locals considered his half of Station Drive as the 'flash' part of town. A few houses had even upgraded to electronic gates, but Liam had never been one for moving with the times. Letting his aging LandCruiser idle, he hopped out and unlatched his double gates, glancing up the driveway towards his house. His pride and joy.

Unlike his neighbours who'd built large brick manors almost three decades ago, Liam had gone for the traditional country look when his parents had given him the land. His modern Queenslander was built on stumps off the ground in a relative L-shape, boasted cream-painted walls, and had a small verandah on the corner with inverted T-shaped steps. Gum trees shaded his greenish lawn and flowering gardens. At the sound of his arrival, Steph scurried out from her new favourite spot beneath the golden cane palms and raced towards him. Her eyes brightened and tongue lolled out the side of her mouth.

Liam grinned as he took her head in his hands. 'Hey, gorgeous girl. I think I recruited us another friend today.'

He hustled Steph into the LandCruiser to keep her safe before driving through the gates. Jumping back out, he shut them, then drove towards the house. 'His name's Louis and he's a border collie just like you. You should like him, Steph. At least, I hope you do because he has a beautiful mummy.'

He hopped out of the car, Steph at his heels. Always the gentleman, Liam let her into the house first. He'd long since gotten over the dog hair the first day Steph had given him puppy-dog eyes outside the door. She'd been three months old and it'd been time for her to start sleeping outside.

That had never happened.

In the kitchen, Liam crouched in front of Steph and took her face in his hands. 'You're a good girl, Stephanie. My favourite girl. But I met a lovely woman today and I might want to get to know her better.' Scratching Steph's ears, Liam stood. 'Right. What do you say to chicken sandwiches? I know you can't resist.'

Liam made a couple of sandwiches, then stepped onto the large deck that filled the inner part of the L-shaped house. Sitting, he fed a morsel of chicken to Steph and put his feet up to contemplate the surprising afternoon.

It had been a long time since he'd felt attracted to a woman. Liam lived a peaceful life with Steph, liked it that way, and was finally taking a chance at seizing his dreams. Renovations to add a café to the Tourist Centre he operated had begun, with a Grand Opening scheduled for April. Now, not only would he be showcasing Elizadale's unique tourism, but his menu would highlight the best bananas in North Queensland, fresh off Shadow Creek Plantation.

Liam's heart swelled as he bit into a sandwich. Diane might have left him with the city lights in her eyes, but no longer would he let that stop him from chasing their dream.

No. *His* dream. It was his. He didn't need a woman to share a dream with, or a dedicated cook to open a café. He had two of the town's best cooks in his sister and aunt, and Liam knew his own way around the kitchen. The menu focused on homestyle country food and easy family-favourites that everyone loved. Surely, he couldn't stuff that up.

He hoped.

But while he had those dreams, he'd always wanted to settle down one day. He'd hardly thought about it since Diane had left, but love wasn't something you could plan. He certainly hadn't woken this morning intending to meet an interesting woman.

Sighing, he bit into his sandwich. One day at a time. Moving fast wasn't his style, unlike his best friend and cousin Adam, the notorious bad boy of Elizadale. Adam constantly told Liam to seize the day and take a chance, but that wasn't how Liam rolled. Ana was in town for a year, which gave him plenty of time to know her and uncover what had prompted her to move to his peaceful town. And whether she was likely to stay.

But it was risky admiring a city girl. Many people used the country for the experience, especially healthcare workers and teachers like Ana. They came to work in a town no one else wanted to live in, then returned to the city to get on with their real lives.

Liam's chest tightened. Was that Ana's plan? If so, she'd be just like the two teachers before her. Hardly worth getting attached to.

He picked up his second sandwich with a sigh. He should have known better with Diane. She'd always talked about going to the city, so he shouldn't have been surprised when she'd abandoned their café plans and taken off to Brisbane.

It had still hurt though. His dreams of a business and family had vanished overnight, leaving him alone and heartbroken. But he'd gone ahead with his plans in the two years since. Now, at twenty-seven, he had a business, a house, and his beloved Steph. Even though he'd enjoyed growing up on Shadow Creek, Liam had always known he was more suited to town life. His father, uncle, and cousins happily managed their thriving property, so Liam had taken his passion for tourism and boosted the reputation of High Ridge, his family's retreat. Located on the mountain with spectacular views over the banana fields, High Ridge provided Aunt Wendy and Lucy with plenty of guests and events to keep them busy. More travellers were stopping by the Tourist Centre and soon people would be able to enjoy all sorts of delicious banana, avocado, and tropical fruit goodies.

Elizadale might be a hidden gem off the beaten track, but it was close enough to the tourist hotspots of Port Douglas, Cairns, and the Atherton Tablelands to attract visitors. Backpackers and caravanning grey nomads often stopped by to enjoy their fresh produce, historic buildings, and shop for country homewares.

Liam finished his sandwich and glanced out over his backyard. He'd done things he could reflect upon proudly, so what else was a man to do with his life in a small town? His position on the town committee and work at the Tourist Centre both gave him joy and gratification. He owned the house that he shared with Steph.

So, perhaps Ana arriving was a sign he should consider dating again. He hadn't bothered since Diane had left and had put all his focus into work instead.

Liam ran his hand through his hair. Knots formed in his belly. He liked Ana. A lot. And she loved border collies.

But 'slow and steady wins the race'.

* * *

Heat surged through Rick Newman's veins, his fists clenching as he glanced at the calendar on the wall. Friday was the day.

Four more sleeps and he'd be out of this cell and on his way to making things right.

Not that it'd be fucking easy. The stupid whore could be anywhere by now. He doubted she'd have left the western suburbs as she'd still been teaching in Liverpool last year, but that damn 'women's refuge' had kept her out of his reach before the trial and he suspected she'd be trying to protect herself once he was free.

But he would find her. She was his, dammit, and if she wanted to live in fear, so be it. He'd told her when she'd sent him to this hellhole that he'd come for her. That no matter what, she'd never escape his clutches. That when he got out, she'd be sorry.

It'd been a promise and he didn't intend to break it.

Rick stood and paced his cell. The bitch had deserved what she'd got, but she'd overreacted and gone to the police. She'd made her choice and put him in prison. But this time, she'd learn her lesson. And when he was done with her ...

Rick glanced around the small room he'd called home these past thirty months. Yeah, he might get sent back here, but so what? He had a record now. His life would never be the same. And prison had been easy. It'd changed him and the stupid slut only had herself to blame. She'd thought he was better off in here, so he'd show her just the type of man she'd made him become. Prison had been an education more than a punishment. And he'd done everything he could to make parole. He'd kept his nose clean, his head down, and lied through his teeth to the judge. Now, they were showing him the door.

Rick smiled and clenched his hands in anticipation. He would find Ana. In today's world, no one could hide.

Chapter Three

Ana stopped by Riley Road Shops on Tuesday to pick up the essentials she hadn't managed to fit into her hatchback. She browsed the independent supermarket, bakery, and fresh produce store, pleasantly surprised by their variety. Carrying the groceries to the car, she passed the hair salon, hardware store, and butcher as she glanced across the road at the Tourist Centre. Construction fencing hid half of the dark brickwork and she frowned. What were they building?

Sighing, Ana loaded the groceries. She wouldn't mind visiting the Tourist Centre as she'd love to browse the local crafts she'd heard they sold. But after the way Liam Maguire had made her body tingle yesterday, it might be best if she kept her distance. Men and romance weren't part of her plan. Especially if the worst happened and she had to run again.

Ana slammed her hatchback closed and forced those worries away. She drove home and pulled into the shade of the carport, then lugged the groceries towards the unit. Sweat rolled down her back beneath the midday sun as she opened the screen and smiled at the kookaburra in the glazed windowpane of the wooden door.

'Hey, Louis!' Ana brought him inside so that he could enjoy the air-conditioning. He curled up on his bed and lowered his head for a nap while she put the groceries away. Then she finished setting up her new home.

Ana ached as she thought of everything she'd left in Sydney. Fine linen, cute ornaments, pretty artworks, and the books. She'd had so many precious things, all now packed away in a storage shed. But with new unread novels on the shelf, treasured knickknacks in her room, and Louis' baby photos on the walls, the unit looked more like home. Curling up on the lounge for the rest of the afternoon, she devoured a few chapters of a romantic suspense novel until dusk approached.

'Come on, Louis! Walk time!'

Not that the tropics were any cooler after the sun had gone down, but they both needed their daily exercise. Ana took a firm grip of Louis' lead, keeping him by her side as they headed for the walkway that circled Elizadale. Striding a block up to Station Drive—the edge of town that overlooked parkland and Shadow Creek—unease settled in her belly as she glanced at her beautiful boy. Louis enjoyed walking but was often distracted by things his instincts wished to herd. Like cars. This led to frustration and since Ana didn't want to deny him walks, she'd usually steer clear of roads. But she didn't have any other choice in Elizadale.

They joined the pathway near the dog park and headed in the opposite direction, weaving their way along the path shaded by various palms and flowering trees. Ana glanced up at them. Maybe she'd learn their names one day.

They paused at the road that cut across the path towards the open gate, where the overhanging slab of wood read *Shadow Creek*. Pushing her hat up off her face, Ana absorbed the majesty of the bushland that spread towards the silhouette of the mountain beyond.

What did the Maguires do out there? And where were the banana trees? Meg had said that Shadow Creek was the most successful banana grower in the region and Ana would admit, she was curious. It'd be interesting to learn about life on the land. She'd never considered how farms worked, what it took to grow produce, or how the people who ran these properties lived.

'Perhaps we'll get to visit one day, Louis.' If she made friends with the Maguires, that was.

For now, she put her energy back into her walk. She didn't follow Station Drive as it curved around the golf course. Instead, she cut down past the greens and emerged onto Abbott Street. Crossing the road, Ana quickened her stride, getting the most of her exercise as she tightened her grip on Louis' lead and admired the soft pink flowers on the trees lining the highway. Parkland spread beside her towards a thicket of bush lining the creek.

Pity she was only in this beautiful town for a year.

A car whizzed past and Louis' ears perked. His gaze followed the sound, but he maintained his stride, his tongue hanging out the side of his mouth as he panted happily. She smiled and the knots in her shoulders loosened.

Then the unmistakable sound of a semi-trailer approached and dread filled Ana's belly. She held Louis tight and slowed her steps. His shoulders dropped. Head lowered.

'No, Louis. Leave it.' The semi-trailer zoomed past and Louis lunged, lifting onto his hind legs and twisting against his collar, barking at the offending truck. Ana groaned and fought down her frustration.

Would it ever end? Exposure, the experts said. But how much exposure did Louis need before he got used to moving vehicles?

She sighed sadly as they continued on. With little traffic, she and Louis thankfully returned home without further incident. But would walking ever be enjoyable if she couldn't snap Louis out of his instincts?

* * *

Ana arrived at the dog park on Wednesday morning to meet Meg and Lola. Unclipping Louis' lead, she rubbed his head. 'Okay, go run.'

Louis ran towards the bushes, following his nose with his fluffy tail in the air. Ana sat on a bench beneath a large ficus— one of the few trees she could name—and watched him.

She'd made the right decision moving here, but it hadn't lessened her fears or anxieties. Crossing her arms over her chest, she exhaled. She and Louis had both suffered trauma and no one was going to protect her, not even the courts. She hadn't wanted Rick to be released and had begged the court to deny parole. But in the end, the only people who'd had her safety in mind were her family. So, along with her sister, Natalia, and their mother, they'd formed a plan that had uprooted their lives. But while they might be safer for it, Ana couldn't stop worrying. Rick could still track her to Elizadale. She just hoped he'd turn Sydney upside down first.

As Louis picked up what she could only describe as a tree branch, Ana forced herself to smile as he dragged it to her feet. He shuffled back and lay low, his eyes focused.

'You want me to throw a tree?' Ana stood and planted a

foot on the branch, snapping off a stick. She tossed it across the park and Louis bolted after it.

'Nice tree.' Ana turned as Meg arrived with a wriggling ball of caramel fluff under her arm.

'He likes the big sticks. So, this is Lola?' Meg placed her in Ana's eagerly outstretched arms. 'She's so cute!'

'Yeah, she is.' Meg sat on the bench. Louis dropped his stick at her feet and Meg threw it.

'How old is she?'

'Four. I got her after uni.'

Ana placed the little dog on the ground and settled beside Meg. 'Did you go to uni straight after school?'

'Yeah, I always knew I wanted to be a teacher and Deb said I'd be good at it. I studied in Townsville and came back here when I graduated because I'm a small-town girl at heart.'

'From what I've gathered, you'll never leave Elizadale.'

'Very true.'

Ana tossed Louis' stick and laughed as Lola tried to chase him, stopping when she realised her little legs wouldn't allow her to keep up.

'So … Ana, tell me. How is it that a woman like you moved to Elizadale all by her lonesome?'

Ana tore her gaze from Louis and glanced at Meg, who crossed her legs and sank back against the bench. Sighing, Ana mimicked her motions. 'It's a pretty uninteresting story.'

'I don't believe that. Leave anyone back home? Almost bring someone with you?'

Ana's throat tightened. She considered sharing her past with Meg and the horrors that lay in it, but it was such a nice day and she didn't want to inform Meg that she may have trouble following her.

'No. I dated a little last year,' she said, trying to keep her voice steady. 'But there was no one but Louis to bring with me.'

'I guess he's the best man to bring with you.'

'I think so.' Ana twisted her fingers in her lap as Meg threw Louis' stick. Her heart lurched as she contemplated the questions on her tongue, but she hadn't been able to shake Liam Maguire from her head, so what was the harm in getting answers? 'I saw the construction at the Tourist Centre. What's going on there?'

'Liam's opening a café! It's always been a dream of his. But like anything, it's taken him a while. I'm excited about it though.' Ana thought Meg would be excited about pretty much anything. 'The Tourist Centre highlights everything about the region and the café will focus on our local produce.'

'Sounds interesting.' Ana didn't know much about tourism or cafés, but it sounded like a solid idea. She'd passed a lot of roadside fruit stands on her drive, as well as many cafés and tourist spots. Considering Elizadale was close to Cairns and the Atherton Tablelands, she'd imagine they'd get their fair share of visitors. She'd also heard wonderful things about the Tablelands and hoped to take a drive there one weekend to explore the waterfalls, parks, and taste local produce. A café like Liam's seemed like just the thing Elizadale needed.

'When does he plan to open it?'

'School holidays, just before Easter. He'll have an opening day, which should bring people from neighbouring towns. He's also contacted the newspaper in Cairns for media exposure.'

'Wow. He's going all out.'

'Yeah, tourism's Liam's passion and he's done a lot for this town and High Ridge.'

Ana frowned as she tossed Louis' stick. 'High Ridge?'

'The holiday retreat out on Shadow Creek. They have a lovely campground, cabins, and many fun activities. That's where Lucy works.'

'Oh, right.' The Maguires seemed to have a lot going on. 'So, tourism's a family thing then?'

'Well, Wendy Maguire opened High Ridge when we were kids, but since Liam took over the Tourist Centre, Elizadale has boomed. We're lucky to have him on the town committee, really.'

Nerves vibrated in Ana's belly as she watched Louis chew his stick, now covered in dirt and saliva. 'Liam sure seems like a nice man.' *They all did until they showed their true colours.*

Ana resisted a sigh. No, she couldn't think like that. She wasn't afraid of men. They weren't all like Rick.

'Liam's awesome. One of the town's ultimate nice guys.'

Ana nodded as she stared absently at the dogs, Louis chewing happily while Lola rolled in the green grass, her little legs wriggling in the air. There was certainly something appealing about Liam. He'd made her blood stir on Monday afternoon and when he'd smiled, her hormones had done a little dance.

But her head remained in the game and getting involved with a man was not the best idea. She'd just moved to town and didn't plan to stay. She couldn't.

Ana glanced at Meg. 'Where's your man, then?'

Meg crossed her arms and examined her pink fingernails. 'My man?'

'Someone as outgoing and influential as you must have a man around somewhere. Or one in her sights.' Liam *had* mentioned Meg's 'love of her life'. 'No one you like around here, Meg?'

This time, Ana gave the elbow nudge. Meg shook her head

at the ground, dropping her arms as a small smile curved the corners of her mouth.

'Nah … I don't … no one notices me around here. I'm just Meg Riley, former Show Queen, part-time country singer, and schoolteacher. As my mum says, too spirited to settle down, even if I am twenty-five and wouldn't mind doing so in the near future. But for now, I'm happy where I am.'

Meg forced a smile and Ana returned the gesture, but she saw what was inside her new friend. Heartache. She'd either been rejected or overlooked for far too long.

'I'm sure he'll come around,' Ana said kindly.

'It doesn't matter. Men are stupid. All they care about up here are their farms.'

'Yeah … men are stupid.' *Or mean, violent, and controlling.*

A bird chirped in the ficus and drew Louis' attention away from his stick. He lifted his head, his gaze following as the bird took flight. Barking, he ran after it. Ana smiled as Lola chased after him on her tiny legs.

'She has no hope,' Meg laughed, relaxing into the bench. Then her eyebrows lifted as she turned to Ana. 'Do you like yoga?'

Ana blinked, her shoulders softening at the change of subject. 'I guess. I've only done a little bit of yoga, but my sister's into it and I took a few classes once.'

'Then you should come with me tomorrow. My friend Grace just started teaching yoga at the community hall. She wants to open her own studio, so we should support her. What do you think?'

It couldn't hurt. Ana had enjoyed the classes she'd attended with Natalia, she just hadn't continued going because Rick hadn't liked her being out of an evening.

So why not? She could strengthen and stretch her body

while supporting a new community business. That's what small towns were all about, right? Supporting local?

'Sounds good. What time?'

* * *

For a small town, yoga was insanely popular. Ana seemed to meet nearly every woman in Elizadale—and a few men—as Meg introduced her around the room.

Grace White was their age, a nurse, and also lived in Jackson Villas with her two friends—Jessica Smithfield, who worked at her family's pub, and Claire Taylor, the hairdresser. Isabella also came and set up her mat on the other side of Meg.

Ana met Meg's mother Sue and her aunt Heather, who ran the homewares store. Ana hadn't visited it yet, but they mainly traded in local crafts and if she needed a throw blanket, tea-towels, or tablecloth, that's where she'd find them.

'We also sell candles, made by my daughter,' Heather said, 'as well as other knickknacks. And if Adam Maguire got his act together and did more woodturning, we'd have his things to sell too.'

Meg glanced at Ana. 'Mum and Aunt Heather are always pestering Adam to make a business out of his woodturning, but he keeps shrugging it off.'

Ana hadn't met Adam, but considering he helped run Shadow Creek, he probably had more to do than spend his days woodturning.

As Grace called the class to attention, she and Meg returned to their mats and Ana glanced around the hall. It was located across the road from Riley House and quite standard, with a stage at the front, tiny kitchen at the back, and a massive wooden floor. Ana could imagine the country dances, bake sales, and other events it had hosted in its many years.

But today, it was yoga. The class was basic, but it'd been a while and Ana was happy just to get her muscles moving. Her pulse raced during sun salutations and warrior pose brought a strong burn to her thighs.

By the end of the class, Ana couldn't stop smiling as she rolled up the mat Meg had loaned her. Ladies huddled in clumps as they hugged goodbye, waved across the room and called out they'd catch each other soon. Everything inside Ana relaxed and clenched at the same time. This was what she'd always wanted. Elizadale was a community. Here, she could be a part of something. She could have friends. A life. She could even settle down.

Her heart plummeted.

If only.

Chapter Four

Nadia Hamilton had lived a good life. Even though she'd lost her husband young and had raised two daughters on her own, she'd done all she could to make their world perfect. It hadn't been easy, and she'd spent many hours working to provide her daughters with everything they'd needed, but it had paid off in spades when she considered the achievements of Natalia and Anastasia.

Nadia's heart ached as she made herself lunch. Her life had consisted of nothing but being a mother for twenty-seven years, a single mother and widow for twenty-one, and she missed her girls. But with Natalia on the other side of the city and Anastasia in another state, she'd started to explore other joys in life, like having friends, going to lunch, and spending the day indulging in unnecessary female pleasures. She even had time to pursue her artistic talents with jewellery making when she wasn't working as store manager of Bras 'n' Things. She'd always loved her art, but as the sole wage earner, she'd had to pursue a steady job, and Bras 'n' Things came with great discounts on pretty lingerie and cute pyjamas.

Mixing her stir-fry, Nadia smiled as she thought about her girls. She couldn't be any prouder of Natalia, who was an intelligent and outgoing general practitioner, and she knew Natalia's father, the late Doctor James Hamilton, would have been proud too.

Just as he'd be proud of their youngest. Ana was as beautiful as her older sister and possessed the patience and heart to educate and mould the minds of young children. The memories of what Ana had been through still haunted Nadia, yet she remained grateful that she'd raised her daughter with enough courage to stand up for herself.

She'd known she'd done her job perfectly the night Ana had arrived on her doorstep for help. Nadia had stood by her daughter through everything—the hospital, the trial, and the months that had followed. She'd expressed her concerns to the court when they'd fought Rick's parole, but the justice system 'rehabilitated' criminals, and apparently, he was no longer a threat to society.

Today, they were letting him out.

Nadia exhaled and forced the knots in her belly away as she reached for a bowl. She'd done her best for Ana, but they'd known Rick wouldn't remain locked up forever. And after seeing the fear in her daughter's eyes, they'd had no choice but to take precautions for her safety. Nadia had suggested Ana get a transfer to the other side of the city, but Ana had wanted to escape Sydney entirely, so she'd supported her daughter's move to Elizadale. She just hoped that one day Ana could come home.

But as long as Ana was safe and happy, Nadia was content.

Having no plans for her Friday off, she'd stayed home and opted for a cashew and vegetable fried rice. Natalia had been an excellent influence upon changing her diet, and even though Nadia should have put more effort into looking after herself years ago, it was never too late to change.

She was about to eat with her two newest babies, twin chihuahuas Cooper and Colin, when the doorbell rang. She wasn't expecting anyone, but she left her lunch and headed to the door as the puppies yapped.

* * *

Nadia Hamilton, Rick thought with spite. The bitch who'd convinced her whore of a daughter to press charges and toss him in the lockup. Fucking mothers could never see the flaws in their children. Ana had deserved what she'd got. She was his and he could do with her as he pleased. It was a man's right. And when he tracked her down, she'd learn her lesson about treating him with respect.

Perhaps he'd teach her mother a lesson too.

Rick arrived in Fairfield in his newly purchased second-hand Subaru Outback and parked outside the little white house. He'd never liked Ana's mother. She was nothing but a gold-digging slut who'd married a rich doctor, popped out a couple of kids, and was forced into work when the husband had literally dropped dead. Ana had always spoken highly of her mother, but the woman wasn't anything special. A bit of a looker, perhaps. It was no secret where her daughters had gotten their good looks.

His lip curled as he studied the house. The mother wouldn't have left it. Ana may have grown up moving from house to house all over Sydney, but the mother had proudly bought this little shithole not long after he'd started dating Ana. She'd still be there and the bitch would tell him where her daughter was or he'd make her. He'd be on his way to Ana within the hour.

Oh, how he'd dreamed of this moment all those long nights in prison.

He stepped onto the street and slammed the door. Power flooded through his veins as he approached the house. The old woman didn't stand a chance.

Rick rang the doorbell. Waited. His heart pounded. Muscles quivered. He was ready to barge in and demand the location of the whore daughter when he heard dogs barking.

The door opened.

A middle-aged man greeted him.

Frustration floored Rick.

'Hello. Can I help you?'

Rick frowned. He had the right house. He was sure of it.

His teeth clenched. 'Nadia Hamilton doesn't still live here, does she?'

'Sorry, mate.' The man shook his head. 'Dunno who lived here before, but we moved in about two months ago.'

Chapter Five

Friday was notoriously busy at the Royal Hotel as workers and families from the farms flocked into town. Liam sat with his cousins in their regular booth. None of them missed a Friday night at the pub no matter how much work there was to do on Shadow Creek.

'So, apparently Meg's bringing the new teacher tonight,' Jack Maguire said, nursing his beer.

'Yeah, I met her on Monday.' Liam lounged back in the booth. 'Seems nice enough. And she's got herself a border collie.'

Beside Liam, Michael Maguire laughed. 'You can't think there's much wrong with her, then.'

Liam shrugged, trying for nonchalance. He hadn't stopped thinking about Ana and failing to see her again these past few days had filled him with disappointment. In a town of two thousand people, you'd think a chance run in would be high. But she'd arrive soon and chat away into the night. He'd put on one of his best shirts, shaved, and was trying his best to relax.

Taking a swig of his beer, Liam glanced at his companions. They might be his cousins, but Jack, Adam, and Michael were the best friends he could ask for. Having grown up together on Shadow Creek, Liam considered these blokes brothers more than cousins. Their bond ran deep and it was up to the four of them to keep an eye on Lucy, who was a vault of secrets, and Lily, who was studying veterinary science in Townsville and the youngest of them all. Their fathers had operated Shadow Creek for thirty years and Jack and Adam would continue to do so in the future.

'How did the farm reports come back this week?' Liam asked, glancing at Jack.

'The same,' he replied. 'No sign of disease and soil's good. Got some spraying to do, but the next two weeks may be slow for us.'

Liam nodded. Like with any type of farming, every day was different on Shadow Creek. Commercial banana production was a tough industry and tightly controlled since Panama tropical race 4 disease was found in North Queensland in 2015. Every two weeks, department officials came to check the monitors around Shadow Creek and provide reports on fertiliser, spraying, and the risk of disease for the crop. Biosecurity was a necessary evil if they were to stay in business and even though Liam no longer lived or worked on the farm, his interest and love for Shadow Creek would run in his veins until the day he died.

'When are you planting that new field?' he asked.

'Probably not until February,' Jack replied. 'Might have some rain by then.'

Adam scoffed, his gaze glued to the bar. 'We won't. I can tell ya that.'

'The rain is a bit late this year,' Liam admitted with a grimace. They were two weeks into January and hadn't had a drop since early December, which was unusual. 'Must be frustrating.'

'Yep,' Jack said as he frowned at Adam. 'What are you staring at?'

'What do you think?' Adam nodded towards the bar. 'Jordan looks good tonight.'

Jack rolled his eyes while Liam and Michael shook their heads. Liam had his back to the bar, but he knew who Adam was checking out because he'd seen her himself on the way in. Jordan Kelly was a popular barmaid and thrived on being the centre of attention.

'Have you not learned your lesson where she's concerned?' Jack said. 'She's not worth it, mate.'

'Yeah, but she's been texting me for a few days now.' Adam took a swig of his beer and shrugged. 'Can't hurt, right?'

Liam sighed. There was no point trying to talk his cousin out of it. Adam enjoyed women, more often than Liam ever had, but when Jordan Kelly beckoned him back into her clutches, trouble often followed.

'Be careful, mate,' Liam warned him. 'Her brothers are here tonight and they'll be watching you like a hawk.'

Adam smirked. 'Only makes things more dangerous. I like things when they're dangerous.'

Liam shook his head. Why he bothered to warn Adam, he didn't know. Adam and Jordan's on-again, off-again, no-strings-attached arrangement was major fuel for the Maguires' lifelong feud with their neighbours, the Kelly brothers. Even though their fathers had grown up together and were best friends, there had been a rift between the younger Maguires and Paul and Harrison Kelly for as long as Liam could remember.

'Jack will have your back when they come after you,' Michael said.

Jack's eyes narrowed. 'Thanks, mate. Adam, if Paul and Harry pick a fight, you're on your own. We were only kicked out of here last month.'

Considering the feud, fights weren't uncommon. In fact, they'd been more frequent these past six months. Liam wasn't sure why, nor did he care to find out. As far as he was concerned, the less they had to do with the Kellys, the better.

If only Adam shared his views. But no matter how many times the feisty pub owner, Georgina, kicked him out of the Royal for fighting, Adam never learned his lesson.

'That wasn't my fault,' Adam protested, before turning his attention to Liam. 'So, tell me about this teacher? She cute?'

Liam resisted a sigh. 'I guess.'

'Blonde?'

'Why are you interested?'

'Why are you not?'

Liam took a long swig of his beer. It wasn't unlike Adam to play twenty questions about a new woman in town, but Liam refused to respond. The last thing he needed was for anyone to think he might be interested in Ana. Yeah, she was bloody gorgeous, but she'd only just arrived in town and he never rushed these things. Besides, pursuing her wouldn't be worth it if she was just another blow-in.

But that thought vanished as Adam let out a low whistle, and Liam turned to the door. The women were late, but they were knock-outs, each having slipped into tight jeans, cute tops, and killer heels. Liam stared. His heart started a rapid thumping as Ana slid into the booth beside him.

He no longer knew what he wanted to do.

* * *

Ana cursed herself. Why hadn't she let Lucy slide in first? Sitting beside Liam was not the best way to smother her attraction for him. Especially when he looked smoking hot in a tight red polo.

Meg made the introductions. 'Ana, this is Jack, Adam, and Michael.'

Ana smiled around the table, glad to meet them all. 'Hello.'

'Hey, Ana.' Adam flashed her a smile that had dangerous written all over it. Strangely, she was instantly charmed. 'Welcome to town.'

'Thank you.'

'You enjoying it so far?' Michael asked.

'More than I planned to.'

Meg snatched Jack's attention and while everyone chatted, Ana found herself caught in Liam's blue gaze.

'You look nice.'

She managed a small smile and ignored the heat that washed through her. 'Thank you. Meg insisted we dress up.'

'You sure did,' Adam said. 'Best-looking ladies in the room.'

'Distracted him from Jordan, anyhow,' Jack muttered.

Meg groaned. 'Adam, not again! Don't you remember what happened last time?'

'That wasn't my fault! I told Paul that Jordan had moved on.'

'He still punched you though. And Jack.'

Ana's spine stiffened and her hands clenched beneath the table. Meg had warned her about the feud, but it didn't stop her heart from lurching. She frowned as Adam merely grinned.

'Don't worry, Meggy. I promise Jack won't get hurt.'

Jack rolled his eyes. 'As if. I'll take Paul any time.'

Ana swallowed, twisting her fingers as she glanced at Liam. She tried to keep her voice steady. 'Why did they fight?'

'Adam and Jack have been fighting with Paul and Harrison Kelly since we were kids. Their sister Jordan isn't the nicest person, but she and Adam see each other on and off. Sometimes, things between us get heated and a fight breaks out. Jack usually backs Adam and you don't get past him in a fight, but Meg disapproves.'

Ana pressed her lips together. Of course, Meg wouldn't like it. Nor did she. Why should anyone? There shouldn't be any reason for the men to fight.

Lucy slapped her hands on the table and Ana jumped. 'Should we get a round of drinks?'

Adam downed the last of his beer. 'Keep 'em comin'!'

It was beers all around and Lucy declared it her shout. Ana slid out of the booth to help her, escaping Liam's warm presence as they waited at the bar. But Jordan served them far too quickly and Ana followed Lucy back to the booth.

Even though she knew better, Ana slid in beside Liam, passing him a beer as she caught up on the conversation. If she focused her attention on everyone else, maybe she could extinguish the heat burning in her belly. Besides, it was nice to find herself part of this interesting group of people and having fun on a Friday night. Ana couldn't remember the last time she'd gone out with friends.

'We've done three of them,' Adam said, leaning casually in the corner with one strong arm resting on the windowsill. 'Little two or four seaters. The big bastard is what we've been putting off.'

'*You've* been putting off,' Jack said, shooting Adam a glare before turning to Liam. 'We'd have had it made ages ago if Adam would pull his finger out.'

'What are you making?' Ana asked.

Adam's dark eyes brightened. 'Tables! Jack and I do a bit of woodwork. Carpentry, woodturning, making shit just because we feel like it.'

'Except when he's practically being *commissioned*,' Liam muttered with a shake of his head.

'Yeah, we're supposed to be making the tables for Liam's café. We have these massive slabs of silky oak, which Jack thought would be perfect.'

'And I thought would look good,' Liam added.

'But no one asked me if I'd make them!' Adam told Ana. 'They conned me, the bastards.'

'Just thought you'd want to contribute to the new family business,' Liam said, smirking. 'And to have your stunning work seen and admired by those who stop by.'

Adam waved the compliment away. 'Yeah, yeah, that's what Mum says about the stuff I made for High Ridge.'

'Don't you enjoy making something with your own hands though?' Ana asked. If she had any creative talent, she'd hone her passion and take pride in it.

'Yeah, he does,' Jack said. 'He just enjoys complaining more.'

Adam's eyes narrowed. 'It takes inspiration.'

'Not to make simple tables, it doesn't,' Liam replied.

'Simple? You call them simple?'

'Commissions don't take inspiration,' Jack said. 'You just need to get the work done.'

'Besides,' Lucy said, 'I bet you'll find plenty of inspiration once the Show approaches.'

'The Show's a competition! I can't have anyone beat me! You know what I mean, Luce. How many times have you won Cake of the Year?'

'You guys enter the Show?' Ana glanced between the Maguires. She knew that's what agricultural shows were all about, showing off animals, baked-goods, and arts and crafts. She'd been to the Sydney Easter Show nearly every year of her life, but she'd gone for the rides and show bags more than to take an interest in what the event was actually about. Now that she was in the country though, she'd likely embrace the animal, craft, and food competitions.

'I tell you, Ana.' Adam placed his beer down. 'The Show is the best weekend of the year and everyone takes part. Jack here is a machine in the woodchop and I always kick Harrison Kelly's arse in the woodturning comp.'

'Except that one year,' Lucy reminded him.

'Doesn't count,' he said, shooting Lucy a glare. When his gaze returned to Ana, it was warmer. 'But basically, it's a weekend full of animals and food and comps.'

'It's lots of fun,' Meg said. 'I love the Show. Jack and Adam usually beat the Kellys at the woodchop, then compete against each other.'

Ana nodded. Looking at Adam and Jack, they seemed the type. 'I've always enjoyed watching the woodchop.'

'It's my favourite,' Meg agreed. 'I also enjoy the horse events.'

'My mare Esme has won Best in Show before,' Lucy said proudly. 'I train horses and compete in some events myself. But Lily, my cousin, is a champion jumper.'

Adam grinned. 'Now that girl has skill.'

Jack nodded. 'I taught her well.'

'You? What about me?'

'You and Cade were too busy getting up to mischief to teach the little sis anything.'

'We taught her how to fight.'

'I'll give you that. As well as lying and stealing.'

Adam frowned. 'She doesn't do those things.'

'She did when you paid her to pick the locks on Mum and Dad's liquor cabinet.'

'She wanted to play with us!'

Ana smiled, enjoying the banter between the brothers. They appeared to be good guys and she liked them all. Jack was lean and rugged in an undeniably sexy manner with his dark hair a little too long, dreamy brown eyes, and shoulders that went for days. Meg looked positively petite beside him and Ana could easily imagine him repeatedly slamming an axe into a log. Adam too, who looked a lot like his brother with that added appeal of rebel. Michael was another version, younger and just as good looking. The three of them were the definition of tall, dark, and handsome, whereas Liam …

Her gaze drifted to her left. Liam had all the physical features of his cousins, yet his eyes were blue, his hair lighter, and she found that more appealing. How or why, she didn't know. Possibly didn't want to find out.

She couldn't believe that all the Maguire men were single.

'So, Ana.' Adam turned his attention back to her. 'You're from Sydney, right?'

'Yep.'

'What made you come here?'

Ana bought time to consider her answer by sipping her beer. 'Honestly, I needed out.' That, at least, was the truth. 'And I wanted to live somewhere smaller. When I saw they wanted a new teacher here, I figured Elizadale sounded like a nice place and applied.'

'It is a lovely town,' Liam agreed. 'Of course, we haven't lived anywhere else.'

'Really?'

'Well, Jack and I both did a year in Toowoomba studying agriculture,' Adam said with a wince. 'Cold, horrid place, that was.'

'But I did my tourism certificates online,' Liam told her. 'And Michael did his building apprenticeship here with Graham Klein.'

Ana nodded. That was normal for small towns too, wasn't it?

'I lived in Cairns for a few months though,' Lucy said. 'It's all right and is our main go-to place for shopping and healthcare and such. Only Jack's had the experience of being flown to Townsville. No one else has ever been that sick.'

'We've been lucky,' Adam said, and Ana agreed. Even though she wanted to know how Jack had landed himself on an emergency plane to Townsville, she knew better than to ask.

Liam's elbow gently nudged hers. 'So, how many years have you been teaching?'

'This will be my fourth,' she replied. 'I like the little kids, so I was glad I got the grade ones.'

Adam's mouth twisted. 'A whole classroom full of noisy kiddos, they couldn't pay you enough.'

Meg laughed. 'We already love you, Adam. No need to flatter us.'

'Oh, Meggy, I'd flatter you anytime.'

Jack shook his head and regarded Ana. 'Do you have brothers or sisters?'

'I have an older sister.'

'Oh, mate.' Adam's eyes gleamed as he glanced at Liam. 'She has a sister.'

Ana laughed. 'Natalia's a doctor in Sydney.'

'Natalia. She sounds hot.' Adam's grin turned wicked and Ana narrowed her eyes.

Lucy sighed. 'Really, Adam? Every woman?'

'What? She's got a nice name. Sorry, Ana. Please continue. Does Natalia look like you?'

Even though her sister would hate it, Ana grinned and decided to play with Adam. She liked him and it wasn't like he'd ever meet Natalia. Hell would freeze over before her sister stepped foot in a small town. 'She's prettier.'

Adam blew out a slow breath. 'Damn ...'

Everyone laughed while Ana leaned back in the booth and picked up her beer. The conversation moved on in an easy, casual manner. She could certainly get used to Friday nights at the pub.

Or maybe not. Ana perused the dinner menu and sighed. She'd expected this problem. She rarely ate out for many reasons, the main one being she could cook anything far better than she could buy elsewhere. But at least in Sydney, she had choices. Elizadale was limited to the two pubs, the takeaway shop, and the roadhouse. And the Royal Hotel had quite the standard pub menu, filled with steaks and burgers, all served with chips and what they called a salad. There wasn't much variety.

Grimacing, she cursed Natalia and her health advice. Then retracted it because Ana wasn't anything less than grateful. Natalia's health scare had probably saved both of their lives, even if it made eating at the Royal Hotel difficult. They didn't have many options for vegetarians.

'Would you like a recommendation?' Liam asked, standing next to her in line.

Ana glanced up from the laminated menu. 'Do you think they could make me the Caesar salad without chicken?' It was that or the garden salad again, which she'd had for lunch on Monday and had found rather ordinary.

'Of course.' His brow furrowed. 'You don't like chicken?'

'I don't eat meat.'

'Oh. Then yeah, they should be able to do that for you. No worries.'

Ana smiled. It wasn't often people judged her for being vegetarian, but it still happened now and then. She approached the register, placed her order, and thanked the girl when she only charged her the garden salad price.

Back in the booth, they continued to chat. Everyone was fun and interesting. She wished she could learn more about Liam but was also grateful that Adam led most of the conversation. She couldn't risk thinking about Liam. And while Adam may have an unsavoury reputation, the bad boy was easy-going and entertaining. He probably got away with a lot of things too since his best friend was a local police officer.

Cade Wilson dropped by their table after dinner to say hello, and Ana blinked. Was there something in the water in Elizadale? Because if the Maguire men were hot, they held nothing against Cade. He was taller, sexier, and *had* to be the town catch. She could only imagine the many hearts he and Adam would have broken together.

By ten o'clock, everyone but Adam was beat.

'You staying, mate?' Jack asked when Adam resumed eyeing Jordan.

'Yeah, doubt I'm going far.'

'You don't care that Paul's still here?' Liam asked.

Adam shrugged. 'Why should I?'

Jack sighed. 'Fine. But remember, you have work in the morning, so you better be there and not hungover.'

'I can promise the first.'

Jack rolled his eyes and turned to Meg. 'Can I give you a ride home, darlin'?'

'Ana and I were going to walk.'

He blinked. 'No, you're not.'

Ana bit back a smile as Meg batted her eyelashes. 'Jack, there will be two of us and the crime rate here is pretty much zilch.'

'There won't be two of you when you go in separate directions,' Liam said.

'Exactly,' Jack agreed. 'I'll drive you ladies home.'

Meg rolled her eyes at Ana. 'Heaven forbid. I guess we better get in the car.'

They left Adam behind and headed outside, calling their goodbyes as Jack escorted them to his ute. Ana tried not to watch Liam or check out his cute butt as he crossed the road towards his LandCruiser.

Shaking her head, she slid into the back of Jack's twin cab ute.

'Have you enjoyed your first week here, Ana?' Jack asked as he pulled out onto the road.

Her heart twisted. 'It's been great. Everywhere I go people know I'm new, are so friendly, and seem to like the idea that I'm a teacher.'

'Yeah, people do like us,' Meg agreed. 'When I was growing up, we had many blow-ins. It's the reason I wanted to become a teacher, so I could come back here and stay. We're actually pretty lucky since your position is the only contracted one.'

Ana was well aware of the tendency people had to do a rural stint for the experience before returning to the city. She'd considered it herself when she'd first graduated and knew that's what people in Elizadale might think of her, that she'd blow in, stay twelve months, and blow out again. Like a golden wattle in the wind. If only her case was that simple.

Yet what Meg said surprised her. 'The rest of you are permanent?'

'Three of our staff have been there since before I was born. Like Deborah. Then there's Elanora, who's also local and unlikely to leave.'

'Huh. I guess I'll find out more about that on Monday.' Jack pulled up outside Jackson Villas. 'Thanks for the ride.'

'No worries.'

Meg turned from the front seat. 'I'll see you at agility training.'

'I'll be there.' And with a last goodbye, Ana stepped out of the ute and waved as she headed inside.

She locked the screen, turned the deadbolt, and applied the chain to the wooden door before sinking against the glazed windowpane and smiling. She'd been afraid it'd be hard to make friends in a small community. At first, she hadn't minded because she could keep to herself, get through her year unnoticed and run away again. But honestly, she was glad that wouldn't be the case. She missed having friends and since Meg and Isabella both went way back with the Maguire family, it was a privilege to be included.

But what was she going to do about her pesky feelings for Liam? She could pretend otherwise, but she was attracted to him. Her heart had danced when he laughed and she'd actively spent most of the evening trying not to look at him.

Ana sighed and pressed her lips together. She didn't want to spend her life running, but right now, she saw no other option. Rick was possessive and thrived on control. She'd realised long ago that there was something seriously wrong with him.

Shaking her head, she strode to the back door to check on Louis. She didn't want to think about Rick. She didn't want to be afraid. But Rick had hurt her once and she knew without a doubt that he'd do it again.

And she couldn't risk her heart over Liam Maguire when she didn't know where she'd be next year.

Chapter Six

Liam glanced up as the gate crashed closed and Adam strode into the dog park, his Jack Russell, Rusty, running off to sniff the bushes.

'Be level with me, mate.'

Liam paused in setting up the hurdle. 'About what?'

'You like Ana. Admit it.'

Liam shook his head. Great. Just what he needed. 'Why do you think that?'

'Please! You couldn't take your eyes off her on Friday night. Granted, she's fucking pretty. So, what you gonna do?'

Liam turned the legs out on the hurdle and set it on the grass. 'Never said I liked her.'

'You're going to go slow, aren't you?'

He sighed. His cousin may be his best mate, but they'd never thought alike when it came to women. Not that it surprised him that Adam had caught his spark of interest in Ana. She brought new life to their group and he'd enjoyed getting to know her on Friday. But even though they'd shared a few lingering gazes and smiles, he'd sensed no great interest on her side. Only resistance.

He frowned. What did that mean?

Shaking the thought away, he glanced at Adam. 'Even if I do like her, doesn't mean I'll rush into anything. Call me old-fashioned, but I like to know someone on a personal level before dating.'

'Yeah. You're old-fashioned.' Adam helped himself to a hurdle and began setting up. 'But I suppose some girls like that.'

Liam rolled his eyes. 'You wouldn't know because you keep hanging out with Jordan. I see you're still breathing though, so did you not take her home Friday night?'

'Sure did. Paul just knows better than to stick his nose in.'

'Paul knows nothing, Adam. He's a bloody wanker.'

The gate opened again as Meg and Lucy arrived. Steph shot across the park in a black-and-white blur to greet Roger, Lucy's German shepherd.

'Hey!' Meg called, leaving Lola to sniff Rusty. 'What are we talking about?'

Adam didn't miss a beat. 'How Paul Kelly's a wanker.'

'Paul is a wanker,' Lucy agreed, crossing her arms over her chest. 'You got Jordan out of the Royal, did you?'

'Sure did. Nothing was stopping her.'

Lucy shook her head. 'Why do you keep going back to her? You should find someone nice to date.'

'Yeah,' Liam agreed, shooting Adam a grin. 'You'd like it, mate. Dating's fun.'

'So why don't you do it?'

'I do it more than you.'

Adam laughed. 'That's debatable.'

'Oh, stop it, you two,' Lucy said. 'Although Adam is right, Liam. You haven't been out with a woman in forever.'

Liam's mouth curved. 'Don't make me retaliate, Luce. At least I tell you who I date.'

His sister frowned and Liam knew he'd struck a chord. It'd become somewhat of a legend, the story of Lucy and her secret lover.

She crossed her arms over her chest and shook her head. 'You still don't want to know.'

Adam shot his hand in the air. 'But I do!'

'We're not talking about this.' Lucy reached for a hurdle and stalked across the park.

The gate opened again, and Liam turned as Ana arrived with the most gorgeous border collie—*male* border collie— he'd ever seen. Her blonde ponytail hung over her shoulder as she told Louis to sit. He obeyed, shivering with excitement. She unclipped his lead, opened the second of the two gates, and Louis raced into the park.

'Hi!' Ana grinned and Liam's stomach knotted. Damn, she was pretty. She wore denim shorts and a pink T-shirt that hugged her slender frame. A stylish brown hat shaded her face.

'Hey.' He moved towards her, swallowing as he glanced at her dog. He'd do better to focus on the dog. 'So, that's Louis? He's beautiful.'

She beamed. 'Yeah. Oh look. He's found Steph.'

His chest swelled as he watched Louis and Steph circle each other, catching a whiff and deciding whether they'd be friends. 'They look good together.'

'Yeah. Two border collies are always better than one.'

Liam laughed. 'See? I knew I could like you.'

He slipped his hands into his pockets, resisting the urge to take Ana into his arms and kiss her passionately. It was amazing how much you could like a person just because they liked your dog.

Blowing out his breath, he called Steph. She looked at him and tilted her head. *What?* Liam tapped his thigh. Steph's mouth fell open and she came running. Louis followed. Steph sat at Liam's feet, panting happily as she raised her paw.

'Good girl. Say hello to Ana, Steph.'

Ana dropped into a crouched position to pat her and Steph's eyes closed in pleasure. 'You're gorgeous, aren't you?'

'Yes, hello, Louis.' As the other dog vied for attention, Liam crouched to pat him. 'Your mummy still loves you. She's just—'

Louis ran out of his arms and across the park, barking at the bird he'd seen take flight.

Ana laughed. 'He has a thing about chasing birds and keeping them out of the yard.'

'Well, he's got to have something to do. Steph herds the galahs in the yard of an afternoon, don't ya, girl?'

Ana stroked Steph's head. 'Do you like to play fetch? That's Louis' favourite game.'

Steph broke all her lady-like tendencies as her tongue darted out to lick Ana's cheek. Horrified, Liam was about to scold her, but Ana merely laughed. His heart did a strange, swishy thing as he cleared his throat. 'Steph loves playing fetch.'

* * *

Ana glanced around the park, amazed by the turn-out. A range of dogs sat waiting around the fenced grassland, from little terriers to big retrievers. Isabella and her King Charles cavalier stood with Meg and Lucy. Evie sat between Isabella's feet on a sparkling pink lead, the picture of a perfect princess who didn't want to dirty her pristine paws. Meanwhile, Cade Wilson added to his appeal with a squirming Jack Russell tucked under his arm. Rusty sprinted across the park to greet them, jumping up Cade's leg until he put the dog down.

But no one looked better than Liam. Ana's nerves continued to vibrate as she watched him set up the equipment, admiring the easy way in which he moved. When everyone had split into groups to begin training, Liam crouched to talk to Louis, his arms strong and tanned beneath the tight cuffs of his crimson shirt. 'So, Louis, what do you want to learn first?' He lifted his gaze to Ana, his large hands rubbing Louis' ears. 'He's okay with basic commands, right?'

Ana swallowed. Dammit, she had to stop checking him out. 'He can sit, stay, and come when he chooses to.'

Liam smiled at Louis. 'We'll just see how you go today, hey? You don't need to be perfect, but I bet you'll pick it up quick. I can see you already have a strong bond with your mummy, so you'll do as she instructs, won't you?'

Ana's heart thumped. How could she *not* like a man who spoke to dogs like that?

Liam stood. 'Let's start with hurdles.'

As they joined the group waiting at a series of low hurdles, Ana glanced around the park. 'You have lots of equipment.'

'Yeah, we've done well.'

'I like the look of the bridge.'

'That's the dog walk. It's an advanced obstacle because it's a bit scary for dogs up there.'

'Right.' Ana glanced at the hurdles. 'What do I do here?'

'Have Louis stay on one side and we'll call him over one

hurdle to start with. He needs to have a release word, something other than "come" as that's an everyday term. But you can use it today if you wish.'

'Okay.' Ana watched a woman call a kelpie over the hurdles.

'As handlers, we get a good workout ourselves, especially when the dog's a beginner and needs to be handled closely. And look at Louis.' Liam grinned. 'He's already watching and learning.'

Louis was watching, but whether he was learning was a different matter.

Ana could certainly get used to this though. Barking and laugher filled the warm air and with Liam beside her—fit, sexy, and smelling incredible—agility sure had its perks.

When it was her turn, Liam instructed her on what to do. 'Let Louis stand and tell him to stay. I'm sure he'll jump over them. We're doing it at this height to build his awareness that there's an obstacle there.'

Ana nodded. That explained why the hurdles were only a few inches off the ground. 'Do you and Steph want to go first?'

Liam shook his head. 'Nah, we'll go next.'

Hoping Louis wouldn't make them both look ridiculous, Ana positioned him in front of the hurdle. 'Okay, stay.' She unclipped his lead and backed up a few paces to the other side of the hurdle. Exhaling and praying that he'd do it, Ana slapped her thighs. 'Come, Louis.'

Louis ran around the hurdle and sat at her feet, rising to plant his paws on her knees.

Ana laughed. 'No, baby.' She took Louis by his collar. 'Come back here.'

Leading him back to the starting position, she risked a glance at Liam. He was grinning. 'It's not funny.'

'No, you're doing a good job. Keep going. He'll get it.'

'How's he doing?' Meg asked, strolling towards them with Lola snuggled in her arms.

'He's going to do it.' Determined to make it happen, Ana dropped her gaze back to Louis. 'Okay, stay.' She hurried around the hurdle again. 'Now, come. Jump, Louis.'

Louis jumped over the first hurdle. Ana shrieked. 'Yes! Good boy! Okay, let's do another. Stay, Louis.' She ran around the next hurdle, pulse racing, and called him again. 'Come! Jump, Louis!'

He jumped over the hurdle and Ana fell to her knees, her heart somersaulting as she threw her arms around her talented dog. 'Good boy! You're so clever. Who's a clever boy?'

Grinning, she clipped Louis' lead on and almost skipped back to Liam. 'Did you see him? He did it!'

His blue eyes shone. 'He was great. So were you.'

Warmth filled her cheeks as she dropped her gaze to Louis, then Steph. 'Your turn, girl.'

Liam led Steph to the starting position. Ana watched, keen to see his dog in action. Liam unclipped her lead and held up his hand rather than verbally commanding her to stay. He moved to the end of the three hurdles without looking back. Steph watched him with her eyes focused, her body forward and her front paw poised, like a runner waiting on her mark.

'Okay, Steph,' Liam said, and Steph took off. She leapt over the hurdles, quick and agile. Ana blinked. When Steph finished, she pranced around Liam's feet, her tongue drooping with pride.

Ana's eyebrows shot up. Steph was incredible.

She glanced at Louis. He looked up at her. 'You're going to learn how to do that.' When Liam and Steph returned, Ana smiled. 'Wow. Steph's awesome.'

'Thanks. She's still young, but I've put a lot of training into her.'

'How long do you think it'll take Louis to be that good?'

'Not long, I reckon, if you come every week.' He sounded confident about that as he rubbed Louis' ears.

Ana smiled. If she got to hang out with Liam, then she'd definitely be there.

She glanced at Louis. 'Was that fun? Do you want to learn how to do this?'

His mouth dropped open in a doggy smile and Ana took that for a yes.

Liam rubbed Louis' head again. 'You'll be a star athlete, won't you, Louis?'

'I hope so. Should we stick with the hurdles for today?'

'Yeah, then we'll give them a go at the tunnels.'

Accepting that plan, Ana ran Louis through the hurdles until he grew bored. Then they moved on. He'd get better with practice, but she wasn't in any hurry because training him was proving to be a lot of fun.

And at least agility was something they could continue doing no matter where they moved onto next.

Chapter Seven

After settling into the staffroom on Monday, Deborah introduced Ana to her colleagues. 'This is Elanora Campbell, our prep teacher.'

'Hi.' Elanora smiled. She was a pretty woman who couldn't be much older than Ana. 'It's great to have you with us.'

'And Joe Cooper, our physical education teacher.'

'Welcome aboard, Ana.' Joe smiled kindly. He looked to be in his thirties and boasted the muscular body of a man who liked his sport.

'And Vivian Roberts.'

Ana shook Vivian's hand. She was an older teacher with greying brown hair and kind eyes behind her glasses.

'And Kate Lewis, Linda Wilson, and David Brennan, who is also our deputy principal.'

'It's lovely to meet you all.'

After Deborah had introduced her to their administration assistants and teacher aids, the principal took a seat at the head of the table to begin the staff meeting. Ana sat beside Meg and during the first hour, she learned more about rural education than any university could have taught her. As education was a serious issue in rural and remote areas, Deborah was under extra pressure to provide quality education to the children of Elizadale. The school had done well last year with their test scores, compared to schools in similar regions, which they hoped to maintain as Deborah outlined new strategies for the upcoming year.

Yet it was no wonder small schools struggled. Elizadale didn't have half the facilities and opportunities that her school in Sydney had. Interschool activities were available but required travelling to Mareeba or Atherton or Port Douglas. Queensland Health still sent Harold the Giraffe to provide health education and the school dentist made an annual appearance. Sports tours came, but they had no sports teams. There was no band or choir. No debate team.

But Meg was right about one thing—they had dedicated teachers. Deborah, Linda, and David had been a team for over thirty years. Meg and Elanora were locals unlikely to leave. Ana didn't know Kate or Vivian's story, but they'd been in Elizadale for some years.

Ana's heart twisted even harder as she interlaced her fingers beneath the table. If only she, too, could give this school more than twelve months.

But she couldn't stay. The year itself was already a big ask.

Shoving those thoughts aside, Ana focused on the changes to the curriculum that Deborah was discussing. The government had altered a few things for other year levels, but not much for grade one. And despite what Elizadale lacked, the school still provided the students most of the classes that would be available to them in the city. All they were missing out on was music and a foreign language, which was unfortunate but not surprising.

When she left the meeting, Ana couldn't wait to get started

as she walked with Meg and Elanora to their section of the school.

'It's set out in a diamond pattern, as you can see. Admin is at the front, we're here on this side, grades three, four, and five are on the other, and six is at the back. This is our lunch area.'

They'd arrived at an undercover concrete area ringed by wooden benches with water bubblers on one side and toilets at the back.

Ana smiled. 'It's cute.'

'The other sections have the same thing,' Elanora said as they continued along the path.

Meg waved her hand towards the three white Besser block buildings. 'And these are our classrooms.'

One sat longways overlooking the other two, which faced each other. Colourful curtains covered the windows and port racks lined the outside walls.

Elanora moved towards the one to their left, while Meg and Ana headed for the facing classrooms. They waved goodbye and Ana stepped inside. Switching on the lights and air-conditioner, she glanced around the room. Desks were stacked at the back, chairs piled in a corner, and cubby shelves lined one wall. With a double whiteboard at the front of the room, the setup wasn't much different from what she was used to.

But she recognised potential. She had a new start, new school, new children to educate. Ana's heart filled with excitement. She'd always loved her job and working with children. And after this morning's meeting and the week she'd spent in Elizadale, there was more to being a teacher here than she'd realised.

Sighing, she sat and opened the curriculum. Wouldn't it be

nice if she could stay? If she could educate children who were disadvantaged simply because they lived in a rural area? Because being a teacher in Elizadale wasn't the same as it was in Sydney. Here, she would be valued. She'd fill an essential role for a basic need. She'd never have to fight to keep her position. And if she stayed … could she maybe take a chance with Liam?

Ana shook her head. No. She couldn't risk daydreaming. It was foolish.

Resting her chin in her hand, she focused on reading the curriculum. It didn't take long. There wasn't much unchanged or that she wasn't familiar with. She placed the pages aside and picked up her class list. She had a class of eleven, which was far smaller than she was used to, but an intimate class meant she could give each student individual attention.

A knock sounded on the door and Ana glanced up to find Deborah letting herself in. 'I thought I'd come see if you needed anything or had any questions.'

'Um …' Ana glanced at the papers in front of her. 'No, I think I'm okay. I was just going over the student list.'

'Good. Do you like your classroom?'

'Yes, it's nice.' She glanced around again, imagining it filled with artwork. 'I'll set it up later in the week.'

'All right. But if there's anything you need, just let me know. We're expecting a delivery on Wednesday so you'll get new stationary then.'

'Okay. Thanks, Deborah.'

'No worries. I'll see you at lunch.'

Deborah left and Ana returned to work. By twelve-thirty, she had her first term planned and a list of ideas for projects. Joining her colleagues in the staffroom, she settled between Meg and Elanora with her potato curry. Chatter filled the room as everyone asked her questions, welcomed her into their tight-knit workplace, and updated each other on their latest news. Ana enjoyed Vivian's stories about her new baby grandson, which had Meg and Elanora's hormones going haywire. She could understand Elanora's reaction since she was trying for a baby with her husband, but Ana wasn't sure what to make of Meg. She was obviously in love but didn't appear to have done anything about it.

'That was a good day,' Ana said when they left work later, almost skipping as she and Meg crossed Riley Road. 'David's quite funny.'

'Yeah, I love David. He was my grade six teacher. Linda's great too. I had her in grade two and four.'

'And Vivian's very excited about being a grandma, isn't she? Those baby pictures got you going a bit.'

'Yeah ... it's something I think about. Vivian's daughter is my age, married with a baby, and I damn well should be too! Many girls I went to school with have had kids and even my younger sister has two. But I'll be twenty-six in August and it doesn't help my mummy hormones when I'm around kids all day. I need a man to wake up and realise he's in love with me so we can get married and have a dozen babies.'

Ana smiled to herself. 'Wake up' was probably the correct term. 'A dozen?'

'Well, two isn't enough.'

'True.' Ana had thought about kids when she'd been with Rick, having imagined three or four. 'It seemed Elanora was getting a little clucky as well. I guess it's hard to "try" though. She's also very nice.'

'Yeah, Elanora's lovely. It's hard to dislike her.'

'Why would you want to dislike her?'

'She's a Kelly,' Meg said, and Ana's eyebrows shot up. 'Paul and Harry's older sister. But we've put El in the neutral zone because she doesn't cause us trouble.'

Ana frowned. 'None of you like the Kellys, but Adam sleeps with Jordan.' Where was the logic in that?

'Yeah, and I still don't understand why. He should steer clear of her. But El's nice and she can't help it if her brothers are a couple of idiots.'

'True,' Ana agreed as they arrived at Jackson Villas. She waved goodbye to Meg and went inside, switching on the air-conditioning to battle the ridiculous heat. She led Louis onto his inside bed to enjoy the cool too, then sank into the lounge. In less than an hour, she'd see Liam again and after the way her heart had gone off on some sort of frenzy yesterday, Ana wasn't sure how much longer she could ignore her feelings. All year? It'd be torture!

She needed to debrief and there was only one person Ana ever turned to for advice, who she missed like a limb torn from her body.

She phoned her sister.

'Ana!' Natalia's pretty face—so much like Ana's—filled the screen as she answered the FaceTime call. 'How is it up there? Are you bored yet?'

Ana laughed as she tucked her legs beneath her. 'Not at all. I'm having a great time. I've met a wonderful group of people and started at the school today. I'm going to love working here.'

'I'm glad to hear it. I was worried you'd go crazy within a week, but you've made it so far.'

'Just because you wouldn't survive without the hustle and bustle of the city.'

Natalia shrugged. 'You never know. I like peace and quiet

on occasion. And I'd love to grow my own food, although I'm sure I'd kill it. So, the school's good, you said?'

'Yeah. I mean, I knew being a teacher in a small town was a highly valued position. Any profession is. But now …' She sighed, unable to express the feeling in words. 'It's going to be great. Deb Maguire, the principal, is lovely. She introduced me to another teacher, Meg, who showed me around. Elizadale's such a sweet place, Nat. Even you'd like it. We're *surrounded* by fruit farms.'

'I do love my fruit! And you never know, I might visit. Have you got a nice house?'

'Yeah, and there's a spare room, so visit any time you like. Louis' yard is small, but there's a park I take him to. And we're getting involved in dog agility!' Ana sighed as she lay down on the lounge. 'Oh, Nat. I need to tell you about Liam.'

'Ooh, Liam? A man?' Natalia smiled, but it didn't quite reach her eyes. 'Are we happy about this?'

'I'm not worried,' she said, understanding Natalia's concern.

'In that case, tell me everything.' She rested her chin on her hand and stared into the camera.

Ana swallowed. Where to start? 'Well … I'm attracted to him, Nat, and he seriously makes my heart do crazy things. Nothing like Rick ever did.'

'All Rick did was make you bleed, cry, and give up everything that was important to you,' Natalia stated dryly.

'Yeah, but before that.' Ana dismissed the unpleasant memories with a wave of her hand. 'When he was romantic, kind, and spoiled me with orchids.'

'When he seduced you into believing in a fairy tale,' she sighed, both wistfulness and resentment in her tone. Natalia winced. 'I'm sorry, Ana. I don't for a second believe that Liam would do the same thing. And if you're keen, then I am too.'

'Well, I'm not sure if I'm keen because I can't stay here, but I think I like Liam. His kindness seems genuine and—oh, the best part!' Ana grinned. 'You want to know the best part?'

'Of course!'

'He's got a border collie named Steph!'

Natalia laughed. 'A girlfriend for Louis! Aww, you could double date!'

'Oh, shut up.' But Ana was laughing too, glad to have her sister again even if they were only together via videophone. She and Natalia had always been the best of friends. Even Rick hadn't managed to separate them, despite his many attempts. 'But yeah … Steph's beautiful.'

Natalia's eyes softened. 'Sounds awesome, Ana. I'm glad Louis has a friend, but you know me. I like the man.' Natalia had her own issues with men, and she too had grown wary after Ana's incident with Rick. But while she jumped back and forth between dating and avoidance, Natalia always loved talking about other people's love-lives. 'So, tell me more. What does Liam do?'

Ana filled Natalia in and told her sister about everyone she'd met. 'And you'll also be pleased to hear that I went to yoga!'

Natalia's eyebrows shot up. 'They have yoga in Elizadale?'

'Yeah, one of the local nurses just started it. It was fun.'

'Yoga is awesome, but I'm into Pilates at the moment. I'm glad you've made friends and you seem happy. I miss you though.'

Ana smiled sadly. 'I miss you too. But I am happy.' She had to remain focused on the positives. 'So, tell me what's up with you?'

Natalia shook her head. 'Nothing much. Bondi's quite different from Burwood, but it's not like I'm not used to living in a new neighbourhood. Work's okay and I've started seeing this new guy from Pilates.'

Ana smiled kindly but didn't get excited. She knew to tread carefully, just like Natalia had about her news of Liam. 'And is he promising?'

'He's all right,' Natalia replied, but Ana didn't miss the disinterest in her sister's eyes. 'But it's unlikely to go anywhere.'

'Fair enough. Work's not giving you trouble?'

'Nah, they're good to me. I wish we did more procedures because I want to work on my excision technique, but they prefer to send everyone to the skin clinic instead. But I did get to extract some gravel from a young guy's knee!'

Ana's eyebrows lifted. Her sister was always excited about getting a scalpel in her hand. 'How so?'

'He'd come off his motorbike a few months ago and had a bit of gravel rash on his knee. It'd been cleaned at the time, but he hadn't been able to kneel since. Bit of an issue being a plumber and all. I could feel there was still gravel beneath the skin, so I got in there and extracted the offending little rock. It was bigger than we'd expected too. Five millimetres in diameter!'

Ana laughed at Natalia's delight. 'Well, I'm glad you got a little blood on your hands.'

'It was pretty cool.' Natalia tucked her blonde hair behind her ear and rolled her eyes. 'Although why anyone rides a motorbike is beyond me.'

Ana had to agree there. Natalia continued to update her on the jewellery their mum was making, then Ana noticed the time and sat upright. It was almost five o'clock!

'Sorry, Nat, I need to go. Meg will be here any minute.'

A cheeky smile spread across her sister's face. 'All right. Have fun. And Ana?'

'Yeah?'

'Don't hold back if you do like Liam. Rick's already taken so much from you. Don't let him take anything else.'

Ana's throat closed over. 'But what about the plan for me to keep moving?'

'Plans change, Ana. Roll with it.'

Chapter Eight

'Even Rusty could see how much you were falling for Ana yesterday!' Adam said, his frustration over Liam's reluctance making his voice rise as the men lounged in their booth. 'You couldn't take your eyes off her, didn't help anyone else all afternoon, and she's a damn catch! Hurry up and buy her dinner, I reckon.'

Liam sighed. 'Mate, just let me do it my way.'

'But your way pisses me off.'

'Leave Liam alone,' Michael told Adam.

Jack shook his head. 'I like how you suggest buying her dinner.'

Adam's spine straightened. 'I'm not unromantic! I've bought plenty of women dinner. I've even bought them flowers. And once, I bought a woman jewellery.'

Michael rolled his eyes. 'Mum doesn't count.'

Adam glared at his brother. 'So? What does that matter? Maybe the woman I want to buy jewellery for hasn't shown up yet.'

'Yes, because one day hell will freeze over and you'll want to settle down with someone,' Jack said sarcastically.

Liam and Michael laughed.

Adam backhanded Jack in the biceps. 'You can't talk. You're pushing thirty and by family law I don't need to settle down until my big brother does. It works in an order, you know.'

'It doesn't work in a bloody order. And you're pushing thirty too.'

'I'm pushing twenty-eight. I don't push thirty until you're thirty.'

Liam shook his head. 'Break it up, you two. Michael will marry before either of ya.'

Jack scoffed. 'Bullshit.'

'Liam might be right,' Michael agreed.

'Yeah.' Liam clapped Michael on the shoulder as he regarded his cousins on the other side of the table. 'You, Jack, don't express or receive feelings for women because if you did, you'd have had her a long time ago.' Liam's eyes narrowed as Jack frowned. 'Don't pretend you don't know what I'm talking about. And, Adam, you're too busy letting Jordan walk all over you to even bother looking for someone else. And you two say I have problems.'

Liam sank into the booth and drank his beer.

Adam raised his eyebrows. 'Who's to say Jordan won't be the woman I end up with?'

'She treats you like trash!' Liam cried. 'If there was any emotional connection between you, you'd have found it long ago.'

'If you marry her, I'll bloody kill you,' Jack said, crossing his arms. 'She's still a Kelly and it's bad enough you're sleeping with her. Now, be a mate and buy us another round.'

Liam went with Adam to the bar where Jordan was serving.

'Hey, stud.' She glanced at Adam with a wicked gleam in her eyes, her body curving against the bar and enhancing their view of her barely concealed chest. 'Another round?'

'Yeah, get in before the ladies get here.'

She laughed and tossed her dark hair over her shoulder. 'You're bad, Adam. As long as you buy me one after work.'

Adam handed over cash. 'Righto.'

Jordan grabbed the beers as Paul and Harrison Kelly walked into the pub. Liam inhaled, preparing himself. Harrison was always the first one to stick his nose in.

'Whatcha doin', Maguire? Planning to screw over my sister again?'

'Just buying a beer, Harry.' Adam lifted the bottle of Great Northern Jordan placed on the bar. 'Cheers.'

Liam gathered the rest of the drinks as Paul swore under his breath. 'Just watch it, Maguire.'

Jordan glared at her brothers. 'Bloody hell, you two. Let it go.'

Liam kicked Adam in the ankle and directed him back to the booth, leaving the Kellys to bicker.

Jack sighed wearily as Liam handed him a beer. 'It'll be your fight, mate. You rile them up, you take the hit.'

Adam shrugged. 'Whatever.'

Liam welcomed the arrival of the ladies.

'Afternoon,' Meg said as she and Lucy slid into the booth beside Jack.

Ana and Isabella sat beside Liam. Damn, Ana looked gorgeous in a pink cotton dress. The colour suited her pale skin and the skirt billowed around her slender legs. Would she ever fail to steal his breath away? He hoped not.

'Hey,' he said.

Her eyes glittered. 'Hey.'

'How is everyone?' Meg asked.

'Adam's about to get his head smashed in by one of the Kellys,' Jack muttered.

'Just be sure to get a few good ones in, Adam,' Lucy said, crossing her arms over her chest.

Meg sighed. 'Seriously, Adam. Don't rile them up. If this continues, Georgina may ban you from the Royal permanently.'

Liam laughed. 'She couldn't do that. He's one of her best customers.'

'Whatever. But I mean it, Adam.'

'Aww, I'm sorry, Meggy.'

'You will be when you and Jack are bleeding again. I'll make Georgina ban you.'

Adam laughed. Meg narrowed her eyes.

'She can do it, mate,' Jack warned. 'You better shut up and do what she says.'

'So …' Meg surveyed the table. 'Michael, what's going on with you?'

Beside Liam, Michael shrugged. 'Not much. Worked on the café today. Made progress on the house over the weekend.'

Ana raised her eyebrows as she glanced at Michael. 'You're building a house?'

'Yeah. This one's my own, so I've been taking my time, showing it plenty of care and attention.'

'He's been at it for eight months and only just put the frame up,' Liam said.

Isabella grinned and folded her arms over the table. 'It's going to be amazing. Michael brought in catalogues so we could help him choose tiles and such. I love decorating, so it was fun to help.' She leaned past Ana to meet Michael's gaze. 'It'll look great when it's done.'

Michael took a swig of his beer. 'I'm glad you think so.'

'Where are you building it?' Ana asked.

'On Shadow Creek.'

She frowned. 'Where do you live now?'

Jack scoffed. 'Some nights he sleeps on his slab.'

'But I'm still in the shack with Jack. We've got this small house we built for Jack, Adam, and Liam to get out of the homestead, and I moved in when I finished high school. We had a great time there until Adam and Liam went solo. But I'll move into my house once the roof is on and the plumbing works in the ensuite.'

'What about the kitchen?'

'Nah, I'll go to the retreat. Mum will feed me.'

'Fair enough.' Ana surveyed the table. 'Who needs drinks?'

Liam lifted his beer. 'We just got another round.'

With drinks for just the girls, Ana and Lucy headed for the bar. Liam released a deep breath and took a swig of his beer. With all the talk about houses, he wondered if Ana would like his. He had given it a lot of attention when he'd helped Michael build it, imagining the possibilities. Diane had only just left, so he'd chosen the design he'd liked and painted the walls a happy shade of eucalyptus, both of which she'd have hated. But it hadn't mattered, because it was *his* home. Yet as he'd chosen the décor, the thought of the right woman and a family joining him one day had never faded.

Slow, he reminded himself. He wanted slow. He liked slow.

But as he shot a glance towards the bar where Ana stood with his sister, Liam frowned. Did he want slow with her?

* * *

Ana's body softened as she left the booth. What had she been thinking sitting beside Liam again? If she didn't want to have feelings for the man, then close proximity certainly wasn't helpful.

'What would you like?' Jordan asked, jolting Ana out of her thoughts.

'We'll have three Diet Cokes and a Great Northern please.'

'Bloody diet shit,' Jordan muttered under her breath as she turned to fill the order. Ana frowned and exchanged a quick glance with Lucy, who simply shook her head.

'You must be the new teacher.' Ana turned towards the voice, surprised to find Paul Kelly speaking to her. She hadn't even noticed she was standing beside him. 'I'm Paul. Nice to meet you.'

He smiled politely and offered his hand, which Ana accepted. What choice did she have? Even if there was a feud raging between the Kellys and her friends, she couldn't be uncivil. Besides, Paul had done nothing to hurt her. And while she didn't care to notice, he also had quite a rugged handsomeness about him.

'I'm Ana. Nice to meet you too.'

He was still smiling as he withdrew his hand, picked up his beer, and turned his gaze to Lucy. 'Hey, Luce.'

Lucy didn't spare him a glance as Jordan placed their drinks on the bar. 'Paul.'

'You're looking well.'

With a beer and three glasses of ice in her hands, Lucy heaved a sigh before facing him. 'Bite me.'

She turned on her heel and stalked back to the booth. Ana stared after her, frowning but not surprised. It wasn't her problem. She took her change and gathered the rest of the drinks. When she returned to the booth, the conversation was back on the Kellys.

'You want me to beat him up, Luce?' Adam asked.

'He's not worth it,' she replied as she scooted out of the seat. 'I'm going to the bathroom.'

Ana sighed as she sipped her drink. 'What happened to make you and the Kellys hate each other so much?'

There had to be a reason, and if she was going to live in Elizadale and be the Kellys' sworn enemy by proxy, then Ana needed to know why.

'Our parents are old friends,' Adam told her brightly, and Ana's frown deepened. 'When we were little, we used to play together. But when Harry and I started school, he turned into quite the bully. Paul's a year between us and Jack. We no longer got along and spent most of our time arguing.'

'It grew from there,' Liam added. 'We became really competitive at school and local events. Thankfully for us, we always seemed to outshine the Kellys.'

'Then Adam and Jordan started seeing each other and that pissed them off even more,' Jack said.

Ana glanced from Adam to Jack, then to Liam. Were they serious? That was it? Sure, it was okay not to like a bully … but none of that sounded like an actual *reason* for the feud.

'Jordan can be quite nasty, as she's been known to tell lies and spread rumours, but Paul and Harry also have a protective older brother complex,' Liam continued. 'They seem to overlook Jordan's actions and I think they prefer to see Adam as using their sister than Jordan as a woman who makes her own choices.'

Adam nodded. 'But it comes in waves, Ana. Sometimes it seems like Paul couldn't give a shit what we did. Then the next thing I know, he's pissed with me again.'

'He's been pretty pissed off these past six months,' Jack said.

Liam frowned. 'Yeah, I've noticed that.'

'But basically, none of them have ever gotten along.' Meg sighed as she crossed her arms over the table. 'And that sometimes destroys our peaceful afternoons because Adam can't keep his mouth shut.'

'Fucking bastard can't tell me who I can and cannot date.'

Meg raised her eyebrows. 'Date?'

Adam shrugged. 'Whatever.'

Ana shook her head. She wasn't sure if it was enough to fight over, but while she may not like it, she didn't know what had happened in the past and shouldn't let it bother her.

As long as they kept their fists to themselves.

Lucy returned and snatched her beer off the table. 'What do you lot say to a game of pool? I think dinner here sounds good tonight.'

Ana resisted a groan. She'd been looking forward to her lasagne, but everyone else agreed and the Caesar salad hadn't been too bad.

'Sounds good, Luce. Shall we team up?' Jack asked.

'I want to be on Jack's team!' Meg shot her hand into the air. Lucy's shoulders sagged.

Adam shook his head. 'All the ladies want to be on Jack's team.'

'That's 'cause I know how to shoot pool.'

'Let's go, bro.' Adam slapped his hands on the table and

Liam swore softly under his breath. 'If you've got Meg, Luce and I'll only beat you anyway.'

'Hey!'

'It's okay, darlin'.' Jack wrapped his arm around Meg's shoulders. Ana sipped her drink to hide her smile. 'We'll show 'em.'

Ana followed her friends to the pool table in the next room by the bistro. As the players grabbed cues, she sat with Liam, Michael, and Isabella at a high table by the window.

Liam leaned on the table beside her, his biceps tensing beneath his tight sleeves. 'This'll be fun. Jack and Adam are competitive and both excellent players.'

Belly fluttering, Ana tore her attention from his arms and sipped her drink. She had to stop noticing these things. 'I've never played.'

'Really? I'll have to teach you. Adam and Jack are good, Lucy's okay, and Meg sucks. That's why she goes on Jack's team because he's legend enough to beat Adam and Lucy with Meg screwing up shots in between.'

'Are you any good?'

'Not as good as Jack.'

'I guess we can play later.' Ana imagined Liam leaning beside her as he guided her to make a shot, his body warm and close to hers. She shivered. 'What about you, Isabella?'

Isabella shook her head, pale hair falling over her face. 'I'm hopeless. Lily tried to teach me once. She's like Jack, of course. She can win a game of pool blindfolded.'

'She sounds interesting.'

Isabella grinned. 'Lil's awesome.'

Meg flipped a coin to see who got to break.

'How was your first day at work?' Liam asked.

'Loved it.' Ana tore her attention from the game. Her knees weakened at the interest in his blue eyes. Thankfully, she was already sitting. 'It's going to be great teaching here. Your mum sure knows what she's doing.'

Meg cheered as she won the toss.

'Yeah, Mum's always wanted to improve education in rural areas. That's why she came here. A year later, she married Dad, so she's had thirty years to make Elizadale State School what it is.'

'She's certainly passionate about it. Was it fun having your mum as the principal?'

'Yeah, she became principal when I was in grade three. I never got into trouble, that was for sure. Wouldn't dare.'

Ana laughed. 'I bet.'

'Adam did though. He and Cade dared all the time and Mum just kept punishing them. By grade five they were wagging school. Cade's dad, who's a copper, would hunt them down, make them ride in the police car, and take them back to school. Almost every day in grade six, that happened. Didn't improve much during high school either.'

Ana shook her head, amused despite herself. 'How'd they think they'd get away with that?'

'Apparently, that's what made it fun. I wouldn't know. I sat at school with Darren making bets on how long it'd take them to get caught.'

Ana smiled. As a group, they turned their attention to the game, which was entertaining but didn't last long. Jack sank three balls in a row and Adam was just as good. Lucy managed to sink one ball and Meg got none. But Jack quickly made up for it. It came down to Meg to win the game.

'Okay, darlin'.' Jack placed his hand on Meg's shoulder. 'Just line it up and shoot. You can do it.'

'Because if you don't, I will,' Adam teased, leaning on his pool cue with a mischievous grin.

Ana crossed her fingers, her heart pounding as Meg leaned over the pool table and lined up her shot.

'Relax your hand, Meg,' Jack coached her, placing his hand over hers. 'It's simple. There you go. Now shoot.'

She shot the eight ball straight into the pocket. Ana laughed. Adam swore. Meg cheered as she turned and threw her arms around Jack.

'Haha!' She laughed, taunting Adam and Lucy as she danced in Jack's embrace. 'Take that, suckers!'

'That's why you play on Jack's team,' Liam told Ana, smiling as Lucy declared best out of three.

Throughout the evening, everyone played pool. Jack never lost and Ana had a great time strategising with Liam while they lost a game to Adam and Lucy. To laugh and gossip and relax among easy company ... oh, she'd missed it.

The pub was almost closing when Jordan Kelly arrived at their booth. 'Hey, Adam. Let's get outta here.'

'Yeah, righto.' Downing the last of his beer, Adam stood and shrugged into his leather jacket. 'My bike's out front.'

'We should get going too,' Meg suggested, glancing at Isabella and Ana.

'I hope you don't plan on walking again,' Jack said.

Meg smiled sweetly. 'Wouldn't dream of it.'

They had just stepped out into the warm night when Paul Kelly called after them. 'Maguire!'

Ana's heart leapt as everyone spun around.

Jack's face hardened. 'What?'

'Fucking talk with your bastard brother.' Paul closed in and poked his finger into Jack's broad chest. Ana stilled. 'Because I tell you, Maguire. If Adam screws over my sister again, you'll both be sorry.'

Ana's hands clenched. A pounding filled her ears.

Jack, however, seemed unperturbed. 'Is that what you tell all the men your sister sees? Or just when she moves back to Adam?'

'Don't you—'

'Stop it!' Meg stepped between the men and pushed Jack back a step. 'Go away, Paul.'

Paul shot them a filthy look, then stalked back into the pub.

'Bastard.'

'Don't rile him up, Jack. Now get in the car.' Meg pointed and Jack did as he was told.

Exhaling, Ana turned to Liam. Her pulse slowed as she raised her eyebrows. 'Seriously?'

'Nothing out of the ordinary really.' His shrugged, then softened his gaze. 'So … I was thinking. What do you say to taking Steph and Louis to the park on Wednesday?'

Ana blinked. Her breath caught. Taking their dogs to the park meant alone time together. Whether or not she'd call that a date …

Natalia's words ricocheted through her mind. *Plans change.* So, before she could stop herself, Ana nodded. 'Yeah, okay. Sounds like fun.'

He smiled. Her heart did another hula-hoop while her stomach sank. What was she doing?

'Great. How's three-thirty?'

'Perfect.'

'I'll see you then. 'Night, Ana.'

'Goodnight, Liam.'

She slipped into the back of Jack's ute, pulse racing. It was just an afternoon at the park, not unlike what she may have done even without his invitation. She shouldn't overanalyse it. It was *not* a date.

But she suppressed her grin the entire ride home.

* * *

In a city of five million people, how would he ever find three lousy women? There were too many schools, GP clinics, and Bras 'n' Things stores. That's if the old woman still worked for that shop.

Rick had to give the slut credit. She'd done a good job of hiding.

He slammed himself back into the car, fury raging. Ana was his, dammit. *His.* She couldn't run away from him. He'd find her. None of them could hide forever. He'd find the bitch mother or the hot sister. Then he'd find Ana. He was a clever man and he knew how to find people. The most infuriating thing was that it seemed Ana wasn't stupid. Her social media existed but appeared unused. Or he just couldn't see much since she'd unfriended him.

Rick swore as he sped out of the shopping centre car park. It had been four days and he still didn't have a lead. He'd known finding her wouldn't be easy, but it wasn't impossible. And when he finally had his hands around her neck, she'd only have herself to blame. Just like last time. If she'd done what he'd wanted, she'd never have needed to be taught a lesson. And if she hadn't thought she could stand up for herself and walk out on him, she wouldn't have pressed charges. She wouldn't have destroyed his life. He'd still have his career.

And because she thought she had that power—because the court had granted her it—he had to show her *he* didn't give her that power.

Nothing would protect her from him now that he was free. Anastasia Hamilton better pray that she'd hidden herself well because he was coming for her.

And that stupid dog too.

Chapter Nine

Liam leaned his hip against the counter and put the phone on speaker, hoping that would help him hear over the hammering vibrating through the Tourist Centre from the construction zone. 'I've confirmed all bookings for High Ridge tomorrow. There should be two cabins free, yes?'

'Yep,' Wendy replied. 'Two cabins, then I'll be almost empty on Friday.'

'Good, because we have that artist retreat coming in.' Considering its serenity and isolation, High Ridge was popular for large groups and they'd hosted many events for artists and writers. Grace White had also mentioned the possibility of a yoga retreat. But they catered for all types and often had couples escaping for a romantic getaway, families who wanted to experience the bush and go horseback riding, and retired travellers who sought peace and quiet.

Liam smiled as he clicked to next weekend on the computer. Once, Wendy's retreat had been small and intimate, but since the Maguire family had bought the Tourist Centre and Liam had got his clutches into the business, High Ridge had boomed. And there would be more to come once the café opened, assuming he could make a success out of it. He didn't know why he doubted himself some days as he had a solid business plan and everyone loved good food. He even had a prime location with the Tourist Centre being the first stop after the roadhouse for drivers veering off the highway between Port Douglas and Cooktown.

But would his idea be too simple? Were people looking for more than smoothies, coffee, and food they could make at home?

Liam sighed. He guessed that's what he'd find out.

Simple had worked for him before though because the Tourist Centre wasn't anything out of the ordinary. Information flyers and local history books filled the shelves and Elizadale's resident artist Jessica Smithfield had painted a historical town timeline on the wall. Liam tended the gardens himself and had sourced local crafts to sell because that's what small towns were all about, helping each other out. He was forever liaising with local artists and seeing what else he could promote about the region. The centre still sold mass-produced souvenirs—postcards, magnets, and a variety of plush Australian animals—but also carried homemade jams, chutneys, and gifts. Isabella Brennan crocheted adorable plush bananas and Rebecca Taylor provided a supply of exclusive scented candles. Lucy loved them so much that she'd convinced him to burn them in the store, which everyone said added a country authenticity to the ambiance.

Liam inhaled and smiled, again grateful for his sister's suggestion. Today, he was burning rosella, his personal favourite.

'Everything's okay out there, then?' he asked Wendy.

'Yes. Thank you, Liam.'

'No worries. What are you cooking tonight?'

'Nothing too fancy. Roast beef with horseradish crust, garlic potatoes, and Yorkshire puddings.'

Liam's stomach rumbled. He shouldn't have asked. No one could pass up Wendy's cooking, least of all her family. Wendy had dreamed of opening her own restaurant and had been working up the culinary chain in Brisbane when she'd visited her sister in Elizadale and landed herself on a farm with the love of her life. She'd sacrificed her city career and had inspired the greatest menu change ever seen at the Royal Hotel. But after Lily had gone to school, she'd renewed her dream and opened High Ridge. Tourists had raved about the food and it'd been a success within a year.

'Sounds good. I don't think I'll make it out there, so I'll probably make some rissoles or something.'

'Do you have plans this afternoon?'

Liam slipped his hand into his pocket. 'Just taking Steph to the park.'

'That's always fun. I should get on though and start preparing dinner.'

'Okay. Thanks, Aunt Wendy.'

When Michael called it a day after lunch, having another project he needed to get to, Liam stepped inside the construction zone to look around. The frame and roof were up, but the wiring and plumbing still hung through the exposed beams.

'We'll hang the plasterboard on Friday, I reckon,' Michael said, standing beside Liam with his hands on his hips. 'But we're cruising along nicely.'

'It's brilliant, mate.' Liam's heart swelled as his dream materialised before him. Once the walls and ceiling were complete, the countertops would go in. Large windows overlooked the highway with the double-door entrance on the corner and an outdoor dining area. Liam would paint the walls a banana-flesh-cream to match the Tourist Centre and with Adam's beautifully crafted tables, he'd have the intimate café he'd always wanted.

'Won't be long now.' Michael clapped Liam on the shoulder. 'I also heard Jess Smithfield is painting you a landscape.'

'Yeah, she won't say what it's of though.'

'Well, you can always trust Jess to produce some quality art.'

Liam couldn't resist a grin. 'You still have that horse she painted you, don't ya?'

Michael gave a lazy shrug. 'How could I throw it out? First present a girl ever gave me.' Michael and Jessica had 'dated' when they were thirteen. 'Plus, she's much better now. I'm sure whatever she gives you will be brilliant.' He nodded towards the front wall. 'Should fit nicely between the windows.'

'That's the plan. Well, thanks, mate.' Liam shook Michael's hand. 'Catch you later.'

Michael left. Liam greeted an elderly couple who stopped by and chatted to them about local sights for a while. When Isabella arrived at one o'clock for her afternoon shift, Liam caught up on some stock ordering. Helping him at the Tourist Centre was only one of Isabella's casual jobs, but he enjoyed having her on the team and she was lovely towards the customers. At three, he left her in charge and drove home to pick up Steph for their date with Ana and Louis.

That's if he should call it a date. Liam wasn't sure and didn't think he needed to put a label on it. He just wanted to spend time with Ana. And Steph wanted to go to the park, so it was a win-win all around.

'Okay, girl. Let's go see Ana and Louis.'

Steph leapt into the back of the LandCruiser. Liam slipped behind the wheel and continued to talk to her, but Steph paid no attention as she stuck her head out the window. People often gave him grief about having a LandCruiser that was almost as old as he was, but why would he want anything else? He'd paid cash, it ran, and modern LandCruisers didn't have the rear windows that opened for dogs to enjoy. He was quite content not being in debt for a flashy car.

He pulled up on the corner of Riley Road and Station Drive and let Steph out. Ana was already in there. Dark denim shorts sat snug on her hips, the rolled cuffs finishing high on her slender thighs while a blue T-shirt clung to her torso. Her blonde hair swished in a long ponytail, exposing her creamy neck and pretty hoop earrings beneath her brown hat. Liam stupidly felt the air clog inside his lungs.

Then Louis ran towards her with a stick in his mouth and dropped it at her feet. Ana picked it up and tossed it. Liam squeezed his eyes closed. Shit. He did not just see that.

His stomach tightened as he let Steph into the park. She darted across the grass, nose down, tail up. Ana spotted her and turned to Liam with a smile. 'Hey!'

'Afternoon, Ana. Been here long?'

'A little while. I went home, sat for five minutes, then decided I'd been sitting all day and wanted to move, so we came early. How was your day?'

'Slow.' He stood beside her and slipped his hands into his pockets. Louis returned and lay at their feet, chewing happily on his stick. Liam resisted the urge to snatch it from him. *Later.* 'I took bookings for the retreat, but that was about it.'

'Do you have activities at the retreat?'

'Yeah. We allow guests to help in the guava orchards and

I want to start banana farm tours, but because of biosecurity guidelines, Dad and Uncle Henry are a little hesitant.'

'Yeah, I heard about that. To protect against disease or something?'

'Panama disease. It's all about controlling the spread of dirt. It's a serious issue, but they only found it in North Queensland in 2015, so quarantine methods continue to develop. We did farm tours before that though, so I'll start them up again eventually. In the meantime, there's always wildlife spotting in the reserve and bushwalks through the National Park.'

'That sounds fun. I enjoy walking, especially along pretty trails.'

'Yeah, the walks are nice. We also offer horseback riding, because horses are Lucy's thing. She takes people on trail rides and overnight campouts.'

'Yeah, you can forget about your campouts.'

Liam smiled as he tore his gaze from Louis. Steph had come to say hello, but Louis was too busy focusing on his stupid stick to pay her any attention. 'You don't like camping?'

She shrugged. 'I've never actually gone camping but sleeping outside doesn't appeal to me.'

'We camped all the time growing up, heading out to find a spot on the weekend to get away from the parents. It was fun, but I'm not exactly the outdoorsman in my family. Lucy loves sleeping under the stars though and Jack and Adam do it all the time. Except, Luce did find a snake in her swag once, which put her off for a while. Adam thought it was hilarious. Thankfully, it was only a harmless python.'

Ana shuddered and clutched her elbows. 'Do you get a lot of snakes out here?'

Liam grinned. Typical city girl. 'A few. This area is home to many venomous ones. But don't worry, I've lived here all my life and a snake hasn't killed me yet.'

She smiled. 'It must have been fun growing up on a banana farm though,' she said, moving to sit on the park bench.

Liam joined her. 'Yeah. There was always work to be done though and with six kids running about, Dad and Uncle Henry had a lot of help. It was usually the slave work, but it wasn't too bad. If they didn't have anything for us to do, Mum and Aunt Wendy sure did.'

Ana crossed her legs. 'I guess your mum and Aunt Wendy get along well?'

Liam nodded, dragging his gaze from her long, tanned legs to meet her eyes. 'Well, Mum and Aunt Wendy are sisters too, so yeah.'

Ana's eyebrows shot up. 'Wow, that's cool. Do you have any other cousins?'

'Nope. Two brothers married two sisters. What about you? Is it just your mum and sister?' It hadn't escaped his notice that she'd yet to mention her father.

'Yeah. My dad died when I was five.'

'Oh.' Liam's stomach sank. 'I'm sorry.'

'It's okay. He died at thirty-seven from sudden cardiac death. One second he was there and the next, he was gone. After that, we moved around Sydney a bit as rent prices changed, but Mum made sure Nat and I had everything we needed.' Ana smiled, the sparkle returning to her eyes. 'My mum's great. She, Natalia, and I are more like friends than anything else these days.'

An ache formed around Liam's heart. Even at five, it would have been hard for a little girl to experience a loss like that. He couldn't imagine growing up with only a few people when his family was so big and close.

'Sounds nice.' And all the stranger that she'd moved so far away. 'So, with names like Ana and Natalia, do you have Russian heritage or something?'

'Yeah, my grandmother was from Moscow. Mum's name is Nadia and I'm actually Anastasia.'

'Anastasia.' He smiled. 'That's pretty.'

She smiled softly. 'Thanks.'

'And your mum never remarried?'

Ana shook her head, her ponytail swishing over her shoulder. 'Nope. I feel bad for making this move and leaving her, but we both knew it was for the best.'

'How far away does Natalia live?'

'Not far, but Nat works six days a week as a GP registrar. She finishes her training in May, but I don't see her hours reducing.'

'Fair enough.' Liam swallowed as he prepared to ask his next question, unsure if he wanted to know the answer. But then Louis pushed his stick towards their feet and as Ana reached down, the focus of his concern changed. He should say something. But what?

She tossed the stick. Liam winced but couldn't tear his eyes away. The stick landed before Louis could catch it midair and his shoulders softened. But his heart continued to pound.

No, he had to say something.

'So ... do you often throw sticks for Louis?'

Ana shrugged. 'He'll chase anything. He loves his ball and never really took to a frisbee, but when we go to a park, he always finds a stick.'

'Yeah, dogs will do that when they want to play.' He cleared his throat. 'But can I make a suggestion?'

'Of course.' She tucked loose hair behind her ear as Louis returned with his stick. This time, Liam beat her to retrieve it. Louis gave him that intense border collie stare, waiting to give chase. But Liam would throw it over his dead body.

He glanced at Ana and said it before he changed his mind. 'Please bring his ball next time. Sticks are incredibly dangerous.'

She frowned. 'Really?'

'Well, yeah.' The tension inside him loosened as he handed Ana the stick. 'See how pointy that end is? One wrong move or a midair catch, it could seriously hurt Louis.'

She pressed her finger to the tip and gasped. 'Oh my God, I never thought ...' She glanced at her eagerly awaiting dog. 'No more sticks for you!'

Louis didn't move, just stared, waiting. Ana turned to Liam. 'When I was little, my friend threw sticks for her dog all the time. I just thought it's what you did.'

Liam nodded. 'I know. I could see you might not be aware of the danger. Many people aren't.'

Her ponytail swished as she shook her head, her eyes wide. 'I wasn't.'

'But I'd hate for an accident to happen and for Louis to get hurt. Many dogs have been killed while chasing, catching, or by chewing sticks. Balls or other fetch toys you can buy won't cut their tongues or pierce their mouths.'

'Oh my God, I never ...' Ana touched the pointy stick again. 'Well, I'm not surprised. Thank you.' She placed her hand briefly over his and everything inside Liam heated. 'I'll make sure I always bring his ball.'

He smiled softly. 'No worries, Ana.'

His heart pounded as she continued to hold his gaze. Then Louis lunged for the stick and she wrenched it away.

'No. Go run, Louis. Play with Steph.'

Louis sat, panting but still waiting. Liam relaxed into the bench and looked around to find Steph sniffing her favourite bushes. Ana placed the stick between them and Louis lay down. After some time passed in silence, Liam frowned. What had he been about to ask Ana?

'So ... I guess you miss your mum and sister?'

She nodded with a sigh. 'Yeah. We're very close and I've never lived this far away.'

His throat tightened. 'Do you think you'll go back after this year's over?'

'I don't know ...' Ana didn't look at him, but something in her voice alerted his sixth sense. She loved her family in Sydney, so why had she moved to Elizadale on the edge of nowhere? She may have wanted a rural experience and she'd taken this job because it had been available, but something didn't add up. And he hated to think of Ana being just another blow-in when she made his blood heat in ways he'd never felt before.

'Well, I think after this year you won't want to move because you'll fall in love with Elizadale.'

Ana smiled, but it didn't reach her eyes. 'You think so?'

'I know so. I may be biased, but there's nothing not to love about North Queensland. At any moment, the rain should come. Everything will grow greener and the rivers will flow. You'll have to see Barron Falls in flood, it's spectacular. Then winter will arrive and you'll freeze, but that means bonfire night at High Ridge. And once Louis becomes better at agility, you won't want to leave. You'll get the chance to renew your contract and you'll be saying yes, Ana.' He flashed her a smile. 'Trust me.'

Maybe by showing her all the amazing places around his

hometown, he might be able to convince her of that too? After all, the only way to stop something from blowing away was to help it grow roots.

Ana smiled, her eyes brightening this time. 'You seem very sure about that.'

'Oh, I am.' Unfamiliar confidence filled his chest and he couldn't bear the thought of not feeling Ana out for a date. Nevertheless, something in the back of his mind told Liam to tread carefully. 'Elizadale is like no other place on earth, Ana.'

'I'll admit I like it. And the country lifestyle.'

Hope rose inside him. 'Really?'

'Yeah. But they have dog sports clubs in Sydney too, so I could easily join one of them.'

'Yeah, but they aren't as awesome as ours.'

Ana laughed and again moved the stick out of Louis' reach. 'Okay, I'll be saying yes or no in October. But what if I told you I was already falling in love with Elizadale?'

Liam ignored the joyous leap of his heart. 'Then I'd say you have a great taste in small towns.'

'I haven't been to many, but this place certainly has charm. I can see why you want to make sure everyone knows it.'

'I am passionate about that,' he agreed. 'I'm glad I'm finally opening the café, anyway.'

'Meg said it's been a dream of yours for a while.'

'Yeah. It was something my ex and I used to talk about. She was a cook, I had the business sense, so it sounded like a good idea. She left a bit more than two years ago, but after a while, I realised I could do it myself. My cooking's all right and I have Lucy and Aunt Wendy to help me. I'm just a little worried about the menu because I want to keep it simple. Pancakes, waffles, milkshakes, smoothies. I don't want to step on the bakery's toes with too many cakes, but I'm afraid it might be too boring.'

She smiled softly. 'I think it sounds just fine, and like an exciting venture. Meg said you're planning a grand opening.'

'Yeah, I got some ads lined up for local papers and will make a big do of it.'

'Should be fun. What's the café called?'

Heat rose in his cheeks, but that didn't stop his grin. 'The Bent Banana.'

Her eyebrows lifted. 'Really?'

He sighed at the laughter in her voice. 'I know. I wish I could have come up with something else, but it came to me, and I laughed myself stupid thinking I couldn't name it that. But after a while, it stuck and I've decided to roll with it.'

'I think it's a fine name. Funny, but not unusual. And it sounds like a place people would want to visit.'

He smiled. 'Thanks. I think so.'

When Louis reached for the stick again, Ana shook her head. 'No, Louis. Go play with Steph.'

At the sound of her name, Steph looked over from the bushes, her black ears perking as she tilted her head. Louis' gaze remained glued to his stick.

'Come on.' Ana stood, calling Louis as she walked towards Steph. Louis followed Ana. Or his stick. Liam wasn't sure which.

'You want to play with Steph, mate,' he said, pushing to his feet. 'You two could have a lot of fun and she tells me she likes you.'

Finally, it seemed Louis noticed Steph and his ears perked as they sniffed each other. Ana laughed as she dropped the stick into the bushes, then crouched to pat both dogs.

'Aren't they beautiful?'

Liam ran his hand down Louis' lush coat. 'He sure is a handsome dog. Where'd you get him?'

'A breeder in Newcastle. I went there and played with seven puppies. It was like heaven. Paid a good fortune for him too, which hadn't been appreciated by a certain someone …' Her mouth thinned and she shook her head. Whatever thought she'd fallen into though quickly passed as her eyes brightened and she said, 'But I wanted Louis, and no one was going to stop me from getting him.'

Liam nodded. 'Boyfriend?'

'Yeah.' She rubbed Louis' head and sighed. 'We'd been living together for a couple of months. He wasn't keen to get a dog but said I could have one if I took the responsibility of looking after it, which I was happy to do. He didn't like that I'd spent so much money on him, even though it was *my* money, but I didn't care. I love Louis and if I wanted to pay for him then I damn well could.'

'Exactly.' Liam had paid a pretty penny for Steph too, but she'd been worth it. 'So … what happened to him?'

Ana's gaze returned to his. 'I left him a few months later.'

Liam resisted a frown. It wasn't like him to pry, but there was something going on behind Ana's pretty eyes. Something that made his pulse spike. He wasn't sure how serious it was as people split up for many reasons, but hopefully it wouldn't get between what he wanted with her. Because even though she still might leave, Liam wanted Ana. He wanted to date, get to know her, and find out what it would be like to press his lips to hers.

But since it probably wasn't a good idea to find that out anytime soon, he tore his gaze from hers and glanced at the dogs. 'So, why'd you name him Louis? You said something about the kings of France?'

Ana smiled, the sparkle returning to her eyes. 'The breeder was called Royal Border Collies, so I figured he needed a regal name. His full name is Louis Jacob Hamilton. And don't look at me like I'm crazy for giving my dog a middle name.'

Laughing, he shook his head. 'I wouldn't do that. Steph's full name is Stephanie Dawn Maguire.'

Ana laughed too. 'Oh my God. People really would think we're crazy.'

'As long as we don't find each other crazy.'

She sighed and stared at him for what felt like an eternity. His heart began pounding again. Hell, he was a goner. Anastasia Hamilton was too beautiful. Her sapphire eyes … golden hair … and she was just as dog-crazy as he was.

'Yeah …' She dropped her gaze to Louis. 'I'll admit, I've become an obsessive dog-mum. But it's just been Louis and I for so long now and I want him to be happy.'

Liam nodded. 'Of course.'

She continued to stroke Louis' back for a moment. 'So … Meg said you know about dog training and obedience too?'

'Yeah, a bit. I did a training course years ago so I could help people and their dogs with behavioural problems.' He frowned as Ana bit down on her pretty lower lip.

'Do you charge much?'

Liam resisted a smile. 'Friends are free.'

'Oh, you don't—'

She ceased her objections as he laid his hand over hers on Louis' back. 'What's the problem, Ana?'

Her gaze returned to his. 'Louis lunges at cars when we're out walking. It's incredibly frustrating. Could you help us with that?'

Smiling softly, he nodded. 'I'd be happy to.'

Chapter Ten

The Royal Hotel came alive on Friday night as locals danced in the outdoor beer garden. Ana sat with her friends sipping Diet Coke after sharing in Meg's bottle of chardonnay, more relaxed than she could remember being in a long time. The jukebox switched between country ballads, the latest pop, and old rock songs, filling the pub with a lively atmosphere where everyone seemed to be enjoying themselves.

Everyone except Paul and Harrison Kelly, who glared at Adam as he danced with their sister.

Beside Ana, Liam crossed his arms over the table as his gaze moved between his cousin and the Kellys. 'They look ready to smash his head in.'

Ana swallowed the lump in her throat. 'They're just dancing.'

'I know that. But Paul and Harry ...' Liam shook his head, his mouth twisting. 'I don't know what their problem is, but they don't like it.'

'Paul and Harry should get over it.'

Liam took a swig of his beer. 'You don't need to tell me.'

Ana glanced out at the crowd. She could see how Adam

and Jordan's proximity would annoy Paul and Harrison, but they were hardly making a spectacle of themselves. Yet the more everyone discussed it, the more Ana's belly roiled with the rising tension. Why couldn't they leave each other alone?

Sighing, she forced her spine to relax and glanced at Liam. Lucy was swaying with a farmhand from Tropic Sun—the banana farm south of Elizadale—and Ana's feet itched to move. She hadn't been out dancing in years, but she'd give it a little longer for Liam to issue an invitation before asking him herself.

When the men left to fetch more drinks, Meg glanced at Ana, curiosity gleaming in her pale eyes. 'You and Liam look extra cheerful tonight.'

Ana tried not to blush and failed. Liam had filled her thoughts these past few days and she feared she might really be falling for him. She could resist and deny it all she wanted, but such a thing was undoubtedly futile. Liam was kind, easy to talk to, and he had a sense of humour, which wasn't something she'd really considered important until now. But it was his dogs-are-people-too mentality that had stolen her heart. She'd been hesitant to ask for help with Louis' car herding problem, but when he'd agreed, hope had risen inside her. She couldn't wait to get started as every moment she spent with Liam made her feel glorious. And that was a definite sign of trouble.

'That's nothing,' Ana said, trying to brush off Meg's curiosity with a wave of her hand. 'We hung out at the park the other day with Steph and Louis. He's just being nice.'

'No, that's not it.' Meg nudged Ana with her elbow. 'Don't hold out on me, girl. Something else is forming between the two of you.'

'I'm not holding out on you. We're just … friends, maybe, who have the same type of dog.'

'So, you haven't been seeing each other outside of here and the dog park?'

Ana shook her head.

'So … nothing's happened?'

Ana laughed at Meg's crestfallen expression. 'No. He's nice, but nothing's happened.' And she should try to keep it that way.

'He is lovely, isn't he?' Meg said, her excitement returning. 'I've always thought he'd be a great guy to have. Not for me, but definitely for you. You're both intelligent and dog-loving people.'

Jack, Liam, and Cade returned with drinks. Liam handed Ana a fresh Diet Coke before leaning his elbow on the table.

'Thank you.'

'No worries.' He glanced out at the crowd, looking quite sexy in his knee-length denim shorts and black polo shirt that stretched across his chest. Her belly fluttered and she forced her attention towards Jack and Cade.

Ana was glad that Cade had joined them tonight. The more she got to know him, the more she liked the young Elizadale cop. He may have run wild in his youth, but with his father being the town sergeant and his mother the strict teacher, Linda Wilson, Cade had pulled himself together and followed in his father's footsteps. Like his parents, he was tough, and Ana still thought he was the hottest man in town. The kind of hot that women knew was out of reach. But she was glad to have him as a potential friend because the day might come when she'd need him.

Shaking her head, she sipped her drink.

Liam glanced at her and Meg. 'All set for school on Monday?'

Meg grinned. 'Yep!'

Ana nodded. 'I arranged my classroom today and have my first term planned. I hope to decorate the walls with lots of artwork.'

Liam smiled and her insides turned to mush. Ana sighed, trying to ease her frustration with her foolish hormones.

Lucy returned to the table and snatched up her drink. 'Hey! What are we talking about?'

'Work stuff. Where's your buddy?' Ana asked.

'Oh, that's Dave. He's pretty nice. I think he likes me.'

'Of course he does, Luce,' Cade said with a devilish grin that rivalled Adam's. 'You look good.'

Ana smiled. Lucy was indeed an attractive woman with a taut, lean body—a credit to her love of horse riding and hiking. She looked amazing in her tight blue jeans and snug black top, her dark hair hanging loose and long over her shoulders.

She laughed and gave Cade a playful shove. 'Aww, thanks, Cade.'

Cade nudged Liam. 'You'll have to beat them off with a stick, mate.'

'She can beat them off herself.'

Lucy sipped her Diet Coke. 'Yep. And have you guys seen the way the fuckhead twins are watching Adam and Jordan? They're rearing for a fight.'

Jack groaned. Ana shared his sentiments.

'It'll happen all right,' Jack muttered. 'But I'm not getting involved 'cause I don't wanna drink at Smithy's.'

Lucy's dance partner returned. 'Gotta shake up the dance floor. Call me if Paul wants to fight!' She waltzed away.

'You've got your work cut out for you with that one, mate,' Cade said, slapping Liam on the back. 'Makes me glad my sister's married.'

'Lucky,' Meg muttered, and Ana didn't miss the usual envy in her voice. Again, she reminded herself to talk to Meg about that. But for now, Ana focused on Cade.

'You have a sister?'

'Yeah, Emma. She's a nurse. Got married a few years ago to her high school sweetheart and has little Naomi, my favourite niece.'

Adam returned to the table—without Jordan—took Jack's beer, and downed half of it.

Jack barely blinked. 'You gonna buy me another one?'

Adam slapped some money on the table. 'I'm not waiting at the bar.'

'You realise that this kind of behaviour with Jordan is what started your last fist fight with Paul and Harry.'

Ana pressed her lips together, her hand tightening around the glass.

Adam shrugged. 'No, last time it's because we weren't "exclusive".' Adam actually used air quotes while Jack and Cade sighed in frustration. 'Hey, don't blame me. She's the one who took up with another bloke. The sooner the moron brothers get it through their heads that Jordan doesn't care about that stuff, the sooner my jaw will stay intact.'

Jack rolled his eyes. 'Why do you put up with her?'

'She uses you, mate. And last time, she got a free car service out of you.'

Ana frowned as Adam waved Cade's comment away. 'Yeah, yeah.'

'Can't you just find someone to settle down with?' Jack asked.

'I don't wanna settle down. Hey, hon.' Jordan joined them and Adam slipped his arm around her waist.

'Ooh, beer, gimme.' Jordan took Jack's beer and sculled the rest.

Meg placed her hand on Jack's arm. 'Want to go to the bar?'

'Seems I have to.' Pushing away from the table, Jack and Meg left.

Jordan placed the glass on the table and glanced up at Adam. 'Let's get outta here.'

'Righto.' Adam lifted his hand in farewell. 'Say bye to Jack for me.'

'Where do you think you're going, Maguire?'

Ana stilled, her heart leaping into her throat at the sound of Paul Kelly's voice.

'Home. You got a problem with that, Kelly?'

'Yeah. I do.' Paul stepped towards Adam, his eyes narrowing.

Ana shot a glance at Liam. Was he going to let this happen? Yeah, she was new in town and had no real idea why the Maguires and Kellys hated each other so much, but surely they didn't need to fight!

Jordan's lip curled. 'Oh, fuck off, Paul.'

Tearing his gaze from Adam to his sister, Paul's eyes flashed. 'Jordan, you have to stop screwing around with Maguire.'

'Hey, look! She can damn well—'

'Don't talk to me about my sister, Maguire! You have no right—'

'I think I have every right to say what I fucking wanna say!'

'Hey!' Jordan shouted, reaching past Paul to take Adam's arm. 'Come on, forget him. Let's just—'

Adam held up his finger. 'One sec, hon.'

'Don't you "hon" my sister!'

'I'll "hon" your sister all I want! You have no fucking say in it, Paul. No say in what either of us does.'

Paul's lips twisted. Ana cringed. 'Then maybe I'll "hon" *your* sister next time she's in town.'

'No, you fucking won't.' Jack's voice could cut glass as he returned to the table with Meg and a full beer in his hand.

'Fuck you, Maguire. Stay out of it.'

Adam's fists clenched at his side. Ana's breath caught. 'Yeah. No, you fucking won't.'

'We'll just see about that. You've got my sister, so I'll—'

Adam's fist collided with Paul's jaw so quickly that Ana didn't see it coming. She gasped as her hands flew to her mouth. Paul stumbled back. Jack advanced. Lucy rushed over. Jordan started shouting more obscenities. Paul came back swinging.

Ana placed her glass on the table, her hand shaking. She tore her gaze from the men, her heart racing and breath catching painfully in her throat as she dropped her head into her hands and tried to block it out. There was a crash and she squeezed her eyes shut.

Blood ... pain ... the swell of darkness. Everything came rushing back.

Then, all too quickly, the shouting stopped and silence fell as bodies scuffled around her. Ana looked up. Cade and Jack had Adam by the arms and Harrison had hold of Paul.

Liam stepped between them. Ana's breath escaped in a whoosh. He held his hand to his cousin's heaving chest.

'Stop it, Adam.'

'You keep *my* sister out of this!' Adam shouted, a small trickle of blood dripping down his chin.

Ana pressed her fingers to her lips. A metallic taste filled her mouth.

Memory. It's just a memory.

'Okay, okay!' A short blonde woman in a Royal Hotel T-shirt hurried over. The men ignored her.

'Fuck you, Maguire! If it wasn't for you—'

'Enough!' The blonde woman screamed it this time and everyone in the pub shut up, leaving only Midnight Oil burning beds on the jukebox.

'Maguire! Kelly!' The blonde was petite, but the fury in her eyes silenced Paul and Adam. 'What have I told you? No fighting in my pub! You know the rules! Get out and I don't want to see your faces for a week! And if this happens again, I'll ban you for life. I mean it!'

'Sorry, Georgina.' Adam shook himself free from Jack and Cade's grip. He reached for his keys by Ana's hand.

She flinched.

But Adam didn't seem to notice as he glanced at Jordan. 'Come on. Let's go.'

'Seriously, Maguire?' Paul called after them as Jordan led Adam out of the beer garden. Jack went with them. 'I thought I said—'

'Shut up, Paul!' Georgina cried and Paul shut up. 'Your sister is a grown woman and does as she pleases. Get over it. Because if you cause another scene in my pub, I'll kick you out of here forever. You got me?'

Georgina advanced, pointing her finger at Paul's face. And even though her head didn't even reach Paul's shoulders, there was no mistaking that Paul took Georgina seriously.

'Sorry, Georgina.'

'Good. Now, get out of my pub.'

Following Georgina's pointed finger, Paul and Harrison left. Chatter quickly resumed. Thankfully, everyone seemed to have been too immersed in the fight to have noticed Ana's reaction.

She took a deep breath and sipped her drink, forcing herself to relax and appear unperturbed. The last thing she wanted to do was explain herself.

'Did you lot cause any trouble?' Georgina asked, eyeing the rest of them with her hands on her tiny hips.

Meg shook her head. 'Sorry. We tried to warn Adam.'

'Then you can stay.' She turned on her heel and strode back inside.

'Well …' Liam turned back to the table, amusement flashing through his eyes. Ana frowned. She didn't see what was so funny. 'Looks like we've got rid of Adam for the week.'

'Can't blame him.' Smirking, Cade rested his elbows on the table. 'I would have punched Paul's smart mouth too.'

Ana raised her eyebrows as she stared at her new friends. Did none of them care that what had just happened was *illegal*? She glared at Cade. He should damn well know better. And Liam …

He took a swig of his beer and met her gaze. Ana forced herself to soften. She'd love to tell them off for treating what had just happened as a normal part of life, but that would only raise questions she didn't want to answer. She didn't know what had come over Adam and Paul. Anger and alcohol weren't a good mix, but Ana suspected it wasn't just that. Adam wasn't doing anything wrong and he had every right to tell Paul to get over it.

It was Paul who puzzled her. What was his problem?

When Jack returned, Ana shoved all thoughts of violence

from her mind. She'd been having a nice evening and she didn't want a stupid testosterone-fuelled fight to ruin it.

'Adam and Jordan left and I had a word to Paul. I ever hear the name "Lily" or a reference come out of his mouth again, I'll punch him myself.'

'All right, Jack.' Meg placed her hand on his shoulder and surveyed the rest of the group. 'So, now that's over, why don't we all go dance?'

Desperate to shake off her tension, Ana downed the last of her drink and jumped to her feet. 'Sounds good.'

Jack sat, sighing heavily. 'I'd love to, darlin', but I'm not in the mood to dance.'

'I'll dance with you, Meg,' Cade offered.

Finally, Liam extended his hand to Ana. 'May I?'

She smiled. 'Of course.'

Ana took Liam's hand, tingles shooting up her arm as he led her to the dance floor. Slipping his arm around her waist, he pulled her close. Her blood warmed and her tension melted away. She fitted into his arms perfectly.

'Now you've witnessed a Kelly-Maguire brawl and you're starting with the kids on Monday. See? You have to admit. Elizadale's growing on you.'

Ana smiled, her knees weakening as they swayed to the slow music. It didn't impress her that he'd shrugged off his cousin's behaviour, but her heart had a mind of its own as it waltzed happily inside her chest. 'It is. But I don't like fighting.'

'You did look a little pale …' His curious eyes searched hers. Ana gulped and quickly dropped her gaze, not caring if it gave her away.

She didn't want to talk about it. Discussing Rick at the park had been hard enough and she didn't like sharing the experience. But she might tell Liam about her past eventually, especially if they did develop a relationship.

'I was just a little … shocked, is all,' she said, shrugging.

'I don't blame you. Honestly, fights don't happen often. Not anymore. But it'd help if Adam stayed away from Jordan.'

Ana returned her gaze to his. She didn't know how much longer she'd last on legs that were turning to jelly. 'You never know. One day, he might meet someone and fall desperately in love.'

Liam laughed, the sound escaping from deep inside his chest and shooting tingles across her skin. 'We'll see. But right now … I don't care about Adam.'

Ana swallowed. She gazed into his alluring blue eyes as a tug of want pulled hard at her belly.

She'd never felt this way about a man before. Never desired one so much. Not with any of her previous dates and certainly not with Rick. And as she danced snug in Liam's arms, everything seemed quite right in the world.

But she couldn't date Liam. As much as she wanted to, Ana didn't have it in her. She didn't want to start something with potential only to lose it. Because she wasn't naïve. Rick would look for her. He would find her. And she would run.

She'd have no choice.

'Liam …'

His hand hardened against her lower back, cutting her protests short. 'It's okay, Ana. Let's just dance.'

She nodded, doing her best to relax. Thinking about what could or couldn't be would only ruin the moment. So instead, she focused on enjoying herself, an easy feat when wrapped in Liam's warm embrace.

* * *

That night, the nightmare returned.

She'd never known such pain. Everything hurt. Her ribs. Her knees. Back. Shoulders. She couldn't move. Her throat was raw. It hurt to breathe. Her screams echoed inside her head.

Rick's footsteps had faded.

Ana lay unmoving, her cheek pressed to the cold wooden floorboards. Maybe if she stayed still, she'd sink into oblivion and the pain would go away.

Then Louis' whimpers cut through the night air and Ana's eyes flew open. The border collie puppy scratched at the back door, crying.

No, she couldn't stay there. She needed to get up. She needed to take Louis and run.

Except this time, Ana couldn't move. In this nightmare, Rick came back.

Chapter Eleven

Ana awoke gasping for air. Sitting up, she clutched the cool sheet to her chest and blinked away the darkness. Her heart pounded. She hadn't had that nightmare for months.

Wrapping her arms around her legs, she dropped her head onto her knees. She took a deep breath and let it out slowly, again and again, just like she'd learned in yoga.

You're okay. You're alive. You got out. You survived.

But he was going to find her. He was going to hurt her again.

Ana lifted her head and ran her hands down her face. No. He *wouldn't* find her. He'd never look for her thousands of kilometres away in a tiny rural town.

Would he?

Ana threw back the sheets and climbed out of bed. Gazing out the window, she was glad to see the glow of the dawn because she'd never get back to sleep now.

She went downstairs, flipping on lights. A cup of tea would help settle her nerves. Black? Camomile? No, peppermint. Definitely peppermint.

She set the jug to boil, then moved to the back door. Louis

lay against the screen on his back, fast asleep with his legs in the air and his white belly exposed. Ana felt bad for disturbing him, but if anything would make her feel better, it was puppy cuddles.

She slid open the door and Louis jolted awake. He scrambled to his feet, wagging his tail and greeting her with a happy smile. Ana drew him inside, made her tea, then sat at the table with her steaming mug. Louis settled at her feet and lay his head on his paws. Sipping the sweet brew, she reminded herself that she was okay. She was safe.

But the moment dawn broke, she called her mum, thanking God for daylight savings and that Sydney was an hour ahead of her. Not that Nadia would have minded if Ana had woken her. She pressed the phone to her ear and waited. For once, Ana was glad that her mum didn't have an iPhone or FaceTime.

'Hey, Mama. Sorry it's early …'

'Not at all, sweetheart. Are you okay?'

Ana took a deep breath and rubbed Louis with her foot. He rolled over to expose his belly. 'I'm all right. I just … I had the nightmare again. About that night. I'm fine,' she hastened to assure her. 'Honestly. I suppose I just wanted to talk to you.'

'Of course, Ana. That's what I'm here for.'

Ana smiled. She'd phoned Nadia earlier in the week to catch up and tell her about work, but right now, Ana just needed to hear her mum's voice. 'I know.'

'So … do you want to talk about it?'

'Not really. Not about that night. But I am still afraid, Mama.'

It had been a long road. Only three years ago, she'd

thought she'd found her happily ever after. Her puppy had been born and she'd been eagerly awaiting his 'gotcha day'. A gorgeous, romantic man had stolen her heart and then …

Ana closed her eyes. She'd seen her psychologist weekly after the incident with Rick and had worked hard to improve her confidence, self-esteem, and reduce her anxieties. Some things still triggered her trauma, like the fighting and yelling that had happened last night, but deep down, the fear lingered. And now that Rick was out of prison …

'Ana, it's okay. I know it can't be easy, but you've done one of the best things you could by moving there. And there's been no word about Rick. I know he's only been out for a week, but he hasn't found Natalia or me, so I doubt he's located you, sweetie. And that's if he's bothering to look. He may not be as vengeful as we feared.'

'Yeah, maybe …' But Ana wasn't sure about that. She knew Rick. He needed to win. 'Just promise me you won't take any chances.'

'I promise, Ana. Don't worry about us, we'll stay safe. As long as you promise me you won't let Rick ruin anything you could have in the future.'

Ana frowned and sipped her tea. 'What do you mean?'

'Natalia told me you've met a man.'

'Oh.' She gazed into her mug, not sure what to say. She wanted to smile, but a ball of dread had formed in her belly. 'Yeah. But since I don't plan to stay here, I don't think …' Ana ran her hand down her face. Who was she kidding? She couldn't pretend what she felt for Liam wasn't real. 'Oh, Mama, I don't know what to do.'

She could almost hear her mother's smile. 'How about you start by telling me about him?'

And as she did, Ana's shoulders loosened. She shoved Rick from her mind and focused on the positives as the sun rose. Their conversation lasted through breakfast.

* * *

That afternoon, Ana braved the heat and humidity as she walked over to Station Drive to visit Meg. She had a lovely home—a small three-bedroom brick house with a formal living area at the front, the kitchen separated by a sliding door, and another sitting room at the back. Ana complimented her home and its simple yet elegant décor.

'It's all right,' Meg agreed as they sat at the dining table with Diet Cokes between them, 'but I don't plan to be here forever. It isn't fun living alone.'

Ana resisted a sigh as Meg absently spun the can round on the table. That was it. Meg commented on her single, unwed status often enough to raise Ana's concerns.

'Well … what's going on between you and Jack? Do you like him?'

'No, there's …' She stared at her drink, an array of emotions passing through her eyes. 'We're just friends. That ship … sailed long ago.'

Meg took a drink. Ana waited, but her friend didn't elaborate. Oh well, she'd broached the subject, but Meg obviously didn't want to talk about herself.

'Okay. Well, since you don't seem to mind talking about other people, can I ask you something?'

Meg's gaze returned to Ana's. 'Sure.'

'Um … why is Liam still single?'

A smile curved her friend's mouth. 'I thought you weren't interested.'

'I never said that. I said nothing has happened between us.'

'But you want it to?'

Ana shrugged and sipped her drink. Meg just laughed.

'Well, you'd think someone would have snatched him up. He did have a serious girlfriend once.'

'The one he wanted to open the café with?'

'He told you about her?'

'Not really.'

'Oh. Yeah, he and Diane were going to open the café. You could say they were high school sweethearts, although they didn't actually "date" until their early twenties. Friends first, you know? Diane was from Mareeba, where we all went to high school, and she wanted to learn to cook. So, she became Wendy Maguire's assistant at High Ridge. But when Liam started talking about building a house, she ran off to the city.'

Ana's eyebrows shot up. 'She didn't want to settle down?'

'Not sure, but she'd always wanted a city life. I never thought she was right for Liam anyway.' Meg's smile brightened. 'I saw the way you two were dancing last night though. Sparks were flying so much *I* almost got zapped!'

Ana's belly warmed at the memory. 'Yeah, it was nice. But I don't know, Meg. I'm not really looking for a relationship right now.'

'Because you just moved to town?'

'Yeah, but also because …'

Sighing, Meg leaned towards her. 'Okay. What happened, Ana? I'm sorry and I don't mean to pry, but I sense there's something you haven't told me. And I saw you last night. You were frightened when Adam and Paul started fighting.'

Ana swallowed the lump in her throat as Meg reached across the table and placed her hand over hers.

'If you don't want to talk about it, that's fine. But whatever it is, don't let it stop you from starting something with Liam. He's a great guy.'

Taking her hand from beneath Meg's, Ana fiddled with the flip-top on her drink. She didn't want to hide her past forever and she didn't need to. She wasn't ashamed and had no reason to be. And she liked Meg, so she could tell her even though Meg refused to talk about her own frail love-life.

'All right. But if I tell you, we need to talk about you afterwards.'

Meg shrugged. 'Fine, but I'm a very uninteresting story.'

Ana doubted that. Taking another sip of her drink, she searched for the right words. 'I was engaged. His name was Rick and he literally swept me off my feet. He took pride in giving me gifts and taking me to flash places, which was nice since I was still a uni student. He proposed a month before I graduated. We'd only been together for a year, so it took me by surprise, but I said yes. I loved him, you see? So, I got my first job, moved in with him ... and then Rick became abusive.' Ana paused for another sip before continuing. 'One night, not long after I brought Louis home, Rick hit me. It really did seem like an accident. He turned around so quickly and I was in the way. He apologised and I forgave him. But a few weeks later, it happened again, and I realised it hadn't been an accident.'

'Oh, Ana.' Meg took Ana's hand again, entwining their fingers. 'I'm sorry.'

Ana smiled sadly. 'Thanks. It was almost three years ago now and I feel I've moved on. I know it's not supposed to be common, although domestic violence is ridiculously abundant. So, I'm not holding back out of fear of it happening again. But Rick ... there'd been no reason for it. In the beginning, he'd been wonderful. But even though I didn't realise it at the time, he isolated me from my uni friends. After we were engaged and I had moved in, he became quite controlling, always wanting to know where I went and who I was seeing. He'd complain when I bought anything or spent too much money, which wasn't much at all. Besides, we had separate bank accounts, so it wasn't his business.'

Ana remembered like it was yesterday and her bones began to ache. 'The second time he hit me, it was completely out of the blue. He came home so angry and he took it out on me. And it wasn't just a few slaps, Meg. He pushed me into walls. Kicked and punched and slapped and … oh God, it was horrible.'

Ana glanced at their hands and swallowed, gathering the strength to continue. 'I lay on the floor, unable to move. Then he literally tossed Louis across the back deck.' She exhaled. 'I screamed. He was only a puppy! So, with a broken wrist, a few cracked ribs and aching like hell, I took Louis and got out of there. I pressed charges and considering my injuries, which involved internal bleeding and a long stay in hospital, he was arrested. For three months, I lived in fear while he was out on bail, but then the trial happened and they sentenced Rick to five years in prison. He only served thirty months.' She paused and swallowed. 'They let him out a week ago. And I know he wants revenge. He told me during the court proceedings that I'd be sorry for pressing charges. He was so adamant and mean about it, so I know he meant it. I couldn't relive the fear I had before the trial, so I applied for a job outside of Sydney. And here I am.'

With a soft smile, Meg squeezed Ana's hand. 'It must be hard to have that as your reason for coming here.'

Ana nodded slowly. 'I've always considered teaching at a rural school, so I'm glad I came. But I *had* thought I'd only move a few hours outside of Sydney. I always liked the idea of Cowra.'

'Well, I've never been to Cowra, but I'm glad you found our little town.'

Ana managed a smile. 'Me too. And if things were different, I'd like to start something with Liam. But I don't plan to stay in Elizadale, Meg. I think the best way to remain safe is to keep moving.'

'But you don't want to be running for the rest of your life. Don't you want roots?'

Ana's heart twisted inside her chest. 'Of course. And no, I don't want to keep running, but I don't know what else to do. Even twelve months in one place seems too long when I don't know what Rick's up to. I sort of hope he'll give up looking when he realises I'm no longer in Sydney. Surely he can't search all of Australia.'

'No. But I'm glad you got out, Ana.'

'People say it's tough, pressing charges. But it wasn't for me. He left me broken and after what he did to Louis …' Ana bit back her fury, her hand clenching against her thigh. 'Thankfully, he wasn't hurt. The vet said he was just sore, and he was quite timid after that. But we helped each other recover. Nothing is worth staying in an abusive relationship for, so it wasn't hard to leave. It was just difficult to keep Rick away afterwards. The trial was tough and I was terrified, but I had many people in my corner. And now … *this* is what's difficult. I've uprooted my life and have to live in perpetual fear, never knowing if I'll turn around one day and find him there.'

Ana took a deep breath as tears threatened to brew.

'I can't imagine what that feels like, Ana. And I don't know why people need to be so cruel. To hit someone like that …'

Meg exhaled and squeezed Ana's hand. 'You're a strong woman. Don't forget that.'

Ana didn't feel very strong right now. In fact, she was defenceless. What if Rick did find her? What would she do? She could pretend she was okay with her plan, but Meg was right. She didn't want to spend her life running and constantly looking over her shoulder.

'You'll be safe in Elizadale, Ana. Trust me. None of us will let anything happen to you. Especially Liam.'

Ana raised her eyebrows. 'Yeah?'

'Liam wouldn't let anything happen to a stranger, let alone someone he cares about. He's honestly there for everyone and always responds in a crisis. I've called him plenty of times if my car broke down or I needed help to move something. He doesn't have a hero complex or anything, he just likes to help. Even if it's a bad or strange or embarrassing situation, he's there for you.' Meg laughed lightly. 'One night, Lucy got herself in a pickle when she spent a few steamy hours in the back of her LandCruiser with her secret lover. They forgot to turn the headlights off and drained the battery. She called Liam to come get her and she wasn't in a decent state, let me tell you.'

Ana returned Meg's smile, her heart lightening.

'But the point is,' Meg continued, 'you can depend on Liam for anything. And no one will hurt you out here, Ana.'

Ana nodded slowly. She believed Meg, but preferring to think of anything else, she asked, 'Lucy had a secret lover?'

Meg sighed. 'Yeah. It was years ago and Lucy refuses to discuss it, even with me, her best friend of twenty years.'

'Hmm …' Ana frowned, puzzled. 'That's interesting.'

'Yeah, but Lucy's always had her secrets. One day, she came here and cried for three hours. I held her while she just cried. She never told me what was wrong. But the next day, she seemed fine again.'

Ana raised her eyebrows. Lucy's situation sounded more mysterious than Meg's story with Jack. 'Did these events happen around the same time?'

'No, the crying was last year.'

'Oh. Probably not related, then.'

'Doubt it. But yeah, if anything escalates, you should take a shot with Liam.'

'I'll see,' Ana sighed, finishing her Diet Coke.

Meg shook her empty can. 'Yeah, let's have another.'

'I'll get them.' Ana gathered the cans and stood. 'But when I get back, we're going to talk about you.'

'Whatever.'

Ana strode into the kitchen. She'd get through to Meg even if it killed her. Placing the cans in the recycling, she turned to the fridge, grabbed two more, and stepped towards the doorway.

And froze.

A snake lay in the corner of Meg's kitchen. Its brown body curled around itself, but there was no mistaking how long it was. Ana's heart started to hammer. She swallowed, searching for her voice as she remembered what she'd always been told and stood very, very still.

'Meg!' The word came out like a squeak.

A chair scraped along the tiles. 'What?'

'Snake!'

Seconds of silence filled the air. 'Where?'

'In the corner by the stove.'

'Okay.' Meg's voice hitched and Ana clutched the cans tighter. 'Don't move.'

Meg came through the hallway to enter the kitchen

behind Ana. She gripped Ana's wrist until she almost yelped. 'Shit.'

The snake moved. They both screamed.

'Get on the bench! Ana, on the bench!'

Meg pushed her towards the kitchen bench. They clambered onto it. Ana shook as she sat back on her heels. The snake's long length stretched along the kitchen tiles. It was over a metre.

'Okay.' Meg took a few deep breaths, her eyes wide. 'I *think* it's a taipan.'

'A taipan!'

Meg shushed her and prised the cans from Ana's hands.

'Sorry,' Ana said. 'I've just never seen a snake before. Apart from at Taronga Zoo, but it was in a glass cabinet and didn't have the ability to *kill you*! How do you know it's a taipan?'

'Because of its head shape. I could be wrong, but I know snakes well enough. Ana, pass me the phone.'

'The phone.' Panicking, Ana looked around frantically. 'Where's the phone?'

'Down there.' Meg pointed to the other end of the bench. Ana crawled over, picked up the landline and handed it to Meg. Her fingers trembled as she dialled. Ana kept her eyes on the snake.

'Jack!' Meg cried. If Ana wasn't so scared, she'd have laughed. 'I have a taipan in my house. I think. A snake, definitely. Can you come get it for me!?'

Ana took deep breaths to calm her racing heart. It made sense that Jack knew what to do with a snake, but who else would Meg call?

'Ana and I are on the kitchen bench … it's by the stove. Thanks, Jack!' Meg hung up. '"Don't panic," he says. Yeah right. Ana, grab one of those knives.'

Ana pulled a knife from the block and handed it to Meg, then grabbed her own. 'What are the knives for?'

'I don't know, but I feel safer.'

'I guess. So, you called Jack?'

'Jack knows how to catch them.'

'Have you had a snake in the house before?'

'We get them a bit around here, but I've never had a snake in this house. You do need to be mindful though, Ana. Snakes love farms and the tropics.'

'I'm so moving after this.'

'No, you can't leave! It's just a stupid snake. It's one of those things you get when you live in the country. Hence why God made men.'

'To catch snakes?'

'They need to be good for something. I don't care what anyone else says. As a woman, there are some things I shouldn't have to do.'

'True.' Ana took a deep breath, but it didn't steady her. 'How'd it get in?'

'Probably through the doggy door. Oh no!' Meg dropped her knife and scurried off the other side of the breakfast bar. 'Lola's snoozing on the lounge. I have to get her. If she comes in here, that snake will eat her!'

Ana tossed her legs over the other side of the bench to follow. 'Should I—'

'No, stay there. Do *not* take your eye off that snake.'

Ana nodded, turning back to keep her eye on Mr Taipan while Meg rushed down the hallway. Of course, she couldn't leave the snake unattended. What if it hid in the pantry and lunged at Meg later when she was making dinner? Ana shuddered, listening to Meg's footsteps as she opened and closed doors.

'I put her in the spare room.' Meg clambered back onto the bench. 'Hopefully Jack won't be much longer.'

Twenty minutes later, Jack called out and came in through the hallway. Seeing them both, he took off his hat and grinned. 'Look at you two armed and dangerous.'

Meg glared at him. 'Shut up. Get the snake out of my house, Jack, then you can laugh at me.'

Jack placed his hands on his hips as he studied the snake. 'Yeah, taipan all right. What were you doing?'

'Ana came in for drinks.'

His dark eyes gleamed. 'Then you both huddled onto the bench with knives?'

Meg continued to glare. 'Shut up.'

Adam strode in armed with what Ana assumed was the snake catching tool and bag. 'Where's our boy? Whoa, he's a big boy, aren't ya, mate?'

'Hold the bag, Adam.' Jack took the metal tool and moved towards the snake.

Meg clutched Ana's hand. Ana squeezed back to reassure her even though she was scared out of her wits. But she had faith that Jack knew what he was doing.

'Not going to hurt you, mate. You're just a little lost, aren't ya?'

Jack had the snake caught before Ana could even freak out. He dropped it into the bag and Adam twisted the top closed before taking the metal catchers from Jack.

'I'll pop him in the ute.'

Adam left. Ana blew out her breath and put her knife down.

'Thanks, Adam!' Meg called.

'Thank God that's over,' Ana said as Meg slid off the bench.

'Thank you, Jack.'

'Anytime, darlin'.'

He drew Meg to his side and she wrapped her arms around his waist. Ana smiled. They sure made a gorgeous couple.

'You know I'll always come. He was a big nasty boy too.'

'Still. You're the best. You and Adam want a beer?'

'Nah, we've gotta go,' he said and Meg stepped away. 'We'll release old mate by some rocks and then we've got a few things to do. Raincheck though, darlin'?'

'Of course.'

'Just keep your doors and windows closed, Meg. Especially at this time of year when it's still so dry. And don't forget to clean your floor. Snakes carry all sorts of diseases. Call me if you have any more slithery friends visit. Same goes, Ana.'

'Don't worry. I'll scream like a girl and have someone over real fast.'

Jack laughed. 'Okay, ladies. Take care.'

Ana hopped off the bench and walked with Jack and Meg to the door, unable to thank him enough.

'Anytime.' Jack tipped his hat and swaggered towards his ute. Ana and Meg waved until he took off down Station Drive.

'God, that was scary,' Ana said.

Meg visibly shuddered. 'I can't stand snakes. They freak me out.'

Ana couldn't withhold her grin. 'Good thing you've got Jack, isn't it?'

Meg rolled her eyes and headed towards the laundry. 'Yeah, yeah. I'm going to mop that floor. Shut those doors, would you, Ana?'

Chapter Twelve

When Ana told Liam about yesterday's encounter with the taipan, his eyes filled with concern and he reached for her shoulders. Ana didn't hide her smile.

'Thank God I wasn't in my house alone else I'd have had no idea what to do.'

'I'm sure you'd have managed and called someone. But just remember, snakes are harmless if left alone.'

'Yeah, so you all say. But that doesn't mean they're not scary.'

Agility training was underway and once again, Ana had gained Liam's undivided attention. He looked good, as usual, and smelled like mango after spending the morning slicing up bucket-loads of the fruit to freeze. But the sweet scent made her insides flutter, so she glanced at Louis. His tongue hung out the side of his mouth as he panted with excitement.

'Should we do hurdles again today?'

He nodded. 'Yeah, let's start there.'

Ana exhaled as she followed Liam towards the hurdles. They laughed and joked as they trained Louis and watched Steph fly over the jumps. Liam was so confident with her and

Steph obeyed him with such trust. Their bond only made Liam even more gorgeous. Whenever Steph finished a task, she'd stand at Liam's feet, her mouth open in a wide smile. She was an energetic girl and so beautiful, proud of herself and pleased with Liam's praise.

The sight brought warmth to Ana's chest. How could she resist a man who had such a big heart for his dog? They made a great team and it wasn't only Steph who was amazing. Liam was far too sexy as he ran with her, his commands clear, their connection unbinding. Ana shamelessly watched his strong calf muscles ripple in the sun.

'You're going to be as amazing as Steph one day, Louis,' Ana whispered as she watched Liam lead Steph through a small course. Sitting beside Louis on the grass, she pulled him close and rubbed his neck. 'You like agility, don't you?'

Louis' gaze darted around the park, a clear sign he wasn't listening. Ana sighed and watched as Steph jumped over the last hurdle and ran to Liam, bouncing around in a circle before placing her paws on his thighs.

'You two are great together,' Ana said when they returned. She stood and dusted her hands on her thighs.

'Thanks. We work hard, don't we, girl?' He beamed at his dog before meeting Ana's gaze. 'So, what are you doing for dinner?'

Ana blinked, her pulse spiking as she tightened Louis' lead around her hand. 'Tonight? Nothing. I'll probably whip something up.'

'Well, I was going to whip something up if you and Louis want to come over. Steph and I would enjoy the company.'

No. It was a bad idea. Such a bad idea. It'd be far more prudent if they only spent time together among the company of their friends. She should refuse. Make up an excuse. Tell him she didn't think it was wise.

But she didn't want to.

'Okay. We'd love to join you.'

Liam's blue eyes lit up and Ana's heart flipflopped. 'Great! If you come around at about six, there'll be plenty of daylight left for Louis and Steph to play.'

'Sounds good. Do you want me to bring anything or do you need any vegetarian ideas—'

He dismissed her question with a wave of his hand. 'I'm sure I can handle it and please, only bring Louis. Now, how about we go do the tunnels?'

Nodding, Ana contained her smile as she followed Liam across the park, but her subconscious continued to reel.

What was she doing? Dinner at Liam's house couldn't *not* be a date. She may want her life back, to have friends and be happy, but she didn't want a broken heart.

Then again, it was only dinner.

Ana sighed as they joined the line at the tunnels. *Relax, dammit!*

But her heart continued to pound. Hopefully, the nerves would pass.

* * *

They didn't pass. Ana's hands tightened around the steering wheel, butterflies fluttering in her belly as she turned into Liam's driveway. Parking next to his LandCruiser, she let out a deep breath. Everything would be okay.

She stepped out of the car and straightened her skirt. She'd had no idea what to wear and had spent too long rummaging through her closet. Jeans would have sufficed, but she'd chosen her favourite white lace sundress because the city girl in her couldn't fathom the idea of wearing anything less to dinner. And looking nice gave her courage.

Letting Louis out of the back seat, everything inside Ana softened as she gazed around the property. The sprawling house was well situated among the shady gum trees, the cream walls shining beneath the dying sun. The many gardens overflowed with palms and flowering bushes. Well-tended buffalo grass enhanced the greenery and split pine logs lined the gravel driveway.

Ana smiled. It was everything she'd expect of a small acreage, and the fact Liam took great pride in his yard filled her heart. Because his home … it was as though he'd conjured it from her dreams.

She quickly shook that thought away and told herself not to be foolish. Stepping onto the verandah, she rang the doorbell.

It wasn't Liam who answered.

'Oh my God, it's true.' Steph let go of the rope tied to the handle and smiled. Despite being forewarned, it was no less surprising.

'Hey.' Liam strode down the hallway and opened the screen door.

'Hi,' she said as Steph and Louis greeted each other with sniffs and wagging tails. 'She really opens the door.'

Liam grinned. 'She really does. Hold on a moment, I need to shut those gates. Houdini here will escape.'

He jogged down the few steps and along the driveway. Ana watched him, admiring the easy way he moved as she held Steph by her collar. When he closed the white wooden and wire gates, Ana unclipped Louis. He and Steph scurried down the stairs and away.

'They certainly don't waste any time,' Liam said, returning to the verandah.

'They're already best friends. So, Steph likes exploring, does she?'

'If I leave the gates open, curiosity will get the better of her. I almost lost her when I rebuilt the fence last year. The clever girl chewed through her lead and ran off for a swim at the golf course. She still hates being tied up.'

Ana's chest tightened. 'Coming home and not finding Louis there is my greatest fear. If he got out, he'd chase a car for sure.'

'Yeah, Steph probably wouldn't do that, but I'd hate to find her gone too. She has a metal chain now if I ever need it, although she tries to chew that too.'

Ana laughed as Liam opened the door and she stepped onto the glossy floorboards in the bright entryway. There was a modest dining room with sheer curtains in front of her and a formal living area with plush blue sofas and grey carpet sat to her left. A sense of welcome washed over her as she followed Liam down a short hallway.

'I was thinking too,' he said over his shoulder, 'that we could work on Louis' car chasing on Wednesday, if you like?'

Ana nodded. Wednesday was the Australia Day public holiday, so she wouldn't have to work. 'That'd be great.'

They arrived in the kitchen and open plan living area, which was simply decorated and tidy. A solid square table sat by the kitchen and two cream lounges faced each other with a wooden coffee table between them. A sliding door led to the covered back deck.

Ana smiled. 'You have a lovely home.'

'Thanks. I try to keep it simple. What would you like to drink? I have beer, water, or white wine.'

'Water's great for now, but I'm happy to have a glass of wine with dinner.' Ana didn't ask what they were having, but the aroma drifting from the oven smelled delicious.

Liam filled them both a glass of water before inviting her onto the deck. Ana lowered herself into a padded chair at his timber table and gazed out at the massive yard. His property backed onto Shadow Creek with a six-foot wooden fence and gate separating him from the bush. A cluster of banana trees brightened one corner and what looked like a mango tree shaded a stone bench.

Ana relaxed and sipped her water. She may have grown up moving around Sydney, but she'd always loved wide-open spaces. They provided such freedom and beauty. A kookaburra laughed overhead as Steph and Louis chased each other around a palm garden.

'This is a fantastic spot you have here.'

'Yeah, it's quiet and there are always birds around. That kookaburra you hear comes every afternoon until dusk and the galahs will settle on the back fence later.'

Ana swallowed. She shouldn't mention it, but the words came before she could stop them. 'I briefly had a nice place in Sydney with a big yard.' The opportunity to have a yard, gardens, and a dog had added to her excitement about moving into Rick's house, all of which she'd enjoyed during the five months she'd lived there. 'I loved having so much space.'

'You don't miss the city?'

'Not really. Some aspects maybe, but I'm only a city girl because that's where I grew up. I've always imagined myself somewhere semi-rural, I just never thought I'd move this far away. But I like Elizadale. It's small and friendly, not including the Kelly brothers, of course.'

Liam's mouth curved as he sipped his water. 'And you're looking forward to school starting tomorrow?'

'Yep.' She grinned. 'I love the first day of school.'

Steph barked at Louis to get him to chase her. He responded and she took off through the garden. As she watched the two border collies, Ana's heart filled.

'Did you always want to be a teacher?'

'I think so.' She tore her gaze from the dogs and met his. Liam looked incredible sitting on his back deck, his long legs stretched out in front of him. Warmth filled her belly as Steph and Louis rustled the palm fronds and the kookaburra laughed in the sunset. Ana cleared her throat and sipped her drink. Perhaps it'd be best if she kept talking. 'I decided to be a teacher in high school and fell in love with it during my first university placement.'

'Teaching can be a rewarding job. I know Mum thinks so.'

Ana's system relaxed again. 'I think it's even more rewarding to teach in a small town.'

They continued to chat as the pink-and-grey galahs settled on the fence. Steph snuck up on the birds in her slow sheepdog trot before bolting at them. They flew off, only to repeat the process. Louis quickly picked up on the game and Ana smiled. She was glad he had a friend. Did dogs make friends? Of course, they did. And it was lovely to see Louis happy again after the months he'd spent timid and frightened.

Liam asked her more about his car herding problem and she explained the best she could. He seemed confident they'd be able to work on it though, and they agreed on a time for Wednesday. Then he told her about his role on the town committee and his goals for The Bent Banana.

'I want it to be a place that the locals can be proud of. And that people from surrounding towns will consider to be a nice weekend outing, like saying to the kids, "Hey, let's go to The Bent Banana".'

Ana nodded, understanding what he meant. Sort of like visiting the Big Banana in Coffs Harbour, although not to that scale. 'I'm sure you'll make it something very special, Liam, even with the simple food.'

'Yeah, the menu should be fine. I hope. It's not all simple. I don't mind cooking and experimenting, but Luce and Aunt Wendy helped out and we made a fabulous choc avocado brownie.'

'Sounds delicious. With Meg's family's avocados?'

'Yep. But I still think people like to eat what they're familiar with, so I'm sticking to the sandwiches, fruit muffins, ice creams, and smoothies. I also plan to make it a dog-friendly place with a separate eating area outside.'

Ana gasped. 'That's a great idea! Then you can sell dog treats!'

Liam paused with his water glass halfway to his mouth. 'Well … yeah. I didn't think about that. I was just going to advertise as dog-friendly and have bright yellow water dishes. You mean homemade dog treats?'

Ana nodded. She and Louis had frequented a dog-friendly café in Sydney and they'd sold the cutest pupcakes. Louis had loved them. 'You could do cakes and bickies. And bananas are popular in dog treats, so it's perfect!'

Liam grinned. 'In that case, you better give me some recipes. Pronto.'

She laughed. 'I'd love to.'

Mind reeling, Ana reached for her drink. She could see it now, sitting outside The Bent Banana feeding Steph and Louis banana bones. Life in Elizadale … the possibilities seemed too good to be true.

'Wow …' Liam slowly shook his head. 'The things you don't think about.'

'I'm sure you would have sorted it if people started asking. But I still think the whole concept is a great idea. I can see it being a wonderful success.'

'I hope so, Ana.'

He may have his doubts, but he seemed confident enough and Ana had no problem providing encouragement. The more she thought about his dream, the more excited she grew herself. The café sounded like Liam, and he deserved it. He'd already achieved so much for Elizadale. They'd won a title for Tidiest Town two years ago, the locals had embraced his dog park idea, and he'd also had a hand in the construction of the walking path around town. His passion for Elizadale was inspiring and it fired a spark inside Ana as she relaxed, laughed, and enjoyed his company.

There was something welcoming about Liam, open and not at all fake. What you saw was what you got. And as unnerving as it was, Ana liked what she saw. Liam was a kind, honest country guy who loved his dog, community, and really liked to chat. If they pursued a relationship, not only could they be lovers but also good friends. And there was something to be said about that. The lust swirling through her body heated while her reasons for why she shouldn't date him faded with the sunset.

Steph and Louis curled up under a tree, panting heavily after their galah herding. The cuckoo clock inside noted the hour. Then Liam surprised Ana by taking her hand in his. Tingles shot up her arm and sent her heart into overdrive.

'I'm glad you're joining me for dinner.'

'Really?' Heat rose in her cheeks as the word tumbled out of her mouth, but she could hardly think when Liam was looking at her as though she were the most precious person in the world.

He brushed his thumb over her knuckles and her hand tingled. 'Yeah. I like you, Ana. Ever since you arrived in town, I haven't been able to stop thinking about you.'

It took everything she had to stop herself from melting. She wanted to share her hesitations, but instead, she smiled and decided to be honest. 'I'd have to say the same. I've enjoyed spending time with you too. And I'm glad you invited me to dinner.'

'So, would you like to do dinner more often? Tomorrow we'll have drinks with the group, but I believe I've seen a veggie burger on the menu at the roadhouse, so we could go grab one of those?'

Ana's pulse slowed. She wanted to join Liam for dinner, dates, and all kinds of fun. Even though her feelings scared her, her mother and sister were right. The plan for her to keep moving hadn't been set in stone. Besides, according to her friends, Liam didn't move fast, so she could make that work for her.

'Sounds lovely, Liam.'

'Yeah, I was thinking about dining out around here earlier and that's when it occurred to me that the menu at the Royal Hotel isn't helpful.'

She shook her head. 'Not really.'

'I'll have to see what Smithy's has,' he considered, his brow furrowing. 'I heard some rumours about a menu change. But anyway. I have no problem cooking vegetarian food, Ana.' He smiled, let go of her hand, and stood. 'Shall we have dinner?'

Liam fed the dogs first, then Ana followed him inside. The

kitchen filled with a spiced tomatoey aroma as he pulled two individual dishes from the oven. Ana's stomach rumbled.

'I have a shepherd's pie I love to make.' He set the hot dishes onto plates, then peeled off the alfoil to reveal crispy-topped mashed potato. 'But I figured I could use beans instead.'

'That's the perfect substitution.' She met his gaze and smiled softly. 'Thank you.'

'It was no problem. I'm keen to see how it tastes.'

Her heart swelled. 'You'll love it.'

Liam switched on the outside lights as they returned to the deck. Summer warmth lingered, but the breeze was cool. Ana settled into her seat while Liam poured them each a small glass of chardonnay.

They dived into their dinner. Liam's eyebrows shot up in approval while Ana resisted a moan. The veggies fell apart in her mouth with the right mix of tomato and herbs. Glancing at him, everything inside her softened further.

'This is delicious, Liam.'

'Very tasty,' he agreed, scooping another forkful. 'These beans are good. Bet they'd go well in a bolognese too.'

'They do. Beans go in just about anything. But I will say I'm impressed. I like that you can cook. I've never known a man who does.'

Liam's eyebrows lifted. 'Seriously?'

'I believe my father was adequate, but Mum was always the cook. As was my grandmother. And I've never dated anyone who had decent kitchen skills.'

'Would I be right in saying you're a great cook?'

Ana grinned. 'I'll make you dinner one night and you can find out.'

'I look forward to it. But yeah, Aunt Wendy insisted on

teaching all six of us kids. It's a handy skill to have if you want to eat.'

Ana laughed. It'd be that way in the country. Sure, there were the pubs and takeaways, but the choices were limited if you didn't know how to cook.

Ana enjoyed her dinner and felt disappointed when they were finished as she knew she'd need to leave soon. But she didn't hurry. They sat and talked for another hour before he offered her some frozen mango. She'd never had it frozen before and found it to be the most delicious thing she'd ever tasted.

Afterwards, she made a move and Liam walked her to her car.

'Thank you for inviting me over.'

'No worries. It was nice to spend some time together.'

'It was. So, I'll see you tomorrow at the pub?'

'Absolutely. Can't miss Monday afternoon drinks. Especially if you're there.'

He reached up and brushed the hair off her face. Ana stilled, her breath catching at his touch. She'd hoped he might kiss her, so resisted the urge to pull away as she held his gaze. When his hand slid down to cup the back of her neck, Ana lifted her chin and welcomed him.

She closed her eyes and responded to the kiss with gentle heat. Her knees weakened at the soft touch of Liam's mouth, then he drew away. Her eyes fluttered open. His gaze pierced through hers, hot, blue, and full of want.

Ana's breath caught. The kiss hadn't been long enough. Thankfully, Liam thought so too as he swooped down and kissed her with more heat, more passion. Fire radiated through her, fuelling the chemistry that'd been bubbling since the day they'd met. Liam wrapped his arm around her waist and drew her closer. Ana surrendered as her body softened and her skirt fluttered around her knees. She felt strong in his arms. Cherished. She changed the angle of their kiss and let everything go.

She could do this every day for the rest of her life. It was the last of first kisses. Somehow, she knew that. And it was incredible.

But she had to go. Now.

Ana pulled away, releasing her grip on Liam's arms and stepping out of his embrace.

He let her go. 'I'm sorry.'

She shook her head, horrified. 'Don't be sorry. That was just … I mean, yeah. We can do that again. I should be going, is all. Else …' She swallowed and blew out her breath. 'Yes, I need to go.'

Heat rose in her cheeks and as he brushed her hair back again, she shivered. What had she been thinking? She was in deep now.

'Yeah, if you don't go, I'll want to kiss you again. I may not want to stop.'

'Trust me,' she breathed. 'It's hard to do so.'

They shared a grin and risked one quick kiss.

'Goodnight, Ana. Safe trip home.'

'Yes, okay. Goodnight.' She took the initiative and unlocked the car. 'Where's Louis?'

She called him and Liam called Steph for good measure. Both border collies ran around from the other side of the house.

'Time to go, Louis. Say goodbye.'

Liam gave him a quick rub between the ears before Louis jumped onto the back seat. Steph leapt in after him.

'No, Steph,' Liam laughed. 'Come here.'

He took Steph by the collar, but she dug in her heels and wouldn't budge. Sighing, Liam simply lifted her out and Ana closed the door before slipping behind the wheel.

'Thanks again. I'll see you tomorrow.'

'I look forward to it,' he replied, smiling and looking far too gorgeous with his arms full of Steph. 'I'll open the gates for you. Goodnight, Anastasia.'

Her heart pounding, she shut the door. Ana waved as she drove through the gates, sharing Louis' sentiments as he whimpered.

Chapter Thirteen

Rick strode through the Monday shoppers, his gut tightening as he entered the lingerie store. Lace and satin knickers lined the walls and empty push-up bras left nothing to the imagination. Fuck, it'd been a long time since he'd touched a woman. Held breasts. Screwed. Prison had offered a lot of things, but he'd sure missed convenient sex. All his blood rushed south until his jeans grew tight. Perhaps when he found Ana, he'd take one last ride before—

'Good morning, sir. Can I help you?'

Rick eyed the middle-aged woman and resisted a grimace. The sexy undergarments she sold would do nothing for her with that flab she tried to conceal around her waist. The thought quickly iced the heat running through his veins. Rick forced his hands to relax and reminded himself why he was there.

'Yeah. Is Nadia Hamilton working today?'

The woman frowned. Her nametag read Helen. 'I'm afraid it's just the two of us,' she said, indicating towards the other old woman.

Rick's hands curled. He swore this was the store Ana had mentioned her bitch mother was moving to. She'd worked at two in the time he'd been with the slut. He'd visited them both, but the whores who worked there hadn't seemed to know who he was talking about, the fucking liars.

'It's just, last time I was here to buy gifts for my girlfriend, she was very helpful. Nadia knows what she likes and I wanted to deal with her again.'

'I'm sorry, sir, but I'm sure we should be able to help you out. What is your girlfriend's size?'

Rick gritted his teeth. 'Can you just tell me when Nadia will be in?'

Helen exchanged a look with the other woman. His pulse spiked. Did she work here? Would she be in another day?

'Nadia Hamilton does not work here,' Helen replied. Her eyes remained kind, but her tone had hardened. Rick wanted to grab her and shake until she spat out the location of the whore mother. 'Would you like to see our selection today and what's on special?'

Rick rolled his eyes, turned, and marched out of the store. Fucking bitches. The lot of them.

* * *

Over the past two weeks, meeting new people had happily overwhelmed Ana, but it was nothing compared to the first day of school. The children arrived in droves, sporting clean uniforms with shiny shoes and glossy books. The older kids ran around smiley faced and excited, but some of Ana's grade ones clung to the hands of their parents with terrified expressions on their young faces. Ana was ready for tears.

The first couple she met were Jason and Rebecca Taylor with their daughter, Lisa. Meg had told Ana that the family operated Tropic Sun and that Rebecca was her paternal cousin. Jason was the only son of John and Millie Taylor, and he managed the banana farm. Lisa seemed rather happy about coming to school, but still clung to her mother's hand.

'Hello, Lisa.' Ana smiled kindly as the little girl blinked her big blue eyes. 'How are you?'

'Good,' she replied in a small voice.

'Do you want to pick a place to sit? You can have any spot here at this group of tables.'

Rebecca and Jason helped Lisa settle in while Ana met parents left, right, and centre, everyone welcoming her with a genuine smile. The noise grew as the classroom filled and the kids greeted their friends. Molly took the desk beside Lisa and three little boys argued over who got to sit in the middle. Ana smiled, her heart threatening to burst before the bell had even rung.

She got her class settled and began the day with housekeeping. She was good with names so didn't forget anybody. As a new teacher, the kids asked her questions that led to a long description of Sydney, where most of them had never been. But Ana didn't mind. She was back in her element, doing what she loved, and she couldn't wipe the smile from her face. Being in the classroom again with young, fresh-faced children eased the stress she'd experienced these past few months. Teaching them would be a pleasure. And if she was still breathing in October, then …

She sighed. *One day at a time.* Next year was a problem for later.

* * *

'That was a long day,' Meg groaned as she and Ana locked their classrooms, exhausted.

'It was.' Ana had enjoyed herself, but she longed to go home, put her feet up, and not get up again for a week.

'Yeah. So, I didn't have time to ask, how was dinner with Liam? You must tell me everything.'

Ana smiled. Even with her busy day, she hadn't stopped thinking about last night. She tingled at the memory of his kiss and quivered for more. 'It was lovely.'

Meg raised her eyebrows. 'That's all I get?'

Ana laughed. 'Fine. We talked a lot. He said he planned to make The Bent Banana dog-friendly and I suggested he sell homemade dog treats.'

'That's an awesome idea!'

'He thought so too. Dinner was delicious and, yes, he kissed me goodnight.'

Meg grinned, skipping as they strolled down School Street. 'Wow! I'm not at all jealous. How was it?'

'What? The kiss?'

'Of course!'

'It was ... amazing.' To say anything less would be an insult. 'It's just ... oh, seriously, Meg! I didn't expect to come here and meet someone. Not like Liam. Don't you think it's too soon?'

Meg wrapped her arm around Ana's shoulders, squeezing gently. 'Ana, haven't we had this discussion? There's no reason you shouldn't date Liam and you need a huge upgrade after your last boyfriend. Just go for it. You know you want to.'

'Yeah ...' She could admit that much. And as for the rest of it, she'd figure it out later. 'We're going to the roadhouse tonight to get burgers.'

'The burgers there are to die for!'

Arriving at Jackson Villas, Ana waved Meg off and headed inside. She dumped her bag onto the dining table, then pulled back the curtains to see Louis.

Ana gasped and pushed open the sliding door. 'Louis!'

Louis stopped digging the hole and dropped his head. He crept towards Ana, his front paws black, head down, and eyes sad. Ana placed her hands on her hips, appalled at the sight before her. The yard was a mess with holes and dirt everywhere. Louis lay at her feet, his head between his paws and eyes squeezed shut. An ache formed around her heart. She couldn't yell at him. Not when he was showing signs of being intimidated. Poor Louis. The last thing she needed was him relapsing. He'd only dug because he was bored. And being bored was her fault.

Ana pressed her lips together, grabbed Louis' nose, and lifted his head. 'Bad boy. That was a very bad boy, Louis. You are not allowed to dig holes.'

Then she sat in the doorway and sighed, lifting Louis into her arms. She cradled him and held him close.

'I'm so sorry, baby. I should have known better. I'm sorry I took you away from your big yard, but you know we had to leave.'

Louis wriggled and Ana let him go. His eyes were happier now that he'd realised she still loved him, but it didn't lessen Ana's guilt over being a bad dog-mummy. She'd brought Louis to Elizadale where he was bored and hot all because they had granted Rick parole. She'd known he wouldn't stay in prison forever, but he hadn't even served half of his five-year sentence. Good behaviour and showing signs of rehabilitation, the court had argued. But Ana knew such claims were fake and believed with all her heart that Rick had done everything he could to be released with the sole intention to find her. And hurt her.

Now Louis had a small backyard and had dug up the grass and gardens.

Fighting back tears, Ana took his head in her hands and buried her face in his soft fur. What could she do? She could try to find another place to live, but the real estate market wasn't exactly booming out here.

Glancing around, she assessed the damage. She could save that plant and the grass would grow back once she filled the holes. Unless Louis dug again tomorrow.

'You have too much energy, don't you? And not enough ways to burn it off. I'm sorry, but if you don't dig, I promise to take you to the park every afternoon.'

She'd taken him to the park or for a walk every day since they'd arrived, so she didn't know why he'd chosen today to dig. Nevertheless, she should have provided her precious boy with the home he needed. A border collie couldn't be locked in a small yard all day no matter how much she walked him.

'Get your ball, Louis.'

He bounded away in search of his tennis ball. If she threw it for a while, he could work off whatever energy he had left. She'd fix the yard later.

Louis dropped his ball at her feet and Ana threw it. Perhaps Liam might have an idea to prevent Louis' boredom. She hated to ask him for help again, but other than leaving Louis with his toys, she didn't know what else to do.

They played until she left for the pub.

'I'll take you for a walk when I get home, no matter how late it is.'

Chapter Fourteen

'Smithy's isn't the same,' Adam grumbled as he and Liam strode into the Smithfield Hotel on Monday afternoon. Located at the opposite end of Abbott Street to the Royal, Smithy's was the first point of call when driving in from the south. It was a modern pub built of rendered brick with a quiet bar in the front, the bistro at the back, and motor-inn rooms at the side. There was nothing better or worse about the Smithfield compared to the Royal, it was simply a matter of preference.

'No one else is gonna meet us down here,' Adam continued.

'No, because they didn't get kicked out of the Royal.'

'If Kelly had said the same thing about your sister, you'd have punched him too.'

Liam didn't argue with him there. They slid onto stools at the bar where Jessica Smithfield was serving.

'Hey. Get kicked out of the Royal again?'

Adam flashed her a smile. 'Now, Jess, why would I need to be kicked out of the Royal to visit you?'

'Because it's the only time you do. Two beers?'

'Yeah. Thanks.'

Jessica took two bottles of Great Northern from the fridge, flicked off their caps, and twirled her bottle opener between her fingers. She placed the beers on the bar with a thud. 'Don't start any fights, Maguire. Luke will kick you out of here for sure.'

'Yeah,' Adam sniggered, picking up his beer. 'Like I'm scared of Luke.'

'You're scared of Georgina and she's a five-foot fairy princess.' Grinning, Jessica moved down the bar.

Adam scowled. 'She's mean.'

'She's right.' Liam laughed. 'Luke will kick you out. He's done it before.'

Luke Smithfield practically ran Smithy's these days, granting his parents a well-deserved break. He was a bulky fitness fanatic, and while Georgina laid down the rules in her pub with her lethal attitude, Luke laid his with muscle.

'Whatever. Tell me about your date.'

'It wasn't a real date.' But as the words left his mouth, Liam frowned. Wasn't it? It certainly had felt like a date.

'You kiss her?' Adam asked.

Liam took a swig of his beer. 'Yeah.'

'That it?'

'Shut it, Adam. You know I don't move that quickly.'

'Yeah. And I suppose with Ana, it'd be best not to rush things. She's the real deal, mate. I'd want to take it at a good pace and get to know her too.'

Placing his beer on the bar, Liam frowned at his cousin. 'Hold on. Are you saying that if you met the right woman that you'd take it slow?'

Adam rolled his eyes. 'Dunno if that'll ever happen, but maybe slower than normal.'

Cade arrived and slid onto the stool on Adam's other side. Liam wasn't surprised he'd joined them since Cade had the major hots for Jessica.

'How's it going?'

'Adam was just saying that if he met the right woman, he'd take it slow.'

Cade laughed. 'That'd be a sight.'

Adam elbowed him in the ribs.

Jessica approached and Cade flashed her a smile. Liam smirked as her hands tightened around the bar. Jessica melted into a puddle every time Cade walked into the Smithfield, but why he hadn't asked her out, Liam didn't know. It wasn't like Cade to move slowly either.

'Hi, Cade.' She greeted him much more pleasantly than she had Liam and Adam. 'What can I get you?'

'I'll just have a beer. How are you?'

'Good.' She turned to take a bottle from the fridge. 'And yourself?'

'Better now.' He grinned and Jessica's hand fumbled as she slid her bottle opener back into her pocket. She placed the beer on the bar and left to serve other patrons.

'Ask her out already,' Adam told Cade before turning back to Liam. 'What are your plans with Ana?'

'We've agreed to see each other. Dinner and such.'

'Well, you got a pretty one, mate,' Cade said.

'She's got great legs,' Adam agreed and Liam jabbed him in the ribs with his elbow. 'What? Like we can't notice?'

'Yeah, she's got great legs,' Cade said and Liam shook his head, even though he'd noticed her legs constantly since she'd arrived in town.

'Anything interesting happen at work today, Cade?' Liam asked, changing the subject. He didn't have a problem talking about Ana, he just didn't want to discuss her with two idiots like Adam and Cade. Even if they were his best friends.

'I drove the patrol car an hour north and back. Booked people for speeding. It was a good day.'

Adam smirked. 'Bet you enjoy the afternoons now that we're drinking at Smithy's again.'

'There are certain perks to Smithy's.' Cade's gaze strayed towards Jessica and stuck. Liam didn't blame him. Jessica was certainly pretty with her slender body and long blonde hair.

When Grace White arrived at the bar beside Liam, Adam wasted no time in sending his charming grin her way. Grace and Adam had once dated each other for six months, making that the only serious relationship he'd ever had. Liam had always thought Grace was good for Adam, but her father's disapproval had destroyed them in the end. Edward White didn't approve of anything unless it made him money.

'Hey, Gracie.'

'Adam. Get kicked out of the Royal again?'

'I don't only come here when Georgina kicks me out. And by the way, Kelly totally deserved it.'

'I'm sure he did. Was it over Jordan again?'

'Always is,' Cade muttered.

'Hey.' Luke Smithfield arrived behind the bar, his eyes flashing at the sight of Adam. 'I see Georgina kicked you out again.'

'I wouldn't sit in your pub if I had any other choice.'

'You won't be sitting in my pub if you keep hitting on my woman either.'

Adam blinked. 'Your woman?'

'Hey, baby.' Luke leaned over the bar to kiss Grace.

Liam's eyebrows shot up. 'I didn't know you two were dating.' But he liked it. They were well suited and if any man could handle the bullshit from Grace's father, it was Luke Smithfield.

'Just since Christmas.' She smiled as Luke handed her a drink. 'And Adam wasn't hitting on me.'

'Not yet,' Cade said.

'Well, let's lay down the law anyway.' Luke turned his gaze to Cade. 'You don't hit on my sister and you, Maguire, don't cause fights and I'll let you drink here until you go back to your own watering hole.'

'I'll take the deal, but I doubt Cade won't hit on your sister.'

'Thanks, mate.'

Finishing his beer, Liam slipped off his stool. 'Well, I'm off to the regular watering hole, so I'll catch you blokes later.'

Leaving Adam and Cade in the hands of Luke, Liam made his way out via the bistro to check out the menu. Rumour was that Luke had wanted to modernise and veer away from the ordinary pub grub and if anyone was to have a vegetarian option, this was where Liam expected to find it.

He respected Luke's idea though as so many people had personal, ethical, or health-restricted dietary requirements. Liam had considered that himself by ensuring he had gluten-free and lactose-free options at The Bent Banana. No matter the reason for food choices, everyone should be able to eat out without fear. And he'd enjoyed cooking for Ana as that shepherd's pie had been delicious. He'd certainly make it again.

But a dinner date would also be on the horizon because health-nut Luke Smithfield hadn't let him down with his new menu.

Liam strode out of the pub with a spring in his step.

* * *

Ana slipped into the booth beside Isabella and poured Diet Coke into her glass of ice.

'Are you going to see Dave anymore?' Meg asked Lucy.

'I dunno. He was nice, but he works on Tropic Sun, is always busy, and you know me ...'

'You flirt and have fun with men for a night, but you never want to date them.'

'He looked cute to me,' Ana said.

Lucy laughed. 'Please. You're attracted to my brother. Your taste is way off. But yeah ... I don't think I want to date Dave.'

'Is that why you're back in your alcohol-free phase?'

Lucy sipped her Diet Coke. 'You know that has nothing to do with anything. Sometimes I just get sick of alcohol.'

'Well, do you want to date any man?' Meg asked. 'You've never had a relationship that lasted longer than a month.'

Lucy shrugged. 'Not really.'

'But Dave was cute,' Isabella reminded her.

'Then you date him.'

'Oh, no. He's too old for me.'

'Well, I would,' Ana laughed, 'but I'm attracted to your brother.'

Lucy smiled. Ana enjoyed these girly chats and it amused her that she was the one with the hot gossip for once. Then she glanced up to see Liam striding into the pub and her toes curled inside her shoes. He smiled as he slipped into the booth beside her.

'Hey, Ana. How are you?'

'Good.' She sipped her drink to prevent a foolish smile from spreading across her face. 'And you?'

'Better now. How was the first day at school?'

'Busy, but really fun.'

When Jack arrived with Michael, Meg insisted on buying him the beer she thought she owed him. Jack informed them he'd released the taipan in the National Park and they continued to talk all sorts of nonsense for the next hour. But Adam's absence didn't go unnoticed.

'He's not happy about being at Smithy's,' Liam said. 'But Cade doesn't mind keeping him company. And guess who Luke's recently snatched up?'

'Who?' Meg and Lucy asked in unison.

'Grace White. Adam was about to chat her up when Luke walked in.'

'Lucky he didn't get his arse kicked out of there too,' Jack commented dryly.

'Yeah.' Liam downed the last of his beer and turned to Ana. 'You want to go grab some dinner?'

She nodded. 'Absolutely.'

'We'll catch you guys later.'

Ana followed Liam out of the booth. As he took her hand, her heart danced and she chose to let her worries go. It wouldn't hurt her to have fun and enjoy her time in Elizadale.

Not tonight, anyway.

* * *

Liam pulled up outside the brightly lit roadhouse, located just off the main highway between Port Douglas and Cooktown. Stepping out of the LandCruiser, he met Ana at the passenger door and slipped his arms around her waist. She smiled, the ends of her blonde ponytail lifting in the breeze.

'I forgot something earlier.' He drew her close and lowered his mouth to hers. Ana's arms wrapped around his neck as she fell into the kiss. Everything inside Liam simmered.

'Hmm …' She pulled away, her eyes fluttering open. 'We better not forget that too often.'

'Agreed.'

He took her hand and led her into the roadhouse. He'd considered taking her to Smithy's instead but decided to save that for a special night since he'd been in the mood for one of Samantha Hudson's burgers all day. She may not be a professional chef like Wendy Maguire, but Samantha had a great mind for food and ran specials such as pizzas, Chinese, or anything else one couldn't regularly buy in Elizadale.

'Hello!' Samantha greeted them from behind the counter. 'I've been expecting you to come in, Liam. It's been a few days.'

'Yeah.' Considering he'd grown up friends with her son Darren, Samantha had become his somewhat third mother. But just because he didn't come over to play anymore, that didn't mean she expected him to visit less.

'Is this your pretty friend I've heard so much about? Ana, right?'

'Yes.' Ana smiled and shook Samantha's hand. 'Nice to meet you.'

'You too. Darren told me you were seeing the new teacher, Liam.'

Liam glanced at Ana. 'I haven't seen Darren in weeks, yet his mother already knows.'

'I heard small towns were like that.'

'So, what can I get you two?'

They ordered two burgers, plus drinks, then sat at a plastic table by the large windows.

'So, people in town are already talking about us,' Ana said, twisting the lid off her Diet Coke.

'Yeah, news spreads fast on the bush telegraph. I guess we have Adam to thank for that.'

'Well, Samantha Hudson seems nice.'

'She is. She liked me as a kid because I was the good influence on Darren. He'd occasionally join Adam and Cade in doing things that got them into trouble, but he preferred to hang with me than wag school.'

'You never wagged school?'

Liam laughed. 'I'd have been stupid to try. My mum would find out and she was the principal. Besides, there aren't many places to hide when wagging in Elizadale. High school in Mareeba was a different story, even though I didn't do it then either. What's ironic is that now Cade's the one who finds kids and takes them back to school.'

'That's because he knows all the good places to hide.' Ana laughed. 'God, I really love this town.'

Liam's heart swelled. 'Told you it was brilliant.'

'Yeah …' Then her eyes clouded and she dropped her gaze to the table. 'I like it, but I don't think it's the best place for Louis. I think he's getting bored. He dug up the backyard today and I feel so bad.'

Her voice broke a little and Liam reached for her hand. 'That's not good, but it isn't your fault.'

'Well, I'm the one who …' She shook her head and sighed again. 'Anyway. He looked like he was having lots of fun, but I feel bad because he has nowhere to run or play. He's stuck in the tiny yard all day while I'm at work.'

Liam nodded. Her yard certainly wasn't ideal, but he didn't need to think hard to offer a solution. 'You could bring him over to play with Steph.'

Ana's eyebrows shot up. 'Really?'

'Yeah.'

'Oh my God, that'd be brilliant!' Grinning, she squeezed his hand. 'Louis would love to play with Steph.'

'Great.' Liam's shoulders relaxed. Louis coming over should be no problem, and Steph would surely love the company. 'Bring him by in the morning, then. They shouldn't get bored with each other and all that land.'

'Definitely not. Thanks, Liam.' She smiled. 'I really appreciate it.'

'Anytime. And maybe after work, we can practise agility or take the dogs for a walk?'

'I'd like that. I was hoping I could train Louis more than once a week.'

'It's a plan, then.'

'It is.'

She grinned so brightly that Liam thought his heart would burst as Samantha delivered their burgers. He shoved a chip into his mouth before he could say something stupid like, 'I'd do anything for you, Ana'.

It may be true, but such a confession was hardly taking it slow. And even though he didn't know why, his inner senses continued to tell him to tread carefully. She may enjoy country life and a stupid part of his brain was beginning to think that helping Ana grow roots wouldn't be all that hard, but shadows flickered behind her eyes as she sipped her drink. Almost as though she had something else on her mind.

But what that was, Liam couldn't work out.

* * *

Rick stormed down Castlereagh Street, his fists clenching as he pushed his way through the crowd. For fuck's sake! Weren't doctors supposed to be listed at their current practices? Not that he was surprised. The hot sister was far smarter than Ana. She'd probably been the one to arrange this whole game.

Because that's exactly what Ana running away was. A game. One that he would damn well win.

Grunting, Rick stopped at the corner and slipped his hands into his pockets. He'd taken the train into the city because he sure as hell wasn't paying for parking. He hadn't expected that the sexy doc would still be working at that prestigious medical practice. The mother had hidden herself away at who-knows-what store and the sister could be shoving her finger up arses anywhere in the city. He'd tried Doctors on Castlereagh Street hoping to pose as a previous patient seeking Natalia Hamilton, but he hadn't expected to find the fucking practice had closed!

The green man appeared on the crossing and Rick stormed across the street, not giving a shit as he bumped into people. He snarled and snaked his way around a little brat who wouldn't fucking walk straight.

Bloody kids.

What was he going to do next? Call the medical board? Bras 'n' Things Head Office? The Department of Education? He wasn't sure how that would help when he didn't even know what fucking state the slut was in.

What state any of them were in.

Shit. The mother and sister could have fucking moved with her! Why hadn't he thought of that? Yeah, the register of GP's still listed the doc as practising in 'Sydney', but that could be bloody well anywhere!

Rick shoved his hand through his hair and jogged down

the steps into the train station. Here he'd been focusing on Sydney when he should be scouring the whole damn country. Not just for Ana, but for all three of those fucking women.

Rick's guts twisted as he slammed his Opal Card on the reader. He wouldn't give up. Things may have become harder, but he had nothing else to do. No job. No friends. No woman to keep his house because the fucking bitch he'd chosen to do so had turned on him. His mother had never betrayed his father like that. She'd recognised discipline when he'd delivered it to her.

But Ana had run to the police. Slandered his good name. She hadn't liked the treatment she'd received all those years ago? She had seen nothing yet.

Standing on the platform, Rick had never felt more determined. It'd make things harder if she had moved out of state because he couldn't leave New South Wales while on parole. And once he found her, he didn't want the authorities coming after him to interfere with his plans. He'd hoped to get his revenge without skipping a check-in.

But he'd worry about that when he found her. And he would. She couldn't hide forever. He'd do every horrible, nasty thing he could think of to her, and she'd pay for the inconvenience she'd caused.

Then he'd strangle the fucking life out of her.

Chapter Fifteen

Ana couldn't be more grateful for Liam's offer to let Louis come and play. The thought of leaving him in their yard again had made her ache, but he certainly expended all his energy playing with Steph on Tuesday. The moment they returned home, he curled up on his bed and fell asleep.

On Wednesday, she attended the Australia Day celebrations at James Abbott Park. The smell of sausages drifted from the CWA tent and kids ran around waving blue and red flags, adding to the overwhelming small-town atmosphere that continued to capture her heart. When the afternoon began to cool, she and Liam took the dogs down to the highway to let Louis watch cars.

'Now, there are a few techniques we could use,' Liam said as they sat on a blanket of fallen pink flowers beneath the trees. Rosy tulips, Liam had called them. 'But you said he knows "look at me", so we'll try that. When he locks a car in his sights, give him the command. Eventually, the hope is he'll use the car as a cue to look at you and stop lunging.'

It sounded good in theory, but Ana still had doubts. She'd tried 'leave it' and that hadn't worked. But Liam seemed confident and she wanted Louis to enjoy his walks without frustrating them both, so it was worth a try.

An hour later, Louis had lunged at four noisy cars and gone ballistic at a truck, but he'd looked at her for the last few and gobbled up his treats. Ana smiled as they stood and Liam rubbed Louis' head.

'It's progress,' he said.

Ana nodded as Louis had indeed done well. 'We'll continue to work on it.'

'Maybe we can go for a walk tomorrow?'

Smiling, she welcomed the flutter inside her chest. 'I'd like that.'

The next morning, she drove Louis to Liam's. This new arrangement may be better for her precious boy, if not inconvenient, but since it meant she could see Liam every day, Ana wouldn't complain. Nor would she let her worries plague her, despite taking a big risk. For the first time in years, she felt like her old self—happy, confident, and willing to take a chance. Since the night she'd escaped Rick as a broken, beaten, and emotional mess, there had been times she'd thought she'd never feel safe again. She'd lived many months in fear and had worked hard to recapture her peace and sense of security.

She'd almost had it too. Then they'd set Rick free.

Her heart clenched as she changed into a blue dress and slipped on a pair of heels. Friday night had arrived and after a wonderful first week at work, Ana planned to enjoy herself. She wouldn't pretend that Rick might not find her in Elizadale, but it would do her mental health no good if she spent every day worrying about it. She'd moved here so she *wouldn't* have to live in fear, and she needed to remember that if she wanted to enjoy life.

But just because she wanted to celebrate her newfound happiness, that didn't mean she'd let her guard down.

Ana fed Louis, then swung by Jackson Villa number one to pick up Isabella.

'You look nice,' Isabella said, locking her screen door with the key.

'Thanks. So do you.' Isabella always looked lovely in pastel dresses with her pale blonde hair cascading over her shoulders.

They strode to the footpath and waited for Meg, who looked stunning as she crossed the road in her skin-tight purple dress.

'We're going to catch some eyes tonight, ladies,' Meg said.

They arrived at the Royal just as Lucy pulled up. It was the first time Ana had seen Lucy in a dress and she looked fantastic in the little black number. Together, they entered, and indeed caught the eyes of some men at the bar.

But there was only one man Ana was interested in.

Liam moved out of the booth with Michael to greet them and everything inside Ana shivered as his blue gaze absorbed her. He reached for her hand and bent to kiss her. 'You look beautiful.'

Ana beamed. 'Thank you.'

She sat beside him while Isabella and Lucy fetched drinks. Ana frowned as she glanced around the table. 'I don't know about you guys, but it doesn't feel right without Adam here.'

Meg shrugged. 'You'll get used to it.'

Ana didn't know about that. She liked Adam, but she didn't approve of him fighting with Paul over something so pointless. And she hated to admit it, but her opinion of him had lessened since then. Adam was a charming man and she didn't want to think of him in any negative context, but she couldn't help it. The bottom line was she didn't condone violence and it'd be nice to have an evening without tension raging between the Maguires and the Kellys.

Lucy and Isabella returned with drinks and settled into the booth. Jack told them what was happening on the farm and Lucy shared anecdotes about guests at the retreat. Then they spoke about Michael's progress on The Bent Banana and his house, a subject that piqued Lucy and Isabella's interest.

'Granite benchtops are the way to go,' Isabella said.

'Definitely,' Ana agreed. 'They're much nicer than laminate.'

'You know that you live in the middle of nowhere, right?' Jack said.

Michael shrugged. 'Yeah, but a bit of luxury doesn't hurt. I need to win a woman over one day.'

'It's lovely to have a nicely finished home,' Isabella said. 'Especially when you live rurally.'

'Absolutely. The house sounds amazing, Michael,' Ana said, looking forward to seeing Michael's masterpiece complete. Then she remembered she didn't plan to still be here and her heart sank.

'It is.' Isabella grinned. 'Michael chose a gorgeous colour scheme. Lily and I helped him pick out paint and tiles.'

Michael smiled. 'You were both a great help. God help me though when Lily wants a house.'

'She wasn't that bad.'

'She's bossy.'

Liam laughed. 'That's nothing we didn't know before.'

'Does she plan to set up a vet clinic here after uni?' Ana asked.

Jack shrugged. 'Apparently. Which isn't a bad idea since

the closest vet is in Mareeba. There are quite a few farms around so she'll get enough business.'

Liam wrapped his arm around Ana's shoulders. 'You'd like Lily, Ana.'

'I'm sure I will,' she said, relaxing against him.

'Is she coming home for her twenty-first, Jack?' Lucy asked.

'April isn't a good time for her with exams.'

Lucy's shoulders slumped. 'That sucks.'

'She's having a party though,' Isabella said. 'She and her housemates are inviting people over.'

Jack frowned. 'She didn't tell me about a party. If she's having one, I'll probably go.'

'It's a Friday, so we could.'

Liam straightened. 'If we take Mum and Dad's LandCruiser, we can fit seven of us. Isabella can squeeze into the back and then no one will miss out.'

Ana smiled. 'Lily would love that. And if it's just a backyard party, don't even tell her you're coming. Just show up.'

Lucy gasped. 'That'll be so much fun! We could make a big deal about not being able to make it, then turn up and cry, "April Fools"!'

Ana laughed at Lucy's excitement.

'It couldn't hurt to drive down for the day.' Jack made it sound like a plan as he turned to Meg. 'You want the last seat, darlin'?'

She smiled sadly. 'I'll have to work.'

'So, you can't either, Ana?' Liam asked.

Surprised to be considered, Ana shook her head. 'Perhaps someone who knows her should go. But it sounds exciting.'

The surprise element would be fun indeed. Natalia would

be twenty-eight in October and even though it wasn't a milestone age, Ana would love to surprise her if she had the opportunity. Perhaps she could turn up unexpectedly during the June holidays? Liam might even go with her.

But the thought of returning to Sydney … Ana's throat tightened. No, it wasn't worth the risk.

Jack placed his beer down with a thud. 'Should we order dinner?'

'Yeah, order me the rib fillet, Jack,' Michael said. 'I'll guard the booth.'

Sighing, Ana followed her friends into the bistro. 'What are you going to have?' she asked Liam.

'I'm thinking the steak sandwich.'

'Sounds good. Would the others think I'm weird if I eat dinner before I come?'

'No. But who cares if they do?'

Ana nodded. Very true. 'Well, I might have the garden salad again.'

'All right. But … hold on. I have an idea.'

Jack finished ordering and Liam approached the register. 'Hey, Hayley. Could I speak to Tom for a sec?'

'Ah … I'll check.'

Hayley poked her head through the kitchen door. Ana frowned as she glanced at Liam. What was he up to?

A man in a black cook's uniform emerged from the kitchen, grinning and extending his hand to Liam. 'Hey, mate. What's up?'

'Hey, Tom. I know you're busy, but I was wondering if you could do me a favour?' Liam gestured towards Ana. 'Ana's new in town and vegetarian. She's been enjoying the salads, but do you maybe have something else you could whip up?'

Ana's belly clenched. She'd never have thought to ask such a thing, but Liam seemed confident while Tom regarded her with thoughtful eyes.

'You're the new teacher,' he said.

'Yeah, I am.'

'My niece Molly is in your class.'

Ana smiled. 'She's a sweet girl.'

'She likes you a lot. But yeah, I can offer you something else.' Tom frowned up at the board. 'I guess our menu's not very vegetarian-friendly.'

'Your salads are delicious,' she said, not wanting him to think otherwise.

'But you'll get bored if you eat them every time you come here. I could do you the chicken alfredo without the chicken? Or a pasta napolitana?'

Ana's shoulders relaxed. She exchanged a glance with Liam and smiled. 'You know, pasta napolitana sounds perfect.'

As Tom had a quick word with Hayley, Liam wrapped his arm around Ana's waist. She leaned into him. 'Thank you.'

'No worries. In small towns, we look after each other.'

Yes, but it wasn't just that. It was all Liam. And, heaven help her, it would break her heart to leave Elizadale.

Chapter Sixteen

Over the next week, Ana began teaching her students addition and started easy spelling lists. She and Liam spent the afternoons together and Louis actually seemed to be making progress on his car herding. He still hated trucks, but every time he looked at her instead of lunging, she praised him with enthusiasm and her heart swelled with pride. Adam had returned to their drinks sessions on Monday and on Friday night, Ana relished the vegetarian alfredo at the Royal Hotel.

They'd moved into February, but the weather showed no signs of cooling down. The midday sun scorched Ana's skin as she strode across the supermarket car park on Saturday. She grabbed a trolley and started up the aisles, trying not to wince at the prices. Some groceries were more expensive given the independence of the store, but Ana found everything she needed in the area of grains and dried plant proteins. What had surprised her most last time though was that they stocked quinoa, and it made her like Elizadale even more.

As she shopped, people greeted her by name and strangers struck up conversation. She was browsing the freezers when one of her students ran over to give her a hug, which was followed by a pleasant chat with Beth's mum about nothing in particular.

After waving them goodbye, Ana consulted her shopping list and sighed. It terrified her how much she loved her new life. Her students were wonderful kids and she enjoyed spending lunchtimes with Meg and Elanora while they supervised their classes and gossiped. And then there was Liam …

Sighing, she reached for a bag of frozen beans. Liam Maguire was one hell of a man. In the fortnight they'd been dating, he'd been nothing but a gentleman without losing a hint of sexy. And every time she thought about how he'd asked Tom to cook her something special, her heart somersaulted until it hurt.

Her only comfort was that they'd take things slow. Starting a relationship with Liam was probably foolish, but she'd be a bigger fool to ignore her feelings. And while she knew that Liam was the polar opposite of Rick Newman, she needed time to ease into a relationship without the pressure for more.

She finished her shopping and drove home. Lugging the groceries to the door, she unlatched the screen with her elbow and shouldered it open just as her phone rang. Knowing it was her mum by the ringtone, she let herself inside and dropped the bags on the floor.

'Hi, Mama!'

'Ana. How are you?'

'Great.' She put the phone on speaker as she shut the wooden door and reached for the air-conditioner remote. 'I had a great first week at work and I love my class. There's this little boy, Thomas, who adores me already. He's very sweet.'

'That's lovely, Ana.'

Moving the groceries to the kitchen, she searched through

her bags for the cold stuff. 'It's sort of like school back in Sydney except with a lot less kids. Having only eleven of them means I can give them each the attention they need. And since Deb insists on having the best little school in the country, we hardly go without. I feel like I can do a lot here.' Ana closed the freezer and left the rest of the groceries as she let Louis inside and lay down on the lounge. 'I hope my next school is just as good. But I think I'd rather be down south. It's too humid here.'

When Nadia remained silent, Ana frowned. 'What is it, Mama?'

'Ana, I have to tell you something.'

'Is everything okay?' She swallowed as her heart began to pound. 'You and Nat?'

'Nat and I are fine. But I got a call from my old store. Rick came looking for me, Ana.'

Ana stilled. She closed her eyes and counted slowly to ten. Taking a deep breath, she told herself not to panic.

'And?' she asked, trying to keep her voice steady.

'I'm not sure, but I told the police. They said they'll look into it. Don't worry about me or Nat. Her work understood the situation and took her off their website. I don't exactly know what I *can* do, but I won't let him find me.'

'It's okay, Mama.' Rick couldn't find her easily. *He couldn't!* But the positive self-talk didn't stop her pulse from racing. 'Thank you for letting me know. But … seriously! What does he think he'll achieve?'

Ana couldn't stop the hysteria filling her voice as she dropped her head into her hand.

'Ana, please don't panic. We've prepared for this, remember? That man was furious, showed no remorse, and threatened to find you when he got out, so we made plans to make sure that wouldn't happen.'

Ana nodded, squeezing her eyes shut. They'd put this plan into place for a reason. Rick wouldn't be the first man who tracked down the woman who'd sent him to prison, but Ana refused to be another victim of the justice system.

You can't rehabilitate a psychopath.

'He's on parole, sweetie. He needs to check in and the parole officer I spoke to said he's been a model citizen.'

Ana's teeth clenched. 'He always was until he tried to beat me to death.'

'I know. But if you get the slightest bit worried or receive any indication that he knows where you are, I want you to go straight to the police. Have you met the police there?'

'I've met Cade, the senior constable. He's a friend of the Maguires and his dad's been a policeman here for decades. But yes, I'll be careful. And if Rick does show up here, we should know about it because everyone knows when people come and go from this town.'

But the moment Ana said it, her stomach sank. That may not be true. Rick could be quite the phantom. The night of the assault, he'd disappeared. It'd taken the police three days to track him down.

He could easily fly into Elizadale under the radar.

* * *

After hanging up with her mum, Ana sat in the back doorway with Louis and stared absently into the yard. She'd desperately hoped that Rick wouldn't bother looking for her. She'd almost convinced herself of that. But it had been a defence mechanism. Denial. Of course, Rick would look! She'd moved two thousand kilometres away! She'd fought his parole and admitted to fearing for her life because she'd seen the promise in his eyes when he'd told her she'd regret sending him to prison.

Her hands clenched. He'd damn well deserved it! No one was allowed to treat another human being like that. He'd hit her. Kicked her. Pushed her down the stairs. If she closed her eyes, she could remember it vividly. Could feel the pain. No one deserved that sort of abuse, especially not from someone who was supposed to love them. That night had been terrifying, horrific, and for a moment, she'd honestly thought he'd kill her. Ana didn't know what had stopped him after her tumble down the stairs. Maybe he'd thought she was dead? She'd certainly lain there quietly for a long time. Until he'd slammed through the back door, picked up a wailing Louis, and tossed him.

She'd screamed, but Rick hadn't come back for her. He'd been angry. Hateful. She'd bled and cried as objects around her had broken. But the stairs had been the worst. The doctors had told her she'd been lucky that her broken bones and internal bleeding hadn't required surgery. But Ana had known from the first moment Rick had hit her that she wouldn't accept the abuse. Gathering her strength, she'd pulled her broken body off the floor, grabbed her keys, and coerced Louis out of his kennel. She'd run before Rick could realise they were leaving. The only thing she'd been thankful for was that her legs had been in working order and that her mother's house had been a short drive away.

Adrenaline had numbed her pain.

Her mother had sprung into action, calling the police before she'd even made sure Ana was okay. Natalia had come to take Louis to the vet while Nadia had driven Ana to the hospital. Sleepy from the medication and fighting for her life, Ana hadn't known it'd taken days to arrest Rick until after the fact. But they'd found him and he'd pleaded not guilty. It'd taken little to convict him, but he'd told her in a lethal whisper that she'd be sorry.

She buried her face into Louis' fur and took a deep, staggering breath. Rick wouldn't find her. He wouldn't look for her in tropical North Queensland. Her Facebook account was still active, but she didn't use it. Only her mum and Natalia knew where she was. She'd remain safe.

But with no way of tracking Rick's progress, anxiety clawed at her throat. Any day now, he could show up at her door, break in, or be waiting for her when she came home.

How could she not be terrified?

'Oh, Louis …'

Giving into her fear, Ana held Louis tight and cried.

Chapter Seventeen

After arriving at the takeaway shop, Liam leaned against the LandCruiser where Steph had her head out the window and called Ana. The phone rang for a while before she answered.

'Hello, Anastasia.' Liam's mouth curved. He liked saying her full name. It was beautiful and downright sexy. 'Steph and I are getting fish and chips and were wondering if you wanted to join us? I can get you a spring roll or pineapple fritters or potato scallops. What do you think?'

It took her a moment to reply. 'Um … Liam, I appreciate it but—'

'Come on, Ana. Steph insists on seeing Louis.' Steph's head tilted at the sound of Louis' name. 'She's crazy about him, so I have to bring her over. And if I do, then I can see you because I'm crazy about you. If you don't want any takeaway, that's fine, but I'm sure there'll be enough chips to go around.'

She remained silent. Liam frowned. Had he done something wrong? Surely not. Or maybe he shouldn't invite himself over like—

'Pineapple fitters sound great,' she replied, and he relaxed at the smile in her tone. 'Just one though.'

'No worries. Steph and I will be there in half an hour, I reckon. It's a bit busy.'

'Okay. I'll tell Louis.'

'See you soon.' He hung up and glanced at Steph. 'You want to go to Louis' house?'

Her mouth fell open. Liam grinned and rubbed her head before heading inside to order. He chatted to some locals until his food was ready, then took the hot paper parcel and drove around the corner to Jackson Villas.

Stepping out of the car, he handed Steph her bucket of dog toys. 'Carry,' he instructed as she took the handle in her mouth. It was a new trick he was teaching her because why should he have to carry her things? Plus, he hoped it'd impress Ana.

Steph carried the bucket to the door. Liam knocked and when Ana answered, his breath caught in his throat. Damn, she was stunning. She'd pulled her hair back into a loose braid, pretty pink stones dangled from her ears, and the black top and denim shorts did wonders for her slim body.

'Hey.' She smiled as she pushed open the screen and glanced down at Steph. 'What have you got there, girl?'

'Hello, Anastasia.' Liam stepped inside and slipped his arm around her waist. She lifted her chin and he pressed his mouth to hers. Ana's hand fell to his chest, gripping his shirt as he kissed her gently.

'Hey.' She pressed her lips together and settled herself back onto her bare heels. 'So … um … what's with the Anastasia?'

'I like your name. It's beautiful, exotic, and I think I'll enjoy calling you that.'

'Oh. Okay. Well … come in. Steph brought toys?'

'She insisted,' Liam said as he followed Ana through the unit. Louis was whimpering at the back door and spinning in excited circles. Steph dropped her bucket and ran, her nails scraping over the tiles. Liam sighed. 'She hasn't mastered the "carry" concept yet.'

Ana laughed. She picked up the toys while Liam let Steph out. The dogs jumped at each other before running into the yard.

'Do you want to eat outside?'

Placing Steph's toys on the table, Ana nodded. 'Yeah, it's not too hot. I'll grab some glasses. Do you want plates?'

He shook his head. 'We've got paper.'

'That's what I thought.'

A tightness formed in Liam's chest as he watched her stride into the kitchen. Something had diminished in Ana's happy persona and those shadows had returned to her eyes. His sixth sense rushed into overdrive.

Something was wrong.

He unwrapped their dinner as Ana returned and placed the glasses on the table. Twisting the cap off the Diet Coke, he poured their drinks. Ana took a chip. Liam broke off a piece of his crumbed fish and forced himself to relax into his chair. He didn't want to pry. Not yet.

'What did you do today?'

She shrugged. 'Just some grocery shopping. Then I talked to my mum.'

'How is she?'

Ana nibbled on a chip. 'She's good. Natalia's good. They both seem happy. But I miss them.'

Liam's heart twisted. 'It must be hard. I wouldn't know as

I've never been away from my family. Maybe your mum and Natalia can come visit?'

'Mum promised she'd try later in the year. She's interested in seeing the Tablelands.'

Liam smiled gently. 'Then maybe I could meet her?'

Ana's eyes brightened a little. 'She'd like that. I told her about you and that we're somewhat dating or "having dinner" often. I think she likes you and she definitely loves Steph.'

He laughed. 'Yeah, but Steph's very lovable. Is your mum a border collie nut too?'

'She's a dog nut. She has two chihuahuas, Cooper and Colin.' Ana bit into her pineapple fritter. A moan escaped her throat and Liam's pulse spiked. 'Wow, that's good.'

'I'm glad you like it.'

'I've never had a pineapple fritter before, but I figured it couldn't be too bad. Apart from the fact the batter and deep fryer completely destroyed perfectly good pineapple.'

'I've never tried it either, so I got one myself.' He reached for his and took a bite. The hot, sticky sweetness melted in his mouth. 'Oh yeah. That's delicious.'

'Your fish looks good too. It's very thick.'

'Yeah, it's Spanish mackerel. Best fish around. They have barramundi at the takeaway shop too, but there's really no comparison.'

'I don't think I've ever had either. Salmon and whiting were the most popular I'd find to eat out or at home.'

He nodded contemplatively as he chewed. 'How long have you been vegetarian?'

Ana sipped her drink. 'Since I was eighteen. Nat was worried about our family cardiac history, you know, because my dad's heart gave out in his thirties? Mum knew that put me and Nat at a risk, so we've always tried being healthy by exercising and eating all the good stuff. Then Nat had a health scare herself. It got her all fired up, so she did a bunch of research and decided giving up meat and the cholesterol that goes with it was the way to go. She made some excellent points and I've always hated to think about where meat comes from, so I decided why not?' Ana shrugged and leaned back in her chair. 'I don't miss it. I also avoid a lot of processed and fatty junk food.'

Liam stared down at the chips spread before them. 'Shit. I'm sorry, I didn't even think. You did tell me about your father.'

'No, don't worry about it.' She placed her hand over his and squeezed, her blue eyes kind. 'I love chips. I just eat them very rarely.'

'Still, I am sorry. Next time, we'll stick to cooking at home. Or go to Smithy's. I checked out their new menu and there's plenty you could eat.'

'Then we'll definitely do that.' She smiled. 'Thanks, Liam.'

'Of course. I don't want you dying young, Ana. And I certainly won't give you grief about however you choose to stay healthy.'

She smiled. 'You have no idea how kind that is. But whatever you do, don't stop surprises like bringing dinner over. It was very thoughtful of you and just what I needed ...'

The sparkle that had returned to her eyes vanished again as she dropped her gaze to the floor. This time, Liam couldn't let it go. He brushed salt off his fingers and took her hand in both of his.

'Ana, what's wrong?'

'Nothing,' she replied a little too innocently. 'I'm fine.'

He didn't believe her. This heavy feeling didn't fill his chest for no reason. He always knew when something was wrong, especially when it involved the people he cared about. And he cared deeply about Anastasia. He might have only known her a few weeks, but that meant she could be keeping thousands of secrets.

'Are you sure?'

Staring at her drink, Ana nodded. 'Yep.'

Liam knew she was lying, but he resisted asking again. If Ana wanted to tell him, she would.

'All right. On the subject of mothers though, I told mine today that I'm seeing you. Or "having dinner" or whatever.'

Ana glanced up. 'What did she say?'

'She likes you as a person and her new teacher, so I believe she doesn't mind the idea. She said she'd like it if I could keep you around so that she won't need to rehire.'

'She said that?' Ana asked with a humourless laugh. 'Well, it'll take a lot more than dinner to keep me here, Liam.'

He took a chance. Standing, he dragged his chair around the table to sit beside her and interlocked their fingers. 'Why don't we just consider ourselves dating?'

Ana raised her eyebrows. 'Yeah? So … you and I seeing each other and … well … doing whatever we end up doing?'

'Absolutely. Steph and Louis might tag along sometimes, but I really like you and I enjoy the time we spend together.'

'So do I,' she admitted softly.

Leaning closer, Liam touched his mouth to hers and slid his fingers into her hair, holding her as she opened herself to the kiss and invited his passion. He wanted nothing tonight other than food and conversation, but that didn't stop desire rushing through his veins as he pulled her closer. She tasted of salt, pineapple, and Ana, delicious and tempting. And damn if she wasn't the woman for him. Liam savoured her taste as his hand brushed her slender waist. He longed to touch her, but he wouldn't rush things.

Liam drew away and laid his forehead against hers. 'You know I'm falling hard for you, right?'

Ana drew back and met his gaze. 'That's okay, because I can't get you out of my head night or day.' She took a deep, shaky breath. 'I'll be honest with you, Liam. I wasn't looking for this when I moved here. I just wanted to get away, find some peace, and then that very first day I met you.'

He smiled. 'I'm sorry if that screwed up your plans.'

She managed a short laugh. 'I didn't have any plans after I arrived here. Just to live, work, and enjoy myself. But I'm glad to be here and that I met you.'

Liam had never been more grateful for anything. He was falling for her quicker than he found comfortable, so it tormented him to know that there was something bothering her. Something had forced Ana to move to Elizadale. He was sure of it. No one packed up and moved across the country to a small town just for fun.

'I'm glad you're here too. So, why don't you tell me what brought you here, Ana? What's bothering you?'

Apprehension flashed through her eyes. Liam's heart leapt.

'How did you know?' she whispered.

He shrugged. 'It's like a sixth sense. I know when something's wrong and you've got it written all over your face. You said you came here to get away and find peace. You don't have to tell me, Ana.' He stroked her cheek again as the sadness in her eyes morphed into panic. 'But if you do, it'll make it easier for me to help you. If you need help. At all. Anytime. I'm here.'

She exhaled, her head dropping into her hands. 'It might ruin the evening.'

'It couldn't.'

She remained silent. He waited patiently. 'Don't change your opinion of me, Liam …'

Her voice hitched and Liam swallowed. This was obviously no little thing. 'I won't,' he promised.

Ana took a deep breath. 'Everything I've told you is true. I've always thought about teaching in a small town and experiencing country living, but it wasn't the reason I moved here. I had to do it for my own protection. My ex-fiancé was released from prison last month and I'd hoped his threats of revenge weren't real. But today, I learned that he's looking for me.'

Liam didn't know what he'd been expecting, but he hadn't thought it as serious as that. Ana wasn't a blow-in. She was a runaway. And looking at her now, her eyes wide and glistening, she was frightened beyond comprehension.

Exhaling, Liam almost pulled her into his arms and promised to protect her. And he would. But he had questions first. 'He threatened you?'

'Only after we'd won our case and they'd handed him his sentence. He said he'd get me back for pressing charges and sending him to prison.'

She dropped her head. Liam placed a soft kiss at her hairline and took a deep breath before asking the question that terrified him. 'What did he go to prison for, Ana?'

He didn't want to jump to conclusions. A million possibilities ran through his mind, some worse than others. But either way, he expected the answer to be horrible.

Ana inhaled before meeting his gaze again. 'Assault and battery. Rick came home one night, angry that I apparently never did anything he wanted. I believe he was still mad about Louis, saying that I spent ridiculous amounts of money on useless things. It happened so fast I never saw it coming. He just hit me. And again and again. Things broke, he yelled, then he pushed me down the stairs. I just … I was scared and hurt and crying. I thought I was going to die before he finally left me alone. It only happened once. I left. I broke my wrist, cracked a few ribs, and had internal bleeding. Mum and I fought his parole, but we lost. So, she and Nat moved houses and I came here. He's been out for three weeks now and apparently went looking for Mum at her old workplace. So, he's looking for me and I have no idea how hard or easy I'll be to find!'

Ana had held herself together, but those last few words broke her. Speechless, Liam pulled her into his arms. He held her tight, trying not to imagine how hurt or scared she must have been. She'd been through something traumatic and he couldn't believe what Rick had done to her, but he was glad she'd told him. It would have taken strength to share her story and she was a strong woman for having removed herself from that situation. Ana was brave and Liam was glad he knew that about her.

But for that experience to have been the driving factor for a long-distance move? For it to have caused Ana to pack up her life, leave her family behind, and escape out of fear? Liam couldn't imagine how that felt.

Closing his eyes, he released a deep, steadying breath.

It didn't matter what had driven Ana to Elizadale because she would be safe here. She was in his arms, in his town, and he didn't let anything happen to the people he cared about.

Liam didn't like to think of himself as protective, he simply liked to be considerate to others.

But when defending someone against a monster, protectiveness was necessary.

'It'll be hard to find you, Ana,' he whispered, placing a kiss in her hair. 'But I promise that if he does, I won't let him near you. Just don't stress, baby. Not when there's nothing to stress about at this very moment. He can't just take off from Sydney while on parole though, can he?'

'People skip out on that all the time. Rick's the vengeful type and he won't stop looking for me. So even though I'd love to stay in Elizadale with you and Meg and everyone, I'm scared that I'll have no choice but to run again.'

Liam's heart clenched as he lifted Ana's chin. 'Please don't run, Ana. If Rick finds you here, I won't let anything happen to you. You've got Jack and Adam who won't let anything happen to you. Meg and Lucy. And we've got Cade. Trust me, you don't need to spend your life running. We'll keep you safe.'

She drew out of his embrace, blinking back tears. 'Thank you for saying that, but I don't think it's that simple. It's terrifying, you know? To realise his threats are real? Men like Rick ... they won't stop until they get what they want. He will find me.'

Liam brushed a lock of hair off her pale face. 'But aren't the parole officers watching him? Making sure he checks in and keeping you and your family updated?'

'Yes.'

'Then you're doing everything right.'

She sighed. 'I know. But—'

He cut her off before she could voice further doubts by touching his lips to her forehead. 'It'll be okay. You can't live your life scared.' He rubbed her back as she drew in a deep breath. 'Thank you for telling me though. I know it must have been difficult.'

'I wanted to tell you eventually. And thank you for listening. I appreciate it.'

'Anytime. But I don't see how that could change my opinion of you. In fact, it makes me like you even more.'

She raised her eyebrows. 'Really?'

'Now I know you're stronger than you look. You may even fit in better around here. Elizadale women are tough.'

The sparkle returned to her eyes. 'Yeah?'

'Meg and Lucy especially. You can see it clearly in Lucy, but Meg's just as stubborn and strong.'

'I've noticed that.'

'Even Lil and Isabella have overcome a lot of difficulties. But you're tough too, Ana, and as long as you're a woman of Elizadale, you'll remain strong.'

'I'm a woman of Elizadale? Wouldn't I need to live here for another twenty years until that happens?'

Liam laughed. Indeed, that seemed to be the case in the country. 'You live here, have an important job here, and are a regular at the pub, so you're almost as local as the rest of us.'

'Aww, thanks.' Smiling, she leaned in to kiss him. He cupped her face, glad he'd made her feel better. He'd do anything to ease her worries. Any day, any time. Because the thought of her running again tore Liam's heart to shreds.

He had to protect her. Had to keep her safe. And if this Rick guy knew what was good for him, he'd stay the hell out of Liam's town.

Chapter Eighteen

Ana arrived at school on Monday with a spring in her step. She hadn't planned to tell Liam about Rick, but she hadn't been able to hide her fear and she was glad she'd talked to him about it.

But the confession hadn't budged the dread that continued to simmer in her belly.

Entering the staffroom, she found Deborah straightening chairs. 'Hey, Deb.'

'Good morning, Ana. How was your weekend?'

Ana didn't miss the underlying question in Deborah's tone or her bubbling curiosity. 'Good. And yours?'

'Oh, fine. My husband and I went horseback riding and had a picnic.'

Ana smiled as she checked her pigeonhole. 'That sounds lovely.'

'It was. How about you?'

Ana resisted a smile as she adjusted the folders in her arms. 'I know why you want to know. Liam said you might get like this.'

Deborah blinked. 'Like what? I'm not like anything. I just want to know how your weekend was. And maybe a little more because my boy mentioned that you're seeing each other.'

Ana shook her head. She couldn't blame Deborah. Mothers were usually interested in their children's love-lives and after the conversation surrounding Vivian's grandson that first week at work, Ana knew Deborah possessed the desire to become a grandparent. But the last thing Ana needed was for the woman to jump ahead and start knitting booties.

'Yeah …' Ana's stomach clenched as Deborah broke into a grin. 'We've been hanging out a little. And I've been taking Louis to agility training.'

'Yes, I heard about your border collie. That's why I wasn't surprised when Liam said he liked you. Lucy said Louis' getting quite good.'

Ana's heart swelled. 'He's learning. But … yeah, you could say that Liam and I are seeing each other.'

Deborah's eyes brightened and Ana's stomach clenched harder.

'I think you'll be good for him, Ana,' Deborah said, placing her hand on Ana's forearm. 'And he for you. He's a sweet boy, my Liam, and I like you too. So, make sure he brings you around for dinner one night. I can't tell him because he won't listen to me.'

A lump formed in Ana's throat. 'Deb, we've only been seeing each other for a fortnight.'

'Then come over in a couple of weeks.'

'Okay. I'll keep it in mind.'

'Good. Now, I'll let you go get ready and I'll see you at the staff meeting.'

'You will.'

Glad the inquisition was over, Ana waved and left.

* * *

'Nice house, mate.' Liam glanced up at the dusk sky through the roof beams of Michael's house, taking a long drink of his beer.

Michael sat beside him in the soon-to-be dining room against the wall frame and smiled fondly. 'It's getting there.'

'One day you may even have indoor plumbing,' Adam said as he returned from a visit to the bushes.

'Yeah, but I don't mind taking my time. You guys remember how it was when we did your houses. I want to enjoy every moment of building this place so I can look back in twenty years and reminisce.'

'Every nail shot with love, hey?' Liam teased.

'Well, I do plan to have a family in here one day.'

Jack thumped his fist on a doorframe. 'We've done some solid work.' As a rather handy bloke, Jack often helped Michael and his mentor Graham when he had the chance.

Liam nodded as he glanced around at the wood and concrete. 'It'll look good when it's done.'

'I hope so,' Michael said. 'Then I can figure out how to convince the right woman to fall in love with me and move in.'

'Got one in your sights?' Adam asked with a laugh.

Michael ignored him and drank his beer.

'You know I'll help you with painting and installing the fittings,' Liam said. 'But I'm always keen to do the landscaping and lay some turf.'

Liam had learned when they'd built Adam's house that there wasn't much he could help with until the walls were up and the roof was on. He was the painter in the family and would help hang doors, install cupboards, and lay floor tiles, which they'd start doing at The Bent Banana next week. But his passion lay in what went on outdoors in the landscaping and gardening.

'It'll be a while before we get to the turf,' Michael said, downing the last of his beer. Jack reached into the esky and handed him another.

They were due at the homestead for a random Thursday night dinner in half an hour but had gathered for a drink at Michael's first to fill in time. All of their dogs—Steph, Rusty, Michael's cattle dog, Sally, and Jack's kelpie, Jill—ran around the site playing in the dirt and sniffing the bushes.

'Mum said Aunty Deb's pretty optimistic about you dating Ana,' Adam said, grabbing another beer. 'You're in the shit now if things go south.'

Liam sighed. 'Yeah, I told Mum. Because I do like Ana. And she might sound optimistic because I think I'm optimistic.'

'Mate, you're optimistic about everything,' Jack said. 'You've only been dating her a few weeks.'

Liam frowned. 'So? You don't think you can know straight away whether or not you want to be with someone?'

'Maybe not straight away.'

'I didn't say I was going to marry her, did I?'

'Not yet,' Michael said.

'Hell, you move so slowly we'll be lucky to ever get a wedding,' Adam said with a laugh. 'But don't tell me that's what you're thinking about, Liam. Like, I'm happy for you. And I like Ana. But still …'

Liam ignored the disapproval in Adam's voice as he lifted his beer and grinned. 'Well … she's pretty damn special.'

He was sure about that. Despite her fears that she'd need to run again, Ana was special. And he'd do everything he could to ensure she felt confident about staying in Elizadale.

Even if Rick did find her.

Adam shook his head. Jack remained his quiet self. Michael, however, laughed and gave Liam a friendly punch in the shoulder.

'Good on ya, mate. Knew you'd be the first one of us to take the fall. Obviously, I figured Jack might one day wake up to himself, but he's still as thick as ever. Ana's a nice girl.'

Liam smiled. 'Yeah, she is. And I don't think Jack's ever going to wake up to himself.'

'I'm ignoring you lot,' Jack commented, his attention on the dogs.

'Ignorant bastard,' Adam muttered under his breath. 'But I'm happy for you too, Liam. You've found a good one. All we need now is for the rest of ya to fall into that ditch while I take the road less travelled and continue on as a single man.'

Jack laughed. 'Mate, you're gonna meet some chick one day who you'll fall flat on your face in love with. And you won't have a clue what to do with her.'

'Yeah,' Adam scoffed. 'Never gonna happen.'

Liam smiled to himself. He could see right through his cousin. Adam might not believe it, but he'd want to settle down one day. Surely no one wanted to deny themselves what he was feeling right now. The joy, the fulfillment. The panic. It was amazing and downright terrifying, but he was willing to embrace it. One day at a time.

But when it was Adam's turn, Liam was pretty sure they'd all enjoy watching him screw it up.

* * *

Liam was still at the Tourist Centre when Ana collected Louis on Monday, so they returned home where she curled up on the lounge and FaceTimed her sister. Natalia was always happy to chat, even if she was in the middle of her daily date with the treadmill, and Ana was keen to tell her about her fabulous weekend. But she let Natalia speak first as her sister usually needed to get work issues off her chest.

'I mean, I love my job, but people still think they can just take a pill and fix all their problems. And you already know how I feel about that. Lifestyle measures need to be implemented first! But no one wants to hear they need to take better care of themselves, they just want drugs.'

'Yeah, I know,' Ana said, having heard all of this before. 'You're not a miracle worker and people need to take responsibility.'

'For most things, yeah! But whatever. What's going on with you? You're the one with the hot country guy.' Natalia grinned. 'What's the latest?'

'What about the man you're dating?' Ana asked, even though she knew it wasn't serious since Natalia hadn't even bothered to tell her his name.

'Yeah, that's over. Nothing bad happened, but I'm taking a break from dating. I don't go anywhere to meet the right people and it's too much effort. There. Your turn.'

Not surprised, Ana didn't press the matter and let her sister live vicariously through her own love-life as she told Natalia about her Saturday afternoon in Mareeba with Liam.

'We didn't do anything special just had lunch and did some necessary shopping. But I was intrigued by the mango wine they make up here, so we stopped by the winery and oh my

God, Nat! It's the best thing ever. I know you don't drink, but even you would love it.'

'That sounds so good it almost tempts me,' she said with a grin. 'Are things getting serious?'

'Sort of … although I don't know what I was thinking.' Ana sighed. 'It can't last.'

'Don't say that! You were thinking that you deserve to have a life and you do. This is a good thing, Ana. I'm happy for you and I'm glad you told him about Rick. Liam sounds like a catch.'

'He is. We're going to Smithy's tonight for Valentine's Day.'

'Ooh? Is it going to be a special night? Have you shaved your legs?'

'I always shave my legs! But I don't know …' Ana bit down on her lower lip. 'I like taking things slow.'

'Yeah, but you've been dating for three weeks now! You've been to dinner at his house and he's come to yours. You can't hold out forever.'

Ana resisted a laugh. Typical Natalia. Her sister enjoyed talking about sex and despite her problems with men, she always had the best advice. But while the thought had crossed Ana's mind, she'd been flattered more than anything when Liam had dropped her home on Saturday evening and left after a few steamy kisses.

But if nothing escalated soon, she'd need to reconsider their definition of 'slow'.

'I know,' Ana said, meeting her sister's gaze on the phone screen. 'But things are comfortable the way they are.'

'Well, hopefully he won't move slow enough to drive you

insane. If so, take things into your own hands and seduce him.' Natalia grinned wickedly. 'Black dresses are the best for that. Plus, it's fun.'

Ana's belly fluttered. She didn't want to think about it. Although ... 'We'll see.'

'Excellent.' Natalia sipped from her water bottle. 'So, what else has been happening?'

'Um ... agility's going well. The Maguires have made plans to visit their sister for her twenty-first birthday. But apart from that, I love my work and Liam swears that any day now the rain will come and not stop for weeks. I sort of can't wait. Apparently, there's a creek and rockpool or something on Shadow Creek that Liam says is better after the rain and he wants to take me there.'

'I believe rain up there is quite different to what we're used to. I just hope you don't get a cyclone.'

'No, there aren't any cyclones brewing.'

'Good.' Natalia hit stop on the treadmill and the whirring ceased. 'My hour's up. But send me pictures if you see any waterfalls. You know how much I love them.'

'There are plenty around here that I'll see eventually, but I'll send you pictures.' Ana checked the time. 'I'd better go. I have to get ready.'

'Okay. Don't worry too much about Rick, Ana. We're keeping an eye on things and we'll let you know if he skips out on parole. We should know before he makes it to Elizadale, I'm sure.'

Ana nodded. She could only hope so.

Chapter Nineteen

Ana and Liam squeezed into the Royal Hotel on Friday night as the beat and drum of live music added to the frenzied atmosphere.

'It's packed!' Ana almost had to shout to be heard.

'Yeah, this happens when The Charlie Boys are playing.'

Her eyebrows shot up. 'The Charlie Boys? Have I heard of them?' They sounded familiar.

'If you're a fan of country music, you should have. They just won their second Golden Guitar at Tamworth. And are Elizadale born and bred.'

Ana wouldn't call herself a fan of country music. She rarely listened to music at all. But she *had* heard of The Charlie Boys and knew that a Golden Guitar Award was a big deal.

'That's awesome. I'll have to look them up. Surely they're on Spotify.'

'Yeah, and I have their CDs at the Tourist Centre.'

Ana smiled, her body instinctively swaying to the pinging guitar and thumping drums, the singer's deep voice melting through her. 'They sound great. It's good that they play here.'

'No matter how big they get, The Charlie Boys will always play at the Royal. It's their home and they were playing here long before they were famous. Meg sometimes sings with them. Her cousin's the lead singer and guitarist.'

Ana laughed to herself. Of course, he was. Meg was related to everyone.

In the booth, their friends were also discussing the band. Ana slid in beside Meg, whose arms were crossed as she shook her head at Adam.

'No. Chaz didn't ask me, so I'm not singing.'

'Oh, come on, Meggy. I bet Chaz will ask you later, so get used to the idea.'

'Not happening.'

Liam grinned. 'They've started on you already?'

'Of course.' Meg's narrowed gaze shot to Adam. '*They* are playing. Not me. I'll sing when they ask.'

'And when will that be?' Ana piped up, raising her eyebrows. If she had to take sides, she'd take Adam's as she'd love to hear Meg sing.

'Probably at the Show. Back in my Show Queen days, I held concerts to raise money for the Royal Flying Doctors and The Charlie Boys played music for me. I mean, I play guitar myself, but it's always nice to have the band.'

Adam grinned. 'She's bloody brilliant. And Chaz will ask her, so you should do it.'

'I'm not going to.'

'Leave her alone, Adam,' Jack said easily.

'Fine. I'll just listen to your CD on the way home.'

Ana's eyebrows shot up. 'You have a CD?' How had she not heard of this? Meg had mentioned being a part-time country singer, but she had a CD? And her cousin had a Golden Guitar?

Meg sighed. 'I released a small album when I was twenty. Only eight songs. But I never made it in the country music scene.'

Something flashed behind Meg's eyes and Ana frowned. Were there more secrets her friend wouldn't talk about?

'You *could* have made it,' Adam mumbled.

Jack elbowed Adam in the ribs. 'Shut up.'

'I have Meg's CD at the Tourist Centre too,' Liam said helpfully.

Ana blinked, lost, which wasn't surprising when she was the new girl in town. But she'd be downloading Meg's songs the moment she got home.

'I think it's time for another round,' Adam said.

'Your shout,' Jack told him, downing the last of his beer.

'What are you drinking, Ana?' Adam asked. 'Coke or beer?'

'Coke, thanks,' she replied as Adam slipped out of the booth.

'Don't cause trouble,' Michael called after him. Adam shot a wicked grin over his shoulder and approached the bar.

Lucy smiled as she crossed her arms over the table and regarded Ana and Liam. 'So, what have you two been up to? It's nice to see you arrive together. Like a real couple.'

Ana's chest swelled as Liam placed his hand over hers. 'We took Steph and Louis for a walk and stopped by the dog park.'

'Uh-oh,' Meg said, her gaze straying across the room. 'Jack, Adam's mouthing off at Kelly.'

Ana's gaze shot to Adam. Jack turned to look … and shrugged. 'He'll be 'right.'

'Go help him with the drinks and get him back here.' Flicking her hands, Meg shooed Jack out of the booth. He didn't argue and slid out. Meg grinned. 'Thanks, Jack.'

'No worries, darlin'.'

Ana's hands clenched beneath the table as she watched Jack approach Adam. She didn't want another fight to break out. Not when it was pointless. But Jack seemed to have it under control as he grabbed the drinks off the bar and kicked his brother in the ankle.

'Fucking bastards. Think they need to have a say in everything,' Adam muttered, sliding into the booth.

'I don't care. I told you to stop pissing them off.'

'I breathe and piss them off. I haven't even seen Jordan in weeks.'

'Good,' Jack said, handing Meg her vodka and Ana a can of Diet Coke.

'She dump you again?' Lucy asked with no sympathy whatsoever.

'Yep. Went over on Aussie Day and she had some other bloke there.' Adam shrugged and relaxed into the booth. He didn't seem too bothered by it. 'Whatever.'

Ana frowned as she turned to Liam. 'That didn't last long.'

'Never does.'

'Right,' she said, sipping her drink. Hopefully, that meant there wouldn't be any more fights with the Kellys and her irrational unease around Adam would fade. She hated that she was jumpy around him because even though he'd hit Paul, she didn't believe Adam would ever be like Rick.

A man arrived at the table and greeted Lucy. Ana quickly placed him as Dave.

'Hey!' Lucy said, rather brightly for someone who'd claimed she didn't plan to see him again.

'Hey. Saw you here and wondered if you wanted to dance?'

'Ah …' Lucy considered for a moment as she took a sip of her drink. 'Sure. Sounds good. Move, please.'

Ana, Liam, and Meg slid out of the booth and Lucy left

with Dave. Ana smiled as they resumed their seats. 'I like Dave.'

Liam took a swig of his beer. 'He seems all right.'

'Perhaps she'll change her mind about dating him,' Meg said, a touch of hope in her voice. 'He is quite cute.'

'What? She doesn't like him?' Liam leaned past Ana to glance at Meg.

'She likes him, but she doesn't want to date anyone.'

Liam sighed. 'As long as he's nice to her.'

'I'm sure he will be,' Ana said. She liked that Liam looked out for his sister but wasn't ridiculously overprotective like the Kellys.

As usual, everyone chatted away, enjoying their night. They were just finishing dinner when a man with long blond hair crouched at their table.

Meg took one look at him, rolled her eyes, and said, 'No.'

'You don't even know what I'm asking.'

'Ask her, Chaz,' Adam encouraged him. 'She'll give in.'

'No, I won't.'

'First, you must be Ana.' He smiled and extended his hand. 'Meg mentioned you'd moved to town. I'm Chaz, her annoying but terrific cousin.'

Ana shook his hand. 'Nice to meet you.'

Chaz glanced back to Meg. 'I was going to ask if you wanted to join us some night. Get your groove on before the Show. What do you say?'

'He won't quit until you agree,' Adam reminded her.

'Why do you want me to sing so much?' she snapped.

'Because you have a beautiful voice and we like to hear it.'

'And I haven't heard you sing,' Ana said.

Meg sighed. 'We'll see,' she told Chaz. 'Ask me later.'

'You wanna join us for a song tonight?'

'No.'

'Not even for "Country Girls Gone Wild"?'

'No.'

'But that's my favourite,' Adam whined.

'Shut up,' Jack growled.

'Fine.' Chaz stood. 'I'll catch you later, then. Gotta get back. Fans awaiting.'

Chaz left, stopping to hug and chat to people on the way. He looked like a laidback guy and was obviously modest in his success. The locals of Elizadale only seemed to get more interesting. Yet it was her new best friend who puzzled Ana the most.

She frowned as she studied Meg. There was something deeper behind her refusal to sing, but before Ana could ask her about it, Liam caught her eye with his soft smile.

'You wanna dance?'

Knowing Meg wouldn't answer her questions anyway, Ana nodded. 'Absolutely.'

'We'll be back,' Liam told their friends before he led Ana into the next room. People played pool or danced on the makeshift dance floor while The Charlie Boys continued to entertain. Liam turned Ana under his arm and pulled her close.

And while it wasn't the first time they'd danced, something sizzled deeper tonight as her body pressed against his. Liam had already proved he could dance, so she wrapped her arms around his neck and followed his lead as they moved and twirled with the crowd. Heat radiated through her body, sending shivers down her spine as his hand rested over the small of her back. Liam smelled incredible, like spice and soap. Ana longed to pull herself close and never let go.

Her belly twisted. If only.

Exhaling, she glanced at Chaz up on the stage. 'I don't know any of their songs, but I like this band.'

'They're awesome. Chaz, Chuck, and Charles have been entertaining us for over a decade.'

Ana laughed. 'So, they really all have the same name?'

'Yep. Although Charles is really Eric Charles. They got their big break eight years ago and have been on the rise since. Meg was actually the one who got them into shows. They started as her backup band, but then the guys decided to take their music seriously, headed to Tamworth, and the rest is history.'

Ana frowned. The Charlie Boys had found success and yet Meg … 'Seems a little strange that Meg doesn't want to sing now. Why didn't she ever get a big break?'

'I don't know,' Liam said, confusion clouding his eyes. 'She was still at uni when Chaz got his, but she later released a few songs as an independent artist, was quite popular, and then … nothing. Elizadale still loves her though, especially the young girls, and she always performs at the Show.'

Nodding, Ana let her curiosity go. If Liam didn't know, then she doubted she'd find out unless Meg opened up. Which was as likely to happen as Ana living without fear and getting her happily-ever-after.

Sighing, her heart sank. But then Liam's hands brushed up her back and her gaze returned to his. 'You look really pretty tonight.'

Heat rose in Ana's cheeks, even though she wasn't sure why. She'd known Liam for almost six weeks now and her feelings for him continued to grow. It both thrilled and terrified her. He only had to look at her and Ana knew she was adored.

Everything inside her twisted. Was running really her only option? Could she stay? Would it be safe to remain in one place?

'Thank you,' she whispered as Liam brushed his lips over hers.

'You're always pretty, Anastasia.' He took his hand from her waist and ran it down the arm she had wrapped around his neck. 'Do you want to do dinner tomorrow night?'

She nodded, blood rushing hot through her body. 'How about I cook?'

His lips curved. 'If you like.'

She'd yet to cook for him and was quite proud of her culinary skills, even though she was up against some tough competition. The man had a professional chef for an aunt, after all. Yet strangely enough, she was confident she'd prove worthy.

'I would,' she said, her arms tightening around his neck. 'Do you have a suggestion?'

'Surprise me.'

Ana's heart swelled as he ran his hand across her lower back, causing her toes to curl inside her shoes. 'I can do that.'

'Should I bring Steph?'

'Of course. You can't disappoint Louis.'

'I'd hate to do that,' he said with a laugh before kissing her again. His mouth was soft, but still possessed the power to send her hormones reeling.

They continued to dance, unwilling to let go of each other. Ana's skin grew hotter with every song and while she enjoyed the way his body fit against hers on the dance floor, she tried desperately not to think about it anywhere else.

Later, Liam drove her home.

'Friday nights are always fun,' she said.

'It's always good to catch up.'

'Yeah. Living here hasn't been boring, anyway. Almost every night I have something to do. I really like yoga.'

'I'm glad,' he said as he turned into Jackson Villas. 'Especially that you're busy and enjoying yourself. I'm just happy spending any time with you.'

'Me too.' After Liam parked the LandCruiser, Ana leaned over to kiss him. It took all her strength to ignore the part of her brain that wished this wasn't goodnight. 'I'll see you tomorrow?'

'You bet.' He slipped his hand into her hair and pulled her back for another kiss. His mouth was warm and gentle and her body ignited in response. She returned his kiss with everything she had, desire surging through her as her grip around his shoulders tightened.

Slow? Why were they taking things slow?

Liam drew away, his eyes dark as he caressed her face. His mouth curved gently. ''Night, Ana.'

Inhaling, Ana pushed aside her frustration, her desires. 'Goodnight.'

He squeezed her hand as she opened the door. 'I'll call you before I come over tomorrow.'

'Okay.'

She smiled and closed the door, her knees shaking as she walked towards her unit. She turned to wave, then stepped inside. Turning all the locks, she sighed, listening as his LandCruiser faded into the night.

She pressed her hand to her chest, but it didn't dull the ache that filled her. She wanted to be with Liam and have him stay the night. Not having felt this level of intimacy in such a long time—if ever—she longed to love, be loved, and wrap herself around his hard, sexy body.

It might be risky to take their relationship to the next level, but she wasn't foolish enough to ignore her desires. It was far too late for that.

Waltzing through the house, Ana opened the back door where Louis sat waiting. She gave him a pat, a kiss, and wished him goodnight before heading upstairs.

In bed, Ana stared up at the dark ceiling, an unfamiliar ache forming around her heart. This year had been about one thing—staying alive. She'd never imagined she'd leave the big smoke for a small farming town in North Queensland, but life never turned out as one expected and she'd been prepared to live a nomadic existence for as long as it took until she felt safe again.

She just hadn't expected to feel that so soon.

Sighing, she rolled over, the wind blowing softly through the window as silence surrounded her. There were no passing cars or partying neighbours. No rumbling trains or noisy pedestrians.

Snuggling into her pillow, Ana couldn't imagine being anywhere else.

But was she safe? Or had the community and friendships she'd found in Elizadale bewitched her into a false sense of security?

Chapter Twenty

Liam and Steph arrived at Jackson Villas just as the streetlights twinkled on. Steph released a soft whine as she looked through the screen door, sensing Louis wasn't far away. Liam grinned as he knocked. 'I feel ya, Steph.'

Ana rushed out of the kitchen, grinning as she pushed the door open. Liam stilled. Steph pulled on the lead and he let her go.

Ana lit up the doorway, her slender body wrapped in a simple black dress. It probably wasn't supposed to be drop-dead sexy, but since when were black dresses not? Her hair tumbled over her shoulders in fluffy golden waves, her legs were a mile long, and she looked incredibly cute barefoot.

'Wow.' The word was a reflex as his gaze roamed down her body and back up. 'You look gorgeous. Do you often hang around the house looking like that?'

'Only when I'm waiting for you.' She rose onto her toes and kissed him. 'And thanks.'

She gestured him inside. Steph had already dashed through the house and was whimpering with Louis, unable to reach him as she scratched at the metal screen door. Liam followed

Ana on lead feet as she bounced across the glossy tiles and let Steph out.

He was in trouble. Watching the way Ana's dress clung to her body and how it swished around her thighs … he wanted his hands on her. He wanted all of her. All of Anastasia Hamilton.

He wanted that dress off.

She spun around, her blonde hair lifting and settling again over her shoulders. 'Would you like a drink? Dinner should be about ten minutes away. I have beer.'

'Beer would be great.'

'I bought Great Northern.' She strode casually into the kitchen, but all Liam saw was a siren. Inhaling, he ordered himself to behave. 'It seems to be the most popular beer around here.'

'Yeah, it's a Cairns company.'

'I thought it must be local,' she said, handing him a cold bottle. She took a Diet Coke for herself, set a dish in the microwave, and they moved to the table. Ana sat, crossing her slender legs as she popped open her drink. 'How was your day?'

'Not bad.' He opened his beer. 'Steph and I took a trip out to High Ridge and had lunch with the family. What about you?'

Needing physical contact, Liam placed his hand over hers and rubbed his thumb over her delicate hand. Ana smiled.

'I cleaned and went to Meg's. We decided to go shopping in Cairns soon. Should be fun.'

'Maybe you could buy more dresses like that one.'

Her smile broadened. She tilted her head and her hair flicked over her shoulder, cheekiness filling her eyes. 'You like it, do you?'

'Well, yeah.' He surveyed her once again. Her long legs were crossed elegantly beneath the table and she'd painted her toenails a glossy pink. Why was that alluring? 'You sure know how to bring a man to his knees, Anastasia.'

Leaning forward, she brushed her lips over his. Her taste lingered and something inside Liam broke. He reached out, slipped his fingers into her hair, and pulled her close, kissing her deeply as she opened and surrendered. Desire rippled through him. He didn't know why he'd pulled away from their steamy kiss last night. He hadn't wanted to. Maybe part of him had felt it was too much of a risk because if they took the next step, it'd break his heart to see her leave, flee, or be hurt again. But the desire he felt for this woman couldn't be quenched and tonight … he would love Anastasia tonight. Reaching for her hip, he pulled her closer and gathered the slinky material in his hand. Ana nipped excitedly at his lower lip, then drew away.

'We better eat. Dinner will burn.'

The words 'let it' lingered on Liam's tongue as he no longer had an appetite for food. But he let her go because they should eat and whatever was in the oven smelled incredible.

'You want any help?'

'No, I'm fine,' she replied, but he stood when she did, leaning against the counter as she moved around the kitchen. She poured the vegetables into a colander and withdrew two trays from the oven. One contained potatoes while the other was a loaf of some kind.

'That looks great.'

She smiled. 'Lentil loaf. I hope you like it.'

'I don't doubt I will,' he said honestly. Food was food and he'd enjoy anything his beautiful Anastasia cooked.

She plated up and they returned to the table. Liam sampled

the loaf and gravy first. It melted in his mouth, a mix of herbs and spices bursting over his tongue.

'Wow. That's delicious.'

She beamed, her blue eyes brightening. 'I'm glad you like it.'

* * *

Ana's heart raced as she ate her spiced potatoes, quite pleased that with very little effort, she'd turned Liam to putty in her hands. Excitement and power shimmied through her. His eyes had been devouring her since he'd arrived.

As usual, Liam looked gorgeous. The blue polo shirt enhanced the brightness of his eyes and the cuffs pulled tight around his strong arms that she desired to have wrapped around her. All night.

But first, she enjoyed her dinner. She'd had no idea what she was going to cook and had gone back and forth between her favourite dishes all morning until deciding on the lentil loaf. Sometimes, it was best to keep it simple and she was glad he liked it. She'd more often than not failed to impress men with her vegetarian meals.

But she shouldn't have worried. Liam had already proven to be openminded. And while she didn't wish to convert him, it was nice to know that their dietary differences shouldn't come between them and that if she wanted to make lentil loaf for dinner, he wouldn't demand she make a separate meatloaf just for him.

Like Rick had.

Her lip curled as she chewed. Ana glanced at the dogs and shoved Rick from her mind.

'I still have to give you those dog-friendly recipes,' she said as Steph and Louis stared at them through the screen door.

'Absolutely. What do you have in mind?'

'Bickies and pupcakes. They're easy to make and just like any other baked-good, except with dogs, we want to avoid additives, sugars, fats, and unsuitable grains.'

'Uh-huh. So, all natural?'

'Pretty much. And it's all normal food, so you can make them in the café without worrying about cross-contamination. Louis' favourite biscuit recipe is just flour, water, and peanut butter. I reckon we get paw-shaped cookie cutters online and call them Peanut Butter Paws.'

Liam grinned around his fork. 'I love it.'

'They'll be a big hit,' Ana said as they finished their dinner. 'I have some natural peanut butter in the cupboard, so we can make them one day and see if Steph likes them.'

'Let's do that this week.'

'And I'll find the other recipes I've tried. I don't remember everything I've made for Louis.' She stood and took their plates to the sink. 'I should probably feed them though. They look hungry.'

'Nah, Steph just doesn't understand being outside.'

Ana laughed. 'I sneaky-let Louis inside on occasion, mainly to enjoy the air-conditioning, but I don't want to get in trouble with the Rileys.'

She fed the dogs, then returned to the table and picked up her can of Diet Coke. 'Do you want to wait before dessert?'

'I think so,' he said, placing his empty beer bottle down. 'What would you like to do instead?'

Her heart hammered, but that didn't stop Ana from offering Liam her most seductive smile. Leaning forward, she took his hand in hers. She hadn't set out to be provocative. It wasn't like her and all she'd done was slip on a black dress.

But Liam obviously liked her cheerful attitude, so Ana rolled with it.

'Whatever you suggest.'

'I want to kiss you.'

'Good plan.'

Liam's mouth met hers, hot and heavy. His fingers dived into her hair and Ana's blood heated, sending a pleasant burn shooting up her spine. As he slipped his arm around her waist, she closed the distance between them and moved onto his lap.

He swooped in, ravishing her until all her thoughts vanished. His fist twisted around her hair and she tilted her head back, his tongue brushing hers as her passion unleashed. A noise escaped from deep within her throat as his hand ran up the side of her dress, coming around to mould her breast. Her lips moved from his and she gasped for air, her body on fire.

His name escaped on a breath as he rained kisses down her throat and sucked gently at her collarbone.

'Anastasia … dessert can wait. You taste so much better.'

Her lips curved, heat settling deep in her belly as she brought her gaze to his. She kissed him once and brushed her fingers down the back of his neck. 'Come upstairs, Liam.'

He released a short breath as she stood and pulled him to his feet. His hands slid down her hips as he kissed her again. Flashing him another inviting smile, she took his hand and led him towards the stairs.

'You planned this, didn't you? Wore a sexy little dress to seduce me?'

'Baby, it wasn't the dress.' She turned when they reached the upper floor and his mouth found hers. He gripped her hips, need radiating from his warm body. Ana ran her hands up his chest and explored the hard ridges beneath his cotton shirt. Her toes curled into the carpet.

'I like the dress,' he whispered, moving his hands down her thighs, 'but I knew I wanted you the day you arrived.'

'Me too,' Ana breathed, unwrapping her arms as he lifted the dress over her head. His gaze roamed down her body, making her feel sexy and powerful. She thanked God again for the discounts at Bras 'n' Things.

'Gorgeous.' On a breath, he captured her lips. 'You're beautiful, Ana.'

Her heart waltzed as she slipped her hands over his hips and down his fine butt. Stumbling backwards, she pulled him into the bedroom and started with his shirt, pushing it up his lean body until he pulled it off. Her fingers splayed over his chest, soaking him in as she committed the moment to memory. Then her hands lowered to his waist and they both worked on unbuckling his pants. Liam kicked them away before he grabbed her around the waist and tumbled them onto the bed.

Touches grew hotter but remained sweet and tender as their entangled bodies overflowed with passion. It'd been so long since Ana had felt wanted, but never had it felt this real as Liam trailed kisses down her body. Touch to touch, breath to breath, whisper to whisper, they moved in perfect harmony. As his hands brushed over her skin, shivers shot down her spine. Her fingers dived into his hair as he kissed and sucked at the tender flesh between her breasts.

Ana smiled and tried to roll him. Liam obliged. Then she began her own exploration, running her hands down his tanned, muscular belly.

They took their time, kissing, touching, and finding the feel of each other. Then her bra clasp came undone. Liam lowered his head to taste her, teasing until she was flirting with the edge of control. Ana had to stop herself from begging.

'Anastasia …' he kept calling her. 'You're so beautiful.'

They slipped off each other's underwear. He touched her and she arched, her breath falling short as her fingernails dug into the back of his hard shoulders. 'Oh, God. I have … stuff … in the … drawer …'

It took a moment, but safe and prepared, Liam captured her mouth with his. Then on one long kiss, he slid into her. Ana gasped, her toes curling over the sheets as she met him. He held her close. Everything fell into place as they moved. Sheets wrinkled, fingers interlocked, and gazes held as they built towards their peaks. They spoke names in whispers and the many syllables of hers on his lips danced over her heart in a precious harmony.

As only he called her Anastasia.

* * *

'You look so sexy in my shirt.' Liam smiled as Ana returned to the bedroom with two steaming bowls of apple crumble. She sat cross-legged on the bed and handed him one.

'You look sexy in my sheets.'

Liam glanced down at the hot pink sheets that graced Ana's bed and frowned. 'Yeah … I don't think I've ever been in sheets so bright before. All of mine are boring colours.'

She spooned dessert into her mouth. 'I like to have colour in my bedroom. Simple and pale aren't my style.'

'Well, I like them. Maybe not the pink,' he admitted, chewing, 'but having colour is nice. This apple crumble is excellent by the way.'

Her eyes brightened. 'Thanks. It's a simple, microwaveable recipe. More apple than crumble, but I like it. So, um …' Her lips pressed around her spoon. 'Do you want to stay? I checked on Steph and Louis and they're happy.'

There wasn't anything he wanted more. The past hour had been amazing. Ana was sexy, responsive, and he didn't want to keep his hands off her. Going home? Not an option. Steph would survive being an outside dog for the night.

'Do you want me to stay?'

She nodded. 'I'd like it if you did. We can have breakfast.'

'If the offer of breakfast is there, then how can I refuse?' He reached across the bed, squeezed her knee, and smiled. 'Of course, I'll stay.'

She grinned. 'Good.'

'But I think I'll have to take my shirt back.'

'Yeah, like that'd be such a terrible thing.' She laughed as she finished her apple crumble, tucked her legs beneath her, and sat back on her heels. 'Maybe that's why I want you to stay.'

Liam tried to suppress his desire until he finished his dessert. 'Then I'll definitely be sticking around.'

She placed her bowl on the bedside table, then crawled towards him, the large collar of his shirt providing him an excellent view of underneath. Ana touched her lips to his and Liam surrendered. His dessert would keep. The crockery cluttered as he blindly reached to place his bowl with hers. He ran his hands up her taut thighs and returned her sweet kiss with a touch of tenderness.

Yep, he was in definite trouble now. But as he brushed his hands up to cup her bottom, the last thing he cared about was the vulnerability of his heart. It was hers, always would be, and as long as he protected her, Ana would never need to leave.

She could stay in Elizadale and enjoy her newfound love of country living. And then one day … well, who knew?

Ana pulled away and met his gaze. Her lips curved in that seductive grin she'd nailed tonight. 'Are you going to take your shirt back?'

Liam laughed. 'Yep.'

In a flash, he had his shirt on the floor and Ana beneath him, pulling the doona up to hide them away from the world.

* * *

Almost at the same moment, thousands of kilometres away in his dingy studio apartment, Rick Newman grinned in triumph. His blood pumped, heart thumped, and fists clenched in anticipation. His hard work had paid off. For a while there, he'd thought he'd never find her. That she was in some ridiculous witness protection or something. But there it was on his computer screen.

Ana Hamilton. Elizadale State School.

Opening Google Maps, Rick searched for the school and frowned when the map landed him in the middle of nowhere. He scrolled out. Far North Queensland. Shit, she'd sure made tracks. Could be worse, she could be in Western Australia. But to get to Elizadale …

Rick swore. He'd need at least three or four days just to drive there. Flying wasn't an option as he couldn't be caught leaving New South Wales. He could sneak over the border in a car, but until the bloody court loosened the leash on his parole, he'd be stupid to make a break for her. They'd know he was gone before he even made it to the backwater town.

Rick sat back in his chair, fury raging as he ran his hands down his face. He had to wait. He had no choice. But he'd found her and that's what was important. Anastasia Hamilton had some time left while he remained compliant with his parole.

But the bitch would be lucky if she saw April.

Chapter Twenty-One

After a glorious Sunday morning of baking dog biscuits and stealing plenty of steamy kisses, Liam and Steph went home. Ana grinned as she closed the door behind them and waltzed through the unit. She stepped onto the patio where Louis lay with his head between his paws.

'Oh, it's not that bad.' She sat in the doorway and dragged Louis onto her lap, cradling him like a baby. He allowed her a cuddle for a few seconds, then began wriggling. Ana let him go as her phone rang. Jumping up, she snatched it off the kitchen bench and wished Nadia had FaceTime as she pressed the phone to her ear. 'Hey, Mama!'

'Morning, Ana. How are you?'

Ana sat back in the doorway as Louis dropped his ball at her feet. She tossed it. 'I'm great. Really, really happy. You better make plans to visit because I'm never leaving this place.'

'Is that so?'

'Yep! I love it here. I have great friends and so many things to do. It's just … life is wonderful, Mama.'

'I'm glad to hear it,' Nadia laughed. 'And how's that man of yours?'

Ana smiled, her heart swelling until she could barely breathe. 'Liam … he's good. Nothing wrong there.'

'Natalia told me things were going well. And that you told him about that other bastard.'

'I did. Oh God! That's not why you called, is it?' Her breath caught and Ana paused with Louis' ball in her hand. He stood as still as a statue, staring intently as she tried not to panic. 'Did something happen?'

'No, Ana. I haven't heard anything. Don't worry.'

She exhaled and threw the ball. 'Yeah, until he finds me and beats me up again.'

She wrapped her arms around her legs and rested her chin on her knees. Taking a deep breath, she forced her pulse to slow as she watched Louis, his tail wagging as he proudly returned his ball.

'That won't happen, Ana. Now, tell me more about Liam. Let's talk about him instead.'

Sighing, Ana shoved thoughts of Rick away and thought instead about the man currently in her life. One who outweighed Rick in every possible way.

'Liam's everything, Mama. He's brilliant. Gorgeous. Kind. And after …' Ana swallowed. She certainly wouldn't mention last night. 'Everything's amazing. I know it's only been a few weeks, but Liam's it.' Her throat closed over. 'He's The One, Mama. I just want to stay here and have everything I can with him.'

The admission almost made her cry. Both with joy and despair. But her mum didn't seem to notice the flaw in that wish.

'Ana, that's wonderful. He sounds like a great man and as long as he feels the same way about you, I'll like him. I promise to make plans to visit.'

Ana blew out her breath and closed her eyes. She had to stop worrying and get the thought of a nomadic life out of her head. Because she didn't *want* to leave, and not just because of Liam. She liked Elizadale and loved her friends. She could see herself settling down here and being happy.

And if Rick found her …

She shook her head. She'd work that out if the time came. Because she didn't want to spend her life running. She didn't want to move from place to place. The thought of making new friends every year or living her life alone? It made her sick. She couldn't do that. Like Natalia said, plans changed, so she needed to let it go. She needed to live while she could and embrace what she had found in Elizadale.

Which was easier said than done.

Opening her eyes, she reached for Louis' ball and threw it. 'I'd love for you to visit, Mama.' Her shoulders softened. Nadia could meet the Maguires, the rest of Ana's friends, and she could show her mum around Elizadale. Ana grinned as excitement surged through her veins. She was one of them now. She was just like Meg, overwhelmed with town pride and the desire to show it off.

'I'll kidnap Natalia and bring her with me.'

'Yes! I'd love to see if she could survive a few days here.'

'I'm sure she'd be fine. Nat was wondering if you'd gone horseback riding as apparently it's something she'd do if she was there.'

'No, but I'm sure I can arrange that for when you visit.' Ana wouldn't mind going riding herself. She'd need to mention it to Liam. 'Lucy takes tourists on rides through the National Park and Liam has a horse. Archer, I think his name is.'

'I'll let Nat know. We'll make plans for the September holidays.'

Ana talked to her mum for a while longer, mostly about what was happening back in Sydney. When she hung up, she turned on the air-conditioner and sat at the table to prepare for this week's classes.

When three o'clock approached, Ana opened the back door. Louis looked over from where he lay beneath the hibiscus, keeping watch on the bird's nest he'd found earlier this week. 'Do you want to go to agility?'

Louis bolted over, his nails scratching against the tiles as he scampered past her towards the door. He skipped around in excited circles, grinning his doggy grin.

'Okay, we're going!' Laughing, she clipped on his lead. Louis remained by the door, whimpering and wagging his tail as she tied her shoes and grabbed her hat. She pulled the door closed and let the screen crash behind her as they headed off, Louis leading them towards the park.

When they arrived, Steph and Roger ran over, making it much harder for Ana to unclip Louis' lead as he strained between the two gates. She let him in and he bolted away with his friends.

'Giving you a hard time there?' Liam asked with a smile.

'He's just excited,' she said as Liam wrapped his arm around her waist and leaned in for a kiss. She grinned into it, her body tingling as his fingers played with the waistband of her shorts. She grabbed his green T-shirt at his hips.

'I've missed you,' he whispered.

Ana laughed. 'Behave. You can come over after practice.'

'Deal.' He took her hand and they joined the rest of their friends.

'Hey, Ana!' Adam called cheerfully.

Meg's eyes twinkled. 'You look quite cheerful today.'

Ana grinned and tried not to glance at Liam. 'I like agility.'

'Where's Bells?' Cade asked.

Meg shrugged. 'Iz will be here soon.'

'We really should walk together,' Ana said, grimacing. But then Isabella always came later considering Evie wasn't interested in agility.

Once training was underway, Liam and Ana worked on the practice obstacles—the dog walk and seesaw that were miniature versions of the real ones. The seesaw was only a metre long, barely off the ground and was designed to get Louis used to things moving beneath his feet.

'You're such a good boy.' Ana grinned as she cuddled and praised him, Louis a genius at the practice dog-walk. 'You're getting really clever.'

'He's becoming too good,' Liam said, rubbing Louis' head. 'I might have to stop helping you. He could almost beat Steph at our event in May.'

Ana raised her eyebrows. 'Beat Steph?'

He smiled. 'I said "almost". Don't think I'll let you win no matter how much you beg.'

Even though she doubted Louis was close to beating Steph, Ana stood and flashed him the grin that had worked so well last night. 'What if I beg in a little black dress?'

'Hmm …' He placed his hand on her hip, his eyes flashing with desire. 'You may get some favours, but you won't win.'

'We'll win next time. Louis is only going to get better.'

'Steph's going to get better too. But I still have to help you else you might not visit as often.'

'I could think of a reason to visit without training.'

He smiled. 'Good. So, how about we go to Smithy's for dinner tonight?'

Ana wrapped her arms around his waist. 'It's a date.'

* * *

A week later, February drew to an end and the rain finally arrived, much to the delight of the community and Liam's family. Jack had been complaining as the rain usually came earlier in the summer. Sometimes even before Christmas. But nevertheless, it was a welcome relief for the farmers. As for Ana, the sunny Elizadale she'd grown to love was now wet, cool, and downright depressing. No matter where she went, the gutters flowed, mud caked her shoes, and she got drenched.

'We don't get rain like this in Sydney,' Ana told Meg and Elanora as they walked to their classrooms. 'Sometimes it's just rain, or drizzle, but this is ridiculous.'

Meg grinned. 'Torrential. I love the rain, at least for the first few days. It's what you get living in this part of the country over your big city. Usually, we'd have weeks and weeks of this, but the rain's late this year.'

'Not good for the farmers,' Elanora sighed.

'But they're expecting this rain to last awhile.' Ana grimaced as they arrived at the flooded lunch shelter. 'By the look of this, I'd say eating inside is included in the wet weather protocol?'

Meg tiptoed around the puddles. 'Yeah, but I've brought a movie so you can both bring your classes over if you like.'

'Sounds good,' Elanora said.

'You're a lifesaver,' Ana agreed. 'I was afraid of the mess they'd make when I gave them arts and crafts.'

'Movies create the least mess. And the least noise.'

'They do.' Ana waved them off. 'I'll see you both later.'

Meg's movie idea was indeed brilliant as they settled the kids in the back of her classroom, where they remained relatively quiet and glued to *Finding Nemo*. Because of the children's protest, Meg let the movie run through to the end of reading time, but she took a stand after that and insisted they'd finish it tomorrow. Ana and Elanora gathered their whining classes and returned to their rooms, where she spent the rest of the afternoon working on literacy skills.

'That was a long day,' Ana sighed, exhausted as she and Meg walked the long way around to the staffroom. Even beneath the covered walkways, they still got wet.

Thankfully, the staff meeting was short. After being locked up with eleven children all day, Ana longed for the booth at the Royal and a nice cold drink.

Meg grabbed the Diet Cokes and Ana sat beside Liam, resting her head on his shoulder.

He placed a kiss in her hair. 'Busy day?'

'Exhausting. I hate the rain.'

'I hate the rain too.' Adam crossed his strong arms with a scowl. 'Bloody messes everything up, gets me wet, and puts Jack in a cranky mood.'

'You put me in a cranky mood with all your whining. If you just did the work instead of complaining about it, you'd be done quicker and wet less.'

'You still work outdoors when it's raining?' Ana asked, not sure why she was surprised.

Adam shrugged. 'There's still humping to do.'

Ana blinked. 'What?'

'Farm-term for picking bananas,' Liam quickly explained. 'It's called "humping" because we carry the bunches on our shoulder.'

'Right.' Ana's spine relaxed. 'Makes sense.'

Lucy sighed as she nursed her beer. 'Are we still going to Meg's after this for a girls' night in?'

Meg grinned. 'Absolutely. I've got kebabs marinating—veggie ones for Ana. We'll watch a movie and talk about men.'

Lucy laughed. 'Even though Ana's the only one of us with anything interesting to gossip about.'

'But there's not much I'll share,' Ana said, squeezing Liam's hand.

'Especially not with my sister.'

Lucy's screwed up her nose. 'Like I'd want to know what you two get up to. It'd gross me out.'

Jack cleared his throat. 'I got some info from Lily about this party. She said it'll be at her house, so I say we leave early so we don't have to rush. Give us plenty of time to get to Townsville.'

'And time for shopping,' Lucy added, sharing a smile with Isabella.

Cade arrived and squeezed in beside Lucy. 'What's up?'

'We're discussing plans for Lily's birthday.'

Cade raised his eyebrows. 'Is she coming back? It's soon, so you guys should have plans for the big twenty-one. I can't believe little Lilypad is twenty-one …'

'Ridiculous, right?' Adam agreed. 'Makes me feel old.'

'No, she's not coming home,' Jack told Cade. 'But we're turning up to her party.'

Cade grinned. 'Turning up? Does that mean you're not telling her?'

Lucy nodded. 'Yep.'

'Awesome. Can I come?'

Adam raised his eyebrows. 'You wanna come? Why?'

Cade shrugged. 'I like parties.'

'Is Mum coming?' Adam asked Jack.

'She would, but she's letting Lucy go, so needs to stay at the retreat. She reckons a twenty-first birthday isn't really her scene and is happy to know we'll be there.'

Shrugging, Adam glanced at Cade. 'There's a spare seat, so come if you want.'

Cade took a swig of his beer. 'I think I will.'

Chapter Twenty-Two

The rain didn't let up for another week. On Wednesday, Ana was enjoying another quiet lunchtime with Meg, the children distracted by *Wreck-It Ralph*, when a flower delivery arrived. The young lady from the nursery knocked and entered Meg's classroom with a beautiful white orchid in a blue glazed pot.

Surprised but flattered, Ana stroked the pretty bloom.

'Wow, it's gorgeous,' Meg said as Ana reached for the card. 'Liam's awfully sweet. Is it a special occasion?'

'Not that I know of. But I do love orchids. I used to …'

She trailed off as she read the note. *A special gift for my special lady. Thinking of you.* Ana's heart lodged in her throat. No. It couldn't be.

'Ana?' Concern filled Meg's voice. 'Are you okay?'

Swallowing, she met Meg's gaze. 'Rick used to send me orchids.'

Her friend's eyes widened. 'Do you think …?'

'I don't know.' Shaking her head, Ana reread the note. It wasn't Liam's handwriting. Her heart pounded. She couldn't move. Had Rick found her? Was he in town? Was he waiting?

Meg placed her hand on Ana's arm. 'Call Liam.'

Nodding, Ana stood. She left the orchid with Meg and slipped out the door on legs that felt like jelly. In her classroom, her hands shook as she fumbled through her bag to find her phone. The handwriting was likely someone's from the nursery, but she had to check.

The phone rang, but Liam didn't answer. Everything inside Ana tightened. 'It's okay. Don't panic. Do *not* panic.'

It could just be a coincidence. He'd been at the nursery, seen the orchid, and thought she'd like it. That's all. He loved plants, so it wouldn't be unusual if he'd stopped by.

But her hands still shook as she opened her text messages. She didn't want to ask if he'd sent it because that could lead to questions and she didn't want Liam to feel bad about scaring her. Instead, she sent: **Thank you for the flower**.

She waited a few minutes, but Liam didn't reply. Closing her eyes, Ana tried to steady her pounding heart with some breathing techniques she'd learned in yoga.

Rick couldn't have found her. If he had, he wouldn't have given himself away by sending her an orchid. She was being silly.

But she kept her phone on her as she returned to Meg's classroom.

'What did he say?'

'Didn't answer. But I think he was heading out to High Ridge this afternoon. Do they have reception out there?'

'Yes, but maybe he's just busy. I'm sure it's okay, Ana. Seeing a pretty orchid and sending it to you sounds like something Liam would do.'

She nodded. Meg was right. Would she be freaking out if the orchid had been roses or sunflowers?

But why wasn't the note signed?

It wasn't until she pulled up outside Riley Road shops after work that a message came through. Meg had insisted that they visit the hairdresser. Not that there was anything Ana wanted to have done, but a trim wouldn't hurt.

She opened the message. **No worries. I thought you'd like it.**

Ana sagged with relief. Running her hand down her face, she glanced over at the orchid riding on the passenger seat and smiled. 'Silly me.'

Climbing out of the car, she joined Meg beneath the shop's awning. 'Liam sent it!'

Meg's shoulders softened. 'Thank God! You actually had me worried!'

Ana managed a laugh. 'Yeah, me too.'

But as they entered the hairdresser, Ana couldn't shake the small ball of dread at the bottom of her belly. It'd been almost eight weeks since Rick had been released and she'd become complacent. She may have a wonderful new life, but she could lose it all in a blink of an eye if he found her.

'Hi, ladies. Be with you in a sec,' Claire Taylor said when they entered the salon.

Meg sat and waved her hand. 'Take your time.'

Ana forced herself to relax as she glanced around. It was set up like any other hairdresser Ana had been to, with a couple of chairs placed before large mirrors, washbasins at the back, and shelves of shampoo lining the window.

'This is a cute place.'

'Yeah, Claire's done well for herself.'

Ana had seen Claire a few times at yoga and she lived with

Grace White and Jessica Smithfield at Jackson Villas. They'd exchanged pleasantries many times when Ana and Louis had returned from their walk.

Claire finished with her customer, then gestured Ana and Meg into chairs. 'Who wants to go first?'

'Meg can. She knows what she wants.'

'Just a trim, thanks, Claire. I want to keep it shoulder length, but what do you think about adding another layer?'

'Hmm ...' Claire examined Meg's wavy blonde hair. 'I don't know. It might increase curl and make your hair bigger.'

'That's what I thought. And I like it as it is. Just do whatever you want.'

Claire pulled her trolley closer and reached for the spray bottle. 'I thought you were going to let it grow.'

'Yeah, but we know that never happens.'

'Fair enough. How are things anyway? Georgina was in the other day ranting about Adam and Paul causing trouble again.'

'Yeah, it's the usual story. Adam and Jordan were on again.'

Claire's lip curled. 'I've never understood what he sees in her.'

'Me neither.'

'She's bloody mean and treats people like shit. Always has.' Claire glanced at Ana. 'Meg, Jordan, and I went to school together.'

Meg met Ana's gaze in the mirror. 'There aren't many girls in town who like her, as you may have guessed.'

'And she's the ultimate boyfriend thief,' Claire said, reaching for a comb and scissors. 'Possessive, controlling, and I've never met anyone more self-centred. She manipulates people to get what she wants, has no boundaries, and even tried to steal Adam off Grace when they were dating. But he didn't stray.'

'Lots of people say bad things about Adam, but he's a decent guy,' Meg said as Claire began cutting her hair. 'I know you once thought so, Claire.'

She smiled. 'Yeah, sometimes you need to find out what all the fuss is about.'

Ana laughed. 'Well, despite his bad boy rep, I think he's all right,' she agreed, even though her body still tensed whenever he and the Kellys started mouthing off at each other.

Claire raised her eyebrow. 'Yeah?'

'Yeah.' Her eyes widened. 'But oh, not like that!'

'Ana's dating Liam,' Meg said.

Claire's shoulders softened. 'I was going to say. Because I had Deb in here last week telling me all about that.'

Heat rose in Ana's cheeks. She could only imagine what Deborah must have said. Thankfully, they didn't remain on that subject for long as Claire asked Ana how she was enjoying Elizadale and they continued to chat during their haircuts.

'That was fun,' Ana said when they left, the rain having granted them a moment's grace. 'Your hair looks lovely.'

Meg fiddled with the end of her blonde waves. 'Thanks. Yours does too. You off to pick up Louis?'

'Yeah. Let's make a run for it while the weather's being friendly.'

They dashed towards their cars, water splashing up their legs as they called cheery goodbyes. Ana slipped inside, smiled at the pretty orchid, and checked her reflection again in the rear-vision mirror. Her hair hung a few inches past her shoulders and smelled clean and fruity from the product Claire had used.

Feeling refreshed, Ana pulled onto Abbott Street and headed for Liam's. The gates were open, so she drove on through, smiling as Liam stepped onto the verandah flanked by the border collies.

'Hey, Ana!'

'Hey.' He held his arms out for her and she fell into his embrace. 'Thank you for my present. How did you know I love orchids?'

His chest rumbled with a laugh. 'Who doesn't like orchids?'

'True. They are pretty.' She'd planned to tell him how the coincidence had scared her, but now it seemed irrelevant. 'How are you?'

'Much better now. You smell incredible.'

'I just visited Claire Taylor. She put something in my hair, but I don't know what it is.'

'Pity.' He placed a kiss in her hair. Ana smiled as she buried her face against his shoulder and wrapped her arms around his waist. 'Want to come in?'

She wanted to, but since he was already lapping her up, Ana knew better. 'Where I'll end up wearing nothing but my beautiful hair?'

'Well, yeah.'

She grinned. His hands brushed up and down her back, heating her blood and accelerating her pulse. 'Not right now,' she said, even though she had no idea why. 'But if you come over for dinner, I'll strip down for dessert.'

'Okay. But I'm going to keep you close and distract you while you're cooking.'

He would too. Liam would like nothing more than to seduce her onto the kitchen floor. She might even let him.

'If I burn dinner, it'll be your fault.'

'I'll eat it anyway.'

'Okay, deal.'

They released each other and Liam grabbed his keys while Ana settled the dogs into his LandCruiser and gathered her things from her car. As they pulled onto Station Drive, the rain returned to hammer fiercely on the windscreen.

Ana sighed miserably. 'I knew I wouldn't get home before it started again. My poor hair!'

'It's just water.' Liam flashed her a sexy grin and squeezed her knee. 'It'll give us an excuse to get undressed.'

She playfully shoved his hand away. 'Don't think you're going to convince me. I said after dinner.'

'Oh, I think I could convince you.'

'Yeah?'

'Yeah.'

Ana ignored him and turned her attention out the window. Was that a challenge? If so, how long would it take for her to surrender?

Probably not long.

Liam pulled up outside Jackson Villas and Ana unclipped her seatbelt.

'I'll get the door if you get the dogs,' she said, jumping out of the car and hugging the potted orchid to her chest as she dashed towards the safety of her front patio. But she didn't get far before Liam grabbed her around the waist. Ana shrieked as he spun her around and smothered her protests with a hot, steamy kiss. Rain ran down her face, saturating her, but Ana didn't care. She kissed him back, the pot pressing between them as their clothes soaked and stuck. His fingers dug into her wet hair and he drew in her lower lip. Ana sighed, accepting defeat as she brushed her tongue against his.

Liam pulled away, his blue eyes gleaming. 'Aww, baby. You're all wet.'

She laughed. God, he was cheeky. 'Get the dogs.'

Liam returned to the car while Ana dashed for cover, pulling open her conveniently unlocked screen door as she fumbled for her keys.

'You really should lock that,' Liam said.

'Nah, too many locks then.'

Liam shook his head as they stepped inside and Ana followed the dogs, hoping to get to the back door before Liam caught her in another passionate embrace. She placed the orchid on the kitchen bench and unclipped their leads. 'Stay out of trouble, you two.'

Tongues lolling, Steph and Louis ran out into the rain. Ana shook her head. Turning, she met Liam's gaze and a wave of desire flooded through her. He gathered her close and she softened, gripping his strong forearms. He looked good with his hair wet, water droplets on his forehead, and his T-shirt moulded to his finely formed body.

Screw dinner.

His mouth descended and Ana clutched him tight. Clearly, the only smart thing to do was to get out of their wet clothes. He trailed kisses down her throat and she gripped his waist, wanting his skin against hers. Heat burned in her thighs as her hands slipped up the front of his shirt, his warm muscles rippling beneath her touch.

'You win, Liam. Let's get out of these clothes.'

'Told you I'd win.'

'Shut up.' She pulled his shirt off over his head. It landed on the floor with a wet plop as her hands splayed across his chest.

He gathered her to him, squishing Ana's arms between their bodies as his mouth found hers. Heat flooded her. They kissed with a hunger that was almost primal and blindly stumbled into the table. Then his hands slid under her butt and she found herself perched on the edge of the glass surface.

Her heart pounded, causing blood to rush south. Liam's fingers brushed over the waistband of her pants and found the skin beneath her blouse, trailing the grooves of her spine. Sparks shot through her. She moaned, her back arching as his hands ran around her hips to her belly. One by one, the buttons of her blouse popped open before he peeled it from her shoulders. She wrapped her legs around his waist and clung, tearing her mouth away to catch her breath.

'We should go upstairs. I don't know about this glass table and I'd hate to explain to the Rileys if we broke it.'

Liam wrapped his arms around her waist and lifted her up. 'It'd be a funny story.'

She laughed. 'Just get me upstairs.'

Ana captured his face in her hands and kissed him again, not caring about the distraction as he crossed to the staircase. But a few steps up, Liam lost his footing. Her stomach plummeted. Shrieking, she clung to him. He tightened his grip on her with one arm and reached for the banister with the other.

'Shit.'

He blew out his breath. 'Sorry, baby.'

'Just put me down.' She unwrapped her legs and he set her on the stairs, kneeling beside her. 'That was close.'

'Should we get up and walk?'

Ana grinned. 'No, I want you now.'

Taking control, she reached for the button of his shorts and flipped it open. Liam didn't protest as he pulled her from her own pants and underwear. He grabbed protection from his wallet, then tossed it and his shorts over the banister as she flipped their positions. Wrapping her arms around his neck, she straddled him and helped get them ready.

'I don't think ...' He reached for her knee and tried to help her find a position.

'We can do it. I just ...'

'Here.' In one movement, he had her there and Ana took him, lowering herself slowly enough to tease and torture. Pleasure she'd never felt before engulfed her. Liam's hands were everywhere, holding her close and running over her satin bra until his fingers twisted into her hair. He pulled her close for a kiss.

Their hearts hammered as they worked towards their peak. Ana fell first, her body exploding over his. Her fingers dug into his flesh as Liam found his own and she rode him through it, his grip tightening around her hair until her scalp ached.

Afterwards, Ana rested her chin on his shoulder and tried to catch her breath. Never had she needed someone so badly that she couldn't even make it up the stairs.

'That was pretty crazy,' he said.

She smiled, brushing her hands up and down his back. Gathering her strength, she lifted her head and met his amused gaze. 'Totally. But I think we should try sex in other places before we return to the stairs.'

'Should we try the shower next?'

'What? Now?'

'Well, we are wet.'

Ana sighed. Would they ever get to dinner? Did it matter if they didn't? Probably, since she'd be hungry, but they'd worry about that later.

'All right.'

They dashed up the stairs.

Chapter Twenty-Three

Rick tossed his pie wrapper towards the bin, missed, and continued through the mall as he waited for his phone to switch on. The new sim card and phone number should cover his tracks. His heart pounded, hand tightening until the blasted thing finally fired up. Scrolling through the contacts, he hit the one he'd saved a few weeks ago and lifted the phone to his ear.

'Hello, Elizadale State School, Mary speaking.'

Rick forced politeness into his tone. 'It's John, from the Department of Education. Would Anastasia Hamilton be there?'

'Of course. One moment, John. I believe she's in the staffroom.'

Rick smiled as the line went quiet. He'd assumed now would be a good time for a lunch break. Stopping on the corner by the park, he waited, pulse racing. Any minute now.

'Hello, this is Anastasia Hamilton.' Her sweet, backstabbing voice filled his ear and everything inside Rick tightened. Heated. His jaw clenched and he almost snapped the phone in half. 'Hello?'

Threats lingered on his tongue. He wanted to scare her. Wanted to call her every filthy name under the sun and tell her she'd soon be sorry.

But he couldn't. Lowering the phone, Rick ended the call. Soon. He'd tell her really soon.

* * *

Ana stepped out of her Yaris as Steph and Louis ran towards her. Smiling softly, she dropped to her knees to hug them while Liam closed the gates. That phone call earlier had been unsettling and she still wasn't sure what it'd been about, but she couldn't do anything about it now as she kissed Louis' head. Then Steph's. Ana laughed as the naughty girl's tongue whipped out to lick her chin. What more could she ask for than to come home to Liam and these two beautiful faces?

'Hey,' she called as he strode over from the gates.

'Hey, baby. How was work?'

'Good. Glad it's the weekend though.' She stood and Liam took her into his arms, the dogs jumping around their feet. Louis lifted to place his muddy paws on her waist, his tongue hanging out the side of his mouth. She rubbed his head.

'Me too. You want to relax for a while or go for a walk?'

Steph's head tilted at the W word. Ana smiled. 'I guess we can't keep these two waiting.'

Liam laughed and glanced at the dogs. 'Who's ready for a walk?'

They bolted towards the gate.

Ana returned to her car for her hat and walking shoes, then slipped them on while Liam grabbed the leads. Steph and Louis didn't move.

'So, something strange happened today,' she said as they set off down Station Drive towards the highway. 'Someone from the Department of Education called, but he was gone by the time I came to the phone.'

'Did you call back?'

'Yeah, but no one seemed to know who had called me. Mary said his name was John.'

Liam frowned as he led Steph around a puddle. Ana walked around too while Louis splashed through. 'That is strange. You sure it was the Department of Education?'

'That's what Mary said. It was a mobile number, so we tried that first and it just rang out.'

Ana tightened her hand around Louis' lead as they crossed the highway towards the parkland. The thought that had been niggling at the back of her mind finally took hold and filled her heart with dread. Swallowing, she glanced up at Liam. 'What if … do you think that phone call could have been Rick?'

'Why would Rick call you?' Liam placed his hand on her lower back and some of the tension eased from her spine.

'Yeah, I know. Silly idea. If he knew where I was, he wouldn't do anything that would alert me. Right?'

'Well, I don't know what goes through the head of someone like him, but I wouldn't call you.'

She sighed and the dread ebbed away. 'That's what I thought. But still … it was strange.'

'When we get home, we'll call the parole board and let them know, hey?'

'Okay.'

Ana enjoyed the rest of their walk and pride filled her heart when Louis didn't lunge at a car once, or the bicycle that rode past. Practice, exposure, and the right verbal cues had finally worked.

When they returned to Liam's, Ana placed a quick call to her contact with the parole board, but all they said was that Rick remained compliant and was still in Sydney. The confirmation reassured her a little, but that still didn't mean he hadn't called her.

Sighing, she got ready for Friday Frenzy. The usual banter and fun passed away their evening and effectively put her at ease.

When she and Liam left, he wrapped his arm around her waist and whispered in her ear. 'You're coming back to my place, right? We'll need to stop by yours to get some things, but I have a surprise for you tomorrow that we should get up early for.'

Intrigued, she planted a quick kiss on his lips. She had no objections to spending the night at his place since they rarely spent nights apart anymore. When they did, Steph and Louis did not appreciate it. They practically pined when separated and if Louis could move into Liam's house, he would. And as they approached the sprawling Queenslander, the verandah light illuminating the front yard to welcome them home, Ana wished she could move in there too.

But she quickly shook that thought away. It was crazy. She hadn't known Liam long, so the idea of living together was ridiculous. He'd certainly think so too with his slow-and-steady-wins-the-race attitude. Besides, Ana liked where their relationship was right now. She took comfort in having her own space. And even though the nights they spent apart felt lonely, Ana enjoyed spreading out in her bed.

At least that's what she kept telling herself—that it was too soon. But after her panic over the orchid and that phone call today, how could she fathom settling down while Rick was still out there? It was best she and Liam enjoyed each other and had fun for as long as they could without planning for the future. It was Steph and Louis who wanted to play house.

But when Ana woke with Liam's mouth on her neck and sunlight slipping through the window, a future with him was all she wanted. Moaning, she rolled to gather him in her arms without opening her eyes.

'Morning, beautiful.' He kissed her and Ana's body melted into the mattress, her leg lifting to wrap around his waist.

'Hey.' She kept her eyes closed and met his kisses, enjoying the lazy contentment.

'You want to join me in the shower?'

'No.' She tightened her grip and buried her face into his naked shoulder. How could he smell so good this early in the morning? 'Stay.'

Sighing, he ran his hand down her bare arm. 'I knew this would be difficult.'

'Hmm …'

'But I have a plan. I want to take you somewhere.'

'Where?'

'It's a surprise.'

She groaned. 'It's not the shower, is it?'

Liam laughed as he placed kisses behind her ear. 'No, although we can do that first.'

'Mmm, okay.'

Lying there a while longer, Ana enjoyed the way his mouth continued to move over her neck and shoulders. Then Liam started complaining again, so she let him drag her out of bed and they spent much longer in the shower than necessary.

Awake now, Ana pulled on the jeans Liam had insisted she bring. She didn't know why and would probably die of heat stroke. Or maybe not since he'd also said to pack swimwear.

'I'm not sure I respond well to surprises,' she said as she brushed her teeth. 'Can you just tell me if it's good?'

'Why wouldn't it be?' He stood behind her and wrapped his arms around her waist, dropping a kiss to her shoulder. 'You'll enjoy it.'

When they were ready to go, Liam called Steph and Louis to the car. They raced over, their white feet and bellies muddy. Ana smiled as they jumped into the back of the LandCruiser. If the dogs were invited, then whatever they were doing had to be fun.

'It doesn't look like it'll rain today,' she said as they pulled out of the driveway.

'I'm counting on it.'

'But it's nice weather. We could spend some time outside.'

'I'm not telling you what we're doing.'

Ana's shoulders slumped. 'Fine. I won't pry.'

But her curiosity peaked when Liam turned off Station Drive and onto Shadow Creek. Ana smiled. She'd been friends with the Maguires for two months but had yet to set foot on their property or visit the banana farm.

'Ahh … what are we doing?'

'Just relax.' Liam placed his hand on her knee. 'We're going to spend the day out here.'

She glanced at the trees and plains that spread far and wide. 'Why don't you have banana trees on this part of the farm?'

'It's another biosecurity measure. The bananas are on the north side of the creek with a dedicated entrance where only workers come and go.'

'Oh. Did you used to grow bananas here?'

'Yeah, once. We were about to rip them out and reduce production when Cyclone Larry hit Innisfail and destroyed almost ninety percent of Australia's banana crop.'

Ana's eyebrows shot up. 'When was that?'

'About fifteen years ago. I was in grade seven and the industry up here wasn't doing too well because Innisfail and Tully are better areas for bananas. But with all their crops sadly gone, the farms around this region flourished. The cost of bananas went up by about four-hundred percent and we kept the banana trees south of the creek.'

'Wow.' She'd been young, but a part of her recalled the time bananas had been an expensive luxury. 'I guess that's farming for you though, right? Luck of nature?'

'Absolutely. But when Panama disease arrived and the government implemented biosecurity, we decided it was easier to quarantine the northern fields.'

'So, what do you do with this land?'

'We keep it for recreational use and farm other fruit.' Liam adjusted his hands on the steering wheel and flashed her a smile. 'At the moment, we have a lychee and a guava orchard.'

'Huh. I'm not sure I've ever had either of those. Guava-flavoured things, yes, but I might have to try them.'

'I can definitely help you with that.'

She smiled. 'Sounds good. So, how long has your family been here?'

'My ancestor, John Maguire, arrived at the same time as Stuart Riley in the eighteen-sixties and began grazing cattle. It wasn't until about twenty years later that the Chinese goldminers introduced bananas to North Queensland. My family planted their first crop after the First World War. Things were tough and they were still grazing cattle, but the industry boomed after the Second World War. When Dad and

Uncle Henry took over, they got rid of the cattle and focused only on bananas, plus whatever else we wanted to grow. Lily wanted guavas and she keeps talking about a pineapple farm. We had mangos when I was a kid, but they were just for local produce. Our bananas are shipped Australia wide.'

Glancing out at the stunning spread of green bushland, Ana asked more questions about how the farming process worked and how many bananas Shadow Creek produced in a year. It fascinated her how one farm could grow so many bananas to help feed Australia one of its favourite fruits.

Liam slowed at an intersection. 'Turning left, you'll find Adam's house. He built it by the creek. Up ahead is the way to High Ridge.' He turned right. 'This road will take us to the homestead.'

Liam continued to talk as they drove, pointing out the turnoffs to Jack's and Michael's houses. Eventually, they arrived at what Ana easily recognised as the main part of the farm. The road looped around a field featuring a massive jacaranda tree and an old wooden swing set. Ana could imagine Liam, Lucy, and their cousins playing on that while growing up. To her left sat a white, double-storey, picture-book farmhouse with a wrap-around verandah, detached garage, and two window nooks on the second floor.

'That's my family home where Mum and Dad live.'

Ana smiled. 'It's beautiful. Are your parents' home today?'

'They won't be far. Mum rarely goes to town on the weekends. We can stop in when we get back and I'll introduce you to my dad.'

'I'd love to meet him.'

'He wants to meet you too.' Liam reached for her hand as they drove past a large shed. 'And this is the official homestead where Aunt Wendy and Uncle Henry live.'

'Wow, it's so big. Lovely wide verandah.'

It was a single-storey, red brick home with a cream tin roof. The verandah overflowed with potted plants, a mix of wooden furniture, and was separated into two where part of the house jutted out. Ana counted five windows across.

'It is nice,' Liam agreed. 'Jack will live there whenever he pulls his head in and gets married.'

Ana smiled as she tore her eyes from the homestead. 'And why isn't he?'

Liam shrugged. 'Who bloody well knows?'

They continued around the loop until Liam parked outside a green tin shed.

'And here we are.' He turned off the ignition and climbed out, giving Ana no time to ask questions as she alighted onto the muddy ground. There was a distinct smell out here, one she recognised as fertiliser. Or, at least, what fertiliser contained. Or, as she heard a soft whinny from the other side of the wall, perhaps it was just the smell of horses.

Liam let the dogs out and Louis chased Steph towards the jacaranda tree. Standing beside Ana, he slipped his arm around her waist. 'What do you think?'

She took in the scenery, breathed in the fresh tropical air, and smiled. 'I love it. Very spacious and pretty.'

Liam smiled. 'I'm glad you like it. So, what do you say we go exploring? I'll show you my favourite spots around Shadow Creek.'

'That sounds lovely, Liam.'

'Ever been on a horse?'

Chapter Twenty-Four

Ana stilled. Been on a horse? Was he serious?

'No,' she replied weakly. 'I've never even touched a horse.'

She may have liked the idea of riding the other day, but she hadn't mentioned it to him since realising how big horses were. And that riding one meant she'd have a large, powerful animal beneath her and that people died riding horses every day.

Liam took her hand and led her to the stable doors. 'Then you've come to the right place. I'll introduce you to a horse today.'

Ana followed him, more out of curiosity than anything. 'Can't we just drive?'

'It's nicer to go on horseback. Driving takes the fun out of it. Unless …' Inside the stables, he turned to her and placed his hands on her shoulders. 'You're not afraid, are you?'

Swallowing, Ana wasn't sure what she was. She didn't mind the idea, but that didn't stop her heart from thumping. Horses were intelligent creatures that always seemed to know what a person was thinking. The closest she'd been to one was at the Show. And frankly, she didn't trust animals that were bigger than she was.

'No, I'm not afraid. But … I don't know, Liam. Shouldn't I start with a few circles around a paddock rather than a long ride through the farm?'

'I'll teach you how to ride first, don't worry. And we'll take it slow. I promise you, Ana. We have people come here all the time who've never ridden before. You'll be fine.'

He took her hand again and led her towards a stall. A brown horse poked its head out of the gate and Ana jumped. It was huge!

'This is Esme. She's Lucy's mare and she loves the young ladies. She has a soft temperament and has been ridden by inexperienced people before, so she'll be nice and calm for you. Esme, this is Ana. She's never ridden before, okay?' As he stroked Esme's face, she actually seemed to be listening to him. Or was it just Ana's imagination trying to settle her nerves? 'I want you to be nice to her, all right? I know you will be.'

He tugged Ana's hand and urged her a step closer. She obliged. There was nothing to be scared of when Liam was there. He wouldn't put her on a horse she couldn't handle.

Swallowing her nerves as she believed horses could sense fear, she reached up and stroked Esme's nose. She was soft and velvety, her eyes blinking at Ana with kind curiosity.

'Hello.' Ana's shoulders relaxed a fraction. 'You're a pretty girl, aren't you?'

'She's a good girl,' Liam said, squeezing Ana's shoulder. 'You stay here and talk to her. Rub her neck too, she likes that. I'll grab the tack.'

Liam left, but Ana didn't mind. Esme couldn't hurt her

when still inside her stall. Besides, if you were friendly to a horse, then the horse would be friendly to you. Right?

God, she hoped so.

'So, you're Lucy's? I can see why she'd like you. You're beautiful and tough, just like she is, hey?' Esme made a sound as though in agreement. Ana took a deep breath and ran her hand down Esme's neck, her reddish-brown mane brushing through her fingers. 'You're going to take me on a tour of Shadow Creek, hey? I hope you know your way around because I sure don't.'

Ana continued to talk to Esme, ignoring what Liam was up to as she allowed her pulse to settle. She was feeling more comfortable with the horse and almost excited about the adventure when Liam returned. He slid a bridle over Esme's head and led her out of the stall. Outside, Ana remained with Esme while he retrieved his own horse. Archer was only slightly taller than Esme, but he was solid and Ana was glad she didn't have to ride him.

'Wow. He's big.'

Liam laughed, securing Archer and taking Ana's hand. 'You want to see big? Come with me.'

He led her back inside and introduced her to the rest of the horses. First there was Bobby, who was Michael's and looked like he was asleep on his feet.

'Lightning is currently in Townsville with Lily,' Liam said, passing by an empty stall with a lightning bolt on the wall. Then he introduced her to a massive black horse who was far larger than the others. 'This is Vendetta, Adam's prize gelding. He's always liked the big dark ones, black preferably, ever since he was eleven and got Vader.'

Ana raised her eyebrows, again questioning Adam's mentality. 'Vader?'

'Yeah. As in Darth Vader. Jack had Yoda and I had Anakin. Lucy named her pony Leia. Thankfully, we'd grown out of the Star Wars theme by the time Archer, Esme, and Vendetta came along. And over here—' He led her to the next stall where another large horse stood, this one of a brown variety. Ana knew there were technical names for the colours, but to her it was just brown. 'This is Jack's horse, Dante.'

'That's a nice name. He's big too. I didn't realise you all needed a horse though …'

'We don't *need* horses,' Liam said, leading her back outside. 'Not for work. But we like horses, so we have them for pleasure riding and to take tourists out with. Besides, there are some parts of the property that are best accessed on horseback. Lucy and Lily both grew up doing horse sports though. Lil has ambitions, but Lucy's more interested in training and breeding these days.'

'But you've all been riding for a long time, haven't you?'

'All our lives. And now, I can teach you.'

Ana glanced at Esme. 'I'm going to be sore tomorrow, aren't I?'

'Maybe, but I'll make it up to you when you resort to bed rest.'

She shook her head and pretended to disapprove. 'You'd love to keep me horizontal all day, wouldn't you?'

He grinned, his eyes wicked. 'Only if you want.'

'How about you just show me what to do, then we'll see, hey?'

As Liam began her lesson, Ana quickly learned that there was a lot more to riding a horse than simply sitting on its back. Liam showed her how to saddle Esme and then settled a white riding helmet onto her head.

'You won't see anyone around here wearing this crap,

except the tourists. But at the moment, baby, you're no better.'
He clipped it under her chin and pressed a kiss to her lips. 'I
wouldn't want you to do yourself a head injury.'

She swallowed. 'This is precautionary, right?'

'Of course. Trust me, Ana. I wouldn't put you on a horse
I didn't think was right for you. Jack and I agreed Esme would
be kind and I believe Lucy gave her a briefing yesterday.'

Taking a breath, Ana nodded as she followed his next
instructions. Liam gave her a leg up and she mounted Esme.
It felt strange with the horse and saddle between her thighs,
but as she wriggled her bum a little, she found a comfortable
seat.

'You'll take a photo of me up here, right?' she asked as
Liam adjusted her stirrups. 'I'll need to send one to Nat. She
was going on about how she wouldn't mind trying to ride.'

'When she visits, we can take her riding too. But sure, I'll
take a photo. Later, when we're out among the paddocks.
How's that?'

The stirrups felt okay, so she nodded as Liam untied Esme
and handed her the reins. They spent some time going over
how to ride and with every lap around the paddock, Ana's
spine relaxed. Steph and Louis sat on the grass by the swing
set, watching her with their heads tilted and ears perked.

'I think I've got the hang of it. I'm happy to go if you think
I'm ready.'

'All right. Stay right there.'

Ana watched as Liam gathered supplies from the car and
packed them into Archer's saddlebags. With his Akubra on his
head, he swung easily onto his horse. Everything inside her
tightened. Damn, he looked good. He might live in town, be
a businessman and about to open a café, but he was still a true

Australian country boy and riding off through the farm was bound to be the ultimate rural date.

'You look hot on a horse.'

He grinned and adjusted his hat. 'What? You think I should do this more often?'

'Well … maybe we could.'

He laughed. 'All right. Let's get going.'

Liam stayed close to her and called for Steph and Louis. The dogs ran over and followed them down the road, Liam stopping for a gate that opened onto a paddock. Steph had obviously ridden with Liam before as she walked slightly to the side of Archer. Considering Louis practically stuck to Steph, Ana wasn't worried about him, especially when there were no cars to chase or anything that should cause them harm.

Except maybe snakes.

Ana shook her head. No, the dogs would be fine. All she had to do was absorb the majestic scenery as she and Liam rode across the paddock. The lush land curved here and there, the grass long from the recent rain. Ana still couldn't identify many of the trees, but they varied in colours and sizes. Up ahead rose the small mountain, which held the National Park. Ana smiled as she breathed in the clean, clear air that still smelled like rain.

Shadow Creek was beautiful.

'How're you going there?' Liam asked as they moved into some bushland and stopped at another gate. He leaned down to open it.

'I'm all right. This is quite enjoyable, actually. And the land is amazing.'

Liam closed the gate behind them and they continued on.

Ana laughed as Steph and Louis raced ahead to herd a flock of sulphur-crested cockatoos. Then Liam held out his hand and, being brave, Ana let go of the reins and took it. His hand squeezed hers as he flashed her a warm smile. Never would she get this anywhere else, no matter where she ran away to next. There was no place like Shadow Creek and no man like Liam Maguire.

Ana's heart ached. She had to stop thinking about it. She didn't *want* to leave. Didn't want to ruin this moment. So, shoving all her worries from her mind, she embraced the romance of being out with Liam beneath the warm sunshine.

And she continued to enjoy it, until almost forty minutes later when they were still riding.

'Are we nearly there?' she asked, adjusting herself in the saddle. Now she realised why the Maguires had great butt, thigh, and stomach muscles.

'Almost. Sorry, I've given you a bit of a tour. But we'll be at Maguire Falls shortly.'

She raised her eyebrows. 'Maguire Falls?'

'That's what we call it. It's a part of the *actual* Shadow Creek near the retreat. See up there?' Liam pointed towards the mountain where a large brick building peeked through the trees to overlook the farm. 'That's High Ridge. What you see is the lodge, where Lucy lives and the guests can gather.'

'Wow. She must love that view.'

'Yeah, she can see all the way over to Adam's place—' he waved his arm somewhere towards the west '—the farm, the Kellys, and even to White Peaks. There are cabins with views, a campground, and walking tracks into the National Park.'

'Can we go there one day?'

'Of course. We could go riding through there too, if you like?'

He flashed her a smile and Ana rolled her eyes. 'We'll see how I go after today. My bum is already sore.'

'Yeah, sorry. We're almost there, I promise. Or do you want to stop?'

She shook her head. 'No, I'll be fine.'

After a few more minutes, the unmistakable sound of rushing water cut through the silence. They weren't far from the retreat when they reached a thicket of trees and Liam swung off Archer.

'We'll walk from here.'

They tied Archer and Esme to a post and Liam slipped his backpack from the saddlebag. Ana followed him along a worn path, Steph and Louis trailing behind them, panting heavily. The gradient increased as they climbed up a few rocky steps and the sound of rushing water grew louder. Then Liam led her around a thicket of bush and they arrived at a clearing overlooking the stunning creek. Up ahead was a small waterfall, maybe two metres tall. The crystal-clear water rushed down a series of rocks and pools beneath the heavy shade of thick, green trees.

'Oh, wow …'

'Beautiful, isn't it?' Liam wrapped his arm around her waist. 'I love this place.'

'I can see why.'

'It's perfect to swim in and have a picnic. The tourists enjoy coming here. It's our own little piece of paradise.'

Paradise indeed. It was the perfect spot to cool down, relax, or have a romantic rendezvous.

'Let's sit down. We'll have something to eat, then take a dip.'

Liam took Ana's hand and led her to a spot closer to the creek. She was about to give Louis permission to swim, but he was already running towards the water and jumped in with a splash. Steph stood on the edge and watched him.

'Doesn't Steph like swimming?' she asked as Liam placed the cooler bag on her lap.

'She'll get in once we do,' he said, offering her a bottle of water. Ana drank and rested her head against Liam's chest. 'I also brought you a vegemite sandwich and an orange.'

Her stomach rumbled with gratitude. 'Thank you.'

They watched the water as they ate. Louis clambered back onto the rock and shook himself, panting happily. Ana smiled as she relaxed against Liam, enjoying the peaceful isolation and musical splash of the waterfall. Time slipped away beneath the gum trees.

'With you here in my arms, Ana,' Liam said, his chin resting on her shoulder, 'I couldn't be happier.'

She smiled, content as she ran her hand over where his clasped around her waist. 'It's been a lovely day, Liam. I've really enjoyed it. Thank you.'

'I'm glad.' He placed a kiss in the curve of her neck. Ana sighed and closed her eyes. 'Are you happy here, Ana?'

'I am.'

'You don't want to leave?'

She swallowed the knot in her throat. 'It's not about *want*, Liam. It's ...'

Pressing her lips together, she glanced down at their hands. Even if Rick found her ... she'd what? Spend her life playing a game of cat and mouse?

'No, Liam.' She interlocked her fingers with his. 'I don't want to leave. I wish I could stay here forever.'

'Good.' He touched his lips to her neck again, then lifted his head. She turned to meet his gaze, finding his eyes warm and bright. 'I love you, Anastasia.'

Everything inside her tightened, then softened. Her heart waltzed as she grinned and lifted her hand to place over Liam's gorgeous cheek. 'Did you bring me here just to tell me that?'

His lips quirked. 'Quite transparent, aren't I? Yeah, I did.'

'Because back home or anywhere else wasn't good enough?'

'I wanted the day to be special. And to bring you here. And to go swimming because it's been so damn hot.'

Ana laughed. She'd tried telling herself otherwise, but she'd loved Liam for many weeks now and there was no going back. She hadn't only answered his question just then, but also made him a promise.

She wouldn't leave.

'I love you too, Liam. And thank you for bringing me here. It was a beautiful gesture.'

Liam kissed her. And deep in her heart, Ana knew she was where she was meant to be.

* * *

The parole officer stepped out of the apartment and lifted his hand in a wave. 'You've done well, Rick. I'm very pleased with your compliance. See you in ten days, hey?'

'Sure thing.' He waved the officer off, closed the door, and grinned. 'Not fucking likely.'

He dashed into the bedroom and grabbed the packed suitcase from the wardrobe. He didn't have a minute to waste. Ten days may be plenty of time to make that ridiculously long trek to Elizadale—the bitch sure had put some distance between them. But he didn't have a clue what he'd find when he got there. He'd need to scout out the place, find out where she lived, who was protecting her.

Not that it mattered. The opportune time would present itself and he'd get the stupid slut. She didn't stand a fucking chance.

Chapter Twenty-Five

Liam's heart pounded as he set up the tables outside The Bent Banana. There was nothing special about them—they were ordinary outdoor settings made of steel—but Adam would arrive soon with his works of art and then his friends were coming to taste test his menu.

Liam swallowed his nerves and reached for a chair. He'd put more work into the menu and made a few last-minute alterations before sending it to the printers, but he'd finally settled on something he was content with. The banana and strawberry muffins that he'd been baking since he was a kid were bound to be a hit, and everyone would love his various flavours of ice cream and sorbet. Wraps and sandwiches always went down well and no one could say no to pancakes. Since meeting Ana though, he'd decided a pasta salad might be more appealing than a standard garden variety and she'd also inspired the apple crumble muffins. Besides, the cosy country kitchen was what he wanted and he was sticking to it. He could adapt and change the menu as he went. Like with any new business venture, there was the risk of failure. But he'd never know until he tried.

Strolling inside, he glanced around the café and slipped his hands into his pockets. The tension eased from his shoulders. How could he fail? He was damn proud of the work he and Michael had done. The café looked fabulous. The windows were open to air out the paint job he'd completed on Friday. They'd installed the counters and all of his equipment had arrived—the stove, display case, and large fridge. Liam couldn't believe the Grand Opening had snuck up on him. It was in two weeks! The trip to Townsville next weekend was inconvenient, but he had everything in order. He'd add the finishing touches—curtains, centrepieces, artwork—then he'd have a café that he could truly call his own.

Grinning, Liam rocked back on his heels. He couldn't wait to show it off to his friends. Only Michael had seen it so far and Liam was keen to know what everyone thought.

Especially Ana.

Liam shook his head. He still had to pinch himself. He had his café *and* the perfect woman. A woman who may have rooted her flighty feet and would stay in Elizadale. He'd been relieved to hear it because even though it still seemed fast, the need to confess his feelings had become too overwhelming.

He loved Anastasia Hamilton and in the week that had passed since their trip to Maguire Falls, speaking those words hadn't lost their spine-shivering quality. He hadn't said them to a woman since Diane and had once feared he never would. But Ana … he'd let go of his fear that she wouldn't stay and accepted what he'd known since that moment he'd first seen her at the Royal. She was The One and he would protect her until his dying breath.

He switched on some music and Kenny Chesney filled the room as Liam checked on the food. The banana ice cream had set nicely, the blenders were ready to whip up smoothies, his brownies were dark and gooey, and the banana bread he'd baked that morning was sliced and ready to serve. He hadn't prepared everything on the menu, just the few specialities he wanted his friends to try. And the treats he and Ana had made for the pups.

Grinning, he eyed the biscuits—peanut butter paws and banana bones—and the pumpkin pupcakes. He didn't know why such treats sounded foolish when any pampered pooch would delightfully gobble them up. He hadn't been sure if people would bring their dogs, but Ana had insisted that dog-friendly cafés were growing in the city. And after a little more research, he'd seen there were quite a few on the Tablelands, which had eased his worries.

The crunch of tyres sounded over gravel and Liam glanced out the window. The Tourist Centre was still open, but at four o'clock on a Saturday, Liam didn't expect many visitors. Thankfully, it was only Jack and Adam.

'Hey!' he called, stepping outside.

'Hey, mate. Got your tables.'

'I sure hope so.'

They strolled around to the back of the ute where six wooden tables gleamed under the dying sun. Liam grinned. They looked fantastic.

'We'll bring the big bastard in later,' Adam said as they lowered the tray-back. 'It'll need a trip all of its own.'

As they carried the tables inside, Liam's pulse slowed. Adam's work was marvellous and nothing less than he'd expected. The tables were square-shaped, rough around the edges, and a fine example of country craftsmanship.

'You did a bloody good job, mate,' Liam said, clapping Adam on the shoulder. 'Thanks.'

'No worries. Glad I could help. They do look good. And

so does this place.' Adam planted his hands on his hips as he glanced around, letting out a low whistle. 'Very nice indeed. Where's Jess's painting?'

'Over here. I haven't hung it yet.' He led his cousins to where the framed canvas lay on the bench, depicting a beautiful scene of the Shadow Creek banana plantation in bright acrylics. 'Nice, hey?'

Adam grinned. 'Shit, she's talented.'

'Sure is. But you should be proud, mate,' Jack said with a rare smile as he gazed about the room. 'Good to see you've finally done it. I'm sure you'll be a hit.'

Liam let out a long breath. 'I hope so.'

He might have doubts about some aspects of the café, but deep down, Liam believed he'd make a success of The Bent Banana. There was still a way to go, but he was a businessman and he'd done all he could to make the right connections. If the café failed, it wouldn't be due to a lack of effort. A news crew was coming to the Grand Opening, as well as people from the Cairns and Mareeba newspapers. He'd hired a jumping castle and Lucy and Aunt Wendy had offered to work in the kitchen. He'd still need casual help and was interviewing a couple of local girls next week. But until then, his family and Isabella were keen to lend a hand, and with Ana about to go on school holidays, she'd promised to be there too.

Soon, the rest of his friends started to arrive. Ana pulled up in her bright yellow Yaris with Steph and Louis. Jack and Adam hadn't brought their dogs, but Michael, Meg, Lucy, Isabella, and Cade did.

Liam laid the outside table with trays of doggy treats. 'See how they like these. Would any of you like a banana milkshake or a guava and mint smoothie?'

Everyone opted to try or share one, so he and Lucy

whipped up mini smoothies, then took out the tray of banana bread, chocolate and avocado brownies, and some guacamole dip to add a savoury. Everyone dug in with enthusiasm, nods and moans surrounding the table as he slipped into the seat beside Ana.

'Good dip,' Adam said.

'And bread,' Isabella added.

'Weren't banana pancakes on the menu?' Michael asked.

'I could do with some damn pancakes,' Adam mumbled. 'Why can't we have pancakes?'

Lucy rolled her eyes. 'Like we really need to taste test the pancakes. We've been eating them since forever.'

'True.' Adam's brow furrowed. 'And did I see Jeph-K Coffee inside?'

Liam nodded. 'Yeah, but I can't showcase local produce and not include the Kellys. Bernie and Liz don't deserve that.'

'I guess. Not that I know why anyone likes coffee. But the brownie's good.'

'The brownies are delicious,' Ana said, placing her hand on Liam's knee. His spine softened.

Isabella lowered her cup. 'I like this guava smoothie.'

Michael laughed. 'You like guava anything.'

Liam smiled, then turned as a red car drove into the car park. Perhaps he did have a visitor after all.

'I can greet them if you like,' Isabella offered, but Liam shook his head.

'It's all right.' He stood and Ana's hand slipped from his leg. But as he began to move inside, the Subaru revved, reversed, and drove away.

Liam frowned, then turned back to the table. That was fine, he'd rather not be disturbed anyway.

'Freddy can't get enough of these banana bones,' Cade said

as Liam slipped back into his seat. 'Dunno why. They taste like shit.'

'You're not supposed to eat them!' Ana laughed. 'Of course, they taste bad! They're just banana, oats, and peanut butter! Sugar is no good for dogs.'

'Yeah, the pumpkin pupcake was bland too,' Lucy said. 'But Roger liked it.'

'So does Sally.'

Liam shook his head, not surprised they'd tried the dog food. He'd done so himself.

'Evie turned her nose up at the pupcake, but she likes the bones.'

'What about the paws?' Liam asked.

'Freddy likes them.'

'So does Lola.'

Liam exhaled. 'Good.'

Ana smiled and squeezed his knee. 'I think, Liam, that you can call this a success.'

'The food's lovely,' Meg agreed.

Lucy nodded. 'It's exactly what you were going for, a fresh country kitchen. And the menu certainly highlights all our best local produce.'

Liam's heart swelled. 'You guys think?'

There were nods and a collective 'yes' around the table. The knots inside Liam loosened. His friends wouldn't lie to him, but they wouldn't say it just to be kind either.

The Bent Banana was going to be awesome.

He reached for a pumpkin cake and relaxed into his seat. 'Excellent. Here, Steph, have a pupcake. But don't you guys fill up! There's still ice cream.'

Adam thumped his fist on the table. 'Hell yeah!'

* * *

Rick smirked as he drove through the dreary town of Elizadale. What a fucking stroke of luck? He'd pulled up at the Tourist Centre and there she was, sitting with a bunch of country hicks with the fucking dog beside her. He'd do a blocky, park, and wait until she left. Locate where she lived. Devise a plan.

Who in their right mind would want to live in this fucking place though? It was nowhere near civilisation. He'd almost died of boredom on the drive, but at least there'd been plenty of free fruit along the way. Yeah, they'd expected him to put money in the secure buckets, but with no one to man the roadside stalls, who could make him?

He turned at the corner near the takeaway shop and pulled over by some footy fields, leaving the air-conditioner running as he eyed the party dining outside the Tourist Centre. He'd thought he'd grab some information about the area, but with the bitch there, he couldn't risk getting out of the car.

Instead, he watched her, tapping his fingers on the steering wheel. His gut tightened and he adjusted himself in his seat. In a matter of days, maybe even hours, he'd have his revenge. Hell, he might have it done and dusted and be back in Sydney before anyone could even suspect him. Rick doubted it, but he didn't care if he ended up back in prison. It'd be worth it.

It felt like an age, but before he could really lose his temper, the happy party separated. Rick watched as the stupid slut loaded two black-and-white mutts into the back of an old LandCruiser. A blond man closed the back doors and kissed her.

Rick's fists clenched. So, there was a man? He shouldn't be surprised. The bitch had always been needy and couldn't possibly survive without someone to freeload off. But what sort of problem could this bloke cause?

She strode to a little yellow shitbox of a car and slid inside. Rick's mouth curved. The LandCruiser tore away after the other cars and the yellow one followed. Rick shoved his Subaru into gear and eased back on the road. He didn't hurry. It wasn't hard to tail someone in a matchbox-size town.

He turned onto the highway, her yellow Yaris up ahead. His blood heated. Heart pounded. Would he get his chance so soon?

She turned at the golf course. He sped up a little and turned too. She pulled into the driveway of a sprawling acre block. His jaw clenched as he slowed to a crawl.

She leapt out of the car beside that old fucking LandCruiser and greeted that blond guy. Rick slammed his hand on the wheel.

Fuck.

He sped away.

Chapter Twenty-Six

'Louis did so well today,' Ana said as they left agility practice.

'He loves the tunnels, that's for sure.' Liam pulled away from the park and headed down Station Drive. 'So, are you excited about the last week of term?'

Ana grinned. She couldn't wait for the Easter break. On Friday, Liam was leaving to gate-crash Lily's birthday party. He'd be home on Sunday and then they had two whole weeks to spend together as they opened The Bent Banana. She may not get a relaxing break, but she looked forward to the café opening. She hadn't played a big part in its preparation, but since contributing the dog treats, she felt connected to The Bent Banana and couldn't wait to share in its joy.

'The last week is always chaotic, but fun. I'd love to catch up on some reading though. I found a new cosy mystery series this week that I want to binge read.'

Liam laughed. 'I'm sure you'll manage that.'

They returned to Liam's, showered and changed, then left for dinner on Shadow Creek. Steph and Louis hadn't been pleased about being left behind.

'Hello!' Deborah called, stepping onto the verandah of the little farmhouse. 'Ana, you look lovely this evening.'

'Thanks, Deb.' She'd worn her white lace sundress again and smiled as she returned Deborah's hug. 'Thank you for inviting me.'

'It's well overdue.' Deborah glared at Liam as she hugged him too. 'Nothing hurries my son along.'

Deborah took Ana's hand, leading her through the open-plan living area and onto the back deck where a man stood to greet her. She'd yet to meet Cliff Maguire as he and Henry had been out when she and Liam had returned from their horse ride the other day. Cliff was tall, appeared quite fit for his age, and had salt-and-peppered hair poking out from beneath his old, weathered Akubra. He smiled and Ana saw what Liam would look like in thirty years.

'Hello, Ana.' Cliff took her hand between both of his. 'Welcome. I've been told that you're a beautiful young woman and am glad to see my son doesn't lie.'

She grinned, flattered, while Liam shook his head at his father. 'Thank you.'

'Take a seat, Ana.' Deborah gestured to the mismatched chairs surrounding the plastic oval table. 'I'll get us some drinks. Lucy should be here soon.'

Considering Ana was already friendly with Liam's mother and sister, it wasn't one of those awkward family dinners. Not to her surprise, Cliff was as charming as the rest of the Maguire men. Liam was so much like him, in both looks and mannerisms, that it was uncanny.

They had a simple barbeque with a colourful salad and homemade veggie burgers all around that quite impressed Ana.

'I could have made beef ones too,' Deborah said as Cliff manned the barbie. 'But I thought it wouldn't hurt to try something new.'

'Food's food,' Cliff laughed. 'And there's nothing wrong with mushrooms.'

Ana smiled. 'Mushroom burgers are the best. You won't be disappointed.'

The food was delicious and went down nicely with a glass of chardonnay and amusing conversation. Before Ana and Liam left, Deborah wrapped up a few spare burgers to take with them, insisting enough that Ana couldn't refuse.

'I'll see you tomorrow, Ana,' Deborah said, hugging them both. 'Thanks for finally bringing her over, Liam.'

Deborah stood on the verandah, and with many pleasantries called back and forth, Ana smiled and waved before climbing into the LandCruiser.

* * *

Rick parked across from the acreage block, glaring at the modern Queenslander surrounded by palm trees, ghost gums, and far too much tropical foliage. Who the hell had the patience to bother with so many gardens?

Fuck, it pissed him off to see Ana looking so happy. And with another dog. The fucking mongrels had sat at the front gate for the past hour. One had started barking and the other had eventually joined in. But the slut and unlucky bastard in her life weren't home. Desperately needing fuel and food earlier, he'd quit watching her for an hour and when he'd returned, the LandCruiser had gone.

Not that it'd be smart of him to go after her while the man

was home. He wasn't that stupid. He needed to get Ana alone. And preferably without the barking, snarling mongrels.

Why the hell she needed two of them, he didn't know. Dogs and kids, that's all she'd ever cared about. Never mind looking after her boyfriend. Her fiancé. Her *husband*. A wife who didn't know her duties was useless. Good thing he'd seen that weakness in her when he had. She'd had no respect for him or their life together or for what he could give her. He could have given her everything.

The bitch hadn't seen that. She hadn't cared about his needs. She'd always wanted to spend time with friends and go to some fitness class or other. He'd stopped that. Then there were the books. Every week, there'd be a new one. And the DVDs. Why the hell had she continued to buy DVDs when he'd subscribed to Netflix? Then there would be a new ornament on the coffee table. New candle holders. A picture. Something else that would collect dust.

Then had come the dog. Spending a bloody fortune on a dog had been her biggest mistake. He'd put his foot down. He couldn't let his woman spend ridiculous amounts of money on useless things. Especially not on something you could pick up cheap at the pound. What would have happened when it'd become *their* money? She'd been crazy to spend over a thousand bucks of her own cash on a damn mutt. She'd have to be bloody stupid if she'd thought she could spend like that after they were married.

Luckily, he hadn't had to marry her. But that didn't mean she'd had to throw him in prison. Did she know what that did to a man? To his ego and reputation? She'd destroyed his life. He had nothing. He was an ex-criminal with a charge that most people found abhorrent.

But none of that mattered anymore. He glanced at the

time. Almost ten o'clock and she still wasn't home. Gritting his teeth, he shoved the car into gear and took off into the night.

The next morning, he returned to the house in time to see the yellow Yaris disappear down the street. He almost followed her, but before he could, the blond guy shutting the gates caught his eye. He climbed into his idling LandCruiser and drove away, leaving the dogs at the gate. Rick tapped his fingers on the wheel for a moment, then followed. He knew Ana worked at the school, so what did this bloke get up to?

Rick tailed the LandCruiser to the Tourist Centre, where the man climbed out and unlocked the front doors. Rick pursed his lips. *Interesting …*

But the place wouldn't be open for another half hour, so Rick headed off to get some breakfast. He bought a bacon and egg roll from the roadhouse, then returned to the Tourist Centre with his heart pounding and jaw tight. He wouldn't confront the bloke, but perhaps he'd get information of some sort.

He strolled inside, but the man wasn't there. A young woman looked up from the desk and flashed him a bright smile. 'Hello!'

He wanted to whack the cheer off her face, but Rick forced his shoulders to relax. He needed to look like a tourist. 'Hi.'

'Is there anything I can help you with today?'

Rick swallowed an impolite retort as he approached the desk. He glanced at the girl's chest and found himself disappointed. But the name on her badge read 'Isabella'.

'Dunno. Anything interesting to do around here?'

'Absolutely. Just passing through?'

'I guess.'

'What are you interested in?'

Rick resisted a smile. Nothing touristy, that's for sure, but he had to play the game. 'Food, I suppose. I saw this café was opening soon.'

He inclined his head to the closed doors off to the side. Isabella's smile widened.

'Yes, it's going to be fantastic, but it doesn't open until next weekend.'

'Why's that?'

She shrugged. 'It's the date the owner decided upon as school holidays should be helpful. Besides, he's going away this weekend.'

Rick's eyebrows lifted, his chest tightening. 'Is that so?'

'Yep. But if you're still around next week—'

'Hey, Iz …'

Rick stilled as a man's voice sounded behind him. Fuck, he hadn't thought this through. Would the slut's new bloke know about him? Seen a picture?

Ducking his head, Rick turned towards the doors. This was a stupid idea.

'Sorry, didn't see you were busy. You 'right, mate?'

Rick's hands curled into fists. Jaw tightened. Rage surged through him as he longed to turn and punch the fucker.

Isabella piped up in her musical voice. 'I was just telling this man about the café.'

'Ah, right. Yeah, we're not open yet, but our Grand Opening should be a blast if you're still in town.'

Rick eyed the doors. He could leave, but with the sudden urge to face this foe, he turned and stared the blond man directly in the eye. 'I don't plan to be.'

'Oh.' The man shrugged. Not a flicker of recognition passed through his pale eyes and Rick's spine relaxed as he checked for a name badge. Liam. 'Well, next time you're passing through.'

'Maybe.' Expelling a breath, Rick forced a touch of friendliness into his tone as he nodded towards Isabella. 'The lady was just telling me you're heading out of town this weekend. I hear there are a lot of nice places to visit. Time away with the missus?'

Liam shook his head. 'Nah, she has to work. Heading off for a family thing.'

It took everything Rick had to swallow his smile. Fuck, friendly people were stupid.

'Right. Well, I might stick around for a few days.' He grabbed an Elizadale flyer off the bench. 'See the sights.'

'There are a few ideas in that one. If you need any more suggestions though, we're more than happy to help.'

Rick grinned, his chest swelling until it almost burst. 'Don't worry. You've helped enough.'

Chapter Twenty-Seven

Ana's legs quivered as she held a prolonged triangle pose. She looked up, activated her quads, and wanted to slap Grace White.

'Keep breathing. Almost there. Just a little more, ladies.'

Grace was pushing them tonight, but Ana focused on the ceiling and did as instructed. She kept breathing and exhaled deeply when Grace said they could rise. She might complain, but her love for yoga grew every week and she always left feeling fantastic. Grace gave everyone the opportunity to either take it easy or push themselves, and Ana always tried putting in a little extra effort. After the past few weeks, she felt stronger, calmer, and much more flexible.

They moved into downward dog and completed a series of lunge poses before lying on their mats for stretching.

Meg sighed when Grace switched off the lights for relaxation. 'Always my favourite part.'

'Mine too.'

Ana let her body relax into the mat, her limbs soft and heavy at the same time. She almost drifted off, but Grace's voice broke her from her reverie just in time.

'So good, as usual,' Meg said as they rolled up their mats. 'I love Grace for bringing yoga to town.'

'She's done a great job,' Ana agreed, glancing around the hall and at the faces that had become so familiar. 'It seems to be growing.'

All the ladies their age attended, most of them Grace's friends. Ana's colleagues, Vivian and Elanora, were there, as well as Linda, with who Ana thought must be her husband. She hadn't met Brett, the senior sergeant, but the tall, solid man couldn't be mistaken for anyone but Cade's father. Ana was glad that the number of men had grown because yoga was for everyone.

Driving home, she parked in the carport and headed for the door. A red car pulled up across the road and sat idling. Her spine tingled as she fumbled for the correct key. Opening the screen, she strode inside and shook off her unease, unsure what that was about. She grabbed the bag she'd packed last night, stupidly having forgot it before yoga, then hurried back to the car to drive to Liam's. Since she was Steph-sitting this weekend, Liam had suggested that Ana stay at his house while he was away because the yard was preferable for the border collies.

Liam let the dogs out of the house after Ana had shut the gates. Louis ran to her, his head down. Whining, he clawed up her leg and she frowned. Louis hadn't whined or displayed signs of separation anxiety for more than a year.

'What's going on?' she asked him, rubbing his soft head.

'Not sure.' Liam frowned as he approached. 'He was quite curious about something going on at the golf course when I got home and wouldn't leave the fence until I dragged him inside for dinner. I couldn't see what he was staring at though.'

'Maybe a wallaby. I've seen a few over there lately.' Ana

shook her head as Louis lowered to his feet. 'You're obsessive, aren't you, Louis?'

'It's in his nature. How was yoga?'

'Excellent.' Liam wrapped his arm around her waist as they headed inside. He had dinner ready to go—chickpea stir-fry on rice—then they headed for bed with the dogs curled on the floor.

'Goodnight, Liam.'

'Night, Ana.' He wrapped his arm around her and pulled her close, inhaling deeply. Closing her eyes against his chest, she knew he needed sleep before his big drive tomorrow. But then again … weren't they entitled to going away sex?

'You're going to cause me to be tired,' he mumbled as she kissed along his stubbly jaw.

'Yeah, but you love me.' Her body warmed as she rolled him onto his back. As usual, it took little to convince him. Holding each other close, they made slow, steamy love between his blue striped sheets. The breeze blew through the window and billowed the curtains above them.

They fell asleep with plenty of time before the alarm sounded at six. Ana groaned as Liam shut off the ringing and moved out of bed, kissing her on the forehead before heading for the shower. At least she didn't have to get up as she snuggled into the pillows. But she wanted to see him off, so she dragged herself out of bed to say goodbye.

'Do you have everything?'

'Yep.'

'You have Lily's gifts?'

'Yep.'

'And you'll let me know when you get there so I know you arrived safely?'

'I will.' Lifting her chin, he kissed her.

'Good. Have fun. I really hope Lily freaks out.'

Liam grinned. 'She will. You can be sure of that. Just look after yourself, Steph, and Louis. Jack will want to leave early on Sunday so we should be back mid-afternoon.'

'I'll miss you.' Slipping her arms around his waist, she hated to think of spending tonight alone. 'You'll think of me, right?'

'Always.'

She smiled. 'I love you.'

'I love you too.'

The LandCruiser was full when Jack pulled up on Station Drive. Ana walked down the driveway with Liam, kissing him once more before leaning over the gate to wave them off.

'Morning, Ana!' Adam called from the passenger window.

'Morning.'

'Cute jammies.'

'Shut it, Adam,' Liam said, tossing his bag into the back before sliding into the middle with Cade and Michael. Rolling down the window, he waved. Ana watched them leave until they turned onto the highway.

Then since she could fit more sleep in before the cuckoo bird chimed the half hour, Ana left the dogs outside and ran back into the house. She tumbled into bed, surrounded by the smell of Liam.

* * *

'Isn't this great, just the two of us?' Meg said.

'Yeah, but I do miss everyone. It's a little weird.'

Meg frowned as she glanced at the large empty seat beside

her. 'I suppose. It's not the same without Jack silent in the corner, Lucy getting all the male attention, Adam's charming remarks, and you and Liam mooning over each other.'

Ana laughed. 'We don't moon!'

'Oh, please. Have you moved in yet?'

'What?'

'Well, you're always at his place. When was the last time you slept at yours? You're paying my parents rent for nothing.'

'I was there on … Tuesday. I'm just staying at his place while he's away to look after Steph.'

Meg quirked her eyebrow. 'This Tuesday?'

'Yes.'

'With him?'

'He's as bad as me, okay! He showed up after the town meeting and I couldn't kick him out. He had chocolate Paddle Pops!'

Meg grinned. 'You really love him, don't you?'

'Yes. I do.'

Ana could barely believe it, but it was the truth. She enjoyed the warmth of falling asleep and waking with him, of sitting down to breakfast and sharing in the camaraderie of the day. She'd never had that before. Rick had been romantic once, but after she'd moved in, he'd grown quiet and distant. He'd get out of bed before her, rarely wait to share their meals together, and they'd even stopped cuddling of a night.

Ana grimaced as she sipped her Diet Coke. How hadn't she noticed the changes after they began living together? Not that it mattered anymore. She was happy in Elizadale and had everything she'd ever wanted with Liam Maguire. She could see her future spread out before her and it was good.

Meg crossed her arms, blew out her breath, and slumped in the booth. 'That's totally unfair. I've lived here my whole life and no one wants to love me.'

Ana resisted a sigh. 'I'm sure somebody does. Or will. Eventually.'

'Enough not to make it up the stairs? Seriously, you have to stop telling me things. I wouldn't be able to walk into your place anymore. You know I haven't had sex in two years? Two years, Ana! I'd kill for that kind of passion.'

Ana laughed. Yes, she'd let a few things slip, but girlfriends did that. And when Ana was happy, she couldn't always control her mouth.

'We're just at that stage in our relationship.' Not that she needed an excuse. Then she thought about what Meg had said and frowned. 'Two years, Meg? Really?'

Sighing, Meg picked up her glass of wine. 'It's not like there's much of a pick around here. I know I could probably get myself a man if I wanted one. I just … don't want anyone.'

No, there was a very specific person who Meg wanted and even though Ana had promised weeks ago to leave it alone, she couldn't help herself.

'You know, from the first week I met you, I could tell you're in love, Meg. And I know you don't want to talk about it—' Ana held up her hands in defence '—but why? Why has that ship with Jack sailed?'

Meg ran her finger around the rim of her wineglass and sighed. Ana wasn't sure what filled her friend's eyes. Was it disappointment, heartache, or simply frustration?

'I don't know. But it's not happening, so not worth talking about. Everyone around here has something they don't talk about. I don't talk about that. Lucy doesn't talk about anything. And even you have a secret.' Her eyes warmed. 'Everything going okay there?'

Ana sighed. It was like talking to a brick wall, so she let Meg have her way. Not that she wanted to talk about Rick.

'I haven't heard anything from my mum since she told me about Rick coming into her old store. And I can't prove if he was behind that phone call. So yeah, I think everything's okay.'

Meg smiled. 'Good. Is your mum still planning to visit in September? Maybe by then you might have actually moved in with Liam.'

'Yeah, she is.' Ana ignored the comment about her living arrangements. 'It'll be great to see her again and I'm sure she'll like Liam. Actually, I can't wait because I've been bitten by that local bug where I seem to have a desire to show off this place.'

'Yeah, I have that bug bad.'

'That bug feeds off you.'

Meg laughed. 'Can I come on the tour?'

'Of course. You know more about this place than I do.' Ana's phone beeped. She pulled it from her bag and smiled. 'A text from Liam. They've arrived at Lily's.'

* * *

Jack parked down the road from Lily's share-house, the tiny street in the popular condensed suburb of Townsville lined with cars. Liam and Cade unloaded the newly stocked esky and carried it between them. Darkness had fallen and the party was in full swing at the rendered house where Lily lived with her two girly housemates. The music played at a decent volume and chatter filled the backyard. Jack entered the house first, which was empty considering everyone was on the patio. Bracing themselves and acting as though they were totally expected, they stepped outside to join the party.

Cade and Liam dropped the esky in the first spot they found, then a shriek cut through the music.

Lily Maguire ran at them.

'Oh my God!' She jumped at Jack, knocking him back a step as she flung her arms around her big brother's neck. Liam grinned. The surprise had been a good call. 'What the hell are you guys doing here?'

Lily blinked as she looked over Jack's shoulder at everyone else, clearly stunned, ecstatic, and overwhelmed as she held her brother tight.

'Hey, Lils,' Jack said. 'Happy birthday.'

'You bloody bastards, this is the best surprise!' Lily stepped back, grinning ear to ear as she pressed her hands to her mouth. Around them, her friends had stopped chatting to watch.

Lily looked wonderful, her long dark hair hanging down her back while her brown eyes sparkled with joy. She wore a singlet top and jeans, nothing fancy as she was still the small and tough Lily Maguire, even if she was now twenty-one and growing up by the day.

Liam shook his head. It'd always felt like he had two younger sisters and he couldn't believe that Lily was no longer little.

'We couldn't help it,' Adam said, gathering Lily into his arms. 'It's April Fools and you know how we love to tease you. Happy birthday.'

'Thanks, Adam. Hey, Mike!'

She hugged Michael before turning to Liam. The six-hour drive and constant bickering was completely worth it as he held his cousin tight. 'Happy birthday, Lil.'

'Thank you. And don't you go far,' she said, her eyes flashing as she stepped away and poked her finger into his chest. 'You have a girl you need to tell me all about.'

He laughed, looking forward to it. 'Okay.'

She caught up with Lucy and Isabella, then turned to Cade. 'You came too, huh?'

'There was a car coming to a party. What did you expect?'

'Aren't you supposed to be a responsible citizen now that you're kinda a police officer and all?'

'I *am* a police officer and I am responsible. Doesn't mean I don't enjoy a good party though.'

'Well, I guess you always have. And I'm thrilled you're all here. Come meet my friends. Everyone!' she called at large. 'This is my family.'

Glad they'd made Lily's day, the Maguires joined the party.

Chapter Twenty-Eight

Ana rose early, let the dogs out, then snuggled back into bed. First day of holidays required a sleep in.

Later, she awoke to the sound of Steph barking. Sitting up, Ana yawned and glanced out the window. It sounded like her playful bark and, indeed, Steph and Louis were just running around the gum trees.

Smiling, she lay back down. Liam's bed was comfortable and she enjoyed being wrapped in the cool sheets, but it was strange to wake up there alone.

Especially since it felt normal.

Her heart clenched as she stared up at the fan circling above her. She wanted to live in this house with Liam. And to spend the rest of her life with him. She knew that, yet her belly still twisted with uncertainty.

Was it possible?

Ana shook her head. She shouldn't be thinking about it. Not when Liam wouldn't be in a hurry to move forward. They may be in love, but sharing a house? That was definitely too fast.

Louis let out a string of loud barks and Ana shot upright. She pushed back the curtains to find him racing along the fence, Steph behind him. Ana's gaze roamed the street and the bushland lining the golf course. What was Louis barking at?

A flock of sulphur-crested cockatoos took flight from the gum trees and Steph bolted after them across the yard. Ana's shoulders relaxed as Louis joined in. She smiled. 'Silly dogs.'

Turning her back on them, Ana went to use Liam's shower. Not her shower. *Liam's*, although she preferred his with its rain showerhead over the tiny cubicle at Jackson Villas. He'd stylishly fitted his bathroom with a mix of cream and white tiles, and the fact they shared similar tastes warmed her up inside. She even had her own toothbrush and a matching towel. Thankfully, Liam hadn't been a man who got weird about things like that. The first time she'd stayed over, she'd been careful, afraid he'd freak out about a woman leaving her things lying around. She hadn't said anything when he'd taken her toothbrush and slipped it into the holder, but the gesture had touched her. She should have known that he wasn't the type to freak out about something as trivial as his girlfriend leaving her toothbrush over.

Liam was sensible. A gentleman. Open, honest, and with no intention of controlling his woman.

Sighing, Ana stepped out of the shower. Wrapping the towel around herself, she ventured into Liam's walk-in robe. He had a few ironed shirts hanging on wooden hangers and various shoes piled haphazardly in the corner. Everything else he kept loosely folded in the drawers while the rest of the space sat empty.

Yet, she'd only placed her bag on the shelf and hadn't gone

as far as unpacking. Was her past making her nervous about moving forward?

'Don't be ridiculous,' she muttered as she dressed. 'You're just being respectful.'

She had to stop thinking about the past though because it *was* holding her back. And she couldn't let it.

With that determination, Ana fetched the dogs their morning treat. Perhaps one day it would be their wardrobe and their shower, but she enjoyed taking it slow and would be content living at Jackson Villas for the rest of the year. Maybe if she signed on for another twelve months at the school, they could reconsider what they each wanted. She'd meant what she'd said at Maguire Falls. She didn't want to leave and no longer believed that a nomadic life would keep her safe. If Rick wanted to find her, he would, no matter how often she moved. She hadn't planned to plant roots, but they'd grown of their own accord and she couldn't rip them out. She didn't want to.

Stepping onto the front verandah, Ana sighed. The dogs were back at the gate. 'Steph! Louis! Come get a bickie!'

Steph came, but Louis needed more coercing. He whined as he climbed the steps and accepted the peanut butter paw. Ana rubbed his head. 'Leave the birds, Louis. Whatever's happening outside this yard is not your concern.'

She sliced a banana to cover her Weet-Bix, then sat on the back deck. The clock cuckooed and she smiled. She loved that clock. There was something authentically country about a bird signalling the time. As Steph and Louis herded the cockatoos, Ana could easily imagine sitting there watching her kids play. She'd always wanted kids.

Did Liam? He was from a big family, so surely he longed to create one of his own. She'd ask him at some point. But one step at a time.

Meg had arrived for lunch and an afternoon movie marathon when Louis started barking again.

'Seriously.' Ana placed the wraps on the kitchen bench. 'That dog. He won't stop barking.'

Meg followed Ana to the front door. 'Is that strange?'

'Well … no. He barks often enough at birds, cats, or if a dog's walking down the street. I think he must just want to chase the wallabies across the road.' She unlatched the screen and stepped onto the verandah. Again, she saw nothing of concern. 'Louis! It's okay!'

Louis glanced over his shoulder, then continued barking. Steph stood beside him, but remained silent.

'Just leave them,' Meg said as Ana stepped back inside. 'That's what dogs do. You'd rather him bark if something's wrong than not bark at all.'

'True.'

Meg and Ana enjoyed falafel wraps, then spread out in the lounge room for an afternoon of tearjerkers.

'You know what?' Ana said while they were in the middle of *The Notebook*. Not that Ana considered it a tearjerker when dying in the arms of your beloved had to be the best way to go. 'I don't like the Maguires being out of town. What if we found another taipan?'

'We'd call Henry or Cliff.' Meg shot her a smile. 'You miss Liam.'

'It's only been a day, so no. But it's weird being in his house alone.'

'Have you picked out which room to make the nursery yet?'

'The middle one,' Ana admitted, knowing Meg wouldn't judge her. Meg had probably done the same thing. 'It's the biggest.'

'Fair enough. I'm going to name my daughter Sophie. It's always been my favourite.'

'That's nice. I don't have a favourite name, just many that I like.'

'Well, be careful because not many good ones go with Maguire.'

Ana smirked. Meg had probably thought long and hard about that too. 'Why not?'

'I don't think names that end in "a" work. Like … well, Ana Maguire actually sounds good.'

Tingles shot down Ana's spine. 'God, don't say that.'

'But you get what I mean?' Meg asked, raising her eyebrows.

'Yeah, I do. I guess that's why you didn't go with Sophia?'

Meg shot Ana a 'don't start' look. 'Sophie is fine.'

For the rest of their afternoon, they watched more soppy movies and discussed topics only girlfriends would talk about—baby names, bridesmaid dresses, and honeymoon locations.

When Meg left to have dinner with her family, Ana tied up her shoes and set off for a walk. She left Steph and Louis because she couldn't safely manage them both on her own and they'd only slow her down. Besides, something outside the front fence still had Louis' full attention, so as she slipped out of the gates, curiosity got the better of her. Crossing the road, Ana trudged through the gum leaves and onto the golf course. She wasn't sure what she was looking for as she studied the ground. She'd seen wallabies occasionally and Louis would undoubtedly want to herd them. But as she gazed out over the lush golf course, she couldn't stop her arms from wrapping around herself. She shuddered. Was Louis trying to tell her something?

Shaking her head, Ana strode off down the green and headed for the footpath. She was being silly. Louis wasn't acting too strangely.

But she couldn't shake her unease as she walked, smiling politely as she passed people she knew. When she returned to Station Drive, she could hear Louis barking from four house blocks away. The rev of an engine cut through the dusk air and she glimpsed a red car disappearing around the bend.

'Louis, I'm almost home!' she called.

Steph raced up to greet her, following Ana along the fence until she reached the gate. Louis didn't move, his gaze fixated on the corner. Slipping through the gate, Ana frowned in the direction the red car had been. Her heart pounded.

'Was someone near the fence, Louis?' She glanced down at the dogs. 'Was someone trying to hurt you?'

Whining, Louis lifted onto his back legs and pawed at her hips. Ana scratched his ears, her belly twisting. 'It's okay, baby. You're both okay. Let's all go inside and calm down.'

Her spine relaxed a fraction as she approached the house. A breeze rustled the palm fronds while a kookaburra laughed and the front verandah light welcomed her home. Because yes, she was home. But as she dragged Steph and Louis inside and latched the screen, a shiver coursed through her as she cast one more look out into the darkening yard. Ana shut the wooden door and turned the deadbolt.

Nothing was wrong. She was safe. Steph and Louis were safe. But a woman on her own could never be too careful.

* * *

Rick sped off down the street. Fucking dogs. He should buy some rat bait and kill them both. That bloody mongrel looked like it wanted to eat him alive. Surely it couldn't remember him. It'd been a four-month-old useless fluffball when Ana had fled into the night.

Rick pulled over by the footy fields. He needed a new plan. And food. He'd never have access to that house while those dogs seemed hellbent on guarding it. He needed the element of surprise. And quiet.

Fuck. Why couldn't it be easy?

* * *

'You'll marry Liam within the year,' Natalia said, her serious confidence leaving Ana with no choice but to laugh.

'I highly doubt that,' she replied as she made herself a cup of peppermint tea. 'Liam's more rational than I am. He doesn't move at warp speed, so it won't be in less than a year.'

Natalia rolled her eyes on FaceTime. 'Right. And he's just letting you stay at his house while he's away. Because that's not serious.'

Ana sat at the breakfast bar and mixed her berry oats, propping her phone against a decorative wooden bowl while she waited for her tea to cool. A pleasant breeze blew through the house while Steph sat at her feet. Louis had returned to the front gate the moment she'd let him out this morning. Seeing the wallabies herself had put her at ease, but Louis hadn't barked at them. He'd just sat and watched.

'Yes, it's serious, but not that serious.'

'Whatever. Don't listen to me. I'm your big sister and therefore know better, but don't take my advice.'

'I just don't want to rush into marriage. I did with the last guy and look how that turned out.'

'Yeah, you ran away to Elizadale and fell madly in love with Liam Maguire. I should tell Mum to hold off on the trip and come when you set a date for the wedding.'

Ana shook her head. 'Stop it, Nat. Just come here in September and you'll see how great Elizadale is. You can meet Liam and the rest of the Maguires and we'll take you horseback riding.'

'Yeah, I'm keen, but I still don't know. Horses are so big.'

'They are. You'll freak when you see Vendetta. He's huge. But Esme's nice and Liam's a good teacher.'

'We'll see. Either way, it might not be that long before I come see you.'

Ana paused with her spoon halfway to her mouth. 'What do you mean?'

'Nothing. I was thinking out loud. But I'll definitely be seeing you in September.'

Natalia started singing the bridal march and Ana ordered herself not to hang up.

'Sorry,' Natalia said when she finished, even though she didn't sound sorry at all. 'But I'm glad you found Liam and that you're staying there. Honestly, I didn't like the idea of you moving every year.'

'Neither did I. I just thought it'd be safer. But now, I don't see how. I'll stay here and build a life.'

Natalia lifted her eyebrows. 'Get married and have babies?'

Ana sighed, wishing her sister would stop. 'Maybe one day, but not any time soon!'

'Why not? You're not getting any younger, Ana.'

'You're older than me and are making no progress in your personal life.'

'I had a date last night. I don't plan on seeing him again because he spent all night trying to convince me that cows were put on this earth to eat. Even though I didn't engage, he wouldn't let up!'

Ana rolled her eyes. 'People. They should keep their opinions to themselves.'

'It's not like *I* gave him any grief. What makes him think I'll see him again when he went out of his way to piss me off? I'm seriously over men.'

Ana smiled morosely. 'I know, Nat. But I'm sure the right one will come along. You want to get married someday, right?'

Honestly, Ana wasn't sure. Her sister enjoyed dating when it went well, but when Ana had been engaged to Rick and they'd been hit by a touch of wedding fever, Natalia had never expressed an interest in marriage herself.

Natalia sighed. 'Maybe … but I'm still not convinced I'll fall in love. I'm going to need a real man if I'm ever going to settle down. I'm over men who have prettier fingernails than I do.'

'Come here, then. No man cares about his fingernails here, I can guarantee you that.'

Natalia grimaced. 'No, I'll need to find a middle ground, I think. But either way, I'm not getting married in the next few months like you.'

Ana let her sister have her fun. What was the harm? She knew marriage wouldn't happen anytime soon.

After Ana hung up, she wiped down the kitchen, swept the floors, and took her clothes out of the wardrobe. After sweeping the dog hair off the back deck, she sat down to play with Steph and Louis. Her silly boy remained mildly distracted, but Steph was happy to lap up the attention. She was a lovely girl, spirited, and much better behaved than Louis had been at her age.

Cuddling the beautiful dog, Ana kissed the top of Steph's head. 'I love you, girl. And I promise I'll always love your daddy.'

Steph panted happily as Louis nudged Ana's hand. 'Yes, I love you too.'

With both border collies in her arms, Ana grinned. Life couldn't get better. Except perhaps if Liam …

White dresses, flowers, and that stupid 'daa-da-da-daa' flashed through her mind. Ana sighed. *Thanks a lot, Natalia.*

Pushing to her feet, Ana glanced down at the dogs. 'Okay, I'm going home. Do you two want to come?'

She'd take Louis, but she couldn't leave Steph behind with sad eyes. So, gathering her stuff, Ana locked up and loaded the dogs onto the back seat of her hatchback. She drove home, needing to catch up on some work before Liam returned this afternoon.

She pulled up inside her carport and hopped out, frowning as she reached for the back door. Was that the same red car parked across the road? She'd never seen it before this week. Had her neighbours just bought it?

Shaking her head, Ana grabbed the dogs' leads and they jumped out of the car. She'd barely had time to shut the door when Louis dragged her towards the unit, his nose down and tail in the air.

'Okay, I'm coming.' He whined as he sniffed the screen door. What the hell was with him? 'It's okay, Louis.'

She reached for the handle, but it didn't budge. Ana froze. Why was the screen door locked?

She tried again. Definitely locked. Staring at the door, her heart pounded. She never locked that door. Not when she was out. Had she ...

Louis clawed at the screen and released three loud barks. Steph whined and looked up at Ana with wide eyes, her ears back. Ana's breath caught in her throat as she lowered her hand. She struggled to inhale.

Could it be ...

She jolted as Louis continued to bark. She backed away. He *was* behaving strangely. Even Steph seemed out of sorts. Unease had filled her ever since that strange phone call and then these past few days she'd been seeing that red car ...

Ana spun around and gasped. The car had New South Wales plates. Holy shit, could Rick—

Steph joined in the barking. Ana turned as a shadow passed over the kookaburra glazed windowpane. Her heart leapt and she almost tripped down the step in her hurry to retreat. Steph and Louis yelped as she yanked on their leads and they all ran back to the car. Ana shoved them through the front door onto the passenger seat, slipped behind the wheel, then slammed the door closed. Locked the car. Turning the key, she reversed and sped away, turning off School Street and onto Riley Road. She paused at the highway, her entire body shaking as her head turned from side to side. Right would take her north to Cooktown or Port Douglas. Both useless. She turned left. Mareeba, then Cairns. She'd hop on a plane back to Sydney and—

A wet nose pressed against her shoulder and Ana jumped, glancing at the dogs. Louis tilted his black-and-white head.

Exhaling, she slowed and pulled the car over. She wrapped her arms around Louis' neck and held him close. Steph inched forward and let out a whimper.

She couldn't run away. Where would she go? What was she supposed to do? She didn't even know if Rick *was* in town.

But then why was the screen door locked? Had he been waiting inside?

Her heart pounded as she reached for her phone. She had to go to the police but first, she made a call.

'Meg! I need you to come. No, I'll come to you. God, I don't know if I should come to you. I might—'

'Ana.' Meg's sharp voice cut through Ana's rambling. 'Calm down. Where are you?'

'In the car. Parked on Abbott Street.'

'Come over. Whatever it is, just come.'

'Okay.'

She hung up.

Chapter Twenty-Nine

The hairs on the back of Ana's neck prickled as she drove the long way to Meg's house. There was no sign of the red car, but terror consumed her, making her skin crawl. She felt violated. But she didn't see anyone she didn't want to see as she turned onto Station Drive.

Ana parked outside Meg's and found her friend waiting. She rushed up the driveway with the dogs, grabbed Meg's arm, and pulled her inside. 'Get in. Quick.'

Meg didn't argue. Locking the screen, Ana slammed the wooden door closed, latched the security chain, and bolted the deadlock. Then she ran through the house and locked the rest of the doors.

'Will you tell me what's going on?' Panic filled Meg's voice.

Ana finally stopped, her chest heaving as she sagged against the wall in the small hallway by the bathroom. 'I think Rick's here.'

Tears filled her eyes as she slid down the wall. Wrapping her arms around her knees, she dropped her head and cried. Louis nudged his nose under her arm to offer comfort and Ana took it, trembling.

She shouldn't be surprised. She'd known he'd come. She'd never underestimated him. Rick was sly, cunning, and evil.

She pulled Louis close and buried her face in his fur.

Meg dropped to her knees and took Ana's hands. 'What do you mean? How?'

Hiccupping, she lifted her head and met her friend's calm eyes. 'I've had this feeling for a few days now. Louis' barking is strange and I keep seeing this red car around. And now, I just went home and found my screen door locked. I never lock it, Meg! Not when I'm out.'

Meg's mouth twisted. 'I know. So, you think—'

'I saw a shadow in the window. Someone was in there.'

Meg blew out her breath. 'Well, you did the right thing, Ana. And if he is here—'

'He's going to kill me, Meg!'

Meg huffed out a breath. 'Oh, Ana.'

'He wants revenge! I knew he'd come. He told me. He hates me for standing up to him, so what else would he consider payback? He won't just hit me this time!'

Ana broke into sobs. It was useless pretending not to be afraid. Elizadale may have provided her with a pretty distraction, but she'd spent the past few months in fear of this very moment.

Meg scooted around beside Ana and pulled her into a hug. 'It'll be okay. I'll keep you close until Liam gets back. But first, we need to call the police.'

Ana was not reassured. 'I need to know if he's here. Then I need him gone! He needs to be back in prison. I didn't want the parole board to let him out early, but they didn't listen. They said he'd been showing signs of good behaviour and was "rehabilitated". I mean, what is that? You can't rehabilitate evil! They said he'd made changes and was safe to re-enter the community. Except *I'm* not safe because he wants revenge!'

'It'll be all right.' Meg's grip tightened, her voice soothing. 'Just calm down. Then you can call Liam and I'll call the police.'

'Okay.' Ana took a deep breath. 'Okay …'

* * *

After a day in Townsville catching up with Lily, Liam stretched out comfortably in the passenger seat while Jack drove them home. He'd beaten Adam out of the front after stopping for lunch in Innisfail and his cousin now sat grumpily between Cade and Michael.

They were turning off the coastal highway and heading for the Tablelands, singing along to an endless stream of country music when Liam's phone interrupted their bad karaoke.

'It's Ana.'

Adam groaned. 'Keep it clean, would ya?' he said as Jack committed sacrilege by turning down Lee Kernaghan.

'Shut up.' Liam answered the call. 'Hey, baby.'

'Liam … um … where are you?'

'Maybe two hours out. Why?' He frowned at the tremor in her voice. 'Are you okay?'

'Um … no, not really. I need you here. I …'

'Just tell him,' Meg said in the background.

Ana took a deep breath. Liam tried not to jump to conclusions as a few popped into his head. But none of them came close to what she told him.

'Liam, I think Rick's here. I don't know where, but he's here.'

Liam straightened, his blood surging as his hand tightened around the phone. That bastard. 'Where are you? Have you seen him?'

'No. But someone was in my unit and I think he may have been watching the house.'

'Where are you?' he asked again, the panic in his voice causing everyone else in the car to fall silent. Fear rose to clog his throat. 'Ana ... baby, please. Don't run.'

She exhaled deeply. 'Don't worry, I haven't. I'm at Meg's. I have Steph and Louis with me.'

'Okay.' Liam closed his eyes and ordered himself to breathe. Of all weekends, of all days, why today? Why now when he was hours away from home and unable to help her? 'Listen to me, Ana. Go to Brett's and wait for me. Cade and I will be there soon.'

Cade leaned forward from the back seat. 'What's going on?'

'Call your dad and tell him Meg and Ana are on their way.'

'Meg's already called Brett,' Ana said. 'We're going in a minute.'

'Good. Tell him everything, Ana. I'll be there as soon as I can. Jack will step on it.'

Jack was already going at a hundred and twenty.

'Okay. And you'll be here in two hours?'

'I'm on my way.'

'Okay. I'll see you soon, Liam.'

'You will. Don't worry, baby. Nothing will happen to you. I love you, Anastasia.'

'I love you too.'

Liam hung up.

'What's going on?' Jack and Cade asked in unison.

Liam blew out his breath. 'Ana's ex-fiancé may be in town.

The man she sent to prison for assaulting her. Who threatened to find her and seek revenge. She came here to get away when he was released and now, he's found her.'

Lucy and Isabella gasped.

'Fucking bastard,' Adam growled.

Cade ran his hand down his face. 'Shit. We better get home.'

Jack's knuckles whitened around the wheel. 'And she's with Meg? He hasn't hurt or seen Ana?'

Liam shook his head. 'Just trying to scare her. May have been inside her home. Jack, let me drive.'

'I'm already doing twenty over the limit and you're in no state to drive, mate.'

'Jack, maybe you should slow down,' Cade advised. 'Or let me drive. We're approaching the range.'

Jack's eyes remained fixed on the road, his jaw tight. Liam's heart pounded. If he were behind the wheel, Liam too would commit all sorts of felonies, but he'd rather return home alive than in a body bag.

Jack exhaled. 'Yeah, okay.'

He pulled over so he and Cade could exchange seats. 'Just get us there as soon as you can, mate.'

* * *

Meg took Ana to the Wilsons' blue, high-set, wooden home at the southern end of Forbes Street next to the golf course. Her pulse continued to pound as she sat in the comfy lounge, the old-style swinging windows open to the cool April breeze. Senior Sergeant Brett Wilson called Sergeant Jim Tibbins to check on Jackson Villas, then listened attentively as Ana told him her story. She'd only seen Brett in passing at yoga, but he was a kind man and his patience put Ana at ease. Linda kept the tea coming. Ten minutes later, Jim phoned to confirm there was evidence of a break-in around the front door.

'He must have naturally locked the screen,' Ana breathed, her hands tightening around the mug.

Brett nodded. 'You were lucky and should be proud of yourself.'

Ana wished she could smile, but the anxiety twisting around her heart prevented her lips from curving. 'I'm proud of Louis,' she admitted. Her precious boy had tried to tell her he'd seen Rick, but she'd been too caught up in her romantic fantasies about the future to notice.

'He's a good boy,' Meg agreed.

'Indeed.' Brett closed his notebook. 'I'll contact the guys in New South Wales and get the parole officer to look for Rick. Then Jim and I will visit the accommodation in town to see if Rick's staying anywhere.'

'I highly doubt it. He's the sort of person who could disappear into thin air if he wanted to. He wouldn't risk staying in a hotel.'

'We'll check it out anyway and see if anyone at the roadhouse saw him. He'd have needed petrol.'

'True.' She hadn't thought of that.

'And you believe he may have been in town for about a week?'

Ana nodded. 'I first noticed that red car on Monday afternoon outside the school.'

'Okay. He'll serve out his sentence for breaking parole and leaving New South Wales, but we'll find him, Ana.' Brett reached across the coffee table and patted her hand. 'Don't worry.'

If only she could. 'Thank you, Brett.'

A knock sounded on the door and Brett stood to let Ron Riley in, who they'd called to sit with the ladies. Ana had met Ron a few times and easily saw why he was so respected. He was approachable, kind, and had a passion for Elizadale that Meg and Liam could only aspire to.

'I'm sorry to hear this has happened to you, Ana,' Ron said after she and Meg gave him an overview of events.

'Thanks. I just hope there hasn't been too much damage to the unit.' He was her landlord after all, but Ron dismissed that with a wave of his hand.

'We can easily repair the property.'

'Now that Ron's here, I'll go catch up with Jim,' Brett said, placing his empty mug down. 'Meg, I want you at your parents' house tonight. It's unlikely this man will target anyone else, but we don't know what he'll do to get to Ana.'

'I second that,' Ron agreed.

'Ana, when Liam arrives, I suggest you go stay on Shadow Creek. Rick knows where you both live, but hopefully we can sneak you out there.' Brett unfolded his tall frame from the lounge. 'I'll only be a few minutes away, but keep the doors locked.'

After he left, Ana sighed and sank into the lounge. Part of her still wished she could climb into her car and disappear, but even though it was hard, she'd done the right thing. She couldn't run. If Rick was in town, they needed to find him and send him back to Sydney. So, she took comfort in her Nerada brew and did her best to chat lightly with Meg, Linda, and Ron, ignoring the shortbread as food wouldn't help right now. She may have chosen bravery, but terror continued to knot inside her belly. She wouldn't be able to relax again until Rick was found and back in Sydney. For now, she had to put her trust in the police and remain calm. She couldn't continue to run scared. Brett seemed like the good sort. He'd do all he could to look after the people in his town.

But she couldn't stop thinking about what would have happened if she'd walked into her house this morning. If it hadn't been for that door and Louis, she could be dead right now.

Ana's hands tightened around her mug. God, she loved that dog.

Ninety minutes after Ana had called, Liam and Cade barged through the front door with their friends behind them.

'Anastasia.' Liam wrapped her in his arms before she'd fully risen from her chair. 'Baby, I'm so sorry.'

'It's okay. I'm fine.' She gripped two handfuls of his shirt, Liam's presence easing some tension from her spine.

'Where's Dad?' Cade asked.

'He went to the station,' Linda said.

Cade pulled his phone from his pocket. 'I'll call him and see what's up.'

'What's the plan?' Liam asked. He stepped back but kept his arm around Ana's waist.

'Brett thinks we should spend the night on Shadow Creek, even though I feel a little weird about having to explain why to your parents.'

'It'll be fine. We'll grab the dogs and some clothes and head out there.'

'I'm not sure how long Rick's been here or what he knows. I'm suspecting since Monday, although I don't know why it took him so long to make his move. Hopefully, he shouldn't find us on Shadow Creek.'

'He probably knows you went to Meg's,' Michael said.

Jack reached for Meg's arm. 'You can't be there alone tonight.'

'Don't worry.' Ron stood. 'She'll be coming with me.'

Jack nodded. 'Good. And Bella, go to your parents, too. He shouldn't know that you're friends with Ana, but I'll sleep better knowing you're not alone.'

'If he's watching us now, he'll know,' Michael said.

'Shit, this is nuts.' Ana covered her face with her hands and shook her head. She couldn't deal with this. Rick was watching them. He'd been watching her for days. She didn't think he'd hurt her friends—his vengeance was with her and her alone. Then again, she'd never thought he'd hurt her either.

'It'll be okay, baby,' Liam said, pulling her back into his arms. 'I promise.'

Everyone sat for a moment to gather themselves. Not long later, Brett returned with Jim and with no news.

'The Smithfields swear nobody of Rick's description checked in. Georgina doesn't think so either. And no one at the caravan park believes he's staying there. I'll go to the roadhouse as soon as—' His phone beeped and Brett pulled it from his pocket. 'Ah, there we go. Pictures. Is this the man, Ana?'

Having removed all photos of Rick from her Facebook page, she'd had nothing to give Brett without going home and finding her external hard drive filled with old photos. But the police had come through for them. Brett showed Ana Rick's mugshot and she nodded, her throat tightening.

'Yep, that's him.'

'Right.' Brett held up his phone, showing the rest of the group. 'If any of you see this man—'

Isabella gasped. Ana's head turned so quickly she almost gave herself whiplash as the young woman pressed her hand to her mouth.

'Oh my God, he was in the Tourist Centre! On Monday. Liam and I …'

Heart in her throat, Ana glanced up at Liam. The blood had drained from his face. 'You saw him?'

Liam's gaze didn't leave the photo as he nodded slowly. 'Yeah. And I told him I'd be out of town.'

Chapter Thirty

The air in the room cooled. Nobody moved. Tears slipped down Isabella's cheeks and Liam's jaw tightened so hard Ana feared he'd break teeth.

'Shit, Ana. I'm so sorry.'

Heart pounding, she reached up to cup his cheek. 'It's okay. You weren't to know and I'm fine.'

'Yeah, but …'

Brett cleared his throat. 'Let's sit down and you and Isabella can tell me what happened.'

They did. Ana's pulse slowed as she listened. Liam's recount of the conversation sounded natural and exactly like something he'd do.

'At least that explains why he waited,' Brett said. 'He knew you'd be alone.'

Ana frowned. 'But I've been alone for days. Why did he wait until this morning?'

'I don't think we could know the answer to that. What's important now is that we keep you safe. And, Liam, don't beat yourself up about this. You did nothing wrong.'

Liam ran his hand down his face and exhaled.

Ana squeezed his leg. 'He's right.'

Brett stood. 'How about you all head off and I'll get down to the roadhouse. Ana, I'll call you if anything comes up.'

Since it was all anyone could do, they left. As she stepped out onto the street, Ana could feel Rick's glare in the back of her head. Shivers ran down her spine, her imagination running wild. What would have happened if she'd left Steph and Louis at Liam's and gone home alone? Rick could have landed a few blows before stabbing her to death. Isn't that what these men did when getting revenge on women who stood up against domestic violence?

God, how would she ever thank Louis?

'Ana, I want you to go with Jack.'

'What?' both Ana and Jack asked, blinking at Liam in surprise.

'Get in the LandCruiser. Jack's going to drop Bella off, then take you and Lucy out to Shadow Creek. Michael will come with me. I'll take Steph and Louis. Where are they?'

'In the backyard playing with Freddy.'

'Right. I'll take your car. Keys?'

Not prepared to argue, Ana handed him her keys.

'Jack, keep an eye out for any red Subaru. Don't let anyone follow you.' Liam kissed Ana's forehead. 'I'll meet you out there.'

Ana nodded. She may be capable of making her own plans to stay safe, but right now, she didn't have it in her. Terror clouded her judgement and she had no choice but to trust Liam. Which she did, because she loved him, and if anyone aside from herself was determined to protect her from harm, it was Liam.

Ana wrapped her arms around him and buried her face against his solid chest. 'Make sure he doesn't follow you.'

'I'll be fine, baby. I'll see you soon.'

He kissed her, then pulled himself away and nudged Michael towards the house.

Ana took a deep breath as Jack laid his hand on her shoulder. 'Let's go, Ana.'

She slipped into the back of the LandCruiser beside Lucy, who reached over and took her hand. Ana managed a small smile. Her friends were there. She was surrounded by people who loved her. People she trusted. Everything would be all right.

Yet such words seemed hopeless.

They drove Isabella back to the Villas before taking her to her parents' house on Station Drive acreage. The Brennan house reminded Ana of an American plantation, built of white cladding with wraparound verandahs circling both floors.

After ten minutes of parking on Station Drive until Jack was satisfied that no one was watching them, they drove out to Shadow Creek, keeping the conversation focused on Lily's birthday party.

'The surprise was the best idea ever,' Lucy told Ana. 'Lily was thrilled. She talked all night, unable to shut up. Then Jack shared embarrassing childhood stories about her.'

Jack laughed. 'It was her twenty-first and you all did it to me. Besides, Lil was cool and everyone enjoyed it.'

'Just wait until you're thirty,' Adam said. 'I'm going to say some nasty things about you.'

'Yeah, but it's no fun when you're in a small town and everyone knows everything. Half of Lily's friends don't even know her.'

'I guess,' Lucy agreed. 'I seriously don't know how she lives with those housemates of hers though. They must drive her crazy with their girly hair and makeup and flirting with all the boys.'

'I don't think I've been chatted up more in my life.' Adam laughed, flashing them his charming grin. Ana could easily believe he'd have been popular with Lily's university friends. 'Cade didn't lap it up though.'

'Yeah, I've never seen him turn down so many girls,' Lucy said. 'Seriously, Ana. It was crazy. I mean, Cade's hot so he had plenty of girls batting their eyelashes at him. But he must seriously love Jessica because he didn't engage with any of them.'

Ana smiled. 'That's kind of sweet.'

They dropped Adam off at his home—a modest brick house overlooking the creek—then Jack took Ana and Lucy to the homestead.

'I don't want to tell your parents what's going on just yet,' Ana said as she and Lucy stood outside the white farmhouse. 'I'd rather wait for Liam.'

'Okay. Do you want to visit Esme with me? We can talk or something? If you want?'

'All right.' Ana would like that. She and Lucy hadn't grown as close as she and Meg had, but Ana liked her just as much. And since she was in love with Lucy's brother, Ana wanted her as a good friend.

'I'll tell Mum that we'll be in the stables so Liam doesn't freak out.'

* * *

No matter how hard he tried, Liam couldn't stop thinking about that conversation with Rick on Monday afternoon. He'd told a complete stranger about his personal plans. He often did. *Yeah, I'm from Shadow Creek. Grew up there. Got a nice place overlooking the golf course. Going to Atherton for the weekend.* These things naturally came up in conversation and so many people did it. Yet this time, the love of his life could have been killed.

There was nothing he could have done differently. The rational part of his brain knew that. But he couldn't help but be angry with himself as he held Ana's hand while she shared her story with his mother. Deborah listened without interrupting, compassion in her nature, although Liam didn't miss the worry in her eyes. But his mum said all the right things and it wasn't until she suggested it that Ana thought to call her mother.

Nadia didn't take the news well and Ana spent quite some time assuring her that everything was under control.

'I have people surrounding me, Mama. The police are supportive and aren't brushing it off. I'll be okay.'

Liam squeezed her hand. 'I won't let you out of my sight.'

Determination steeled his spine, clenched his jaw, and hardened every muscle in his body. Nothing would happen to Ana under his watch. Nothing. He'd had the man in his sights once and hadn't even known it. But he'd never seen a picture. He hadn't asked and Ana had never offered. In hindsight, that had foolish.

But Liam couldn't change that now and despite his resolve, he couldn't shake the worry that continued to build around his heart. His chest had been in a constant state of tightness since he'd received Ana's phone call. His pulse hadn't stopped pounding. He'd maintained a level head, but he couldn't contain his fury.

This whole situation was wrong. In a perfect world, Ana shouldn't have been subjected to it. But they didn't live in a perfect world and while Rick was in town, Ana wasn't safe. Liam didn't follow the news, but he'd seen enough headlines to know that her situation was a big problem that many women unfortunately faced. And far too many were killed.

Liam's fists clenched. He blew out his breath and watched as Ana helped his mother in the kitchen. Warmth eased the tension in his chest and he managed a small smile. He'd captured a blow-in. She'd planted her roots. He loved her and he wouldn't let her fly away again, whether it be by running or at the hands of evil.

Nothing would happen to her.

His mum, bless her, attempted to keep their spirits up by preparing a vegetable lasagne.

'It's always been Lucy's favourite when she's upset,' Deborah explained as she pureed tomatoes. 'And I've always found comfort in pasta. Are these enough vegetables, Ana?'

'They're fine, Deb,' Ana said, smiling softly as she sliced onions. 'Any vegetables will do.'

They only had carrots, onions, and mushrooms to add to the tomato sauce, but Liam didn't see how that couldn't be delicious. They assembled the lasagne, then stretched out on the deck overlooking the green paddocks towards the mountain. His dad arrived home from the farm and they conversed happily over dinner, then locked up before bed. Considering their isolation, locking up the house was rare.

Ana snuggled beneath the blankets, but Liam was too wired to sleep. He stood in his childhood bedroom and stared out the window into the dark night. Every little crack alerted his senses. The wind pricked his ears. God only knew what moved. Rick had waltzed right on into his workplace. Broken into Ana's house. What would stop him from finding them out here?

'Liam, you need to sleep,' Ana said, pushing up onto her elbows.

'I'm not tired.'

'Then can you at least come hold me? I can't rest when you're like this.'

He turned to her and forced his spine to relax. His anger didn't help when she was the one terrified. She didn't deserve this. Any of it. Thinking of what she'd been through by knowing Rick was to be released, trying to fight it, and then fleeing up here made his blood boil. He'd like to think she'd found some peace with him and her new friends, but the fear of Rick finding her had never vanished. Now that he had, the least Liam could do was hold her while she tried to get some rest.

He'd prefer her to be in a dreamless sleep than awake and afraid.

'Okay.' He crossed the room and slipped into the double bed beside her before pulling her close. Ana laid her head on his chest against the rapid pounding of his heart. He might be putting on a good show of anger, but deep down, he, too, was terrified. Rick was a big man. Tall and broad. What damage could he inflict if he got his hands on her?

No. Don't think about it. It isn't going to happen.

'I have you, Ana,' he whispered, stroking her long blonde hair. 'Just go to sleep. You're safe.'

She took a deep, staggering breath and trembled. 'I can't.'

'Yes, you can.' He pressed his lips to her hair. 'Just close your eyes. Empty your thoughts. Sleep.'

'I can still feel his hands on me, Liam.' Her voice was barely a whisper. 'You have no idea what he … it was a total bashing. The doctors said I was lucky to be alive. And I … I can't go through it again.'

Her hands lifted to her mouth as tears formed in her eyes. Liam held her and rocked, pressing his face into her hair and trying to rope in his temper. He didn't want to hear more, but he didn't want to stop her either.

'I thought I was going to die, Liam. Even after I escaped. I was in so much pain by the time I got to Mum's. The adrenaline wore off and I thought I'd die on the way to the hospital. They ran so many scans. ICU was awful. They treated my bruises. Who treats bruises, Liam? Usually, you wait for them to go away.'

'Not the bad ones …'

'I had a kidney bleed and all other sorts of things. And the pain medication …' She shook her head and buried her face against his chest, muffling the rest of her words. 'For weeks, I was on medication for pain. I felt foggy and drugged and so tired.'

Liam took a deep breath, holding onto his control. How could a man do that? How could a man use a small, beautiful, vulnerable woman as a punching bag and toss her down the stairs?

'You're a strong woman, Anastasia. Trust me. You will survive this. He won't get his hands on you again.'

'He's going to kill me, Liam.'

His arms tightened around her. 'No. Don't even think about that.'

'You didn't see the way he looked at me.' Lifting her head, she looked terrified. 'You didn't witness his fury during those hearings. You didn't see the hate in his eyes as he watched me tell the court what happened. Or hear the venom in his voice when he said he'd get me back for this. That I'd be sorry.' She drew in a staggering breath, then let it out again. 'He'll kill me, Liam. It's what these men do. Ever since it happened to me,

I've seen all the domestic violence headlines. I know what happens to women like me. They've been stabbed and shot. Burned. Beaten to death. Only then are these men locked up for good. When it's too late for their victims. Parole isn't enough. A domestic violence order isn't enough. I was safe while he was in prison, but now …' She hiccupped as tears broke free. 'Liam, I'm going to be another statistic!'

He shook his head and gathered her close. Held her tight. Maybe too tight, but she didn't seem to mind. He didn't want to hear it. Didn't want to think about it. He just held her and let her cry.

'You will *not* be a statistic. I know it doesn't seem fair, Ana. I get it. But he won't touch you.'

'I never did anything to deserve this!'

'I know.' He focused all his attention on his breathing. On staying still. But what he really wanted was to leap up and break something. Kick the wall in. Hunt Rick down and break his neck.

Liam didn't understand it. He didn't know why anyone would hurt someone else, especially someone they loved. It tore his heart apart to see Ana frightened. It would shatter him to see her hurt. And if Rick touched her, Liam didn't know what he would do.

He'd be capable of anything.

He loosened his grip to a gentle hold and kissed the top of Ana's head. He wasn't sure if it was for her or his own comfort.

'You did nothing, baby. No one deserves what he did to you. It wasn't your fault, he has serious problems of his own.'

'I paid twelve hundred dollars for a dog he didn't want. That pissed him off.'

Liam smiled, twirling her hair through his fingers. 'Steph was dearer.'

'Are we crazy for spending that much money on a dog?'

'Have you seen our dogs? They're worth every cent.'

She yawned. 'They sure are. But getting Louis was definitely the catalyst. I may have paid more attention to him than Rick, but he was a puppy and I was training him. It all went downhill from there.'

Liam had questions but didn't ask them. Instead, he smiled softly and focused on the more comforting subject. 'Yeah, but Louis was a gorgeous puppy.' He'd seen all the pictures. 'He was naughty though, chewing your outdoor setting. But I guess that's what puppies do.' He took a deep breath and relaxed against the pillows. 'When Steph was a baby, I couldn't let her out of my sight. She slept with me and came to the Tourist Centre during the day. I spoiled her rotten. Still do, I suppose. But when they're puppies, you just do that. They're too cute to say no to.'

Remembering how soft he'd been with Steph, Liam wondered what he'd be like with a human baby. His chest constricted. He'd never given a lot of thought to children, but they'd always been in his plans. He'd adore them to pieces. And how could he not when they'd be as beautiful as their mother?

Smiling, he stroked Ana's pretty blonde hair. Her hand lay over his ribs, her eyes closed and lips softly parted. Yeah, she was his future. They'd have children. One day. There was no need to rush these things.

'You know I love you, right?' he whispered. She didn't respond. 'Ana?'

She was asleep. Liam exhaled and kissed her forehead. She looked so peaceful.

But he stayed awake a while longer, glaring out into the darkness.

Chapter Thirty-One

Ana returned from the shower to find Liam staring out the bedroom window. Shadows rimmed his eyes and his unshaven jaw remained tense. Her heart ached as she pressed her lips together. She knew these past twenty-four hours hadn't only been hard on her.

'You didn't sleep well, did you?' she asked, placing her folded pyjamas into the bag Liam had packed her. She hadn't been sure what he'd grab in his haste, but the three-quarter jeans and pink singlet and blouse she wore worked well.

Ana crossed the room, stood behind him, and slipped her arms around his waist. She inhaled and buried her face against his shoulder. Liam sighed and rubbed her arms affectionately.

'I caught a few winks.' He turned and joined her in the embrace. 'How are you?'

'I'll be okay.' She inhaled deeply, her hands hardening on his back. 'After having slept on it though, I don't think hiding here is going to solve anything. We should go back to town and lure him out so that Cade and Brett can send him home.'

Liam's spine straightened. 'And what? Use you as bait?'

'No. Bait is defenceless and weak, and I'm not either. We'll go to town and eventually, he'll show up. He won't stalk and terrorise me for long. Rick's a control freak and even though everything has to be done his way, he also has no patience.'

Liam shook his head. His grip around her waist tightened. 'I won't risk him coming to hurt you. It's a ridiculous idea. I'm not having it.'

Ana smiled gently and brushed her hands up and down his back. 'He won't get to me.'

Liam swallowed. His jaw tightened and blue eyes turned to steel. 'Ana, baby, there are two ways he can do this. He could show up and give us time to get Cade and Brett there, hopefully before he beats you up. Or he can sneak up on us and leave you bleeding and broken again.'

Ana swallowed as she considered those options. Yes, anything could happen. But anything could also happen if they stayed on Shadow Creek, and they couldn't do that indefinitely.

'He'll confront me sooner or later, Liam. I'd rather it be sooner.'

He nodded slowly, but his eyes didn't soften. 'Ana, we can't put you at risk.'

'I'm at risk no matter what and we won't catch him by hiding out here.'

'Then what do you suggest?'

She exhaled. 'We go back to town and I act as though I'm not afraid. We go live our lives. Carefully.'

He raised his eyebrows. 'Is that what you want?'

She nodded, confident about that. 'It's not like I'll be alone. I don't want to hide anymore, Liam. He scared me. It worked. I ran. But if I hide, he hides. If I don't, he'll come for me and we can send him back to where he belongs. I don't want to be afraid and I don't want him to have this power over me.

Elizadale is where I want to be and I won't let Rick destroy that. I want him gone and out of my life for good.'

Liam's eyes searched hers. His shoulders relaxed. 'I guess I can't argue with that.'

She smiled. 'Good.'

Ana stretched up onto her toes and kissed him. She meant every word. She needed to protect her life and everything she'd found in Elizadale, but she wouldn't be complacent. Her heart pounded and her knees felt strangely wobbly, but she was safe. She wouldn't be alone. She trusted Liam, trusted Cade and Brett, and everything would be over soon if she remained calm and didn't give into her fear.

She and Liam arrived downstairs where Deborah was cooking breakfast, the rich smell of pancakes filling the air. She offered them each a cheery good morning as they sat at the table. But when Ana shared her plans for the day, Deborah stilled, horrified.

'You're not going back to town!' She shook her head vigorously. 'No. I won't hear of it. Cade and Brett will find this man and send him packing. There's no need to put yourself at risk, Anastasia. None at all.'

Ana sighed. Deborah's use of her full name sounded like an echo of her own mother.

'I won't be putting myself at risk,' she explained gently. 'If I stay here, he'll still find me eventually. So, I need to go back. We'll remain in public. Yes, I'm afraid of what could happen, but what can he do to me in a crowd?'

'What crowd? Elizadale's a tiny place, Ana! You can't lose yourself here.'

'But we can all gather at the park with the dogs and hang out at the Royal. He won't walk into the pub and start bashing me.'

Deborah's shoulders softened, but her frown remained. 'Well … if you think it'll work.'

'We'll be smart,' Liam said. 'I'll call Brett and let him know.'

'But you'll come back tonight, yes?'

Ana nodded. 'If we don't find Rick and it'll put you at ease, then yes. We'll come back tonight.'

* * *

'You're going back to town?' Lucy asked, following Liam upstairs as he went to grab their bags.

'Yes. For some dumb reason, we are.'

He'd still rather stay on Shadow Creek, but Ana did have a point. She needed to go back to town and resume her life if not for anything else but to feel less victimised. He couldn't discourage her in that after everything she'd already sacrificed.

'Well, I'm sure everything will be okay,' Lucy said. 'But I'm glad you're coming back tonight. You're tough, Liam, but I don't think it's wise to stay in town.'

He turned to face his sister. 'What's not wise is being here with you and Mum in the house. You never know what could happen, Luce. We don't know what Rick's capable of, which is why I'd much rather leave it to Cade and Brett. But I also know that's not possible. If they haven't found him yet, then Rick obviously doesn't want to be found. So, I don't know what to do.'

Liam ran his hand down his face, exhaled, and picked up their bags. 'I'm at a loss here, Luce. All I know is that I have to look after Ana.'

'That's all you can do, Liam.' She wrapped her arm around his shoulders. 'We can always count on you. That bastard is bloody stupid if he thinks he can get anywhere near my brother's girl.'

'Thanks, Luce.' He was grateful for the support, but if he came up against Rick, Liam wasn't sure what he'd do. He wasn't the type to fight like Jack and Adam were, but a man had to do what a man had to do. 'You're a good sister, you know that, right? And I love you.'

Lucy grinned. 'I'm the most awesome sister in the world.'

'Yeah, except for when you're being a pain in the arse.'

'I wouldn't be awesome if I wasn't. And because I'm awesome, I'm telling you now that you should marry Ana. Trust me, Liam. You don't want to wait. If you love her, you should just do it.'

'You *are* a pain in my arse,' he said, ignoring the tightness in his chest. 'But you're also awesome. If she wants to, Luce, I'll marry Ana one day. But I won't have you or anyone else bugging me about it.'

'Suit yourself,' she said as he moved from her embrace and out the door. She followed him, leaning over the banister as he fled downstairs. 'But you know I'm right. You never know what could happen, Liam! The sooner the better!'

'I'm ignoring you! Bye, Luce!'

Liam put her unnerving advice out of mind as he arrived outside to find Ana chatting with his mum. 'All set?'

'Yep. Thanks for having us, Deb.'

'We're always here for you when you need us.' Deborah pulled her into a hug. 'Please come back tonight, although I hope they find Rick today.'

'Me too.'

They collected Steph and Louis and climbed into the LandCruiser, waving goodbye before driving back to

Elizadale. Exhaling, Liam forced himself to relax. Everything would be okay. He had this.

But he couldn't unclench his hands from the wheel.

'We need to stay in public,' he said. 'We'll stop by my place to get that work you need, then we'll go to the park and let the dogs run around. There'll be other people nearby, but we'll ring Meg and I'm sure Adam will come too.'

'Sounds good. Thanks.' She placed her hand on his thigh and squeezed. 'I'm sorry, but I can't hide. I love living here and I'm not going to let Rick take that away from me.'

'I understand.' He took her hand. 'We just need to remain sharp.'

'Yep.' She let out a deep breath. 'How about I call Adam and see if he wants to hang out?'

Adam said he'd love to bring Rusty to the park and suggested they wind down the afternoon with a beer in someone's backyard. Liam agreed because why not? By the end of the day, a beer might be just what they needed.

They returned to town and drove to his house. Ana wanted her lesson plans for next term to work on and he'd forgotten food for Steph and Louis, who'd eaten leftover chicken last night. Leaving the car idling and the air-conditioning on for the dogs, they alighted and crossed the front yard.

A hard feeling formed inside Liam's chest as he considered what Lucy had said. He loved Ana and marriage wouldn't happen in the timeframe Lucy suggested, but as he unlocked the door and let Ana inside, he knew his sister had a point. Anastasia Hamilton was the woman he wanted to spend his life with. They had so much fun and had come to know each other well over the past few weeks.

Liam scratched the itch at the back of his neck as he

grabbed his hat off the hook by the door. Ana's footsteps echoed towards the kitchen. Maybe he'd wait until July or August and see how he felt about marriage then. He'd have to buy her a ring. Suss her out and discover what she liked. Maybe make a phone call to Natalia because she should know. Or should he let Ana choose it?

He headed for the kitchen, cursing Lucy for forcing these ideas into his head. It was too fast. He was probably going to start panicking now that—

There was a thump. A cry. The sound of papers scattering to the floor.

Liam ran the few steps into the kitchen.

Ana was on the floor.

Pain filled the back of his head and his vision blurred.

Everything went black.

Chapter Thirty-Two

A dog barked. Liam's head throbbed. He squeezed his eyes tighter and curled his fists over the hard wooden floor. Was that Louis? Shit. What had—

His eyes flew open. Heart lurched. Lifting his head, he blinked. And blinked again.

Anastasia was gone.

'Fuck.' The word strangled from his throat as he pushed to his feet. His legs shook. Vision blurred. Adrenaline sent his pulse skyrocketing. Nothing was going to stop him.

Liam ran.

'Ana!'

He bolted through the broken glass door and charged down the steps into the yard. Chest heaving, he glanced around. The back gate was swinging in the wind.

He ran.

The barking grew dimmer. The pain in his head subsided. Liam flew through the gate onto Shadow Creek.

He paused. Blinked. Shit. What was he doing? Where should he go? Pressing his hands to his forehead, he spun around. What the fuck had happened?

That bastard had been waiting inside. He'd hit her. He'd hit him. Shit, how long had he been unconscious?

Liam dashed back into his yard, pulled out his phone, and dialled.

'Cade, get to my place now! Ana's gone. He was waiting for us. Knocked me out. But she's fucking gone!'

'On my way.'

The line went dead. Liam heaved the phone across the yard. Swearing, he kicked the fence. Then he reached up to touch his aching head. There was a massive bump, but no blood.

Adrenaline surged as he took off through the back gate onto Shadow Creek, running until he realised he had no idea where he was going. They were nowhere in sight. Rick could have taken Ana in any direction. He could have had a car waiting on the highway. He could have hightailed it through the bush.

Swearing, Liam turned and ran back to his yard, slamming the gate behind him. He retrieved his phone. A crack split the screen, but it still worked. It was ten-thirty. When had they arrived? He hadn't a clue. But he didn't think he'd been unconscious for long.

He shook his head. Blinked. Fuck, his head throbbed.

How had this happened? Why hadn't he gone in first? Sure, it was his house and it should be safe …

The dog was barking. Shit. Steph and Louis were still in the car.

He strode towards the LandCruiser, squeezing his eyes closed and pinching the bridge of his nose. Fury washed over him. He wanted to go after Ana, but how? What was he supposed to do? Where was Cade?

He opened the back of the LandCruiser and stilled. His heart leapt. 'Where's Steph?'

Louis sat on his haunches, trembling, his head down. Liam scurried into the back to peer over the seats. 'Steph!'

Tyres crunched over gravel behind him. Liam scrambled out of the car as Brett and Cade pulled up.

Cade slammed the door and strode towards Liam. 'What happened?'

Liam struggled to find the words. He wanted to break down, but couldn't. He needed to remain a full flight of fury until he had Ana back. And Steph.

The bastard had taken his woman and his dog.

'We went inside. She went into the kitchen. There was a thump. I was just behind her and got knocked out. Couldn't have been more than twenty minutes ago. Woke up and she was gone. He must have broken in. There was glass and … she's gone! She's fucking gone! And he took Steph!'

Tears formed in his eyes. Shit. Shit, shit, *shit*. He was *not* going to break.

'Sit down, mate.' Cade forced Liam to rest against the back of the LandCruiser.

'I'll check inside,' Brett said, striding towards the house.

'How's your head?'

'My head's fine.'

'Vision?'

'Fine.'

'We'll still call the doctor. Now, which way do you think Rick went?'

'Out the back gate. It was open.'

Another engine roared into the driveway. Liam glanced up to see Adam's ute spraying crusher dust.

'What happened?' Adam slammed out of the car with the engine still running. Jack hopped out of the passenger side.

'I called him,' Cade told Liam.

Brett returned. 'He must have worked quickly. The good news is that the blood on the floor looks old and was found on the glass, so I doubt it's Ana's.'

That should have brought Liam relief, but it didn't. There was no place for relief right now. Not until he had both of his girls back.

'Let's head out the back,' Cade said, striding away. Adam quickly caught up. If they were going to track anything, Adam was the man to have.

Leaving Louis in the air-conditioning, Liam shut the LandCruiser and followed. Everything blurred and he had no idea what was going on, but Jack stayed by his side as Adam and Cade talked about tracks. After the months Adam had spent up at the Cape a few years ago having impromptu tracking lessons with an Aboriginal stockman, he was the man to have.

'One set,' Adam said as they rushed along Shadow Creek behind the acreage lots. Thankfully, the ground was still soft from the rain. 'And Steph's. Why would he take the dog?'

'Because he's a fucking bastard,' Liam growled.

'He must have carried Ana then,' Cade said.

Liam's throat closed over. His blood raged. How dare that man lay a hand on his Anastasia? How dare he? Liam kept up with his friends, wanting to help, but he could only think of Ana. And Steph. Why would Rick take Steph? He hated Louis, but ...

Liam's fists curled. Had he mistaken Steph for Louis?

Shit. Rick wanted revenge upon Ana *and* her dog. If he

could hurt a woman, he could hurt a dog. The chances of getting Steph back …

Liam shook his head. He couldn't think about that. But Ana … what sort of things would Rick do to Ana when she was unconscious?

Unspeakable things. Things Liam didn't want to think about. Things that kept him running.

Within minutes, they were on the edge of Shadow Creek by the highway.

Jack bent to pick up the broken wires resting in the dirt. 'Fence is cut.'

'Definite tyre tracks,' Cade said, nodding at the ground. 'He had the car waiting.'

'Fuck!' Liam pulled at his hair as he whirled on his friends. 'She could be bloody anywhere!'

'We'll find her, mate.' Cade placed his hand on Liam's shoulder. 'Let's go back and get the cars.'

Liam turned and raced back the way they came, ignoring the pain in his head. His heart hammered. Ana was in a car. She could be anywhere. He might never see her or Steph again.

Fuck, he was going to lose them both!

Back in Liam's yard, Brett contacted the Mareeba police. With Rick's car being at the southern end of town and Mareeba the quickest way down the coast, Liam didn't expect Rick would have gone in any other direction. Mareeba agreed to send a patrol car, but Liam only hoped they made it that far. They may have even gone north or over to Port Douglas.

'Cade, take the car,' Brett said. 'I'll go with Jack and head south. Cade, you and Adam drive towards Port Douglas. Liam, stay here and call the doctor.'

'Like hell!'

'Mate, he knocked you unconscious.' Cade placed his hand on Liam's shoulder. 'You're in no state to drive and need to be checked out—'

'Screw that. I'll be checked out later.'

Cade looked ready to argue as Adam wrenched open the door to the patrol car. 'Quit wasting time. Liam, grab Louis and come with us.'

Liam didn't need telling twice. Blinking away the dizziness, he ran to the LandCruiser and grabbed Louis' lead. 'Come on, mate. Let's go get our girls.'

* * *

Ana woke to a familiar ache in her face, unable to stop herself from crying out as her head whipped back against something hard. Her eyes squeezed shut as the blistering sun bore down on her. She tried lifting her hand to shield her face, but found herself restrained.

An animal whimpered.

Then that voice …

'Finally, you stupid bitch. Wouldn't think a knock to the head would have kept you out so long.'

Her cheek stung. Air rasped in her aching throat. Her eyes watered and heart hammered inside her chest. Ana took a deep, painful breath. She would not be afraid. There was no point. She'd run to Elizadale, she'd run again yesterday, but she couldn't run now. Last time, she'd begged and wept. Today, she'd do no such thing.

She opened her eyes to find bush surrounding her, the

trees thick and gum leaves scattered over the grassy ground, still soft from the recent rain. She didn't recognise the place. Why would she?

She sat with her back against a tree and her legs stretched out before her. Rope wrapped around her hips and forearms, successfully restraining her hands to her body, her body to the tree.

Then Ana lifted her head and met Rick's dark, menacing eyes.

He crouched before her, wearing a rugged black T-shirt and old jeans with holes in the knees. He'd grown bigger since she'd last seen him, mostly in muscle size. Her throat constricted as she considered what that meant.

His lips curved in a slow, evil smile. Hate flickered in his dark eyes. 'Hello, Ana.'

'What the fuck are you doing?' she cried, anger surging through her. No, she would not be afraid. She had every reason to be, but she wouldn't give him that power. 'You tied me to a damn tree!'

'Couldn't take any chances.' He grinned, obviously proud of himself. She was defenceless and couldn't run, which only added to his evil game.

The whine cut through the air again and Ana's gaze darted right. Steph was tethered to another tree, crouched low and whimpering.

Ana gasped. 'What are you doing with Steph?'

Rick frowned. 'You mean the dog? What do you think I'm doing with it? You bought the mutt against my wishes—'

'I did not! You said I could have Louis. *Louis.* That's Steph! You have the wrong dog!'

'A dog's a dog.'

Ana stilled. She couldn't breathe. 'Don't hurt her, Rick. She's not mine. She's innocent. Don't you dare hurt her.'

Rick's eyes gleamed. The look on his face was worse than that day in the courtroom, full of hate and a desire to cause horrific pain. He'd certainly changed, and not for the better like the court had assured her. He was no longer the attractive accountant. His arms were thicker, hair longer, and everything about him screamed dangerous.

She could see the next few minutes unfolding. Rick wouldn't care that he had the wrong dog. He'd torture and kill the poor pup just to prove a point before he did the same to her.

Ana wanted to scream. She wanted to cry.

She would do neither.

Rick rose to his full height and paced back and forth in front of her. 'I'll do what I want. You have no power, Ana. You think you did well and you've had all sorts of fun since throwing me into a cage.'

'You put yourself in there, Rick.' It took control, but Ana managed to keep her voice even. Her gaze darted between him and Steph. Terrified, the poor girl trembled as she kept her head down. Her mouth moved among the gum leaves.

Ana looked at Rick and swallowed her fear. 'You're going to go back to prison when the police find you.'

He laughed, a deep cackle of a man who had nothing to lose. 'And you think that'll bother me? You think that once you chuck a man in prison that he'll change? Become someone better?' Rick crouched and braced his hands against the tree on either side of her head. Despite herself, Ana trembled as he leaned in close. 'You're just as naïve as the courts. You threw me in there with rapists and murderers.' His voice turned deadly and she hated that it terrified her. 'Men who've done worse things than what I did to you. You think that it'd change me for the better? No, it just taught me a few things, didn't it!'

A strong backhand met her face. Ana gasped as pain shot through her. It was always shocking, even when you knew it was coming. She blinked back the tears that formed in her eyes.

'You obviously didn't learn the right things,' she said, unable to look at him.

'I learned plenty. Like how to express my anger in other ways besides physical violence. But you know what? Hitting people is much more satisfying.'

His fist collided with her stomach. Ana hunched over, gasping for air as another hand flew across her face.

Steph barked, high pitched and in quick succession.

'You ruined my life, you bitch!' He grabbed her throat and pressed her against the tree, her head colliding with the bark. Ana saw stars. She closed her eyes and focused on anything but the agony. 'And now, I'm going to end yours. At least then when I go back to prison, I'll have a rap sheet worthy of the place.'

'You think that'll make you some sort of hero amongst your prison buddies? You're fucked up, Rick.'

Not that she was surprised. She'd known he wouldn't just hit her this time, but hopefully he might draw it out. She'd take the abuse until she could run. Or help arrived. If she could keep him from killing her and Steph for as long as possible, she'd take anything he threw at her.

'Maybe,' he agreed, a ghost of a smile spreading across his face. 'But this is what you made me, Ana. What did you think? That you could run up here and I wouldn't find you? I'd fucking find you. I'd have found you today or in ten years. Did you really want to live your life knowing that?'

Ana blew out her breath. No, but Rick hadn't given her any other choice. She'd known he'd come for her. But how had he managed to grab her?

She and Liam had returned to town. They'd gone inside. Then … 'Were you waiting for us at Liam's?'

He smirked. 'Your boyfriend's house? Yeah.'

'What did you do to him?'

Rick shrugged. 'Hit him over the head. Dunno if or when he'll wake up. So, don't expect anyone to be looking for you as he's probably still sprawled on the floor.'

Ana swallowed, her heart pounding. She couldn't bear it. Liam had to be all right. If not, Adam and Meg were expecting to meet them at the park. Surely, they'd realise something was wrong. They'd find Liam.

Steph shuffled in the gum leaves.

'So, you grabbed me and the wrong dog?'

'A dog's a dog. The other one was barking and snarling. This one was crouched in the corner. Figured I'd take the one that wouldn't eat me.'

If Ana could smile, she would. Louis didn't forget. But Steph …

'Let her go, Rick. Please. Just let her go.'

'No. You need to learn your lesson, Ana. You have no one to blame but yourself.'

'How is this my fault?' she cried. 'You think you're powerful because you can hurt a dog? You hit me because I was what? A good girlfriend? Cooked your meals? *Separate* meals? Because I washed and cleaned and kept your home tidy while you never lifted a finger? Oh, that's right!' She mustered enough courage to roll her eyes. 'I didn't do everything you said. I wasn't your damn slave, Rick!'

Another backhand made Ana's tear ducts flood, much to her humiliation.

'Finally. Not as brave as you think you are. You think you're some strong, independent, tough country woman? You're nothing but a city whore, Ana. Just the same the weak student you were when I first met you, seeking the happy family life with fairy tale expectations.' He gripped her arms. Hard. His fingers dug in until she thought her bones would snap. But even though her breathing had turned raspy and her eyes were wet, she wouldn't give in. She wouldn't plead or weep uncontrollably.

Rick's lip curled. 'Thought you'd find happily ever after out here, did you? You're a fucking dreamer, Ana. Life isn't as rosy as you think.'

'Let me go.' It was hot. She couldn't breathe.

'What?' His hands squeezed until she winced. She wanted to scream, but held it in. She wouldn't give him the satisfaction.

'I said, let me go!' She tried to wriggle her legs, but he'd bound her feet and stuck a stick behind her knees so that she couldn't bend them. It didn't stop her from trying, but she quickly realised it was a lost cause.

He released her. Ana exhaled.

Then he hit her. She tasted blood. Her face stung and her wrists burned from where the rope cut into her body. There was no getting out of this.

Rick's foot collided with her hip. She cried out. Leaves scattered and a growl cut through the air. Ana's eyes flew open to see Steph lunge and clamp her jaw around Rick's leg.

'Fuck!' Rick howled. 'Get off!'

'Steph!' Ana stared, terror overshadowing her pride. Half of Steph's lead trailed behind her, the other half still attached to the tree.

Ana's eyebrows lifted. Steph had chewed through it! She was free and yet—

Rick's boot collided with Steph's body.

Ana screamed.

Steph landed and rolled on the scattered leaves a few feet away. She scrambled to her feet, her eyes wide and ears back.

'Run, Steph!'

Steph ran.

Chapter Thirty-Three

Rick ran after Steph, then drew to a halt and placed his hands on his hips. 'Bloody mongrel. Hope it gets hit by a truck.'

Fear clogged Ana's throat, but she quickly swallowed it. Steph would be okay. If it'd been Louis, she'd be terrified, but Liam had always said Steph had no interest in herding cars. Just like he said never to tie her up because she chews through leads.

Bloody smart dog.

Rick raked his fingers through his hair as he turned back to Ana. 'Be grateful I'm not going to kill the bloody thing in front of you.'

Ana *was* grateful, but she didn't say so.

'As for you though …' He strolled towards her. Paused.

Ana swallowed.

Rick considered her for a moment, then reached for the rope at her waist. 'I think I might untie you.'

Ana blinked. 'What?'

'You're boring to push around when tied to a tree.'

A spark of hope filled her chest. This was her chance to escape too.

Except Rick pulled a piece of rope from his pocket and tied it around her wrist. Then he grabbed the other one and pulled her arm across her body. An involuntary cry shuddered from her throat as the rope holding her down burned across her skin.

Wincing, she pressed her teeth into her bottom lip and concentrated on her breathing as he untied the rope around her waist. He lifted her with one hand under her arm. She complied and stood. Rick shoved her. Unable to use her hands to break her fall, Ana landed with a groan. Pain shot through her hip. She closed her eyes and breathed, inhaling the scent of the earth as tears ran loose, streamed down her face, and into the dirt.

There was no hope. None. And if they didn't find her soon, wherever she was, she'd prefer to die. Liam would understand. It had to be better than this torture.

'Don't think you can run, Ana,' Rick said as the rope around her feet loosened. He stood near her head, so he hadn't done that on purpose. 'There's no escape for you.'

She wouldn't satisfy him with a response. The cut on her cheek stung, rocks pressed into her arms and pain throbbed in her knee.

Rick's boot collided with her stomach. Ana cried out, curling into herself. She might even throw up.

Then Rick was on his knees. He flipped her over, pinned her down by her shoulders, and screamed. 'Look at me! Look at me, you bitch!'

She did as she was told, opening her eyes to meet his murderous face. He'd kill her and kill her soon. It didn't seem like he wanted to drag it out. Not now that he didn't have Steph to torture first. And Liam …

No, Liam wouldn't understand. She'd just let Rick kill her? Like hell.

'Get off me, you bastard.' Using her fused hands, Ana whacked Rick in the guts and dislodged her legs from beneath his. The rope around her ankles loosened as the one behind her knees slipped. The stick moved. But it didn't do her much good. Rick's strength didn't waver. Ana struggled as he pulled her to her feet and tilted her head back until her eyes watered.

Ana stopped fighting.

'You're no match for me, Ana. No matter how strong you think you are.'

He pushed her into the tree before kicking her feet from under her. Ana crashed back to the ground and pain shot through her shoulder. Her arm scraped a rock and tore the sleeve of her blouse. Blood drenched the fabric. The rope around her ankles moved. She was almost free.

Rick grabbed her head and pushed her forward. The bark scratched her face as he held her. Ana tried to catch her breath, her chest heaving.

'Don't struggle.' He pulled at her bra and snapped it hard against her spine. She flinched. 'I'm going to have you first.'

* * *

'There!' Adam cried, jolting Liam out of his dizziness. He leaned forward to peer out the windscreen. The red Subaru was parked on the side of the road. 'And is that ... it's Steph!'

Cade slammed on the brakes. He pulled over and Liam leapt from the car. Steph crept towards him, whining as she rose to place her paws on his hips. Liam gathered her in his arms and held her tight. Steph's body softened as she whimpered.

'It's okay, girl. I've got you.'

He kissed her head, relieved to see her. Ana couldn't be far.

Cade radioed in their location as Liam glanced out over Kelly Coffee Plantation. They weren't near the coffee trees, more on the border in unused bushland.

His vision blurred as he glanced at Steph. 'Where's Ana, girl?'

Steph whined. He dropped his cheek to where her snout rested on his shoulder. Poor girl, she must have gotten such a fright.

'There's a set of footprints identical to those left on Shadow Creek,' Adam called, glancing at the ground.

'Dad's on his way.' Cade shut the drivers' door and strode around the cruiser to join Liam. 'How's Steph?'

'Not good. Hopefully only frightened.'

'Put her with Louis, she'll be okay.'

Cade opened the back door where Louis eagerly awaited Steph. Her ears perked as Liam placed her on the seat, but she showed little excitement. His vision fuzzed and he clutched the top of the door.

'You 'right, mate?'

Liam blinked. 'Yeah. I just ...'

The world swam before him, and Liam's knees buckled. Cade gripped his arm and helped him to the ground.

'Easy, mate.'

Liam let out a deep breath and pressed the heels of his hands into his eyes. He had to get a grip. Had to get to Ana. She couldn't be far.

'Oi, you guys coming?' Adam called. 'These tracks lead straight into the bushland.'

'Be right there!' Cade called over his shoulder before glancing back at Liam. 'Come on, mate. I can't wait—'

Liam pushed himself into a crouched position, but could barely see straight, let alone stand. It was so bright. His head pounded. He could hardly breathe.

He was bloody useless. He needed to get to Ana, but he couldn't move. There was only one thing he could do.

So, heart breaking, he shoved Cade in the shoulder. 'Go. I'll be right behind you.'

Liam sank back against the car as the blurred images of his best mates raced into the bushland.

* * *

Rick slapped her again as Ana fought back, wriggling her feet and legs free. Her heart hammered until she feared her ribs would crack. She could hardly use her hands, but she kept her legs kicking as Rick held her down.

She'd fight until the very end. No matter how many times he hit her, she hit back. Not well, but that didn't matter. The pain intensified. By now, her face must be one massive bruise. Her right eye was already swollen, but Ana didn't care. The rope around her ankles loosened and she finally kicked it free. The knot around her knees slid down.

'Get off me!' she cried, her knees colliding with his back as he straddled her. Rick didn't seem to notice—or care—that her legs were moving. It had no effect anyway, no matter how many times she kicked him. 'Get your fucking hands off me!'

Rick wasn't backing down. He gripped one of her tied

wrists to hold them still and grabbed her blouse at the throat. The ripping sound shot further fear through her. She wouldn't take this. He could hit her all he wanted. She'd hit him back. But rape? She'd prefer he kill her now.

'Stop wriggling!' He slapped her again, but it didn't faze Ana. She might never feel her cheeks again, but she wouldn't let him violate her in that way.

'No!' She freed her legs and went for the straight kick. Her shin collided with the back of his head. Her leg burned and she cried out. Rick grunted, but he didn't stop.

He tore her shirt open all the way and squeezed her breasts. Hard.

Ana screamed. She kicked and prayed. She tried to roll or push him away. Doing everything she could, she landed another good blow against his ribs. But it only made him hit her harder.

It was time for bargaining. 'Rick, please. Let me go. Run and I won't make them come after you. Just live your life.'

'Not going to happen.' Hatred filled his voice. Ana shrieked and resumed kicking, even though it was hopeless.

Her bra strap ripped.

Footsteps crunched over leaves. Then the unmistakable venomous voice of Constable Cade Wilson cut through the air. 'Hands where I can see them. Stand up and step away from the lady.'

Ana collapsed. Her vision blurred and chest heaved as she tried to catch her breath. Rick glanced over her head at Cade, his face thunderous. She doubted he'd do anything stupid when there was undoubtedly a gun pointed at him, but it didn't stop his detestable mouth from moving.

'What, Officer? You going to shoot me?'

'Try me.'

Rick's lip curled, then his dark gaze dropped towards Ana. 'Should have stabbed you back in the kitchen.'

Ana's heart couldn't possibly pound any faster.

'I said step away!'

In one last vengeful move, Rick pressed his hand to her bruised stomach. She winced. 'Next time, bitch. They can't hold me forever.'

Rick stood.

'Take five steps to your left and get down on your knees with your hands behind your head.'

Rick moved out of her line of vision. Ana closed her eyes and tried to stop the tears that threatened. Cade continued to talk, but she tuned him out.

'Ana.'

Gasping, her eyes flew open to find Adam kneeling beside her.

'Hey, it's okay,' he said, his face gentle. 'You're okay.'

Exhausted, Ana blew out her breath. Tears slipped down her cheeks.

'Adam, I'm taking Rick back to the car. Dad shouldn't be far away. Follow with Ana when she's ready. How is she?'

'She'll be fine,' he replied as Ana broke into sobs. Cade and Rick's footsteps soon faded.

Adam placed his hand over hers. 'Come on, Ana. Sit up for me, hey?'

His other hand went to her back as he helped her into a seated position. Touching the rope around her wrists, he pulled a pocketknife from his boot. She didn't ask why he had one, just let him cut the rope and toss it over his shoulder.

Then his dark gaze rested on her face. 'Oh, cuz, we better get you to Doctor Brennan.'

Ana nodded, barely flinching as Adam gently drew her

blouse together. Watching his hands, they didn't frighten her anymore. There was nothing aggressive about Adam. Nothing hateful.

She swallowed. 'Where's Liam? Is he okay?'

'He took a knock to the head, but he's okay. Left him at the car but he might …'

Adam trailed off at the sound of racing footsteps. 'Ana!'

'Liam!'

Gum leaves rustled as Liam slid to his knees beside her. 'Anastasia, thank God!'

Ana burst into tears. She reached for him and Liam gathered her close. He almost squeezed the remaining oxygen from her lungs, but she didn't care. Mustering all her strength, she squeezed him back.

'I'm sorry. I'm so sorry, baby.'

She cried uncontrollably, unable to breathe as she clung to him. She nestled her face against his chest in a position that didn't make her ache and let it all out.

Liam stroked her hair. 'You're okay. We've got him now and you'll be okay. I'm so sorry.'

Ana struggled to inhale, the pain excruciating in her raw throat. When she could, she gathered herself and pulled away. Liam gently wiped her tears.

'Oh, baby …'

'How bad is it?'

He smiled kindly. 'You're beautiful, Ana. But we'll get you to the doctor and have her check you out.'

'Perhaps we should get back to the roadside,' Adam agreed, moving towards them. 'Brett should be there by now, so you won't need to see that fuckhead, Ana.' He offered her his hand. 'Come on.'

Liam struggled to his feet and they both helped Ana up.

She glanced down at the mess that were her clothes. Her bra still held, but a rip split her singlet and her shirt had fallen open again to reveal a dark bruise forming on her belly. Self-consciously, she pulled her blouse across her exposed body.

'Here.' Adam pulled his shirt off over his head, revealing a dark blue singlet. 'Put this on. It might smell, but at least it'll cover you.'

'Thanks, mate.' Liam helped slip it over her head and Ana lifted her arms through, wincing at the ache in her shoulders. Liam stumbled.

'You okay?' she asked.

'Bloody dizzy.'

'Cade told him to stay at the house, but he wouldn't listen,' Adam said. 'And it doesn't look like you're in any shape to walk either.'

'I hurt my ankle when they were tied together.'

'You can lean on me,' Liam offered, wrapping his arm around her waist, but Adam shook his head.

'You'll both fall over. I'll carry Ana and you can lean on me. Don't argue.'

Ana nodded, too exhausted to do anything but agree. Liam released her hand so she could wrap her arm around Adam's neck as he carefully scooped her into his arms. She hurt all over, but as Liam placed one hand on her shoulder and the other on Adam's, she'd never felt safer.

'Okay. Let's get out of here,' Adam said. 'Liam, don't fall over.'

'I'm 'right, mate.'

Awkwardly, they made their way out of the trees. It felt strange being in Adam's arms, but he'd been right in that she was in no state to walk. Neither, it seemed, was Liam. He stumbled, grunted, and shook his head, but managed to stay upright. Exhaling, she gave into her exhaustion and closed her eyes. The sun filtered through the trees and Adam started to sweat, but Ana didn't care. She held on, grateful he'd been there to help her. She'd never met anyone who could be so naughty, charming, and incredibly kind.

'Thank you, Adam.'

'No worries. Anyone with a conscience would have helped you. No need to thank me.'

'But I do.'

Liam nodded. 'Me too, mate. You were bloody great today.'

'You're a nice guy, Adam. If there's anything I can do for you one day, let me know.'

Adam laughed, the sound so much like Liam's it made Ana want to smile. 'You don't owe me anything. I'm just glad I could help and that you're okay because seeing the two of you together …'

Adam paused long enough to make Ana lift her head. She'd frown if it didn't hurt. 'Adam?'

He exhaled. 'Never mind. Crazy thoughts. I just want you two to be happy. That's all.'

Chapter Thirty-Four

Brett drove Ana and Liam to Elizadale Medical, where they were met by Doctor Joanne Brennan. She helped Ana into the treatment room and examined her thoroughly, expressing plenty of concern over her bruises while Brett directed Grace on how to photograph Ana for evidence. She continued to ache as Joanne and Grace took various x-rays, then she lay on the treatment bed while Grace cleaned her cuts. Relief washed through her when Joanne announced her ribs and facial bones were intact.

'I recommend plenty of rest for the next forty-eight hours, Ana,' Joanne said as she took her blood pressure again to check for signs of internal bleeding. If her blood pressure held steady, Joanne said there was no reason to send her to Cairns. 'And be mindful. I want to see you again tomorrow and if you feel anything is wrong, call me immediately. I live three houses down from Liam.'

Ana nodded, grateful. She'd seen Joanne at yoga but hadn't really met her until today and liked her immensely. She was just the kind of compassionate woman one would want as their local physician.

'I will,' Ana promised. 'But I only took two blows to the stomach and I'm feeling all right. My face does hurt though.'

'You're very lucky, Ana. It doesn't look as bad as what you said happened last time.'

Ana exhaled. 'Yeah, last time was a lot worse.'

'I hope he goes away for a long time. I'm sure Brett and Cade will have plenty to pin him for and the New South Wales police won't be happy.'

'Do you think they'll charge him with attempted murder?'

Joanne shrugged. 'I don't know the law well, but maybe. He's got parole violation and two accounts of assault, anyway. Rick will serve out his sentence and more. Just go to the police station the moment you're done here to give a statement.'

Brett had already asked her to, so Ana nodded. 'I will.'

'Good. I want Rick to pay for this, Ana. No one gets away with hurting people in my town. Especially when they need to come to me for treatment.'

'The people here must really love you.'

Joanne smiled softly. 'Well, I've been here almost thirty years. I've seen many people come and go. I remember when Deb and I discovered she was pregnant with Liam, so yeah. It's been a long time. It's going to be hard to step back from this place.'

Ana's heart sank. 'You're stepping back?'

'I'm hoping to. It's time for a change and I have things I want to do, but I'm not going to leave. I'm getting a junior doctor, someone who wants to put their skills to use in a rural practice. It'll be good for the town, I think. And it'll give me more time with David so we can go away on school holidays and enjoy life.'

'That sounds lovely. I suppose you can't be the only town doctor forever.'

'It'll be good to have two. I've had a few registrars in my time and believe me, this place works better with two doctors.'

'As long as you're happy about it. I hope it works out.'

'I hope so too. Anyway. I'm going to get you some pain meds. The swelling should go down in a couple of days, but you'll be bruised for a while, I'm afraid. I'll go see if Meg's brought you a change of clothes. Be right back.'

* * *

Liam paced the waiting room, his hands on his head. He'd had the x-ray Joanne had insisted upon, but his headache had subsided and he felt fine. His head did, anyway. His heart and soul were a different story.

Meg sat beside Jack and Adam. Michael had taken Steph to the vet in Mareeba with Louis for support. Ana said Steph had only taken one kick, so he wasn't too worried, but Liam had wanted her checked over regardless.

Ana, however, had taken a bloody beating.

Joanne stepped into to the waiting room and Liam shot to her side. 'She okay?'

'Ana's just fine.' Joanne placed her hand on his arm. Liam exhaled, his shoulders sagging. 'But I'll want to talk to you in a minute. Meg, can I have those clothes?'

Meg handed over the bag she'd brought from Ana's place and Joanne returned to the treatment room. But Liam didn't feel any better as he sank into a seat and dropped his head into his hands.

Ana was safe. That was all he kept telling himself. He could barely comprehend what she'd been through and hated that he'd failed her. But she was still here, alive, and she was going to be all right.

When Joanne said he could see her, Liam was up in a flash. He walked into the treatment room where Ana sat on the edge of the bed, her scratches and cuts cleaned with those on her arms and knees bandaged. But her face … Liam wanted to storm into the police station and murder Rick with his bare hands.

He tried not to let that anger show though as he slipped his arm around Ana's shoulders and placed a kiss on her forehead. He sat beside her and she leaned into him as Joanne gave them both instructions.

'Ana will need rest, Liam, and plenty of fluids because she's exhausted. I want the bruises, especially those on her face, to be iced and she must avoid heat for the next two days. That includes the shower. Ana understands this and I want to make sure you do too. You look after her, okay?'

'I will.' He glanced at Ana and brushed his hand up and down her arm. 'I'll take care of her for the rest of my life.'

Ana's lips barely curved, but he recognised her smile by the sparkle in her eyes. She opened her mouth to say something, then squeezed his hand instead.

Joanne moved towards the door. 'You're free to go. I'll see you both tomorrow for a check-up. The police need that statement, so go there now.'

They thanked Joanne and left the room. Meg's hands flew to her mouth when she saw Ana, tears filling her eyes. Ana assured her that she was okay, but Jack had to pull Meg into a chair and calm her down. Ana made their follow-up appointments with Grace, then with warm wishes from their friends, Adam drove them to the police station since Joanne insisted that Liam couldn't drive.

She let him sit with her while she gave the statement. Liam maintained a firm grip on his control and his shoulders tensed during the dramatic points, but he kept his cool and held Ana's hand supportively as she spoke.

Knowing that bastard was in the building though, Liam wanted to bash him around and see how he liked it. Tie him to a fucking tree or knock him out.

He couldn't be more grateful for Cade and Adam's timely arrival. At least they'd managed to save her. Ana told them Rick had been clear about his intentions—wanting to kill Steph, then rape and kill Ana—so Brett and Cade had the case in the bag.

Then finally, it was over. Liam led Ana out of the station.

* * *

Outside, Ana sighed and leaned into Liam. His arms went around her as she rested her sore face against his chest. 'Take me home, Liam. I just want to go home.'

He kissed the top of her head. 'Okay. Adam's on his way to pick us up and Michael texted saying he's back at Jackson Villas with Steph and Louis. She's fine, of course. We'll let Louis inside so he can curl up with you and make you feel better.'

Heat flooded her already hot cheeks and her belly knotted. 'Actually … I think I'd be more comfortable at your place. Then I won't have the stairs and Steph and Louis won't be in that little yard.'

Liam let out a small laugh. 'When you said "home", you meant my place, didn't you?'

Ana squeezed her eyes shut, wincing with pain and embarrassment. 'I'm sorry. I wasn't thinking. I didn't mean home, I just meant—'

'Ana, it's okay.' Liam placed his finger under her chin and

lifted her gaze. Amusement overshone the anguish in his blue eyes. 'You've practically been living there anyway. Louis certainly has. And if you want it to be your home … it could be.'

Ana's heart leapt. 'What? Are you … asking me to move in with you?'

His throat bobbed as he swallowed. 'What would you say if I was?'

'Um …' Hell yes! It was all she'd dreamed about this past week. But now wasn't the best time to be making life-altering decisions. She wasn't thinking straight and he probably wasn't either. Moving in together after two months? Wasn't that Liam's definition of too fast?

'I think I want to,' she replied slowly, 'but my head's not with it right now, so let's pick up Steph and Louis and we can discuss it later.'

'Okay.' Adam pulled up and Liam kept his arm around her waist as they walked towards the LandCruiser. 'But just so you know, I don't think I've ever wanted anything more.'

Speechless, Ana slipped into the car.

Chapter Thirty-Five

Ana had asked Liam to call her mother. She'd come home, fallen into bed, and had been asleep in seconds, but that was the one thing she'd requested.

He'd stared at the phone for eternity before making the call. Despite telling himself it hadn't been his fault, guilt still clawed at his heart. He knew he'd done his best and that Rick had surprised them, but how could he confess to Nadia that he'd failed to protect Ana like he'd promised?

Liam slumped onto the lounge. He couldn't overthink it else he'd send himself crazy with all the ways he could have prevented today's events. He could have gone in first. Or left Ana in the car. They could never have come back to town at all.

But Rick had wanted Ana. He'd have done anything to get her. And whether Liam had gone in first or not—

Exhaling, he ran his hand down his face. No. He had to stop it. It had happened, but it was over. He may feel guilty, but Ana was alive because of the friendships she'd found in Elizadale. They'd all been there to help her, just as he'd promised.

Which was what he told Nadia. She didn't take it well, but she was grateful for everyone involved and that Rick was back in custody. As he moved about the kitchen preparing dinner, Liam did his best to answer her questions about what had happened, what Joanne had said, and how Ana was feeling.

'Well, if you say she's okay …'

'She is, Nadia,' he said, slicing carrots. 'But I can get her to call you when she wakes.'

'Please do. I don't care how late it is. But I'm glad you're both okay, Liam. And that your dog is too.'

'Yeah, she's been running around with Louis, but I expect she might be a bit timid for a while. I'll work on it with her though. At least she had the chance to bite the bastard. I'd have liked to bite him.' Or punch him, kick him, knock him into a tree …

Nadia managed a light laugh. 'Oh, Liam. And please thank your cop friend and cousin for me too.'

'I will.'

'And you're sure I don't have to fly up there?'

'I don't think so. I'll look after her. But if Ana wants you here, I'll buy you a plane ticket immediately.'

Nadia sighed. 'Okay. It's hard for me because I want to look after her, but I know I don't need to. You love her and I know you're there for her. Thank you for calling me, Liam. I look forward to officially meeting you.'

'Me too.'

After hanging up, he fed the dogs, then wondered what he was actually making for dinner. He'd set potatoes to boil and had cut up carrots. He'd throw in some frozen beans and cauliflower. Usually, he'd grill up a piece of steak or chicken to go with that, and he might, but as for Ana … he had a tin of black beans but wasn't sure what to do with that right now.

Sighing, he opened the freezer. He thought he'd done well adapting to her vegetarianism, but if she was going to live here, then he'd need to do better and have things on hand in case—

Ah, lentil cakes! Ana had made them a few weeks ago they'd been delicious. Liam took two out, heated them up, and served dinner. Checking on Ana and finding her still sleeping, he covered her plate and placed it in the fridge. Then, since he didn't have an appetite either, he did the same with his and went to lie down with her.

He wrapped his arm around her waist, careful not to disturb her. It'd been a crazy few days and he'd missed her while he'd been away, but knowing she'd been at home with his dog had been comforting.

Then he'd almost lost her.

Today had been the most terrifying day of his life. Liam didn't want to imagine what else could have happened. It could have been much worse and he never wanted to experience that terror again.

He closed his eyes, Lucy's words ricocheting through his mind. *The sooner the better.*

He understood that now. You never knew what could happen from one day to the next and today had been a prime example. Adam and Cade had found Ana scared and beaten, but a few minutes difference could have changed that. She could have been raped and dead.

He squeezed his eyes tighter. Exhaled. This must be what gratitude felt like as he lay there with her warm and breathing in his arms. In his bed. In his house.

Their house.

Yes, he wanted it to be their house because Lucy was right. Life was too short and too precious to take things slow and steady. Why wait for something that you already knew you wanted? Anastasia Hamilton was the only woman he'd ever truly loved. Life without her and Louis didn't make sense.

Liam smiled softly to himself. He may be in over his head, but after today's rollercoaster of emotions, he couldn't be happier about it.

* * *

Ana ached as she stretched out in Liam's bed. Beside her, the mattress sank as he moved.

'Hey, baby. You okay?'

'Yeah …' She opened her eyes and blinked sleepily. 'I'm sore though. Could you get me those pain meds?'

'Sure.' He climbed out of bed and left the room. Ana groaned as she pushed herself into a seated position. At least the pain wasn't as bad as last time, but her face sure stung.

Liam returned and handed her the box of medication with a glass of water. 'Are you hungry? I cooked dinner.'

She nodded and swallowed the pills, her parched throat relieved by the water. 'Thanks. I guess I could eat. I need to go to the toilet first though.'

'You do that then while I reheat dinner.'

Ana moved into the bathroom, still tired, but her stomach growled as she washed her hands. She slowly made her way into the kitchen where Liam was setting two plates at the small table. Ana's heart thudded. She was lucky to have him. Lucky that she was still able to sit there with him tonight.

'You sleep okay?' he asked as she eased into a chair.

'Yeah. I'd expected some nightmares, but so far, so good. They might still come though.'

'If they do, I'll be there to wake you from them.' His words were gentle, but his actions were not as he stabbed beans with his fork.

Ana reached across the table and placed her hand over his. 'It's okay, Liam. I'm okay.'

Sighing, he dropped his fork and took her hand in both of his. He lifted it to his lips. 'I know. I'm sorry.'

'I love you, Liam.'

'I love you too, Anastasia. More than anything.'

She held his gaze for a moment, but he didn't say anything more. Instead, they dug into their dinner, both ravenous.

'What did Mama say when you called her?'

'She was shocked and upset, but mostly okay. She wants you to call her, no matter how late. I think she just wants to hear your voice.'

After they'd cleared their plates, Ana suggested they sit outside. She'd call her mum, but right now, she just wanted a few moments with Liam.

She lowered herself into a comfortable padded chair as Steph and Louis uncurled themselves from their outdoor beds. Ana smiled as Louis lay his head in her lap and she rubbed his ears.

'So, how about it?' Liam asked. 'Would you and Louis like to live with us?'

Ana swallowed. She glanced quickly at Louis, then back to Liam. 'Well ... yeah, but don't you think it's too soon? I mean, we've only known each other a couple of months. And I don't want today to ...'

'Nothing about today is influencing my thoughts. But is that a problem for you? That it's too soon?'

It was quick. Never would she have considered living with a man she'd been dating less than three months.

But Liam was different. She'd always known that.

She shook her head. 'No.'

'Me neither. I love you, Anastasia. So, do you want to live with us? Louis' keen.'

Louis smiled widely, sending her pleading 'go on' eyes. And even though her face ached, it didn't stop her from breaking into a smile herself. 'Yes, Liam. I do. Louis and I would love to live with you and Steph.'

He grinned, rubbing Steph's ears before sliding out of his chair. On his knees, he took a few steps over to take her hand in his. The cuckoo clock inside struck twelve.

'Kiss me.'

She laughed, wondering if he was crazy. 'What?'

'Just do it.'

'But I—'

'I'll be gentle. You're beautiful, Anastasia. Now, kiss me.'

She leaned in and placed her lips on his. It was weird considering they were swollen, sore, and didn't feel normal, but she kissed him anyway. Liam ran his hands up her arms and caressed her shoulders, his kiss featherlight.

When the cuckoo bird went back inside the clock, he drew away and interlocked his fingers with hers. 'Do you want to marry me?'

Ana didn't blink this time. She stared at him, her heart jumping into her throat. 'What?'

'You're going to make me say it again?' But he didn't seem to mind as his blue eyes sparkled. 'Live with me. Marry me. Be my wife. I love you and I'll never let you go. So, Anastasia Jane Hamilton, will you marry me?'

He was serious. Tears stupidly sprang to her eyes and she smiled. No longer did she feel like the broken Ana, but herself, and the most magnificent man she'd ever met was on his knees asking her to marry him.

Unable to speak as her traumatised throat closed up, she nodded. She tried wiping the tears away, but they kept coming.

Finally, she found her voice. 'Yes, Liam. Oh my God, yes.'

Ana slid to her knees and went into his arms.

'I love you, Anastasia.' He lifted his hand to wipe the tears from her bruised cheeks.

'I love you too,' she said as Steph and Louis nosed their way into the embrace.

Ana and Liam opened their arms to let them in. She kissed the top of Steph's head and smiled at Louis. Together, the four of them would make the perfect little family as they held each other on the back patio of their beautiful home.

Epilogue

A week later, Liam sat outside The Bent Banana with Ana by his side and the dogs curled beneath their chairs. Grand Opening Day had arrived, rushing Liam, Lucy, and Isabella off their feet for most of the morning. His favourite country music played softly from the speakers while more people than he'd expected gathered around the tables or spread out on the grass. Dogs lapped up the biscuits and pupcakes while children ran around on a sugar high between their parents and the jumping castle, their faces painted thanks to Jessica Smithfield's artistic talents.

Liam's heart filled until he was afraid it'd burst. He glanced at Ana and rubbed his thumb over her knuckles, fiddling with the ring he'd placed on her finger three days ago. 'I'm glad you came.'

She smiled softly beneath the brim of her hat. 'I didn't want to miss it. Besides, everyone's been so kind.'

Ana twirled the daisy her student, Molly, had brought her between her fingers. Liam had understood her hesitation about leaving the house. Cuts still grazed her cheeks and her eyes were black. Ana had worried that she'd frighten her students if they saw her beaten and bruised, but word had spread and a few parents had called, offering their best wishes and promising they'd explain the situation to their children. Thankfully, Ana had the holidays to heal, but the warm words had boosted her confidence. She'd been to the supermarket and the dog park a couple of times, where everyone they encountered had been kind and supportive.

But she'd been determined not to miss out on his big day and Liam had been glad to hear she wouldn't hide. Ana had nothing to be ashamed of. Her bruises would heal and life would go on.

And a beautiful life it would be.

Her hand squeezed his. 'It's been a wonderful day, Liam.'

He blew out his breath and gazed around again. The locals had come in droves to support the café. Liam didn't know why he was surprised. Elizadale had always been a fine example of community spirit.

'I guess I still can't believe it.'

'Well, believe it, baby. The Bent Banana has opened with a bang and will be a success.'

Grinning, Liam leaned over to kiss her. Music and laughter surrounded them. Kids shouted. Dogs barked. The scent of pancakes and coffee filled the air and ice cream lingered on her lips.

He had his café. He had his dog. And he had his woman, the bravest and fiercest person he'd never known.

Drawing away, he cupped her cheek. 'I'm so glad you came to Elizadale.'

'Me too. It's the home I never knew I always wanted. And I'll stay here forever with you.'

Louis chose that moment to rear up and place his paws on

Ana's knees. She laughed and her phone beeped. Liam took a sip of his banana smoothie while Ana swiped at the screen. 'It's Nat!'

'Yeah? What's she up to?'

Ana opened the message. Her hand flew to her mouth as she gasped, then squealed. 'Oh my God! Natalia's coming to Elizadale!'

the Man From
Shadow Creek

Can the spirited doctor help the troubled bad boy shed his reputation and feel worthy of her love?

Adam Maguire wore the title of Elizadale's bad boy with pride, until he woke in the park with no memory of the night before. Fearing the unknown, Adam re-evaluates his history of reckless behaviour and decides to build a business out of his passion for woodwork. But with his devious ex determined to lure him back, Adam doubts he will ever be free from his past.

Doctor Natalia Hamilton has escaped the city after suffering harassment that left her confidence shattered. Reunited with her sister in Elizadale, Natalia hopes the small-town vibe will help her rediscover the value of her work. Dating is the last thing on her mind when she's been constantly burned by romance. Until Adam rides in on his motorcycle and takes her breath away.

As sparks ignite between the unlikely couple, Adam and Natalia begin to trust again. But when a story about his forgotten night is revealed, can Adam determine the truth from a web of lies? Or is it already too late for him to start over?

Author's Note

Inspiration comes from many places and this story is special to me. Elizadale formed in my mind when I used to drive through the isolated Townsville suburb of Oonoonba in 2011. I'd approach through bush, slow into this little 'town', then speed up again and leave. Eventually, I was inspired to use this beautiful 'small town' sensation to write a rural romance, so I took Ana and Liam from their Townsville dog park and popped them down in the outback town of Stuart Plains.

Yes, that's right. I won't hide that this series used to be set in outback Queensland and that Shadow Creek used to be a cattle station. There was once the mighty Stuart River, inspired by the ferocious Burdekin, and Stuart Falls was essentially Barron Falls. Adam and Jack were diehard rodeo cowboys and the series contained musters, rodeos, and lots of outback fun. I pursued publishers with this story for years with no success and eventually, felt it was time to put it aside.

Then in January 2021, my decision to adopt a full vegan lifestyle changed my life. It improved my confidence, my health, my work as an exercise physiologist, and my writing. Because while I loved Stuart Plains and this book (then horribly called *Stuart's White Knight*), I asked myself, 'Do I still want to write about cattlemen?'. Now, I have nothing against cattlemen personally and am not out to change people, but I did wonder if it was time for an experiment. After all, the Maguires could farm anything.

So, I considered the many locations and the farms I'd like to work with, but in the end, I stuck with North Queensland. Bananas were the winner because they're a big industry in the Innisfail region, but a coastal location didn't mimic my original setting. So, since Mareeba and Lakeland also farm bananas, I dropped my newly named Elizadale in between them, right on top of Mount Molloy. I diversified the farms by making the Kellys coffee growers and adding an avocado farm to Meg's family, but White Peaks remained a cattle station. After doing this, I realised how many more opportunities I had to develop this series and the stories I'd drafted. The Bent Banana was born out of this change—Liam's story about naming it is my true story—and the development of Jack and Adam into banana farmers and woodworkers has greatly enhanced their characters and books as well.

As I said, this was meant to be an experiment, but after four chapters in, there was no going back. I fell in love with Elizadale, banana farming, the diversity, and the many new directions I could see this series going. These books are my passion and I'm thrilled I can tell these rural stories outside the usual trend of animal farming. I have no agenda and continue to read and love all types of rural fiction, but I write about small towns and people who farm produce. What I call 'vegan rural romance'.

Acknowledgements

The road to this book has been a long journey, so thank you to everyone who has allowed me to talk about Shadow Creek with them. Without the contests at Romance Writers of Australia and Romance Writers of New Zealand, I'd never have been able to develop this story into something I'm proud of, so thank you to these organisations and the readers who provided invaluable feedback. Thank you to the publishers who considered this novel for your encouragement. This may not have been a story you could take on, but your interest in my work boosted my confidence. Thank you to the Queensland Writers Centre and Lori-Jay Ellis for the advice I received during the 2021 *Publishable* program and for boosting my courage. Thank you Belinda Pollard and Edwina Shaw for your assessments and advice.

This book wouldn't have been possible without my local writing network. Thank you to those who attend my popular fiction workshops for your support and encouragement. Guiding you towards achieving your writing dreams brings me such joy. Thank you to my readers Linda Wright, Barbara Strickland, Deeanna West, Jill Staunton, and Mum.

*

Jill Staunton, I will always be grateful for you. Your advice and friendship over the years has transformed me as a writer. Thank you for being the person I can turn to and trust for guidance and a confidence boost. You've gifted me that time and time again. *Home Among the Palm Trees* wouldn't be the same without you.

Thank you Linda and Deeanna for your support as I've bounced ideas off you and constantly sought your advice. I value my friendship with you both and wouldn't have had the courage to do this without you.

Mum. There is no good place to start. Thank you for being by my side throughout this journey and for encouraging me to pursue my writing dream. You've been there from the beginning with this book, from the moment I wanted to write about two people who fell in love over their mutual love of border collies. Thank you for telling me, 'He can't kidnap the dog! The dog won't know what's going on! Kidnap the woman!', which created the theme of this story. Thank you for helping me build this small town, Shadow Creek, and for naming the Maguire family. You've heard this story many times, have helped me plot this series, and it wouldn't be the same without you. Thank you for holding my hand during the tough times and for enjoying all the happy moments with me. I wouldn't have been able to independently publish this book without your support.

A major credit goes to my brother Chris. Thank you for planting the seed that inspired me to go vegan. This improved many aspects of my life, but it also gave me the motivation to restyle this series and fall in love with it again. Thank you for encouraging me to pursue this publishing path and for your advice on tweaking the beautiful cover. I'm sorry it couldn't be 'more dog, less human'.

So, thank you to my cover designer, Danielle, for taking my brief and giving me this beautiful cover! You've captured Ana and Louis in a moment I could never have imagined. Thank you to my editor Alex for guiding me towards improving this story. I learned a lot from your editorial advice and cannot believe the transformation this manuscript undertook.

Thank you to the writing community for showing me there are many ways to find success. Matt B Lewis and Davina Stone, you were my inspiration. Thank you Joanne Austen Brown and Frances Dall'Alba for your advice on independent publishing.

Mum and Ian, thank you for accompanying me for an afternoon of taste testing at Fruit Forest Farm, and a big thanks goes to the Gaia family for taking me on a tour through your banana farm.

Most of all, thank you Dillon and Jacob. Dillon, you'll live forever in my heart and as Louis. You came into my life when I was an eight-year-old girl and left when I was a grown woman who knew it was time to take you to the vet. I'll always remember you as the perfect boy who couldn't live without a ball, even if that meant ripping the husk off a coconut to find one. You are the reason I cannot live without a border collie and why Jacob came into my life. This book wouldn't have transformed without my baby boy. Thank you, Jacob, for your barking, inability to walk without herding cars, and for chewing through your lead to chase the hose. You fill my life with love, fun, and too much cuteness.

Last but not least, thank YOU for picking up this book! I hope you enjoyed your first visit to Elizadale and want to find out what happens next. I promise you, a lot more is to come.

The *Shadow Creek* series